LINDA LAEL MILLER

New York Times bestselling author Linda Lael Miller started writing at age ten and has made a name for herself in both contemporary and historical romance. Her bold and innovative style has made her a favorite among readers. Named by *Romantic Times Magazine* as "The Most Outstanding Writer of Sensual Romance," Linda Lael Miller never disappoints.

SUSAN MALLERY

Susan Mallery is the bestselling author of over forty books for Harlequin/Silhouette. She makes her home in the Pacific Northwest with her handsome prince of a husband and her two adorable-but-not-bright cats.

DARING MOVES

LINDA
LAEL
MILLER

MARRIAGE ON DEMAND

SUSAN
MALLERY

Silhouette Books

Published by Silhouette Books
America's Publisher of Contemporary Romance

SILHOUETTE BOOKS

Copyright in the collection:
© 2001 by Harlequin Books S.A.

ISBN 0-373-48434-8

Cover illustration © Tracy Walker/i2i Art

The publisher acknowledges the copyright holders
of the individual works as follows:

DARING MOVES
Copyright © 1990 by Linda Lael Miller

MARRIAGE ON DEMAND
Copyright © 1995 by Susan W. Macias

This edition published by arrangement with Harlequin Books S.A.

® and TM are trademarks of Harlequin Books S.A., used under license. Trademarks indicated with ® are registered in the United States Patent and Trademark Office, the Canadian Trade Marks Office and in other countries.

Visit Silhouette at www.eHarlequin.com

Printed in U.S.A.

DARING MOVES
by Linda Lael Miller

* * *

For Melba.
Your friendship was a gift from H.P.

Chapter 1

The line of people waiting for an autograph reached from the bookstore down the length of the mall to the specialty luggage shop. With a sigh, Amanda Scott bought a cup of coffee from a nearby French bakery, bravely forgoing the delicate, flaky pastries inside the glass counter, and took her place behind a man in an expensive tweed overcoat.

Distractedly he turned and glanced at her, as though somehow finding her to blame for the delay. Then he pushed up his sleeve and consulted a slim gold watch. He was a couple of inches taller than Amanda, with brown hair that was only slightly too long and hazel eyes flecked with green, and he needed a shave.

Never one to pass the time in silence if an excuse to chat presented itself, Amanda took a steadying sip of her coffee and announced, "I'm buying Dr. Marshall's book for my sister, Eunice. She's going through a nasty divorce." The runaway bestseller was called *Gathering Up the Pieces*, and it was meant for people who had suffered some personal loss or setback.

The stranger turned to look back at her. The pleasantly mingled scents of new snow and English Leather seemed to surround him. "Are you talking to me?" he inquired, drawing his brows together in puzzlement.

Amanda fortified herself with another sip of coffee. She hadn't meant to flirt; it was just that waiting could be so tedious. "Actually, I was," she admitted.

He surprised her with a brief but brilliant smile that practically set her back on the heels of her snow boots. In the next second his expression turned grave, but he extended a gloved hand.

"Jordan Richards," he said formally.

Gulping down the mouthful of coffee she'd just taken, Amanda returned the gesture. "Amanda Scott," she managed. "I don't usually strike up conversations with strange men in shopping malls, you understand. It's just that I was bored."

Again that blinding grin, as bright as sunlight on water.

"I see," said Jordan Richards.

The line moved a little, and they both stepped forward. Amanda suddenly felt shy, and wished she hadn't gotten off the bus at the mall. Maybe she should have gone straight home to her cozy apartment and her cat.

She reminded herself that Eunice would benefit by reading the book and that, with this purchase, her Christmas shopping would be finished. After today she could hide in her work, like a soldier crouching in a foxhole, until the holidays and all their painful associations were past.

"Too bad about Eunice," Jordan Richards remarked.

"I'll give her your condolences," Amanda promised, a smile lighting her aquamarine eyes.

The line advanced, and so did Amanda and Jordan.

"Good," he said.

Amanda finished her coffee, crumpled the cup and tossed it into a nearby trash bin. Beside the bin there was a sign that read Is Therapy For You? Attend A Free Minisession With Dr. Marshall After The Book Signing. Beneath was a diagram of the mall, with the public auditorium colored in.

"So," she ventured, "are you buying *Gathering Up the Pieces* for yourself or somebody else?"

"I'm sending it to my grandmother," Jordan answered, consulting his watch again.

Amanda wondered if he had to be somewhere else later, or if he was just an impatient person.

"What happened to her?" she asked sympathetically.

Jordan looked reluctant, but after a few moments and another step forward as the line progressed, he said, "She had some pretty heavy-duty surgery a while back."

"Oh," Amanda said, and without thinking, she reached out and patted his arm so as not to let the mention of the unknown grandmother's misfortune pass without some response from her.

Something softened in Jordan Richards's manner at the small demonstration. "Are you attending the 'free minisession'?" he asked, gesturing toward the sign. The expression in his eyes said he fully expected her to answer no.

Amanda smiled and lifted one shoulder in a shrug. "Why not? I've got the rest of the afternoon to blow, and I could learn something."

Jordan looked thoughtful. "I suppose nobody has to talk if they don't want to."

"Of course not," Amanda replied confidently, even though she had no idea what would be required. Some of the self-help groups could get pretty wild; she'd heard of people walking across burning coals in their bare feet, or letting themselves be dunked in hot tubs.

"I'll go if you'll sit beside me," Jordan said.

Amanda considered the suggestion only briefly. The mall was a well-lit place, crowded with Christmas shoppers. If Jordan Richards were some kind of weirdo—and that seemed unlikely, unless crackpots were dressing like models in *Gentlemen's Quarterly* these days—she would be perfectly safe. "Okay," she said with another shrug.

After the decision was made, they lapsed into a companionable silence. Nearly fifteen minutes had passed by the time Jordan reached the author's table.

Dr. Eugene Marshall, the famous psychology guru, signed his name in a confident scrawl and handed Jordan a book.

Amanda had her volume autographed and followed her new acquaintance to the cash register.

Once they'd both paid, they left the store together.

There was already a mob gathered at the double doors of the mall's community auditorium, and according to a sign on an easel, the minisession would start in another ten minutes.

Jordan glanced at the line of fast-food places across the concourse. "Would you like some coffee or something?"

Amanda shook her head, then reached up to pull her light, shoulder-length hair from under the collar of her coat. "No, thanks. What kind of work do you do, Mr. Richards?"

"'Jordan,'" he corrected. He took off his overcoat and draped it over one arm, then loosened his tie and collar slightly. "What kind of work do you think I do?"

Amanda assessed him, narrowing her blue eyes. Jordan looked fit, and he even had a bit of a suntan, but she doubted he worked with his hands. His clothes marked him as an upper-management type, and so did that gold watch he kept checking. "You're a stockbroker," she guessed.

He chuckled. "Close. I'm a partner in an investment firm. What do you do?"

People were starting to move into the auditorium and take seats, and Amanda and Jordan moved along with them. With a half smile, she answered, "Guess."

He considered her thoughtfully. "You're a flight attendant for a major airline," he decided after several moments had passed.

Amanda took his conjecture as a compliment, even though it was wrong. "I'm the assistant manager of the Evergreen Hotel." They found seats near the middle of the auditorium, and Jordan took the one on the aisle. Amanda was just daring to hope she was making a favorable impression, when her stomach rumbled.

"And you haven't had lunch yet," Jordan stated with another of those lethal, quicksilver grins. "It just so happens that I'm a little hungry myself. How about something from that Chinese fast-food place I saw out there—after we're done with the minisession, I mean?"

Again Amanda smiled. She seemed to be smiling a lot, which was odd, because she hadn't felt truly happy since before James Brockman had swept into her life, turned it upside down and swept out again. "I'd like that," she heard herself say.

Just then Dr. Marshall walked out onto the auditorium stage. At his appearance, Jordan became noticeably uncomfortable, shifting in his seat and drawing one Italian-leather-shod foot up to rest on the opposite knee.

The famous author introduced himself, just in case someone who had never watched a TV talk show might have wandered in, and announced that he wanted the audience to break up into groups of twelve.

Jordan looked even more discomfited, and probably wouldn't have participated if a group hadn't formed around him and Amanda. To make things even more interesting, at least to Amanda's way of thinking, the handsome, silver-haired Dr. Marshall chose their group to work with, while his assistants took the others.

"All right, people," he began in a tone of pleasant authority, "let's get started." His knowing gray eyes swept the small gathering. "Why does everybody look so worried? This will be relatively painless—all we're going to do is talk about ourselves a little." He looked at Amanda. "What's your name?" he asked directly. "And what's the worst thing that's happened to you in the past year?"

She swallowed. "Amanda Scott. And—the worst thing?"

Dr. Marshall nodded with kindly amusement.

All of the sudden Amanda wished she'd gone to a matinee or stayed home to clean her apartment. She didn't want to talk about James, especially not in front of strangers, but she was basically an honest person and *James* was the worst thing that had happened to her in a very long time. Not looking at Jordan, she answered, "I fell in love with a man and he turned out to be married."

"What did you do when you found out?" the doctor asked reasonably.

"I cried a lot," Amanda answered, forgetting for the moment that there were twelve other people listening in, including Jordan.

"Did you break off the relationship?" Dr. Marshall pressed.

Amanda still felt the pain and humiliation she'd known when James's wife had stormed into her office and made a scene. Before that, Amanda hadn't even suspected the terrible truth. "Yes," she replied softly with a miserable nod.

"Is this experience still affecting your life?"

Amanda wished she dared to glance at Jordan to see how he was reacting, but she didn't have the courage. She lowered her eyes. "I guess it is."

"Did you stop trusting men?"

Considering all the dates she'd refused in the months since she'd disentangled herself from James, Amanda supposed she had stopped trusting men. Even worse, she'd stopped trusting her own instincts. "Yes," she answered very softly.

Dr. Marshall reached out to touch her shoulder. "I'm not going to pretend you can solve your problems just by sitting in on a minisession, or even by reading my book, but I think it's time for you to stop hiding and take some risks. Agreed?"

Amanda was surprised at the man's insight. "Agreed," she said, and right then and there she made up her mind to read Eunice's copy of *Gathering Up the Pieces* before she wrapped it.

The doctor's attention shifted to the man sitting on Amanda's left. He said he'd lost his job, and the fact that Christmas was coming up made things harder. A woman in the row behind Amanda talked about her child's serious illness. Finally, after about twenty minutes had passed, everyone had spoken except Jordan.

He rubbed his chin, which was already showing a five o'clock shadow, and cleared his throat. Amanda, feeling his tension and reluctance as though they were her own, laid her hand gently on his arm.

"The worst thing that ever happened to me," he said in a low, almost inaudible voice, "was losing my wife."

"How did it happen?" the doctor asked.

Jordan looked as though he wanted to bolt out of his chair

and stride up the aisle to the doors, but he answered the question. "A motorcycle accident."

"Were you driving?" Dr. Marshall's expression was sympathetic.

"Yes," Jordan replied after a long silence.

"And you're still not ready to talk about it," the doctor deduced.

"That's right," Jordan said. And he got up and walked slowly up the aisle and out of the auditorium.

Amanda followed, catching up just outside. She didn't quite dare to touch his arm again, yet he slowed down at the sound of her footsteps. "How about that Chinese food you promised me?" she asked gently.

Jordan met her eyes, and for just a moment, she saw straight through to his soul. What pain he'd suffered.

"Sure," he replied, and his voice was hoarse.

"I'm all through with my Christmas shopping," Amanda announced once they were seated at a table, Number Three Regulars in front of them from the Chinese fast-food place. "How about you?"

"My secretary does mine," Jordan responded. He looked relieved at her choice of topic.

"That's above and beyond the call of duty," Amanda remarked lightly. "I hope you're giving her something terrific."

Jordan smiled at that. "She gets a sizable bonus."

"Good."

It was obvious Jordan was feeling better. His eyes twinkled, and some of the strain had left his face.

"I'm glad company policy meets with your approval."

It was surprising, considering her unfortunate and all-too-recent experiences with James, but it wasn't until that moment that Amanda realized that she hadn't checked Jordan's hand for a wedding band. She glanced at the appropriate finger, even though she knew it would be bare, and saw a white strip where the ring had been.

"Like I said, I'm a widower," he told her with a slight smile, obviously having read her glance accurately.

"I'm sorry," Amanda told him.

He speared a piece of sweet-and-sour chicken. "It's been three years."

It seemed to Amanda that the white space on his ring finger should have filled in after three years. "That's quite a while," she said, wondering if she should just get up from her chair, collect her book and her coat and leave. In the end she didn't, because a glance at her watch told her it was still forty minutes until the next bus left. Besides, she was hungry.

Jordan sighed. "Sometimes it seems like three centuries."

Amanda bit her lower lip, then burst out, "You aren't one of those creeps who goes around saying he doesn't have a wife when he really does, are you? I mean, you could have remarried."

He looked very tired all of a sudden, and pale beneath his tan. Amanda wondered why he hadn't gotten around to shaving.

"No," he said. "I'm not married."

Amanda dropped her eyes to her food, ashamed that she'd asked the question, even though she wouldn't have taken it back. The experience with James had taught her that a woman couldn't be too careful about such things.

"Amanda?"

She lifted her gaze to see him studying her. "What?"

"What was his name?"

"What was whose name?"

"The guy who told you he wasn't married."

Amanda cleared her throat and shifted nervously in her chair. The thought of James didn't cause her pain anymore, but she didn't know Jordan Richards well enough to tell him just how badly she'd been hoodwinked. A sudden, crazy panic seized her. "Gosh, look at the time," she said, pulling back her sleeve to check her watch a split second after she'd spoken. "I'd better get home." She bolted out of her chair and put her coat back on, then reached for her purse and the bag from the bookstore. She laid a five-dollar bill on the table to pay for her dinner. "It was nice meeting you."

Jordan frowned and slowly pushed back his chair, then stood. "Wait a minute, Amanda. You're not playing fair."

He was right. Jordan hadn't run away, however much he had probably wanted to, and she wouldn't, either.

She sank back into her seat, all too aware that people at surrounding tables were looking on with interest.

"You're not ready to talk about him," Jordan said, sitting down again, "and I'm not ready to talk about her. Deal?"

"Deal," Amanda said.

They discussed the Seattle Seahawks after that, and the Chinese artifacts on display at one of the museums. Then Jordan walked with her to the nearest corner and waited until the bus pulled up.

"Goodbye, Amanda," he said as she climbed the steps.

She dropped her change into the slot and smiled over one shoulder. "Thanks for the company."

He waved as the bus pulled away, and Amanda ached with a bittersweet loneliness she'd never known before, not even in the awful days after her breakup with James.

When Amanda arrived at her apartment building on Seattle's Queen Anne Hill, she was still thinking about Jordan. He'd wanted to offer to drive her home, she knew, but he'd had the good grace not to, and Amanda liked him for that.

In her mailbox she found a sheaf of bills waiting for her. "I'll never save enough to start a bed and breakfast at this rate," she complained to her black-and-white long-haired cat, Gershwin, when he met her at the door.

Gershwin was unsympathetic. As usual, he was interested only in his dinner.

After flipping on the lights, dropping her purse and the book onto the hall table and hanging her coat on the brass-plated tree that was really too large for that little space, Amanda went into the kitchenette.

Gershwin purred and wound himself around her ankles as she opened a can of cat food, but when she scraped it out onto his dish, he abandoned her without compunction.

While Gershwin gobbled, Amanda went back to the mail she'd picked up in the lobby and flipped through it again. Three bills, a you-may-have-already-won and a letter from Eunice.

Amanda set the other envelopes down and opened the crisp

blue one with her sister's return address printed in italics in one corner. She was disappointed when she realized that the letter was just another litany of Eunice's soon-to-be-ex-husband's sins, and she set it aside to finish later.

In the bathroom she started water running into her huge claw-footed tub, then stripped off the skirt and sweater she'd worn to the mall. After disposing of her underthings and panty hose, Amanda climbed into the soothing water.

Gershwin pushed the door open in that officious way cats have and bounded up to stand on the tub's edge with perfect balance. Like a tightrope walker, he strolled back and forth along the chipped porcelain, telling Amanda about his day in a series of companionable meows.

Amanda listened politely as she bathed, but her mind was wandering. She was thinking about Jordan Richards and that recently removed wedding band of his.

She sighed. All her instincts told her he was telling the truth about his marital status, but those same instincts had once insisted that James was all right, too.

Amanda was waiting when the bus pulled up at her corner the next morning. The weather was a little warmer, and the snow, so unusual in Seattle, was already melting.

Fifteen minutes later Amanda walked through the huge revolving door of the Evergreen Hotel. Its lush Oriental carpets were soft beneath the soles of her shoes, and crystal chandeliers winked overhead, their multicolored reflections blazing in the floor-to-ceiling mirrors.

Amanda took the elevator to the third floor, where the hotel's business offices were. As she was passing through the small reception area, Mindy Simmons hailed her from her desk.

"Mr. Mansfield is sick today," she said in an undertone. Mindy was small and pretty, with long brown hair and expressive green eyes. "Your desk is buried in messages."

Amanda went into her office and started dealing with problems. The plumbing in the presidential suite was on the fritz, so she called to make sure Maintenance was on top of the situation. A Mrs. Edman in 1203 suspected one of the maids of stealing her pearl earring, and someone had mixed up some dates at the reception desk—two couples were expecting to occupy the bridal suite on the same night.

It was noon when Amanda finished straightening everything out—Mrs. Edman's pearl earring had fallen behind the television set, the plumbing in the presidential suite was back in working order and each of the newlywed couples would have rooms to themselves. At Mindy's suggestion, she and Amanda went to the busy Westlake Mall for lunch, buying salads at one of the fast-food restaurants and taking a table near a window.

"Two more weeks and I start my vacation," Mindy stated enthusiastically, pouring dressing from a little carton over her salad. "Christmas at Big Mountain. I can hardly wait."

Amanda would just as soon have skipped Christmas altogether if she could have gotten the rest of the world to go along with the idea, but of course she didn't say that. "You and Pete will have a great time at the ski resort."

Mindy was chewing, and she swallowed before answering. "It's just great of his parents to take us along—we could never have afforded it on our own."

With a nod, Amanda poked her fork into a cherry tomato.

"What are you doing over the holidays?" Mindy asked.

Amanda forced a smile. "I'm going to be working," she reminded her friend.

"I know that, but what about a tree and presents and a turkey?"

"I'll have all those things at my mom and stepdad's place."

Mindy, who knew about James and all the dashed hopes he'd left in his wake, looked sympathetic. "You need to meet a new man."

Amanda bristled a little. "It just so happens that a woman can have a perfectly happy life without a man hanging around."

Mindy looked doubtful. "Sure," she said.

"Besides, I met someone just yesterday."

"Who?"

Amanda concentrated on her salad for several long moments. "His name is Jordan Richards, and—"

"Jordan Richards?" Mindy interrupted excitedly. "Wow! How did you ever manage to meet him?"

A little insulted that Mindy seemed to think Jordan was so far out of her orbit that even meeting him was a feat to get excited about, Amanda frowned. "We were in line together at a bookstore. Do you know him?"

"Not exactly," Mindy admitted, subsiding a little. "But my father-in-law does. Jordan Richards practically doubled his retirement fund for him, and they're always writing about him in the financial section of the Sunday paper."

"I didn't know you read that section," Amanda remarked.

"I don't," Mindy admitted readily, unwrapping a bread stick. "But we have dinner with my in-laws practically every Sunday, and that's all Pete and his dad ever talk about. Did he ask you out?"

"Who?"

"Jordan Richards, silly."

Amanda shook her head. "No, we just had Chinese food together and talked a little." She deliberately left out the part about how they'd gone to the minitherapy session and the way she'd reacted when Jordan had asked her about James.

Mindy looked disappointed. "Well, he did ask for your number, didn't he?"

"No. But he knows where I work. If he wants to call, I suppose he will."

A delighted smile lit Mindy's face. Positive thinking was an art form with her. "He'll call. I just know it."

Amanda grinned. "If he does, I won't be able to accept the glory—I owe it all to an article I read in *Cosmo*. I think it was called 'Big Girls Should Talk to Strangers,' or something like that."

Mindy lifted her diet cola in a rousing roast. "Here's to Jordan Richards and a red-hot romance!"

With a chuckle, Amanda touched her cup to Mindy's and drank a toast to something that would probably never happen.

Back at the hotel more crises were waiting to be solved, and there was a message on Amanda's desk, scrawled by the typist who'd filled in for Mindy during lunch. Jordan Richards had called.

A peculiar tightness constricted Amanda's throat, and a flutter started in the pit of her stomach. Mindy's toast echoed in her ears: *"Here's to Jordan Richards and a red-hot romance."*

Amanda laid down the message, telling herself she didn't have time to return the call, then picked it up again. Before she knew it, her finger was punching out the numbers.

"Striner, Striner and Richards," sang a receptionist's voice at the other end of the line.

Amanda drew a deep breath, squared her shoulders and exhaled. "This is Amanda Scott," she said in her most professional voice. "I'm returning a call from Jordan Richards."

"One moment, please."

After a series of clicks and buzzes another female voice came on the line. "Jordan Richards's office. May I help you?"

Again Amanda gave her name. And again she was careful to say she was returning a call that had originated with Jordan.

There was another buzz, then Jordan's deep, crisp voice saying, "Richards."

Amanda hadn't expected a simple thing like the man saying his name to affect her the way it did. It was the strangest sensation to feel dizzy over something like that. She dropped into the swivel chair behind her desk. "Hi. It's Amanda."

"Amanda."

Coming from him, her own name had the same strange impact as his had had.

"How are you?" he asked.

Amanda swallowed. She was a professional with a very responsible job. It was ridiculous to be overwhelmed by something so simple and ordinary as the timbre of a man's voice. "I'm fine," she answered. Nothing more imaginative came to her, and she sat there behind her broad desk, blushing like an eighth-grade schoolgirl trying to work up the courage to ask a boy to a sock hop.

His low, masculine chuckle came over the wire to surround her like a mystical caress. "If I promise not to ask any more questions about you know who, will you go out with me? Some friends of mine are having an informal dinner tonight on their houseboat.''

Amanda still felt foolish for talking about James in the therapy session, then practically bolting when Jordan brought him up again over Chinese food. Lately she just seemed to be a mass of contradictions, feeling one way one minute, another the next. What it all came down to was the fact that Dr. Marshall was right—she needed to start taking chances again. ''Sounds like fun,'' she said after drawing a deep breath.

''Pick you up at seven?''

''Yes.'' And she gave him her address. A little thrill went through her as she laid the receiver back on its cradle, but there was no more time to think about Jordan. The telephone immediately rang again.

''Amanda Scott.''

The chef's assistant was calling. A pipe had broken, and the kitchen was flooding fast.

''Just another manic day,'' Amanda muttered as she hurried off to investigate.

Chapter 2

It was ten minutes after six when Amanda got off the bus in front of her apartment building and dashed inside. After collecting her mail, she hurried up the stairs and jammed her key into the lock. Jordan was picking her up in less than an hour, and she had a hundred things to do to get ready.

Since he'd told her the evening would be a casual one, she selected gray woolen slacks and a cobalt-blue blouse. After a hasty shower, she put on fresh makeup and quickly wove her hair into a French braid.

Gershwin stood on the back of the toilet the whole time she was getting ready, lamenting the treatment of house cats in contemporary America. She had just given him his dinner when a knock sounded at the door.

Amanda's heart lurched like a dizzy ballet dancer, and she wondered why she was being such a ninny. Jordan Richards was just a man, nothing more. And so what if he was successful? She met a lot of men like him in her line of work.

She opened the door and knew a moment of pure exaltation at the look of approval in Jordan's eyes.

"Hi," he said. He wore jeans and a sport shirt, and his hands rested comfortably in the pockets of his brown leather jacket. "You look fantastic."

Amanda thought he looked pretty fantastic himself, but she didn't say so because she'd used up that week's quota of bold moves by talking about James in front of people she didn't know. "Thanks," she said, stepping back to admit him.

Gershwin did a couple of turns around Jordan's ankles and meowed his approval. With a chuckle, Jordan bent to pick him up. "Look at the size of this guy. Is he on steroids or what?"

Amanda laughed. "No, but I suspect him of throwing wild parties and sending out for pizza when I'm not around."

After scratching the cat once behind the ears, Jordan set him down again with a chuckle, but his eyes were serious when he looked at Amanda.

Something in his expression made her breasts grow heavy and her nipples tighten beneath the smooth silk of her blouse. "I suppose we'd better go," she said, sounding somewhat lame even to her own ears.

"Right," Jordan agreed. His voice had the same effect on Amanda it had had earlier. She felt the starch go out of her knees and she was breathless, as though she'd accidentally stepped onto a runaway skateboard.

She took her blue cloth coat from the coat tree, and Jordan helped her into it. She felt his fingertips brush her nape as he lifted her braid from beneath the collar, and hoped he didn't notice that she trembled ever so slightly at his touch.

His car, a sleek black Porsche—Amanda decided then and there that he didn't have kids of his own—was parked at the curb. Jordan opened the passenger door and walked around to get behind the wheel after Amanda was settled.

Soon they were streaking toward Lake Union. It was only when he switched on the windshield wipers that Amanda realized it was raining.

"Have you lived in Seattle long?" she asked, uncomfortable with a silence Jordan hadn't seemed to mind.

"I live on Vashon Island now—I've been somewhere in the vicinity all my life," he answered. "What about you?"

"Seattle's home," Amanda replied.

"Have you ever wanted to live anywhere else?"

She smiled. "Sure. Paris, London, Rome. But after I graduated from college, I was hired to work at the Evergreen, so I settled down here."

"You know what they say—life is what happens while we're making other plans. I always intended to work on Wall Street myself."

"Do you regret staying here?"

Amanda had expected a quick, light denial. Instead she received a sober glance and a low, "Sometimes, yes. Things might have been very different if I'd gone to New York."

For some reason Amanda's gaze was drawn to the pale line across Jordan's left-hand ring finger. Although the windows were closed and the heater was going, Amanda suppressed a shiver. She didn't say anything until Lake Union, with its diamondlike trim of lit houseboats, came into sight. Since the holidays were approaching, the place was even more of a spectacle than usual.

"It looks like a tangle of Christmas tree lights."

Jordan surprised her with one of his fleeting, devastating grins.

"You have a colorful way of putting things, Amanda Scott."

She smiled. "Do your friends like living on a houseboat?"

"I think so," he answered, "but they're planning to move in the spring. They're expecting a baby."

Although lots of children were growing up on Lake Union, Amanda could understand why Jordan's friends would want to bring their little one up on dry land. Her thoughts turned bittersweet as she wondered whether she would ever have a child of her own. She was already twenty-eight—time was running out.

As he pulled the car into a parking lot near the wharves and shut the engine off, she sat up a little straighter, realizing that she'd left his remark dangling. "I'm sorry...I...how nice for them that they're having a baby."

Unexpectedly Jordan reached out and closed his hand over Amanda's. "Did I say something wrong?" he asked with a gentleness that almost brought tears to her eyes.

Amanda shook her head. "Of course not. Let's go in—I'm anxious to meet your friends."

David and Claudia Chamberlin were an attractive couple in their early thirties, he with dark hair and eyes, she with very fair coloring and green eyes. They were both architects, and framed drawings and photographs of their work graced the walls of the small but elegantly furnished houseboat.

Amanda thought of her own humble apartment with Gershwin as its outstanding feature, and wondered if Jordan thought she was dull.

Claudia seemed genuinely interested in her, though, and her greeting was warm. "It's good to see Jordan back in circulation—finally," she confided in a whisper when she and Amanda were alone beside the table where an array of wonderful food was being set out by the caterer's helpers.

Amanda didn't reply to the comment right away, but her gaze strayed to Jordan, who was standing only a few feet away, talking with David. "I guess it's been pretty hard for him," she ventured, pretending to know more than she did.

"The worst," Claudia agreed. She pulled Amanda a little distance farther from the men. "We thought he'd never get over losing Becky."

Uneasily Amanda recalled the pale stripe Jordan's wedding band had left on his finger. Perhaps, she reflected warily, there was a corresponding mark on his soul.

Later, when Amanda had met everyone in the room and mingled accordingly, Jordan laid her coat gently over her shoulders. "How about going out on deck with me for a few minutes?" he asked quietly. "I need some air."

Once again Amanda felt that peculiar lurching sensation deep inside. "Sure," she said with a wary glance at the rain-beaded windows.

"The rain stopped a little while ago," Jordan assured her with a slight grin.

The way he seemed to know what she was thinking was disconcerting.

They left the main cabin through a door on the side, and because the deck was slippery, Jordan put a strong arm around

Amanda's waist. She was fully independent, but she still liked the feeling of being looked after.

The lights of the harbor twinkled on the dark waters of the lake, and Jordan studied them for a while before asking, "So, what do you think of Claudia and David?"

Amanda smiled. "They're pretty interesting," she replied. "I suppose you know they were married in India when they were there with the Peace Corps."

Jordan propped an elbow on the railing and nodded. "David and Claudia are nothing if not unconventional. That's one of the reasons I like them so much."

Amanda was slightly deflated, though she tried hard not to reveal the fact. With her ordinary job, cat and apartment, she knew she must seem prosaic compared to the Chamberlins. Perhaps it was the strange sense of hopelessness she felt that made her reckless enough to ask, "What about your wife? Was she unconventional?"

He turned away from her to stare out at the water, and for a long moment she was sure he didn't intend to answer. Finally, however, he said in a low voice, "She had a degree in marine biology, but she didn't work after the kids were born."

It was the first mention he'd made of any children—Amanda had been convinced, in fact, that he had none. "Kids?" she asked in a small and puzzled voice.

Jordan looked at her in a way that was almost, but not quite, defensive. "There are two—Jessica's five and Lisa's four."

Amanda knew a peculiar joy, as though she'd stumbled upon an unexpected treasure. She couldn't help the quick, eager smile that curved her lips. "I thought—well, when you were driving a Porsche—"

He smiled back at her in an oddly somber way. "Jessie and Lisa live with my sister over in Port Townsend."

Amanda's jubilation deflated. "They live with your sister? I don't understand."

Jordan sighed. "Becky died two weeks after the accident, and I was in the hospital for close to three months. Karen— my sister—and her husband, Paul, took the kids. By the time

I got back on my feet, the four of them had become a family. I couldn't see breaking it up."

An overwhelming sadness caused Amanda to grip the railing for a moment to keep from being swept away by the sheer power of the emotion.

Reading her expression, Jordan gently touched the tip of her nose. "Ready to call it a night? You look tired."

Amanda nodded, too close to tears to speak. She had a tendency to empathize with other people's joys and sorrows, and she was momentarily crushed by the weight of what Jordan had been through.

"I see my daughters often," he assured her, tenderness glinting in his eyes. He kissed her lightly on the mouth, then took her elbow and escorted her back inside the cabin.

They said their goodbyes to David and Claudia Chamberlin, then walked up the wharf to Jordan's car. He was a perfect gentleman, opening the door for Amanda, and she settled wearily into the suede passenger seat.

Back at Amanda's building, Jordan again helped her out of the car, and he walked her to her door. Amanda waited until the last possible second to decide whether she was going to invite him in, breaking her own suspense by blurting out, "Would you like a cup of coffee or something?"

Jordan's hazel eyes twinkled as he placed one hand on either side of the doorjamb, effectively trapping Amanda between his arms. "Not tonight," he said softly.

Amanda's blue eyes widened in confusion. "Don't look now," she replied in a burst of daring cowardice, "but you're sending out conflicting messages."

He chuckled, and his lips touched hers, very tenderly.

Amanda felt a jolt of spiritual electricity spark through her system, burning away every memory of James's touch. Surprise made her draw back from Jordan so suddenly that her head bumped hard against the door.

Jordan lowered one hand to caress her crown, and she felt the French braid coming undone beneath his fingers.

"Careful," he murmured, and then he kissed her again.

This time there was hunger in his touch, and a sweet, frightening power that made Amanda's knees unsteady.

She laid her hands lightly on his chest, trying to ground this second mystical shock, but he interpreted the contact differently and drew back.

"Good night, Amanda," he said quietly. He waited until she'd unlocked her door with a trembling hand, and then he walked away.

Inside the apartment Amanda flipped on the living room light, crossed to the sofa and sagged onto it. She felt as though she were leaning over the edge of a great canyon and the rocks were slipping away beneath her feet.

Gershwin hurled himself into her lap with a loud meow, and she ran one hand distractedly along his silky back. Dr. Marshall had said it was time she started taking chances, and she had an awful feeling she was on the brink of the biggest risk of her life.

The massive redwood-and-glass house overlooking Puget Sound was dark and unwelcoming that night when Jordan pulled into the driveway and reached for the small remote control device lying on his dashboard. He'd barely made the last ferry to the island, and he was tired.

As the garage door rolled upward, he thought of Amanda, and shifted uncomfortably on the seat. He would have given half his stock portfolio to have her sitting beside him now, to talk with her over coffee in the kitchen or wine in front of the fireplace...

To take her to his bed.

Jordan got out of the car and slammed the door behind him. The garage was dark, but he didn't flip on a light until he reached the kitchen. Becky had always said he had the night vision of a vampire.

Becky. He clung to the memory of her smile, her laughter, her perfume. She'd been tiny and spirited, with dark hair and eyes, and it seemed to Jordan that she'd never been far from his side, even after her death. He'd loved her to an excruciating degree, but for the past few months she'd been steadily receding from his mind and heart. Now, with the coming of Amanda, her image seemed to be growing more indistinct with every passing moment.

Jordan glanced into the laundry room, needing something real and mundane to focus on. A pile of jeans, sweatshirts and towels lay on the floor, so he crammed as much as he could into the washing machine, then added soap and turned the dial. A comforting, ordinary sound resulted.

Returning to the kitchen, Jordan shrugged out of his leather jacket and laid it over one of the bar stools at the counter. He opened the refrigerator, studied its contents without actually focusing on a single item, then closed it again. He wasn't hungry for anything except Amanda, and it was too soon for that.

Too soon, he reflected with a rueful grin as he walked through the dining room to the front entryway and the stairs. He hadn't bothered with such niceties as timing with the women he'd dated over the past two years—in truth, their feelings just hadn't mattered much to him, though he'd never been deliberately unkind.

He trailed his hand over the top of the polished oak banister as he climbed the stairs. With Amanda, things were different. Timing was crucial, and so were her feelings.

The empty house yawned around Jordan as he opened his bedroom door and went inside. In the adjoining bathroom he took off his clothes and dropped them neatly into the hamper, then stepped into the shower.

Thinking of Amanda again, he turned on the cold water and endured its biting chill until some of the intolerable heat had abated. But while he was brushing his teeth, Amanda sneaked back into his mind.

He saw her standing on the deck of the Chamberlins' boat, looking up at him with that curious vulnerability showing in her blue-green eyes. It was as though she didn't know how beautiful she was, or how strong, and yet she had to, because she was out there making a life for herself.

Rubbing his now-stubbled chin, Jordan wandered into the bedroom, threw back the covers and slid between the sheets. He felt the first stirrings of rage as he thought about the mysterious James and the damage he'd done to Amanda's soul. Jordan had seen the bruises in her eyes every time she'd looked at him, and the memory made him want to find the bastard who'd hurt her and systematically tear him apart.

Jordan turned onto his stomach and tried to put the scattered images of the past two days out of his thoughts. This time, just before he dropped off to sleep, was reserved for thoughts of Becky, as always.

He waited, but his late wife's face didn't form in his mind. He could only see Amanda, with her wide, trusting blue eyes, her soft, spun-honey hair, her shapely and inviting body. He wanted her with a desperation that made his loins ache.

Furious, Jordan slammed one fist into the mattress and flipped onto his back, training all his considerable energy on remembering Becky's face.

He couldn't.

After several minutes of concentrated effort, all of it fruitless, panic seized him, and he bolted upright, switched on the lamp and reached for the picture on his nightstand.

Becky smiled back at him from the photograph as if to say, *Don't worry, sweetheart. Everything will be okay.*

With a raspy sigh, Jordan set the picture back on the table and turned out the light. Becky's favorite reassurance didn't work that night. Maybe things would be okay in the long run, but there was a lot of emotional white water between him and any kind of happy ending.

It was Saturday morning, and Amanda luxuriated in the fact that she didn't have to put on makeup, style her hair, or even get dressed if she didn't want to. She really tried to be lazy, but she felt strangely ambitious, and there was no getting around it.

She climbed out of bed and padded barefoot into the kitchen, where she got the coffee maker going and fed Gershwin. Then she had a quick shower and dressed in battered jeans, a Seahawks T-shirt and sneakers.

She was industriously vacuuming the living room rug, when the telephone rang.

The sound was certainly nothing unusual, but it fairly stopped Amanda's heart. She kicked the switch on the vacuum cleaner with her toe and lunged for the telephone, hoping to hear Jordan's voice since she hadn't seen or heard from him in nearly a week.

Instead it was her mother. "Hello, darling," said Marion Whitfield. "You sound breathless. Were you just coming in from the store or something?"

Amanda sank onto the couch. "No, I was only doing housework," she replied, feeling deflated even though she loved and admired this woman who had made a life for herself and both her daughters after the man of the house had walked out on them all.

"That's nice," Marion commented, for she was a great believer in positive reinforcement. "Listen, I called to ask if you'd like to go Christmas shopping with me. We could have lunch, too, and maybe even take in a movie."

Amanda sighed. She still didn't feel great about Christmas, and the stores and restaurants would be jam-packed. The theaters, of course, would be full of screaming children left there by harried mothers trying to complete their shopping. "I think I'll just stay home, if you don't mind." She stated the refusal in a kindly tone, not wanting to hurt her mother's feelings.

"Is everything all right?"

Amanda caught one fingernail between her teeth for a moment before answering, "Mostly, yes."

"It's time you put that nasty experience with James Brockman behind you," Marion said forthrightly.

The two women were friends, as well as mother and daughter, and Amanda was not normally secretive with Marion. However, the thing with Jordan was too new and too fragile to be discussed; after all, he might never call again. "I'm trying, Mom," she replied.

"Well, Bob and I want you to come over for dinner soon. Like tomorrow, for instance."

"I'll let you know," Amanda promised quickly as the doorbell made its irritating buzz. "And stop worrying about me, okay?"

"Okay," Marion answered without conviction just before Amanda hung up.

Amanda expected one of the neighbor children, or maybe the postman with a package, so when she opened the door and found Jordan standing in the hallway, she felt as though she'd just run into a wall at full tilt.

For his part, Jordan looked a little bewildered, as though he might be surprised to find himself at Amanda's door. "I should have called," he said.

Amanda recovered herself. "Come in," she replied with a smile.

He hesitated for a moment, then stepped into the apartment, his hands tucked into the pockets of his jacket. He was wearing jeans and a green turtleneck, and his brown hair was damp from the Seattle drizzle. "I was wondering if you'd like to go out to lunch or something."

Amanda glanced at the clock on the mantel and was amazed to see that it was nearly noon. The morning had flown by in a flurry of housecleaning. "Sure," she said. "I'll just clean up a little—"

He reached out and caught hold of her hand when she would have disappeared into her bedroom. "You look fine," he told her, and his voice was very low, like the rumble of an earthquake deep down in the ground.

By sheer force of will, Amanda shored up her knees, only to have him pull her close and lock his hands lightly behind the small of her back. A hot flush made her cheeks ache, and she had to force herself to meet his eyes.

Jordan chuckled. "Do I really scare you so much?" he asked.

Amanda wet her lips with the tip of her tongue in an unconscious display of nervousness. "Yes."

"Why?"

The question was reasonable, but Amanda didn't know the answer. "I'm not sure."

He grinned. "Where would you like to go for lunch?"

She would have been content not to go out at all, preferring just to stand there in his arms all afternoon, breathing in his scent and enjoying the lean, hard feel of his body against hers. She gave herself an inward shake. "You know, I just refused a similar invitation from my mother, and she would have thrown in a movie."

Jordan laughed and smoothed Amanda's bangs back from her forehead. "All right, so will I."

But Amanda shook her head. "Too many munchkins screaming and throwing popcorn."

His expression changed almost imperceptibly. "Don't you like kids?"

"I love them," Amanda answered, "except when they're traveling in herds."

Jordan chuckled again and gave her another light kiss. "Okay, we'll go to something R-rated. Nobody under seventeen admitted without a parent."

"You've got a deal," Amanda replied.

Just as he was helping her get into her coat, the telephone rang. Praying there wasn't a disaster at the Evergreen to be taken care of, Amanda answered, "Hello?"

"Hello, Amanda." She hadn't heard that voice in six long months, and the sound of it stunned her. It was James.

Grimacing at Jordan, she spoke into the receiver. "I don't want to talk to you, now or ever."

"Please don't hang up," James said quickly.

Amanda bit down on her lip and lowered her eyes. "What is it?"

"Madge is divorcing me."

She drew a deep breath and let it out again. "Congratulations, James," she said, not with cruelty but with resignation. After all, it was no great surprise, and she had no idea why he felt compelled to share the news with her.

"I'd like for you and me to get back together," he said in that familiar tone that had once rendered her pliant and gullible.

"There's absolutely no chance of that," Amanda replied, forcing herself to meet Jordan's gaze again. He was standing at the door, his hand on the knob, watching her with concern but not condemnation. "Goodbye, James." With that, she placed the receiver back in its cradle.

Jordan remained where he was for a long moment, then he crossed the room to where Amanda stood, bundled in her coat, and gently lifted her hair out from under her collar. "Still want to go out?" he asked quietly.

Amanda was oddly shaken, but she nodded, and they left the apartment together. The phone began ringing again when they reached the top of the stairs, but this time Amanda made no effort to answer it.

"I guess I can't blame him for being persistent," Jordan remarked when they were seated in the Porsche. "You're a beautiful woman, Amanda."

She sighed, ignoring the compliment because it didn't register. "I'll never forgive James for lying to me the way he did," she got out. Tears stung her eyes as she remembered the blinding pain of his deceit.

Jordan pulled out into the rainy-day traffic and kept his eyes on the road. "He wants you back," he guessed.

Amanda noticed that his hands tensed slightly around the steering wheel.

"That's what he said," she confessed, staring out at the decorated streets but not really seeing them.

"Do you believe him?"

Amanda shrugged. "It doesn't matter whether I do or not. I've made my decision and I'm not going to change my mind." She found some tissue in her purse and resolutely dried her eyes, trying in vain to convince herself that Jordan hadn't noticed she was crying.

He drove to a pizza joint across the street from a mall north of the city. "This okay?" he asked, bringing the sleek car to a stop in one of the few parking spaces available. "We could order takeout if you'd rather not go in."

Amanda drew a deep breath, composing herself. The time with James was behind her, and she wanted to keep it there, to enjoy the here and now with Jordan. Christmas crowds or none. "Let's eat here," she said.

He favored her with a half grin and came around to open her door for her. As she stood, she accidentally brushed against him, and felt that familiar twisting ache deep inside herself.

She was going to end up making love with Jordan Richards, she just knew it. It was inevitable.

The realization that he was reading her thoughts once more made Amanda blush, and she drew back when he took her hand. His grip only became firmer, however, and she didn't try to pull away again. She was in the mood to follow where Jordan might lead—which, to Amanda's way of thinking, made it a darned good thing they were approaching the door of a pizza parlor instead of a bedroom.

Chapter 3

The pizza was uncommonly good, it seemed to Amanda, but memories of the R-rated movie they saw afterward made her fidget in the passenger seat of Jordan's Porsche. "I've never heard of anybody doing that with an ice cube," she remarked with a slight frown.

Jordan laughed. "That was interesting, all right."

"Do you think it was symbolic?"

He was still grinning. "No. It was definitely hormones, pure and simple."

Amanda finally relaxed a little and managed to smile. "You're probably right."

Since there were a lot of cars parked in front of Amanda's building, a sleek silver Mercedes among them, Jordan parked almost a block away. It seemed natural to hold hands as they walked back to the entrance.

Amanda was stunned to see James sitting on the bottom step of the stairway leading up to the second floor. He was wearing his usual three-piece tailor-made suit, a necessity for a corporate chief executive officer like himself, and his silver gray hair looked as dashing as ever. His tanned face showed signs of strain, however, and the once-over he gave Jordan was one of cordial contempt.

Amanda's first instinct was to let go of Jordan's hand, but he tightened his grip when she tried.

Meanwhile James had risen from his seat on the stairs. "We have to talk," he said to Amanda.

She shook her head, grateful now for Jordan's presence and his grasp on her hand. "There's nothing to say."

The man she had once loved arched an eyebrow. "Isn't there? You could start by introducing me to the new man in your life."

It was Jordan who spoke. "Jordan Richards," he said evenly, without offering his hand.

James studied him with new interest flickering in his shrewd eyes. "Brockman," he answered. "James Brockman."

A glance at Jordan revealed that he recognized the name—anyone active in the business world would have—but he clearly wasn't the least bit intimidated. He simply nodded an acknowledgment.

Amanda ran her tongue over her lips. "Let us pass, James," she said. She'd never spoken so authoritatively to him before, but she took no pleasure in the achievement because she knew she wouldn't have managed it if Jordan hadn't been there.

James did not look at Amanda, but at Jordan. Some challenge passed between them, and the air was charged with static electricity for several moments. Then James stepped aside to lean against the banister, leaving barely enough room for Jordan and Amanda to walk by.

"Richards."

Jordan stopped, still holding Amanda's hand, and looked back at James over one shoulder in inquiry.

"I'll call your office Monday morning. I'd be interested to know what we have in common—where investments are concerned, naturally."

Amanda felt her face heat. Again she tried to pull away from Jordan; again he restrained her. "Naturally," Jordan responded coldly, and then he continued up the stairway, bringing Amanda with him.

"I'm sorry," she said the moment they were alone in her apartment. She was leaning against the closed door.

"Why?" Jordan asked, reaching out to unbutton her coat. He helped her out of it, then hung it on the brass tree. Amanda watched him with injury in her eyes as he removed his jacket and put it with her coat.

She had been leaning against the door again, and she thrust herself away. "Because of James, of course."

"It wasn't your fault he came here."

She sighed and stopped in the tiny entryway, her back to Jordan, the fingers of one hand pressed to her right temple. She knew he was right, but she was slightly nauseous all the same. "That remark he made about what the two of you might have in common…"

Jordan reached out and took her shoulders in his hands, turning her gently to face him. "Your past is your own business, Amanda. I'm interested in the woman you are now, not the woman you were six months or six years ago."

Amanda blinked, then bit her upper lip for a moment. "But he meant—"

He touched her lip with an index finger. "I know what he meant," he said with hoarse gentleness. "When and if it happens for us, Amanda, you won't be the first woman I've been with. I'm not going to condemn you because I'm not the first man."

With that, the subject of that aspect of Amanda's relationship with James was closed forever. In fact, it was almost as though the subject hadn't been broached. "Would you like some coffee or something?" she asked, feeling better.

Jordan grinned. "Sure."

When Amanda came out of the kitchenette minutes later, carrying two mugs of instant coffee, Jordan was studying the blue-and-white patchwork quilt hanging on the wall behind her couch. Gershwin seemed to have become an appendage to his right ankle.

"Did you make this?"

Amanda nodded proudly. "I designed it, too."

Jordan looked impressed. "So there's more to you than the

mild-mannered assistant hotel manager who gets her Christmas shopping done early,'' he teased.

She smiled. ''A little, yes.'' She extended one mug of coffee and he took it, lifting it to his lips. ''I had a good time today, Jordan.''

When Amanda sat down on the couch, Jordan did, too. His nearness brought images from the movie they'd seen back to her mind. ''So did I,'' he answered, putting his coffee down on the rickety cocktail table.

Damn that guy with the ice cube, Amanda fretted to herself as Jordan put his hands on her shoulders again and slowly drew her close. It seemed to her that a small eternity passed before their lips touched, igniting the soft suspense Amanda felt into a flame of awareness.

The tip of his tongue encircled her lips, and when they parted at his silent bidding, he took immediate advantage. Somehow Amanda found herself lying down on the sofa instead of sitting up, and when Jordan finally pulled away from her mouth, she arched her neck. He kissed the pulse point at the base of her throat, then progressed to the one beneath her right ear. In the meantime, Amanda could feel her T-shirt being worked slowly up her rib cage.

When he unsnapped her bra and laid it aside, revealing her ripe breasts, Amanda closed her eyes and lifted her back slightly in a silent offering.

He encircled one taut nipple with feather-light kisses, and Amanda moaned softly when he captured the morsel between his lips and began to suckle. She entangled her hands in his hair and spread her legs, one foot high on the sofa back, the other on the floor, to accommodate him.

The eloquent pressure of his desire made Amanda ache to be taken, but she was too breathless to speak, too swept up in the gentle incursion to ask for conquering. When she felt the snap on her jeans give way, followed soon after by the zipper, she only lifted her hips so the jeans could be peeled away. They vanished, along with her panties and her sneakers, and Jordan began to caress her intimately with one hand while he enjoyed her other breast.

The ordinary light in the living room turned colors and made strange patterns in front of Amanda's eyes as Jordan kissed his way down over her satiny, quivering belly to her thighs.

She whimpered when he burrowed into her deepest secret, gave a lusty cry when he plundered that secret with his mouth. Her hips shot upward, and Jordan cupped his hands beneath her bottom, holding her in his hands as he would sparkling water from a stream. "Jordan," she gasped, turning her head from side to side in a fever of passion when he showed her absolutely no mercy.

He flung her over the savage brink, leaving her to convulse repeatedly at the top of an invisible geyser. When the last trace of response had been wrung from her, he lowered her gently back to the sofa.

She lay there watching him, the back of one hand resting against her mouth, her body covered in a fine mist of perspiration. Jordan was sitting up, one of her bare legs draped across his lap, his eyes gentle as he laid a hand on Amanda's trembling belly as if to soothe it.

"I want you," she said brazenly when she could speak.

Jordan smiled and traced the outline of her jaw with one finger, then the circumferences of both her nipples. "Not this time, Mandy," he answered, his voice hardly more than a ragged whisper.

Amanda was both surprised and insulted. "What the hell do you mean, 'not this time'? Were you just trying to prove—"

Jordan interrupted her tirade by bending to kiss her lips. "I wasn't trying to prove anything. I just don't want you hating my guts when you wake up tomorrow."

Amanda's body, so long untouched by a man, was primed for a loving it wasn't going to receive. "You're too late," she spat, bolting to an upright position and righting her bra and T-shirt. "I *already* hate your guts!"

Jordan obligingly fetched her jeans and panties from the floor where he'd tossed them earlier. "Probably, but you'll forgive me when the time is right."

She squirmed back into the rest of her clothes, then stood

looking down at Jordan, one finger waggling. ''No, I won't!'' she argued hotly.

He clasped her hips in his hands and brought her forward, then softly nipped the place he'd just pillaged so sweetly. Even through her jeans, Amanda felt a piercing response to the contact; a shock went through her, and she gave a soft cry of mingled protest and surrender.

Jordan drew back and gave her a swat on the bottom. ''See? You'll forgive me.''

Amanda would have whirled away then, but Jordan caught her by the hand and wrenched her onto his lap. When she would have risen, he restricted her by catching hold of her hands and imprisoning them behind her back.

With his free hand, he pushed her T-shirt up in front again, then boldly cupped a lace-covered breast that throbbed to be bared to him once more. ''It's going to be very good when we make love,'' he said firmly, ''but that isn't going to happen yet.''

Amanda squirmed, infuriated and confused. ''Then why don't you let me go?'' she breathed.

He chuckled. ''Because I want to make damn sure you don't forget that preview of how it's going to be.''

''Of all the arrogance—''

Jordan pulled down one side of her bra, causing the breast to spring triumphantly to freedom. ''I've got plenty of that,'' he breathed against a peak that strained toward him.

Amanda moaned despite herself when he took her into his mouth again.

''Umm,'' he murmured, blatant in his enjoyment.

Utter and complete surprise possessed Amanda when she realized she was being propelled to another release, with Jordan merely gripping her hands behind her and feasting on her breast. She didn't want him to know, and yet her body was already betraying her with feverish jerks and twists.

She bit down hard on her lower lip and tried to keep herself still, but she couldn't. She was moving at lightning speed toward a collision with a comet.

Jordan lifted his mouth from her breast just long enough to

mutter, "So it's like that, is it?" before driving her hard up against her own nature as a woman.

She surrendered in a burst of surprised gasps and sagged against Jordan, resting her head on his shoulder when it was finally over. "H-how did that happen?"

Still caressing her breast, Jordan spoke against her ear. "No idea," he answered, "but it damned near made me change my mind about waiting."

Amanda lay against his chest until she'd recovered the ability to stand and to breathe properly, then she rose from his lap, snapped her bra and pulled down her T-shirt. In a vain effort to regain her dignity, she squared her shoulders and plunged the splayed fingers of both hands through her hair. "You don't find me attractive—that's it, isn't it?"

"That's the most ridiculous question I've ever been asked," Jordan answered, rising a little awkwardly—and painfully, it seemed to Amanda—from the sofa. "I wouldn't have done the things I just did if I didn't."

"Then why don't you want me?"

"Believe me, I do want you. Too badly to risk lousing things up so soon."

Amanda wasn't satisfied with that answer, so she turned on one heel and fled into the bathroom, where she splashed cold water on her face and brushed her love-tousled hair. When she came out, half fearing that Jordan would be gone, she found him standing at the window, gazing out at the city.

Calmer, she stood behind him, slipped her arms around his lean waist and kissed his nape. "Stay for supper?"

He turned in her embrace to smile down into her eyes. "That depends on what's on the menu."

Amanda was mildly affronted, remembering his rejection. "It isn't me," she stated with a small pout, "so you can relax."

He laughed and gave her another playful swat on the bottom. "Take it from me, Mandy—I'm not relaxed."

She grinned, glad to know he was suffering justly, and kissed his chin, which was already darkening with the shadow of a beard. "Nobody has called me 'Mandy' since first grade," she said.

"Good."

"Why is that good?" Amanda inquired, snuggling close.

"Because it saves me the trouble of thinking up some cutesy nickname like 'babycakes' or 'buttercup.'"

She laughed. "I can't imagine you calling me 'buttercup' with a straight face."

"I don't think I could," he replied, bending his head to kiss her thoroughly. Amanda's knees were weak when he finally drew back.

"You delight in tormenting me," she protested.

His eyes twinkled. "What's for supper?"

"Grilled cheese sandwiches, unless we go to the market," Amanda answered.

"The market it is," Jordan replied. Once again, in the entryway he helped Amanda into her coat.

"You have good manners for a rascal," Amanda remarked quite seriously.

Jordan laughed. "Thank you—I think."

They walked to a small store on the corner, where food was overpriced but fresh and plentiful. Amanda selected two steaks, vegetables for a salad and potatoes for baking.

"Does your fireplace work?" Jordan asked, lingering in front of a display of synthetic logs.

Amanda nodded, wondering if she could stand the romance of a crackling fire when Jordan was so determined not to make love to her. "Are you trying to drive me crazy, or what?" she countered, her eyes snapping with irritation.

He gave her one of his nuclear grins, then picked up two of the logs and carried them to the checkout counter, where he threw down a twenty-dollar bill. He would have paid for the food, too, except that Amanda wouldn't let him.

She did permit him to carry everything back to the apartment, however, thinking it might drain off some of his excess energy.

When they were back in Amanda's apartment, he moved the screen from in front of the fireplace as Gershwin meowed curiously at his elbow. After opening the damper, he laid one of the logs he'd bought in the grate. Amanda glanced at the label on the other log and saw it was meant to last a full three hours.

She grinned as she got her favorite skillet out of the drawer underneath the stove. Two logs totaled six hours. Maybe Jordan would change his mind about waiting before that much time slipped past.

Dusting his hands together, he came into the kitchenette, and Amanda could see the flicker of the fire reflected on the shiny front of her refrigerator door. Without being asked, he took the vegetables out of the bag and began washing them at the sink.

Amanda went to his side, handing him both the potatoes. "You're pretty handy in a kitchen, fella," she remarked in a teasing, sultry voice.

Jordan's eyes danced when he looked at her, and his expression said he was pretty handy in a few other rooms, too. "Thanks." He scrubbed the potatoes and handed them back to Amanda, who put a little swing in her hips as she walked away because she knew he was watching.

He laughed. "You need a spanking."

Amanda poked the potatoes with a fork and set them in the tiny microwave oven her mother and stepfather had given her the Christmas before. "Very kinky, Mr. Richards."

Jordan chuckled as he went back to chopping vegetables, and Amanda found the wooden salad bowl she'd bought in Hawaii and set it on the counter beside him.

They ate at the glass table in Amanda's living room, the fire dancing on the hearth and casting its image on their wineglasses. Darkness had long since settled over the city, and Amanda wondered why she hadn't noticed when the daylight fled.

"Tell me about your daughters," she said when the meal was nearly over.

Jordan pushed his plate away and took a sip of his wine before replying. "They're normal kids, I guess. They like to watch *Sesame Street*, have me read the funny papers to them, things like that."

Amanda felt sad, but if someone had asked, she would have had to admit she wasn't thinking about Jordan's children at all.

She was remembering how it felt when her dad had gone away that long-ago Christmas Day, swearing never to come back. And he hadn't. "Do you miss them?" she asked.

"Yes," he admitted frankly. "But I know they're better off with Karen and Paul."

"Why?" Amanda dared to ask.

Jordan lifted his shoulders in a slight shrug. "I told you— my sister and her husband took them in when I was in the hospital. I'm more like an uncle to them than a father. They wouldn't understand if I uprooted them now."

Amanda wasn't so sure, but she didn't say that because she knew she'd already overstepped her bounds in some ways. If Jordan didn't want to raise his own children, that was his business, but it made Amanda wonder what would happen if the two of them were ever married and had babies. If she died, would he just send the kids to live with someone else?

She refilled her wineglass and took a healthy sip.

There was a look of quiet understanding in Jordan's eyes as he watched her. "What have I done now?" he asked.

"Nothing," Amanda lied, setting her glass down and jumping up to begin clearing the table.

Jordan rose from his chair and elbowed her aside. "Go and sit by the fire. I'll take care of this."

Apparently giving orders had become a habit with Jordan over the course of his successful career. "I'll help," she insisted, following him into the kitchen with the salad bowl in her hands.

Jordan scraped and rinsed the plates, and Amanda put them, along with the silverware and glasses, into the dishwasher.

"Somebody trained you rather well," she commented grudgingly.

He gave her a meltdown grin. "Thanks for noticing," he said with a slight leer.

Amanda's face turned pink. "I was talking about cooking and doing dishes!"

Jordan smiled at her discomfiture. "Oh," he said, but he sounded patently unconvinced.

Amanda put what remained of the salad in a smaller bowl,

covered that tightly with plastic wrap, then stuck it into the refrigerator. She longed to ask him what kind of wife Becky had been, but she didn't dare. She knew he'd say she'd been wonderful, and Amanda wasn't feeling grown-up enough to deal with that.

He was leaning against the sink, watching her, his arms folded in front of his chest. "James is a lot older than you are," he said.

The remark was so out of left field that Amanda was momentarily stunned by it. "I know," she finally managed, standing in the doorway that led to the living room.

"Where did you meet him?"

Amanda couldn't think why she was answering, since they had agreed not to talk about James, but answer she did. "At the hotel," she replied with a sigh. "He taught a management seminar there a year and a half ago."

"And you went?"

She couldn't read Jordan's mood either in his eyes or his voice, and she was unsettled by the question. "Yes. He asked me out to dinner the first night, and after that I saw him whenever he was in Seattle on business."

Jordan crossed the room and enfolded Amanda in his arms, and the relief she felt was totally out of proportion to the circumstances.

"I have to know one thing, Mandy. Do you love him?"

She shook her head. "No." She tasted wine on Jordan's lips when he kissed her. And she tasted wanting. *Do you still love Becky?* she longed to ask, but she was too afraid of the answer to voice the question.

Slipping his arm around her waist, Jordan ushered Amanda into the living room, where they sat on a hooked rug in front of the fireplace. He gripped her hand and stared into the flames in the silence for a long time, then he turned, looked into her fire-lit eyes and said, "I'm sorry, Mandy. I didn't have any right to ask about James."

She let her head rest against the place where his arm and shoulder met. "It's okay. I made a fool of myself, and I can admit that now."

Jordan caught her chin in his hand and wouldn't let her look away. "Let's get one thing straight here," he said in gentle reproach. "The only mistake you made was trusting the bastard. He's the fool."

Amanda sighed. "That's a refreshing opinion. Most people either say or imply that I should have known better."

"Not this people," Jordan answered, tasting her lips.

Although it seemed impossible, Amanda wanted Jordan more now than she had on the couch earlier when he'd brought her face to face with her own womanhood. She longed to take him by the hand and lead him to her bed, but the thought of a second rebuff stopped her. In fact, she supposed it was about time she started taking the advice her mother had given her in ninth grade and play hard to get.

She moved a little apart from Jordan, stiffened her shoulders and raised her chin. "Maybe you should go," she said.

Jordan showed no signs of leaving. Instead he put his hands on Amanda's shoulders and lowered her to the hooked rug, stretching out beside her and laying one hand brazenly on her breast. The nipple tightened obediently beneath his palm.

Amanda moved to rise, but Jordan pressed her back down again, this time with a consuming kiss. "Don't you dare start anything you don't intend to finish," she ordered in a raspy whisper when at last he'd drawn away from her mouth. Having obtained the response he wanted from her right breast, he was now working on her left.

"I'll finish it," he vowed in a husky murmur, "when the time is right."

He lowered his hand to her belly, covering it with splayed fingers, and Amanda's heart pounded beneath her T-shirt. She pulled on his nape until his mouth again joined with hers, and the punishment for this audacious act was the unsnapping of her jeans.

"Damn it, Jordan, I don't like being teased."

He pulled at the zipper, and then his hand was in between her jeans and her panties, just resting there, soaking up her warmth, making her grow moist. That part of her body was like an exotic orchid flowering in a hothouse.

"Tough," he replied with a cocky grin just before he bent and scraped one hidden nipple lightly with his teeth, causing it to leap to attention.

Amanda's formidable pride was almost gone, and she had to grasp the rug and bite down on her lower lip to keep from begging him to make love to her.

"This night is just for you," he told her, his hand making a fiery circle at the junction of her thighs. "Why can't you accept that?"

"Because it isn't normal, that's why," Amanda gasped, trying to hold her hips still but finding it impossible. "You're a man. You're supposed to have just one thing on your mind. You're supposed to be trying to jump my bones."

He laughed at that. "What a chauvinistic thing to say."

Amanda groaned as he continued his sweet devilment. "I've never seen anything in *Cosmopolitan* that told what to d-do when this happens," she complained.

Again Jordan laughed. "I can tell you what to do," he said when he'd recovered himself a little. "Enjoy it."

Amanda was beginning to breathe hard. "Damn you, Jordan—I'll make you pay for this!"

"I'm counting on that," he said against her mouth.

Moments later Amanda was soaring again. She dug her fingers into Jordan's shoulders while she plunged her heels into the rug, and everyone in the apartment building would have known how well he'd loved her if he hadn't clamped his mouth over hers and swallowed her cries.

"If this is some kind of power game," Amanda sputtered five minutes later when she could manage to speak, fastening her jeans and sitting up again, "I don't want to play."

"You could have fooled me," Jordan responded.

Amanda gave a strangled cry of frustration and anger. "I can't imagine why I keep letting you get away with this."

"I can," he replied. "It feels good, and it's been a long time. Right?"

Amanda let her forehead rest against his shoulder, embarrassed. "Yes," she confessed.

He kissed the top of her head. "I should have dessert before dinner more often," he teased.

Amanda groaned, unable to look at him, and he chuckled and lifted her chin for a light kiss. "You're impossible," she murmured.

"And I'm leaving," he added with a glance at his watch. "It's time you were in bed."

Bleakness filled Amanda at the thought of climbing into bed alone, and she was just about to protest, when Jordan laid a finger to her nose and asked, "Will you go Christmas shopping with me tomorrow?"

Amanda would have gone to Zanzibar. "Yes," she answered like a hypnotized person.

Jordan kissed her again, leaving her lips warm and slightly swollen. "Good night," he said. And then, after a backward look and a wave, he was gone.

Chapter 4

The telephone jangled just as Amanda finished with her makeup the next morning. She'd managed to camouflage the shadows under her eyes—the result of sleeping only a few hours—with a cover stick.

"Hello?" she blurted into the receiver of her bedside telephone, hoping Jordan wasn't calling to back out of their shopping trip.

"If I remember correctly," her mother began dryly without returning the customary greeting, "you were supposed to call last night and let us know whether you were coming over for supper."

Amanda stretched the phone cord as far as her closet, where she took out black wool slacks. "Sorry, Mom," she answered contritely. "I forgot, but you'll be glad to know it was because of a man." She went to the dresser for her pink cashmere sweater while waiting for her mother to digest her last remark.

"A man?" Marion echoed, unable to hide the pleasure in her voice.

"And James was here yesterday," Amanda went on after pulling the sweater on over her head.

Marion drew in her breath. "Don't tell me you're seeing him again—"

"Of course not, Mom," Amanda scolded, propping the receiver between her shoulder and her ear while she wriggled into the sleek black pants.

"You're deliberately confusing me," Marion accused.

Amanda sighed. "Listen, I'll tell you everything tomorrow, okay? I'll stop by after work and catch you up on all the latest developments."

"So there is somebody besides James?" Marion pressed, sounding pleased.

"Yep," Amanda answered just as the door buzzer sounded. "Gotta go—he's here."

"'Bye," Marion said cooperatively, and promptly hung up.

Amanda was brushing her hair as she hurried through the apartment to open the door. She was smiling, since she expected Jordan, but she found a delivery man from one of the more posh department stores in the hallway, instead. He was holding two silver gift boxes, one large and one fairly small. "Ms. A. Scott?" he asked.

Amanda nodded, mystified.

"These are for you—special express delivery," the man said, holding on to the packages while he shoved a clipboard at Amanda. "Sign on line twenty-seven."

She found the appropriate line and scrawled her name there, and the man gave her the packages in return for the clipboard.

After depositing the boxes on the couch and rummaging through her purse for a tip, she closed the door and lifted the lid off the smaller box. A skimpy aqua bikini lay inside, but there was no card or note to explain.

She opened the large box and gasped, faced with the rich, unmistakable splendor of sable. A small envelope lay on top, but Amanda didn't need to read it to know the gifts were from James.

As a matter of curiosity, she looked at the card: "Honeymoon in Hawaii, then on to Copenhagen? Call me. James."

With a sigh, Amanda tossed down the card. She was just

about to call the store and ask to return the two boxes, when there was a knock at the door.

She rushed to open it and found Jordan standing in the hallway, looking spectacular in blue jeans, a lightweight yellow sweater and a tweed sport jacket.

"Hi," he said, his bright hazel eyes registering approval as he looked at her.

"Come in," Amanda replied, stepping back and holding the door open wide. "I'm just about finished with my hair. Pour yourself a cup of coffee and I'll be right out."

He stopped her when she would have turned away from him, and lightly entangled the fingers of one hand in her hair. "Don't change it," he said hoarsely. "It looks great."

Amanda's heart was beating a little faster just because he was close and because he was touching her. Since she didn't know what to say, she didn't speak.

Jordan kissed her lightly on the lips. "Good morning, Mandy," he said, and his voice was still husky. Amanda had a vision of him carrying her off to bed, and heat flooded her entire body, a blush rising in her cheeks.

"Good morning," she replied, her voice barely more than a squeak. "How about that coffee?"

His gaze had shifted to the boxes on the couch. "What's this?" There was a teasing reproach in his eyes when they returned to her face. "Opening your presents before Christmas, Mandy? For shame."

Amanda had completely forgotten the unwanted gifts, and the reminder deflated her spirits a little. "I'm sending them back," she said, hoping Jordan wouldn't pursue the subject.

His expression sobered. "James?"

Amanda licked her lips, then nodded nervously. She wasn't entirely displeased to see a muscle in Jordan's cheek grow taut, then relax again.

"Persistent, isn't he?"

"Yes," Amanda admitted. "He is." And after that there seemed to be nothing more to say—about James, anyway.

"Let's go," Jordan told her, kissing her forehead. "We'll get some breakfast on the way."

Amanda disappeared into the bedroom to put on her shoes, and when she came out, Jordan was studying the quilt over her couch again, his hands in his hip pockets.

"You know, you have a real talent for this," he said.

Amanda smiled. James had always been impatient with her quilting, saying she ought to save the needlework for when she was old and had nothing better to do. "Thanks."

Jordan followed her out of the apartment and waited patiently while she locked the door. He held her elbow lightly as they went down the stairs, once again giving her the wonderful sensation of being protected.

The sun was shining, which was cause for rejoicing in Seattle at that time of year, and Amanda felt happy as Jordan closed the car door after her.

When he slid behind the wheel, he just sat there for a few minutes and looked at her. Then he put a hand in her hair again. "Excuse me, lady," he said, his voice low, "but has anybody told you this morning that you're beautiful?"

Amanda flushed, but her eyes were sparkling. "No, sir," she answered, playing the game. "They haven't."

He leaned toward her and gave her a lingering kiss that made a sweet languor blossom inside her.

"There's an oversight that needs correcting," he murmured afterward. "You're beautiful."

Amanda was trembling when he finally turned to start the ignition, fasten his seat belt and steer the car out into the light Sunday morning traffic. Something was terribly wrong in this relationship, she reflected. It was supposed to be the man who wanted to head straight for the bedroom, while the woman held out for knowing each other better.

And yet it was all Amanda could do not to drag Jordan out of the car and back up the stairs to her apartment.

"What's the matter?" Jordan asked, tossing a mischievous glance her way that said he well knew the answer to that question.

Amanda folded her arms and looked straight ahead as they sped up a freeway ramp. The familiar green-and-white signs slipped by overhead. "Nothing," she said.

He sighed. "I hate it when women do that. You ask them what's wrong and they say 'nothing,' and all the while you know they're ready to burst into tears or clout you with the nearest blunt object."

Amanda turned in her seat and studied his profile for a few moments, one fingernail caught between her teeth. "I wasn't about to do either of those things," she finally said. She didn't quite have the fortitude to go the rest of the way and admit she was wondering why he didn't seem to want her.

Jordan reached out and laid a hand gently on her knee, once again sending all her vital organs into a state of alarm.

"What's the problem, then?"

She drew in a deep breath for courage and let it out slowly. "If we sleep together, you'll be the second man I've ever been with in my life, so it's not like I'm hot to trot or anything. But I usually have to fight guys off, not wait for them to decide the time is right."

He was clearly suppressing a smile, which didn't help.

"'Hot to trot'? I didn't think anybody said that anymore."

"Jordan."

He favored her with a high-potency grin. "Believe me, Mandy, I'm a normal man and I want you. But you're going to have to wait, because I've got no intention of—forgive me— screwing this up."

Amanda sighed and folded her arms. "Exactly what is it you're waiting for?"

His wonderful eyes were crinkled with laughter, even though his mouth was unsmiling.

"Exactly what is it you want me to do?" he countered. "Pull the car over to the side of the freeway and, as you put it last night, 'jump your bones'?"

Amanda blushed. "You make me sound like some kind of loose woman," she accused.

He took her hand and squeezed it reassuringly. "I can't even imagine that," he said in a soothing voice. "Now what do you say we change the subject for a while?"

That seemed like the only solution. "Okay," Amanda agreed. "Remember how you admired the quilt I made?"

Jordan nodded, switching lanes to be in position for an up-coming exit. "It's great."

"Well, I've been designing and making quilts for years. Someday I hope to open a bed and breakfast somewhere, with a little craft shop on the premises."

He grinned as he took the exit. "I'm surprised. Given your job and the fact that you live in the city, I thought you were inclined toward more sophisticated dreams."

"I was," Amanda said, recalling some of the glamorous, exciting adventures she had had with James. "But life changes a person. And I've always liked making quilts. I've been selling them at craft shows for a long time, and saving as much money as I could for the bed and breakfast."

Jordan was undoubtedly thinking of her humble apartment when he said, "You must have a pretty solid nest egg."

Amanda sighed, feeling discouraged all over again. "Not really. The real estate market is hot around here, what with so many people moving up from California, and the prices are high."

They had left the freeway, and Jordan pulled the car into the parking lot of a family-style restaurant near the mall. "Working capital is one of my specialties, Mandy. Maybe I can help you."

Amanda surprised even herself when she shook her head so fast. She guessed it was partly pride that made her do that, and partly disappointment that he wasn't trying to talk her out of establishing a business in favor of something else. Like getting married and starting a family.

"Did we just hit another tricky subject?" Jordan asked good-naturedly, when he and Amanda were walking toward the restaurant.

She shrugged. "I want the bed and breakfast to be all my own."

Jordan opened the door for her. "What if you decide to get married or something?"

Amanda felt a little thrill, even though she knew Jordan wasn't on the verge of proposing. She would have refused even if he had. "I guess I'll cross that bridge when I come to it."

A few minutes later they were seated at a small table and given menus. They made their selections and sipped the coffee the waitress had brought while they waited for the food.

"Who are we shopping for today?" Amanda asked, to get the conversation going again. Jordan was sitting across from her, systematically making love to her with his eyes, and she was desperate to distract him.

"Jessie and Lisa mostly, though I still need to get something for Karen and Paul."

Something made Amanda ask, "What about your parents?"

Sadness flickered in the depths of Jordan's eyes, but only for a moment. "They were killed in a car accident when I was in college," he replied.

Amanda reached out on impulse and took his hand. It seemed to her that Jordan had had more than his share of tragedy in his life, and she suddenly wanted to share her mother and stepfather with him. "I'm sorry."

He changed the subject so abruptly his remark was almost a rebuff. "What do you think Karen would like?"

Amanda was annoyed and a little hurt. "How would I know? I've never even met the woman."

The waitress returned with their breakfast, setting bacon and eggs in front of Jordan and giving Amanda wheat toast and a fruit compote. When they were alone again, Jordan replied, "Karen's thirty-five, a little on the chubby side—and totally devoted to Paul and the girls."

Amanda tried to picture the woman and failed. "Do she and Paul have children of their own?"

Jordan was mashing his eggs into his hash browns. "No."

She speared a melon ball and chewed it distractedly. "That's sad," she said after swallowing.

"These things happen," Jordan replied.

Amanda looked straight into his eyes. "I guess Karen would be pretty upset if she ever had to give Jessica and Lisa back to you," she ventured to say.

He returned her bold, assessing stare. "I wouldn't do that to her or to the girls," he said, and there was no hint of mischief about him this time. He was completely serious.

Things were a little strained between them throughout the rest of the meal, but as soon as they reached the toy store at the mall, they were both caught up in the spirit of the season. They bought games for the girls, and dolls, and little china tea sets.

Amanda couldn't remember the last time she'd had so much fun, and her eyes were sparkling as they stuffed everything into the back of the Porsche.

From the toy store they headed to a big-name department store where, after great deliberation, they chose expensive perfume and bath powder for Karen and a sweater for her husband.

They had lunch in a fast-food hamburger place jammed to the rafters with excited kids, and by the time they returned to Amanda's apartment, she was exhausted.

"Coming in?" she asked at the door because, in spite of everything he'd said about waiting, she'd been entertaining a discreet fantasy all morning.

Jordan shook his head. "Not today," he said. "I've got to drive up to Port Townsend and look in on the kids."

Amanda was hurt that he didn't want to take her along, but she hid it well. After all, she didn't have the right to any injured feelings. "Say hello for me," she said softly.

He kissed her, lightly at first, then with an authority that brought the fantasy to the forefront of her mind. Amanda surreptitiously gripped the doorknob to keep from sliding to the floor.

"I'll be out of town most of next week," he said when the kiss was over. "Is it okay if I call?"

Is it okay? She would be shattered if he didn't. "Sure," she answered in a tone that said it wouldn't matter one way or the other because she'd be busy with her glamorous, sophisticated life.

Jordan waited until she'd unlocked the door and stepped safely inside, then she heard him walking away.

She tossed aside her purse, kicked off her shoes and hung up her coat. The coming week yawned before her like an abyss.

Ignoring the boxes still sitting on her couch, she bent distractedly to pet a meowing Gershwin, then stumbled into her bedroom, stripped off her clothes and crawled back into the unmade bed. All those hours she hadn't slept the night before were catching up with her.

Later she awoke to full darkness, the weight of Gershwin curled up on her stomach and the ringing of the phone.

Groping with one hand, she found the receiver, brought it to her ear and yawned, "Hello?"

"It's Mom," Marion announced. "How are you, dear?"

Amanda yawned again. "Tired. And hungry."

"Perfect," Marion responded with her customary good cheer and indefatigable energy. "Drag yourself over here, and I'll serve you a home-cooked meal that will put hair on your chest."

Amanda giggled, rubbing her eyes and stretching. The movement made Gershwin jump down from her stomach and land with a solid *thump* on the floor. "There's one flaw in your proposal, Mom. Who needs hair on their chest?"

Marion laughed. "Just get in your car and drive over here. Or should I send Bob, so you don't have to go wandering around in that dark parking lot behind your building?"

"There's an attendant," Amanda said, sitting up. "I'll drive over as soon as I've had a quick shower to revive myself."

Marion agreed, and the conversation came to an amicable end.

With her hair pulled back into a ponytail, Amanda was wearing jeans, a football jersey and sneakers when she arrived at her parents' house in another part of the city. And she was making a determined effort not to think about Jordan and the fact that he hadn't asked her to go to Port Townsend with him.

Her mother, a slender, attractive woman with shoulder-length hennaed hair and skillfully applied makeup, met her at the front door. Marion looked wonderful in her trim green jumpsuit, and her smile and hug were both warm.

"Bob's in the living room, cussing that string of Christmas tree lights that always goes on the blink," the older woman confided in a merry whisper.

Amanda laughed and wandered into the front room. There were cards everywhere—they lined the top of the piano, the mantel and were arranged into the shape of a Christmas tree on one wall. Amanda had been putting hers in a desk drawer that year.

"Hi, Bob," she said, giving her stepfather a hug. He was a tall man, with thinning blond hair and kindly blue eyes, and he'd been very good to Marion. Amanda loved him for that reason, if for no other.

He was standing beside a fresh-smelling, undecorated pine tree, which was, as usual, set up in front of the bay window facing the street. The infamous string of lights was in his hands. "I don't know why she won't let me throw these darned things out and buy new ones," he fussed in a conspiratorial whisper. "It's not as if we couldn't afford to."

Amanda chuckled. "Mom's sentimental about those lights," she reminded him. "They've been on the tree since Eunice and I were babies."

"Speaking of your sister," Marion remarked from the kitchen doorway, wiping her hands on her white apron, "we had a call from her today. She's coming home for Christmas."

Amanda was pleased. This was a hard time in Eunice's life; she needed to get away from the wreckage of her marriage, if only for a week or two. "What about her job at the university?"

Marion shrugged. "I guess she's taking time off. Bob and I are picking her up at the airport late next Friday night."

Amanda left Bob to his Christmas tree light quandary and followed her mother into the bright, fragrant kitchen, where they had had so many talks before. "Seattle will be a shock to Eunice after Southern California," she remarked.

Marion gave her a playful flick with a dish towel. "Forget the harmless chitchat," she said with a grin. "What's going on in your life these days? Who's the new man, and what the devil was James doing, dropping by?"

Drawing up a battered metal stool, Amanda sat down at the breakfast counter Bob had built when he remodeled the kitchen, and started cutting up the salad vegetables her mother indicated. "James is getting divorced," she said, avoiding Marion's gaze. "Evidently he has some idea that we can get back together."

"I presume you set him straight on that."

"I did." Amanda sighed. "But I'm not sure he's getting the message. He sent me a sable jacket and a silk bikini today, along with an invitation to Hawaii and Copenhagen."

The oven door slammed a touch too hard after Marion pulled a pan of fragrant lasagna from it. "You'd never guess he was such a scumbag, would you?"

Amanda grinned and tossed a handful of chopped celery into the salad bowl. "You've got to stop watching all those cop shows, Mom. It's affecting your vocabulary."

"No way," replied Marion, who had a minor crush on Don Johnson. "So, who's the other guy?"

"Did I say there was another guy?"

"I think so," Marion replied airily, "but you wouldn't have had to. There's a sparkle in your eyes and your cheeks are pink."

"His name is Jordan Richards," Amanda said. Personally she attributed any sparkle in her eyes or color in her cheeks to the nap she'd taken.

Marion stopped slicing the lasagna to look directly at her daughter. "And?"

"And he makes me crazy, that's what."

Marion beamed. "That's a good sign."

Amanda wondered if her mother would still be of the same opinion if she knew just how hard her daughter had fallen. And how bold she'd been. "I guess so."

"What does he do for a living?" Bob asked from the kitchen doorway. Since it was a classic parental question, Amanda didn't take offense.

"He's a partner in an investment firm—Striner, Striner and Richards."

Bob whistled and tucked his hands in his pockets. "That's the big time, all right."

"Amanda doesn't care how much money he makes," Marion said with mock haughtiness. "She just wants his body."

At this, both Amanda and Bob laughed.

"Mom!" Amanda protested.

"It's true," Marion insisted. "I'd know that look anywhere. Now let's all sit down and eat."

They trooped into the dining room, where Marion had set a festive table using the special Christmas dishes that always came out of storage, along with the nativity set, on the first of December. Despite the good food and the conversation, Amanda's mind was on Jordan.

"About those presents James sent you," Marion began when she and Amanda were alone in the kitchen again, washing dishes while Bob fought it out with the Christmas tree lights. "You are sending them back, aren't you?"

Amanda favored her mother with a rueful smile. "Of course I am. First thing tomorrow."

"Some women would have their heads turned, you know, by such expensive things."

"Expensive is right. All James wants in return for his presents is my soul. What a bargain."

Marion finished washing the last pot, drained the sink and washed her hands. "I'm glad you're wise enough to see that."

Amanda shrugged. "I don't know how smart I am," she replied. "The only reason I'm so sure about everything where James is concerned is that I don't love him anymore. I'm not sure what I'd do if I still cared."

"I am," Marion said confidently. "You've always had a good head on your shoulders. That's why I think this new man must really be something."

Amanda indulged in a smile as she shook out the dish towel and hung it on the rack to dry. "He is." But her smile faded as she thought of those two little girls living far away from their father with an aunt and uncle, and of Becky, cut down before she'd even had a chance to live.

"What is it?" Marion wanted to know. She had already poured two cups full of coffee, and she carried them to the kitchen table while waiting for Amanda to answer.

Amanda sank dejectedly into one of the chairs and cupped her hands around a steaming mug. "He's a widower, and I think—well, I think he might have some problems with commitment.''

''Don't they all?'' Marion asked, stirring artificial sweetener into her coffee.

''Bob didn't,'' Amanda pointed out, her voice solemn. ''He loved you enough to marry you, even though he knew you had two teenage daughters and a pile of debts.''

Marion looked thoughtful. ''How long have you known this man?''

''Not very long,'' Amanda confessed. ''About ten days, I guess.''

Marion chuckled and shook her head. ''And you're already bandying words like 'commitment' about?''

''No. I'm only *thinking* words like 'commitment.'''

''I see. Well, this is serious. Why do you think he wouldn't want to settle down?''

Amanda ran the tip of her index finger around the rim of her coffee mug. ''He has two little girls, and they don't live with him—his sister and brother-in-law are raising them. He sort of bristled when I asked him about it.''

Marion laid a hand on her daughter's arm. ''You're a little gun-shy, dear, and that's natural after what happened with James. Just give yourself some time.''

Time. Jordan was asking the same thing of her. Didn't anyone act on impulse anymore?

Marion smiled at her daughter's frustrated expression. ''Just take life one day at a time, Amanda, and everything will work out.''

Amanda nodded, and after chatting briefly with her mother about Eunice's upcoming visit, she put on her coat, kissed both her parents goodbye and went out to her nondescript car.

''You be careful to park where the attendant can see you,'' Bob instructed her just before she pulled away from the curb.

The attendant was on duty, and Amanda parked where there was plenty of light.

It turned out, however, that it was the inside of her building that she should have looked out for, not the parking lot.

James was sitting on the stairs again, and this time she didn't have Jordan along to act as a buffer.

"I'm glad you're here," Amanda said in a cold voice. "You can take back the fur and the bikini."

James's handsome, distinguished face fell. "You still haven't forgiven me, have you?" he asked in a pained voice, spreading his hands wide for emphasis. "Baby, how many times do I have to tell you? Madge and I haven't been in love for years."

Amanda ached as she remembered Madge Brockman's raging agony during the confrontation. "Maybe *you* haven't been," she muttered sadly.

James either didn't hear the remark or chose to ignore it. "Just let me talk to you. Please."

Having summoned up the courage she needed, Amanda passed him on the narrow stairway. "Nothing you can say will change my mind, James." She reached her door and unlocked it as he made to follow her. "So just take your presents and give them to some other fool."

Suddenly James caught her elbow in a hard grasp and wrenched her around to face him. "You're in love with Richards, aren't you? The boy wonder! You think he's pretty hot stuff, I'll bet! Well, let me tell you something—I could buy and sell him ten times over!"

Amanda pulled free of James, stormed over to the couch, picked up the boxes and shoved them at him. "Take these and get out!"

He stared at her as though she'd lost her mind.

"And while you're at it, you can just take everything *else* you've ever given me, too!"

With that, she strode into the bedroom and yanked open her jewelry box, intending to return the gold bracelet and pearl earrings she'd forgotten about. She only became aware that James had followed her when he cried out.

Turning, Amanda saw him clasp his chest with one hand and topple to the floor.

Chapter 5

James's face was contorted with pain, and he was only partially conscious. "Help—me—" he groaned.

Amanda lunged for the phone on her bedside table, punched 911 and barked out her address when someone came on the line. She followed that with a brief description of the problem.

"Someone will be there in a few minutes," the woman on the telephone assured her. "Is the patient conscious?"

James was clearly in agony, but he was awake. "Yes."

"Then just cover him up and make him as comfortable as you can—and try to reassure him. The paramedics will take care of everything else when they get there."

Amanda hung up and draped James with a quilt dragged from her bed. When it was in place, she knelt beside him and grasped his hand.

"It's going to be okay, James," she said, her eyes stinging with tears. "Everything is going to be okay."

His free hand was clenched against his chest. "Hurts—so much…crushing…"

"I know," Amanda whispered, holding his knuckles to her

lips. She could hear sirens in the distance. "Help will be here soon."

A loud knock sounded at the door just a few minutes later.

"In here!" Amanda called, and soon two paramedics burst into the bedroom, bringing a stretcher and some other equipment. She scrambled out of the way and perched on the end of her bed, still unmade from her nap earlier, watching as James was examined, loaded onto the stretcher and given oxygen and an IV.

"Any history of heart disease?" one of the men asked Amanda as he and his partner lifted the stretcher.

"I—I don't know," Amanda whispered.

"We'll be taking him to Harborview Hospital, if you'd like to come along," the other volunteered.

Amanda only sat there, gripping the edge of the mattress and shaking her head, unable to tell them she wasn't James's wife.

When the telephone rang a full hour later, she was still sitting in the exact same place.

"H-hello?"

Jordan's voice was warm and low. "Hello, Mandy. Is something wrong?"

Amanda dragged her forearm across her face, wiping away tears that had long since dried. *James had a heart attack in my bedroom,* she imagined herself answering.

She couldn't explain the situation to Jordan over the phone, she decided, sinking her teeth into her lower lip.

"Mandy?" Jordan prompted when the silence had stretched on too long.

"I thought you were in Port Townsend," she managed in a small voice that was hoarse from crying.

"I just got back," he answered. "As a matter of fact, I'm spending the night in a hotel out by the airport, since my plane leaves so early tomorrow."

Amanda swallowed hard and did her best to sound ordinary. There would be time enough to tell Jordan what had happened when he got back from his business trip. "Wh-where are you going?"

"Chicago. Mandy, what's the matter?"

She closed her eyes. "We can talk about it when you get home."

There was a long pause while he digested that. "Is this something I should know about?"

Amanda nodded, even though he wasn't there to see her. "Yes," she admitted, "but I can't talk about it like this. I have to be with you."

"I could get in the car and be there in half an hour."

Amanda would have given anything short of her very soul to have Jordan there in the room with her, to be held and comforted by him. But she'd only known him a little while, and she had no right to make demands. "I'll be okay," she said softly.

After that, there didn't seem to be much to say. Jordan promised to phone her from Chicago the first chance he got and Amanda wished him well, then the call was over.

Amanda had barely replaced the receiver, when the bell jangled again, startling her. If it had been Jordan she would have relented and asked him to come over, but the voice on the other end of the line was a woman's.

"Well, I must say, I half expected you to be at the hospital, clutching James's hand and swearing your undying love."

Amanda closed her eyes again, feeling as though she'd been struck. The caller was Madge Brockman, James's estranged wife. "Mrs. Brockman, I—"

"Don't lie to me, please. I just spoke to someone on the hospital staff, and they told me James had suffered a heart attack 'at the home of a friend.' It didn't take a genius to figure out just who that 'friend' might be."

Deciding to let the innuendos pass unchallenged, Amanda asked, "Is James going to be all right?"

"He's in critical condition. I'm flying in tonight to sit with him."

It was a relief to know James wouldn't be going through this difficult time alone. "Mrs. Brockman, I'm very sorry—for everything."

The woman hung up with a slam, leaving Amanda holding the receiver in one trembling hand and listening to a dial tone.

Slowly she put down the phone, then crouched to unplug it from the outlet. After disconnecting the living room phone, as well, she took a long, hot shower and crawled into bed.

The sound of her alarm and faceful of bright sunshine woke her early the next morning. The memory of James lying on her bedroom floor in terrible pain was still all too fresh in her mind.

But Amanda had a job, so, even though she would have preferred to stay in bed with her face turned to the wall, she fed the cat, showered, dressed and put on makeup. Once she'd pinned her hair up in a businesslike chignon, she reconnected the telephones and called the hospital.

James was in stable condition.

Longing for Jordan, who might have been able to put the situation into some kind of perspective, Amanda pulled on her coat and gloves and left her apartment.

Late that afternoon, just as she was preparing to go home for the day, Jordan called. He was getting ready to have dinner with some clients, and there was something clipped about his voice. Something distant.

"Feeling better?" he asked.

Amanda heard a whole glacier of emotion shifting beneath the tip of the iceberg. "Not a whole lot," she admitted, "but it's nothing for you to worry about."

She could almost see him hooking his cuff links. "I read about James in the afternoon edition of the paper, Amanda."

So he knew about the heart attack, and she was no longer 'Mandy.' "Word gets around," she managed, propping one elbow on her desk and sinking her forehead into her palm.

"Is that what you didn't want to talk about last night?"

There was no point in trying to evade the question further. "Yes. It happened in my bedroom, Jordan."

He was quiet for a long time. Much too long.

"Jordan?"

"I'm here. What was he doing in your bedroom, or don't I have the right to ask?"

Tears were brimming in Amanda's eyes, and she prayed no one would step into her office and catch her displaying such unprofessional emotions. "Of course you have the right. He came over because he wanted to persuade me to start seeing him again. I told him to take back the things he gave me, and then I remembered some jewelry he'd given me a long time ago. I went to get them, and he followed me.'' She drew in a shaky breath, then let it out again. ''He got very angry, and he was yelling at me. He just—just fell to the floor.''

''My God,'' Jordan rasped. ''What kind of shape is he in now?''

''When I called the hospital this morning, he was stable.''

Jordan's voice was husky. ''Mandy, I'm sorry.''

Amanda didn't know whether he meant he was sorry for doubting her, or he was sorry about James's misfortune. ''I wish you were here,'' she said, testing the water. Everything would ride on his reply.

''So do I,'' he answered.

Relief flooded over Amanda. ''You're not angry?''

He sighed. ''No. I guess I just lost my head for a little while there. Do you want me to come back tonight, Mandy? There's a flight at midnight.''

''No.'' She shook her head. ''Stay there and set the financial world on its ear. I'll be okay.''

''Promise?''

For the first time since before James's collapse, Amanda smiled. ''I promise.''

''In that case, I'll be back sometime on Friday night. How about penciling me into your busy schedule, Ms. Scott?''

Amanda chuckled. ''Consider yourself penciled.''

''In fact,'' he went on, ''have a bag packed. I'll stop and pick you up on my way home from the airport.''

''Have a bag packed?'' Amanda echoed. ''Wait a minute, Jordan. What are you proposing here?''

He hesitated only a moment before answering, ''I want you to spend the weekend at my place.''

Amanda's throat tightened. ''Is this the Jordan I know—the one who insists on taking things slow and easy?''

''The same,'' Jordan replied, his words husky. ''I need to have you under the same roof with me, Mandy. Whether we sleep together is entirely up to you.''

She plucked some tissue from the box on her desk and began wiping away the mascara stains on her cheeks. "That's mighty mannerly of you, Mr. Richards," she drawled.

"See you Friday," he replied.

And after just a few more words, Amanda hung up.

It was some time before she got out of her chair, though. She'd had some violent ups and downs in the past twenty-four hours, and her emotional equilibrium was not what it might have been.

After taking a few minutes to sit with her head resting on her folded arms, Amanda finished up a report she'd been working on, then slipped into the ladies' room to repair her makeup. Leaving the elevator on the first floor of the hotel, she encountered Madge Brockman.

Mrs. Brockman was a slender, attractive brunette, expensively dressed and clearly well educated. There were huge shadows under her eyes.

"Hello, Amanda," she said.

At first Amanda thought it was just extraordinarily bad luck that she'd run into Mrs. Brockman, but moments later she realized the woman had been waiting in the lobby for her. "Hello, Mrs. Brockman. How is James?"

James's wife reached for Amanda's arm, then let her hand fall back to her side. "I was wondering if you wouldn't have a drink with me or something," she said awkwardly. "So we could talk."

Amanda took a deep breath. "If there's going to be a scene—"

Madge shook her head quickly. "There won't be, I promise."

Hoping Mrs. Brockman meant what she'd said, Amanda followed her into the cocktail lounge, where they took a quiet table in a corner. When the waiter came, Amanda asked for a diet cola and Mrs. Brockman ordered a gin and tonic.

"The doctor tells me James is going to live," Mrs. Brockman said when the drinks had arrived and the waiter was gone again.

Amanda dared a slight smile. "That's wonderful."

Madge looked at her with tormented eyes. "James admitted he went to your apartment on his own last night, and not because you'd invited him. He—he's a proud man, my James, so it wasn't easy for him to say that you'd rejected him."

Not knowing what to say, Amanda simply waited, her hands folded in her lap, her diet cola untouched.

"He's agreed to come back home to California with me when he gets out of the hospital," Mrs. Brockman went on. "I don't know if that's a new start or what, but I do know this much—I love James. If there's any way we can begin again, well, I want a fighting chance."

"It's over between James and me," Amanda said gently. "It has been for months and months."

Mrs. Brockman's eyes held a flicker of hope. "You were telling the truth six months ago when I confronted you in your office, weren't you? You honestly didn't know James was married."

Amanda sighed. "That's right. As soon as I found out, I broke it off."

"But you loved him, didn't you?"

Amanda felt a twinge of the pain that time and hard work and Jordan had finally healed. "Yes."

"Then why didn't you hold on? Why didn't you fight for him?"

"If he'd been my husband instead of yours, I would have," Amanda answered, reaching for her purse. She wasn't going to be able to choke down so much as a sip of that cola. "I'm not cut out to be the Other Woman, Mrs. Brockman. I want a man I don't have to share."

Madge Brockman smiled sadly as Amanda stood up. "Have you found one?"

"I hope so," Amanda answered. Then she laid a hand lightly on Mrs. Brockman's shoulder, just for a moment, before walking away.

Jordan arrived at seven o'clock on Friday night, looking slightly wan, his expensive suit wrinkled from the trip. "Hi, Mandy," he said, reaching out to gather her close.

Dressed for the island in blue jeans, walking boots and a heavy beige cable-knit sweater, Amanda went into his arms without hesitation. "Hi," she answered, tilting her head back for his kiss.

He tasted her mouth before moving on to possess it entirely. "I don't suppose you're going to be merciful enough to tell me what you've decided," he said, sounding a little breathless, when the long kiss was over.

"About what?" Amanda asked with feigned innocence, and kissed the beard-stubbled underside of his chin. Of course she knew he wanted to know what the sleeping arrangements would be on the island that night.

Jordan laughed hoarsely and gave her a swat. "You know damn well 'about what'!" he lectured.

Despite the weariness she felt, Amanda grinned at him. "If you guess right, I'll tell you," she teased.

He studied her with tired, laughing, hungry eyes. "Okay, here's my guess. You're going to say you want to sleep in the guest room."

Amanda rocked back on her heels, resting against his hands, which were interwoven behind her, and said nothing.

"Well?" Jordan prodded.

"You guessed wrong," Amanda told him.

"Thank God," he groaned.

Amanda laughed. "Let's go—we'll miss the ferry."

Jordan's lips, warm and moist, touched hers. "We could just stay here—"

"No way, Mr. Richards," Amanda protested, pulling back. "You invited me to go away for the weekend and I want to *go away.*"

"What about the cat?" Jordan reasoned as Gershwin jumped onto the back of an easy chair and meowed plaintively.

"My landlady is going to take care of him," Amanda said, pulling out of Jordan's embrace and picking up her suitcase and overnight case. "Here," she said, shoving the suitcase at him.

"I like a subtle woman," Jordan muttered, accepting it.

Soon they were leaving the heart of the city behind for West

Seattle, where they caught the Southworth ferry. Once they were on board the enormous white boat, however, they remained in the car instead of going upstairs to the snack bar with most of the other passengers.

"I've missed you," Jordan said, leaning back in the seat, resting his hand on Amanda's upper thigh and gripping her fingers.

"And I've missed you," Amanda answered. They'd already run through all the small talk; Jordan had told her about his business trip and she'd detailed her hectic week. By tacit agreement, they hadn't discussed James's heart attack.

Jordan splayed the fingers of his left hand and ran them through his rumpled hair, then gave a heavy sigh. He moved his thumb soothingly over Amanda's knuckles. "Do you have any idea how much I want you?"

She lifted his hand to her mouth and kissed it. "How much?"

He chuckled. "Enough to wish this were a van instead of a sports car." Jordan turned in the seat and cupped Amanda's chin in his hand. "You're sure you're ready for this?" he asked gently.

Amanda nodded. "I'm sure. How about you?"

Jordan grinned. "I've been ready since I turned around and saw you standing in line behind me."

"You have not."

"Okay," he admitted, "it started after that, when you threw five bucks on the table to pay for your Chinese food. For just a moment, when you thought I was going to refuse it, you had blue fire in your eyes."

"And?"

"And I had this fantasy about the whole mall being deserted—except for us, of course. I made love to you right there on the table."

Amanda felt a hot shiver go through her. "Jordan?"

His lips were moving against hers. "Yes?"

"We're fogging up the windows. People will notice that."

He chuckled and drew back. "Maybe we should go upstairs and have some coffee or something, then."

She felt the rough texture of his cheek against her palm.
"Then what kind of fantasies would you be having?"

"I'd probably start imagining that we were right here, alone
in a dark car, with nobody around." Slowly he unbuttoned the
front of her coat. "I suppose I'd picture myself touching you
like this." He curved his fingers around her breast.

Even through the weight of her sweater and the lacy barrier
of her bra, Amanda could feel his caress in every nerve. "Jordan."

He moved his hand beneath the sweater and then, to the
accompaniment of a little gasp of surprised pleasure from
Amanda, beneath the bra. Cupping her warm breast, he rolled
the nipple gently between his fingers. "I'd be thinking about
doing this, no doubt."

Amanda was squirming a little, and her breath was quickening. "Damn it, Jordan—this isn't funny. Someone could
walk by!"

"Not likely," he murmured, touching his mouth to hers as
he continued to fondle her.

Although she knew she should, Amanda couldn't bring herself to push his hand away. What he was doing felt too good.
"S-someone might see—they'd think…"

Jordan bent his head to kiss the pulse point at the base of
her throat. "They'd think we were necking. And they'd be
right." Satisfied that he'd set one nipple to throbbing, he pro-
ceeded to attend the other. "Ummm. Where were you on prom
night, lady?"

"Out with somebody like you," Amanda gasped breathlessly.

Jordan chuckled and continued nibbling at her throat. She
felt the snap on her jeans pop, heard the faint whisper of the
zipper. "Did he do this?"

The windows were definitely fogging up. "No…" Amanda
moaned as he slid his fingers down her warm abdomen to find
what they sought.

"Lift up your sweater," Jordan said. "I want to taste you."

Amanda whimpered a halfhearted protest even as she
obeyed, but when she felt his mouth close over a distended

nipple, she groaned out loud and entangled her fingers in his hair. In the meantime he continued the other delicious mischief, causing Amanda to fidget on the seat.

She ran her hands down his back, then up to his hair again in a frantic search for a place to touch him and make him feel what she was feeling. His name fell repeatedly from her lips in a breathless, senseless litany of passion.

Just as the ferry horn sounded, Amanda arched her back and cried out in release. Her body buckled over and over again against Jordan's hand before she sagged into the seat, temporarily soothed. Gradually her breathing steadied.

"Rat," she said when her good sense returned. She righted her bra and pulled her sweater down while Jordan zipped and snapped her jeans. Not two seconds after that, the first of the passengers returning from the upper deck walked past the car and waved.

Amanda's cheeks glowed as Jordan drove off the ferry minutes later.

"Relax, Mandy," he said, shoving a tape into the slot on the dashboard. The car filled with soft music. "I'm on your side, remember?"

She ran her tongue over her lips and turned in the seat to look at him. Her body was still quivering like a resonating string on some exotic instrument. "I'm not angry—just surprised. Nobody's ever been able to make me forget where I was."

"Good," Jordan replied, turning the Porsche onto a paved road lined with towering pine trees. "I'd be something less than thrilled if that was a regular thing with you."

Amanda gazed out the window for a moment, then looked back at Jordan. "Is it a regular thing with you?" she asked, almost in a whisper.

He looked at her, but she couldn't read his expression in the darkness. "There have been women since Becky, if that's what you mean. But if it'll make you feel better, none of them has ever had quite the same effect on me that you do. And I've never taken any of them to the island."

Amanda didn't know whether she felt better or not. She

peered at his towering house as they pulled into the driveway, but all she could see was a shadowy shape and a lot of dark windows.

The garage door opened at the push of a button, and Jordan pulled in and got out, then turned on the lights before coming around to open Amanda's door for her. Gripping the handle of her suitcase in one hand, the other hand pressed to the small of her back, he escorted her through a side door and into a spacious, well-designed kitchen.

Amanda stopped when he set the suitcase down on the floor. "Did you live here with Becky?" she blurted. She'd known she wouldn't have the courage to ask if she waited too long.

"No," Jordan answered, taking the overnight case from her hand and setting it on the counter.

She shrugged out of her coat, avoiding his eyes. "Oh."

"Are you hungry or anything?" Jordan asked, glancing around the kitchen as though he expected it to be changed somehow from the last time he'd seen it.

"I could use a cup of coffee," Amanda admitted. "Maybe with a little brandy in it."

Jordan chuckled and disappeared with her coat. When he came back, he was minus his suit jacket and one hand was at his throat, loosening his tie. "The coffee maker's there on the counter," he said, pointing. "The other stuff is in the cupboard above it. Why don't you start the coffee brewing while I bring my stuff in from the car?"

It sounded like a reasonable idea to Amanda, and she was thankful for something to occupy her. What she and Jordan were about to do was as old as time, but she felt like the first virgin ever to be deflowered. She nodded and busily set about making coffee.

Jordan made one trip to the garage and then went upstairs. When he returned, he stood behind Amanda and put his arms around her. "Are you sure you want coffee? It's late, and that's the regular stuff."

His lips moved against her nape, and she couldn't help the tremor that went through her. "I guess not," she managed to say.

Without another word, Jordan lifted her into his arms and carried her through the dark house and up a set of stairs. The light was on in his spacious bedroom, and Amanda murmured an exclamation at the low-key luxury of the place.

The bed was enormous, and it faced a big-screen TV equipped with a VCR and heaven-only-knows-what other kinds of high-tech electronic equipment. One wall was made entirely of windows, while another was lined with mirrors, and the gray carpet was deep and plush.

Amanda glanced nervously at the mirrors and saw her own wide eyes looking back at her.

Jordan kicked off his shoes, flung his tie aside and vanished into the bathroom, whistling and unbuttoning his shirt as he went. A few moments later Amanda heard the sound of a shower running.

Quickly she scrambled off the bed and found her suitcase, still feeling like a shy virgin. Suddenly the skimpy black nightgown she'd brought along didn't look sturdy enough, so she helped herself to a heavy terry-cloth robe from Jordan's closet. After hastily stripping, she wrapped herself in the robe and tied the belt with a double knot.

When Jordan came out sometime later, he was wearing nothing but a towel around his waist. His hair was blow-dried and combed back from his face, and his eyes twinkled at Amanda when he saw her sitting fitfully on the edge of the chair farthest from the bed.

"Scared?" he asked, approaching her and pulling her gently to her feet.

"Of course not," Amanda lied. The truth was, she was terrified.

Jordan undid the double knot at her waist as though it were nothing. "I guess I should have invited you to share my shower," he said, his voice a leisurely rumble.

"I had one at home," Amanda was quick to point out.

He opened the robe, laid it aside and looked at her, slowly and thoroughly, before meeting her eyes again. His lips quirked. "You're awfully nervous, considering how mad you were when I wouldn't make love to you last week."

Amanda moved to close the robe, but Jordan grasped her wrists and stopped her. He subjected her to another lingering assessment before pushing the garment off her shoulders with warm, gentle hands. It fell silently to the floor.

"We—we could turn the light out," she dared to suggest as Jordan lifted her again and carried her back to the bed.

"We could," he agreed, stretching out beside her, "but we're not going to."

He'd shaved, and his face was smooth and fragrant. He took her mouth and mastered it skillfully, leaving Amanda dizzy and disoriented when he drew away.

Tenderly he turned Amanda's head so that she was facing the mirrors, and a moan lodged in her throat when she saw him move his hand toward her breast.

"Jordan," she whispered.

"Shhh," he murmured against the tingling flesh of her neck, and Amanda was quiet, her eyes widening as she watched her conquering begin.

Chapter 6

The dark blue velour bedspread felt incredibly soft against Amanda's bare skin, and she forgot the mirrored wall and even the lights as Jordan kissed and caressed her. Although she tried, she couldn't hold back the soft moans that escaped her, or the whispered pleas for release.

But Jordan would not be hurried. "All in good time, Mandy," he assured her, his mouth at her throat. "All in good time. Just relax."

"Relax?" Amanda gave a rueful semihysterical chuckle at the word. "Now? Are you crazy?"

He trailed his lips down over her collarbone, over the plump rounding of one breast. "Ummm-hmm," he said just before he took her nipple into his mouth. In the meantime he was stroking the tender skin on the insides of Amanda's thighs.

"Stop teasing me," she whimpered, moving her hands through his hair and over the muscular sleekness of his back.

"Never," he paused long enough to say. He left off tormenting Amanda to reach for a pillow, which he deftly tucked underneath her bottom. And then he caressed her in earnest.

Amanda was frantic. Jordan had been subjecting her to various kinds of foreplay for a week, and she simply couldn't wait any longer for gratification. Her body demanded it.

"Jordan," she pleaded, half-blind with the need of him, "*now*. Oh, please—"

She felt him part her legs, then come to rest between them. "Mandy," he rasped like a man being consumed by invisible fire. In one fierce, beautiful thrust, he was a part of her, but then he lay very still. "Mandy, open your eyes and look at me."

She obeyed, but she could barely focus on his features because she was caught up in a whirlwind of sensation. The pillow raised her to him like a pagan offering, and her body was still reacting to the single stroke he'd allowed her. "Jordan," she pleaded, and all her desperation, all her need, echoed in the name.

He kissed her thoroughly, his tongue staking the same claim that the other part of his body was making on her. Finally he began to move upon her, slowly at first, making her ask for every motion of his powerful hips, but as Amanda's passion heated, so did his own. Soon they were parting and coming together again in a wild, primitive rhythm.

Amanda was the first to scale the peak, and the splintering explosion in her senses was everything she'd hoped it would be. Her body arched like a bow with the string drawn tight, and her cries of surrender echoed off the walls.

Jordan was more restrained, but Amanda saw a panorama of emotions crossed his face as he gave himself up to her in a series of short, frenzied thrusts.

They lay on their sides, facing each other, legs still entwined, for long minutes after their lovemaking had ended.

Jordan gave a raspy chuckle.

"What's funny?" Amanda asked softly, winding a tendril of his rich brown hair around one finger.

"I was just thinking of the first time I saw you. You were bored with waiting in line, so you struck up a conversation. I wondered if you were a member of some weird religious sect."

Amanda gave him a playful punch in the chest.

He laughed and leaned over to kiss her. "Let's go down to the kitchen," he said when it was over. "I'm starving."

Jordan rose off the bed and retrieved the yellow bathrobe from the floor, tossing it to Amanda. He took a hooded one of striped silk from the closet and put that on. Together, they went downstairs.

Jordan plundered the cupboards, while Amanda perched on a stool, watching him and sipping a cup of the coffee she'd made earlier. He finally decided on popcorn and thrust a bag into the microwave.

"This is a great house," Amanda said as the oven's motor began to whir. "What I've seen of it, anyway."

Jordan was busy digging through another cupboard for a serving bowl that suited him. "Thanks."

"And it's pretty big." Saying those words gave Amanda the same sense of breathless anticipation she would have felt if she'd walked outside with the intention of plunging a toe into the frigid sound.

He set a red bowl on the counter with a thump, and the grin he gave her was tinged with exasperation. "Big enough for a couple of kids, I suppose," he said.

Amanda shrugged and lifted her eyebrows. "Seems like you could fit Jessica and Lisa in here somewhere."

The popcorn was snapping like muted gunfire inside its colorful paper bag. For just a moment, Jordan's eyes snapped, too. "We've been over that, Amanda," he said.

She took another sip of her coffee. "Okay. I was just wondering why you'd want a house like this when you live all alone."

The bell on the microwave chimed, and Jordan took the popcorn out, carefully opened the bag and dumped the contents into the bowl. The fragrance filled the kitchen, causing Amanda to decide she was hungry, after all.

"Jordan?" she prompted when he didn't reply.

He picked up a kernel and tossed it at her. "How about cooling it with the questions I can't answer?"

Amanda sighed and wriggled off the stool. "I'm sorry," she

said. "Your living arrangements are none of my business, anyway."

Jordan didn't counter that statement. He simply took up the
bowl and started back through the house and up the stairs.
Amanda had no choice but to follow.

Returning to the bed, they settled themselves under the
covers, with pillows at their backs, the popcorn between them,
and Jordan switched on the gigantic TV screen.

The news was on. "I'm not in the mood to be depressed,"
Jordan said, working the remote control device with his thumb
until a cable channel came on.

Amanda settled against his shoulder and crunched thoughtfully on a mouthful of popcorn. "I've seen this movie before,"
she said. "It's good."

Jordan slipped an arm around her and plunged the opposite
hand into the bowl. "I'll take your word for it."

Images flickered across the screen, the popcorn diminished
until there were only yellow kernels in the bottom of the bowl
and the moon rose high and beautiful beyond the wall of windows. Amanda sighed and closed her eyes, feeling warm and
contented.

The next thing she knew, it was morning, and Jordan was
lying beside her, propped up on one elbow, smiling. "Hi," he
said. He'd showered, and his breath smelled of mint toothpaste.

Amanda was well aware she hadn't and hers didn't. "Hi,"
she responded, speaking into the covers.

Jordan laughed and kissed her forehead. "Breakfast in
twenty minutes," he said, and then he rose off the bed and
walked away, wearing only a pair of jeans.

The moment he was gone, Amanda dashed to the bathroom.
When he returned in the prescribed twenty minutes, he was
carrying a tray and Amanda was sitting cross-legged in the
middle of the bed. She'd exchanged Jordan's robe for a short
nightgown of turquoise silk, and she grinned when she saw the
tray in his hands.

"Room service! I'm impressed, Mr. Richards."

He set the food tray carefully in her lap, and Amanda's stomach rumbled in anticipation as she looked under various lids, finding sliced banana, toast, orange juice and two slices of crisp bacon. "Our services are *très* expensive, *madame*," he teased in a very good French accent.

"Put it on my credit card," Amanda bantered back, and picked up a slice of bacon and bit into it.

Jordan chuckled, still playing the Frenchman. "Oh, but *madame*, this we cannot do." He reached out to touch the tip of her right breast with his index finger, making the nipple turn button-hard beneath its covering of silk. "Zee policy is strictly cash and carry."

Amanda's eyes were sparkling as she widened them in mock horror. "We have a terrible problem then, *monsieur*, for I haven't a franc to my name. Not a single, solitary one!"

"This is a true pity," Jordan continued, laying a light, exploratory finger to Amanda's knee and drawing it slowly down to her ankle. "I am afraid you cannot leave this room until you have made proper restitution."

Amanda ate in silence for a time, while Jordan lingered, watching her with mischievous expectancy in his eyes. "Aren't you going to eat?" she asked, forgetting the game for a moment, and she went red the instant the words were out of her mouth.

Jordan chuckled, took the tray from her lap and set it aside. "About the price of your room, *madame*. Some agreement must be reached."

Recovered from her earlier embarrassment, Amanda slipped her arms around Jordan's neck and kissed him softly on the lips. "I'm sure we can work out something to our mutual satisfaction, *monsieur*."

He drew the silk nightgown gently over her head and tossed it away. *"Oui,"* he answered, laying a hand to her bare thigh even as he pressed her back onto the pillows.

Amanda groaned as he moved his hand from her thigh to her stomach, and when instinct caused her to draw up her knees, he claimed her with a finger in a sudden motion of his hand.

The sensation was exquisite, and Amanda arched her neck,

her eyes drifting closed as Jordan choreographed a dance for her eager body. She groaned as Jordan's tongue tamed a pulsing nipple.

"Of course," he told her in that same accented English, "the customer, she must always have satisfaction first."

Only moments later, Amanda was caught in the throes of a climax that caused her to thrash on the bed and call Jordan's name even as she clutched blindly at his shoulders.

"Easy," he told her, moving his warm lips against her neck. "Nice and easy."

Amanda sagged back to the mattress, her breath coming in fevered gasps, her eyes smoldering as she watched Jordan slip out of his jeans and poise himself above her. "No more waiting," she said. "I want you, Jordan."

He gave her only a portion of his magnificence at first, but then, when she traced the circumference of each of his nipples with a fingertip, he gave a low growl and plunged into her in earnest. And the whole splendid rite began all over again.

"A Christmas tree?" Amanda echoed, standing in the middle of Jordan's living room with its high, beamed ceilings and breathtaking view of the mountains and Puget Sound. She was wearing jeans, sneakers and a sweatshirt, like Jordan, and there was a cozy fire snapping on the raised hearth.

"Is that so strange?" Jordan asked. "After all, it is December."

Amanda assessed the towering tinted glass window that let in the view. "It would be a shame to cover that up," she said.

Jordan pinched her cheek. "Thank you, Ebenezer Scrooge," he teased. Then he widened his eyes at her. "What is it with you and Christmas, anyway?"

With a sigh, Amanda collapsed into a cushy chair upholstered in dark blue brushed cotton, her arms folded. "I guess I'd like to let it just sort of slip past unnoticed."

"Fat chance," Jordan replied, perching on the arm of her chair. "It's everywhere."

"Yeah," Amanda said, lowering her eyes.

He put a finger under her chin and lifted. "What is it, Mandy?"

She tried to smile. "My dad left at Christmas," she admitted, her voice small as she momentarily became a little girl again.

"Ouch," Jordan whispered, pulling her to her feet. Then he sank into the chair and drew Amanda onto his lap. "That was a dirty trick."

"You don't know the half of it," Amanda reflected, staring out at mountains she didn't really see. "We never heard another word from him, ever. He didn't even take his presents."

Jordan pressed Amanda's head against his shoulder. "Know what?" he asked softly. "Hating Christmas isn't going to change what happened."

She lifted her head so that she could look into Jordan's eyes. "It's the hardest time of the year when you've lost somebody you loved."

He kissed her forehead. "Believe me, Mandy, I know that. The first year after Becky died, Jessie asked me to write a letter to Santa Claus for her. She wanted him to bring her mother back."

Amanda smoothed the hair at Jordan's temple, even though it wasn't rumpled. "What did you do?"

"My first impulse was to get falling-down drunk and stay that way until spring." He sighed. "I didn't, of course. With some help from my sister, I explained to Jessie that even Santa couldn't pull off anything that big. It was tough, but we all got through it."

"Don't you miss them?" Amanda dared to ask, her voice barely more than a breath. "Jessica and Lisa, I mean?"

"Every day of my life," Jordan replied, "but I've got to think about what's best for them." His tone said the conversation was over, and so did his action. He got out of the chair, propelling Amanda to her feet in the process. "Let's go cut a Christmas tree."

Amanda smiled. "I haven't done that since I was still at home. My stepdad used to take my sister and me along every year—we drove all the way to Issaquah."

"So," Jordan teased with a light in his eyes, "your memories of Christmas aren't all bad."

Recalling how hard Bob had tried to make up not only for Marion's loss, but the girls', as well, Amanda had a warm feeling. "You're right," she admitted.

Jordan squinted at her and twisted the end of an imaginary mustache. This time his accent was Viennese, and he was, according to Amanda's best guess, Sigmund Freud. "Absolutely of course I am right," he said.

And then he pulled Amanda close and kissed her soundly, and she found herself wanting to go back upstairs.

That wasn't in the cards, however. Jordan had decided to cut down a Christmas tree, and his purpose was evidently unshakable. They put on coats, climbed into the small, late-model pickup truck parked beside the Porsche and sped off toward the tree farm.

Slogging up and down the rows of Christmas trees while the attendant walked behind them with a chain saw at the ready, Amanda actually felt festive. The piney smell was pungent, the air crisp, the sky painfully blue.

"How about this one?" Jordan said, pausing to inspect a twelve-footer.

Amanda looked at him in bewilderment. "What about it?"

Jordan gave her a wry glance. "Do you like it?" he asked patiently.

Amanda couldn't think why it mattered whether she liked the tree or not, but she nodded. "It's beautiful."

"We'll take this one," Jordan told the attendant.

They stood back while the man in the plaid woolen coat and blue overalls felled the tree, and followed when he dragged it off toward the truck.

By the time the tree had been paid for and tied down in the back of Jordan's truck, it was noon and Amanda was famished.

Jordan favored her with a sidelong grin when they were seated in the cab. "Hungry?"

"How do you always know?" Amanda demanded, half surprised and half exasperated. A person couldn't have a private thought around this man.

"I'm psychic," Jordan teased, starting the engine. "Of course, the fact that you haven't eaten in four hours and your stomach is rumbling helped me come to the conclusion. How does seafood sound?"

"Wonderful," Amanda replied. The scent of the tree was on her clothes and Jordan's, and she loved its pungency.

They drove to a café overlooking the water and took a table next to a window, where they could see a ferry passing, along with the occasional intrepid sailboat and a number of other small vessels. Jordan flirted with the middle-aged waitress, who obviously knew him and gave Amanda a kindly assessment with heavily made-up eyes.

"So, Jordan Richards," the older woman teased, "you've been stepping out on me."

Jordan grinned. "Sorry, Wanda."

Wanda swatted him on the shoulder with a plastic-covered menu. "I'm always the last to know," she said. Her eyes came back to Amanda again. "Since Jordan doesn't have enough manners to introduce us, we'll just have to handle the job ourselves. My name's Wanda Carson."

Amanda smiled and held out her hand. "Amanda Scott," she replied.

After shaking Amanda's hand, Wanda laid the menus down and said, "We got a real good special today. It's baked chicken with rice."

Jordan ordered the special, perhaps to atone for 'stepping out on' Wanda, but Amanda had her heart set on seafood, so she ordered deep-fried prawns and French fries.

Amanda couldn't remember ever enjoying a meal more than she did that one, but honesty would have forced her to admit it was not the food but the company that made it special.

On the way back to Jordan's house, they stopped at a variety store, which was crowded with shopping carts and people, and bought an enormous tree stand, strings of lights, colorful glass ornaments and tinsel. "I gave away the stuff Becky and I had," he admitted offhandedly while they waited in line to pay.

A bittersweet pang squeezed Amanda's heart at the thought, but she only smiled.

They spent a good hour just dragging the massive tree inside the house and setting it up. It fell over repeatedly, and Jordan finally had to put hooks in the wall and tie it in place. It towered to the ceiling, every needle of its fresh, green branches filling the room with perfume.

"It's beautiful," Amanda vowed, resting her hands on her hips.

Jordan was bringing a high stepladder in from the garage. "So are you," he told her, setting the ladder up beside the tree. "In fact, why don't you come over here?"

Amanda laughed and shook her head. "No thanks. This fly knows a spider when she sees one."

Assuming a pretend glower, Jordan stomped over to Amanda, put his fingers against her ribs and tickled her until she toppled onto the couch, shrieking with laughter.

Then he pinned her down with his body and stretched her arms far above her head. "Hello, fly," he said, his eyes twinkling as he placed his mouth on hers.

"Hello, spider," Amanda responded, her lips touching his. Just as the piney scent of the tree pervaded the house, Jordan's closeness permeated her senses.

Things might have progressed from there if the telephone hadn't rung, but it did, and Jordan reached over Amanda's head to grasp the receiver. There was a note of impatience in his voice when he answered, but his expression changed completely when the caller spoke.

He sat up on the edge of the couch, Amanda apparently forgotten. "Hi, Jessie. I'm fine, honey. How are you?"

Amanda suddenly felt like an eavesdropper. She got up from the couch and tiptoed out of the living room and up the stairs. She was pacing back and forth across the bedroom, when she noticed an overturned photograph on the bedside table.

An ache twisted in the pit of her stomach as she walked over, grasped the photograph and set it upright. A beautiful dark-haired woman smiled at her from the picture, her eyes full of love and laughter.

"Hello, Becky," Amanda whispered sadly, recalling the

white stripe on Jordan's finger where his wedding band had been.

Becky seemed to regard her with kind understanding.

Amanda set the photo carefully back on the bedside table and stood up. A fathomless sorrow filled her; she felt as though she'd made love to another woman's husband. But this time she'd known what she was doing.

Turning her back on the picture, Amanda found her suitcase and her overnighter and packed them both. She was just snapping the catches on the suitcase, when the door opened and Jordan came in.

His gaze shifted from Amanda to the photograph and back again. "Is this about the picture?" he asked quietly.

Amanda lowered her head. "I'm not sure."

"Not good enough, Mandy." Jordan's voice was husky. "Until ten minutes ago when my daughters called, everything was okay. Then you came up here and saw the picture, and you packed your clothes."

She made herself look at him, and it hurt that he lingered in the doorway instead of crossing the room to take her into his arms. "I guess I feel like this is her house and you're her husband. It's kind of like being the other woman all over again."

"That's crazy."

Amanda shook her head. "No, it isn't. Look at your left hand, Jordan. You can still see where the wedding band was. When did you take it off? Two weeks ago? Last month?"

Jordan folded his arms. "What does it matter when I took it off? The point is, I'm not wearing it anymore. And as for the picture, I just forgot to put it away, that's all."

"The night we had dinner at my place, you told me I wasn't ready for a relationship. I think maybe *you're* the one who isn't ready, Jordan."

He sprang away from the door frame, strode across the room and took the suitcase and overnighter from Amanda's hands, tossing them aside with a clatter. "Remember me? I'm the guy whose mind you blew in that bed over there," he bit out. "Damn it, have you forgotten the way it was with us?"

"That isn't the issue!" Amanda cried, frustrated and confused.

"Isn't it?" Jordan asked, clasping her wrists in his hands and wrenching her close to him. "You're scared, Amanda, so you're looking for an excuse to make a quick exit. That way you won't have to face what's really happening here."

Amanda swallowed hard. "What *is* happening here?" she asked miserably.

Jordan withdrew from her, albeit reluctantly, except for the grip he'd taken on her hand. "I don't know exactly," he confessed, calmer now. "But I think we'd damn well better find out, don't you?"

At Amanda's nod, he led her out of the bedroom and down the stairs again. She sank despondently into an easy chair while he built up the fire on the hearth.

"I don't want to be the other woman, Jordan," she said when he turned to face her.

He crossed the room, knelt in front of her and placed one of her blue-jeaned legs over each arm of the chair, setting her afire all over again as he stroked the insides of her thighs. "You're the *only* woman," he answered, and he nipped at one of her nipples through the bra and sweatshirt that covered it. "Show me your breasts, Mandy."

It was a measure of her obsession with him that she pulled up her sweatshirt and unfastened the front catch on her bra so that she spilled out into full view. He grasped her knees, holding them up on the arms of the chair as he leaned forward to tease one nipple with his tongue.

Amanda remembered that there was somebody else in Jordan's life, but she couldn't remember a face or a name. Perspiration glowed on her upper lip as Jordan took his pleasure at her breasts, moving his right hand from one knee to the other, slowly following an erotic path.

Finally, when Amanda was half-delirious with wanting, he kissed his way down over her belly and lightly bit her through the denim at the crossroads of her thighs.

Amanda moaned helplessly and moved to close her legs, and Jordan allowed that, but only long enough to unsnap her jeans

and dispose of them, along with her panties and shoes. Then he put her knees back into their original position, opened his own jeans and took her in a powerful, possessive thrust so pleasurable that she nearly fainted.

She longed to embrace Jordan with her legs, as well as her arms, but he didn't permit it. It was a battle of sorts, but Amanda couldn't be sure who was the loser, since every lunge Jordan made wrung a cry of delight from her throat.

Her climax made her give a long, low scream as she pressed her head into the chair's back. Jordan, both hands still holding her knees, uttered a desolate groan as his body convulsed and he spilled himself into Amanda.

Once the gasping aftermath was over and Amanda's breathing and heart rate had gone back to normal, she was angry. Jordan hadn't forced her, but he had turned her own body against her, and that was a power no one had ever had over Amanda before.

She moved to fasten her bra, but Jordan, still breathing hard, his eyes flashing with challenge, interrupted the action and took her tingling breasts gently but firmly into his hands. "We're not through, Amanda," he ground out.

"The hell we aren't!" she sputtered.

Keeping his hands where they were, he turned his head and lightly kissed the back of her knee.

Amanda trembled. "Damn it, Jordan…"

He moved his lips along her inner thigh, leaving a trail of fire behind them, and slid one of his hands down to rest on her lower abdomen, finding the hidden plum and making a small circle around it with the pad of his thumb. "Yes?" he answered at his leisure.

A whimper escaped Amanda, and Jordan chuckled at the sound, still working his lethal magic. "You were saying?" he prompted huskily.

Amanda reached backward to grasp the top of the chair, fearing she would fly away like a rocket if she didn't. "We're n-not through," she concluded.

Her reward was another baptism in sweet fire, and it made a believer out of her through and through.

* * *

The next day was cold and pristinely beautiful, and Jordan and Amanda decided to leave the tree undecorated and take a drive around the island. That was when Amanda saw the house.

It stood between Jordan's place and the ferry terminal, and she couldn't imagine why she hadn't noticed it before. It was white with green shutters, and very Victorian, and there was even a lighthouse within walking distance. Best of all a For Sale sign stood in the yard, swinging slowly in the salty breeze.

"Jordan, stop!" Amanda cried, barely able to restrain herself from reaching out and grasping the steering wheel.

After giving her one half-amused, half-bewildered look, Jordan steered the truck onto the rocky, rutted driveway leading past a tumbledown mailbox and a few discarded tires and empty rabbit pens.

Amanda was out of the truck a moment after they came to a jolting halt.

Chapter 7

The grass in the yard was overgrown, and the outside of the building needed paint, but neither of these facts dampened Amanda's enthusiasm. She hurried around the back of the house and found a screened porch that ran the full length of the place. On the upper floor there were lots of windows, providing an unobstructed view of the water and the mountains.

It was the perfect place for a bed and breakfast, and Amanda felt a thrill of excitement race through her blood.

A moment later, though, as Jordan caught up to her, her spirits plummeted. The place had obviously been neglected for a long time and would cost far more than she had to spend. People were willing to pay a premium price for waterfront property.

"I could help you," Jordan suggested, reading her mind.

Amanda quickly shook her head. A personal loan could poison their relationship if things went wrong later on, and besides, she wanted the accomplishment to be her own.

After they'd walked around the house and looked into the windows, Amanda wrote down the name of the real estate company and the phone number, tucking the information into her purse.

She could hardly wait to get to a telephone, and Jordan, discerning this, headed straight for the café where Wanda worked. While he chatted with the waitress and ordered clubhouse sandwiches, Amanda dialed the real estate agency's number and got an answering machine. She left her name and her numbers for home and work in Seattle and returned to the table.

"No luck?" Jordan asked as she sat down across from him in the booth and reached for the cup of coffee he'd ordered for her.

"They'll get in touch," Amanda answered with a little shrug. "I don't know why I'm so excited. I probably won't be able to afford the place, anyway."

Jordan's eyes twinkled as he looked at her. "That was a negative thing to say," he scolded. "You're not going to get anywhere in life if you don't believe in yourself."

"Thank you, Norman Vincent Peale," Amanda said somewhat irritably as she wriggled out of her coat and set it aside. "Just because you could probably write a check for the place on the spot doesn't mean I'd be able to."

The clubhouse sandwiches arrived, and Jordan picked up a potato chip and crunched it between his teeth. "Okay, so I have a knack with money. I should have—it's my business. And I don't understand why you won't let me help."

"I have my reasons, Jordan."

"Like what?"

Amanda shrugged. "Suppose in two days or two weeks we decide we don't want to see each other anymore. If I owed you a big chunk of money, things could get pretty sticky."

Jordan shook his head. "That's just an excuse, Mandy. People borrow money to start businesses every day of the week."

In the short time they'd known each other, Amanda had to admit that Jordan had learned to read her well. "I want it to be mine," she confessed. "Is that too much to ask?"

"Nope," Jordan replied good-naturedly, and after that they dropped the subject and talked of other things.

They spent the rest of the afternoon exploring the beach fronting the property Amanda wanted to buy, and the time sped by. Too soon the weekend was over and Jordan was putting her suitcase and overnighter in the back of the Porsche.

Even the prospect of separation was difficult for Amanda. "How about having dinner at my place before you come back?" she asked somewhat shyly as Jordan pushed the button to turn on the answering machine in his study.

He smiled at her. "Smooth talker," he teased.

Amanda barely stopped herself from suggesting that he bring fresh clothes and a toothbrush, as well. All her life she'd been a patient, methodical person, but where this man was concerned, she had a dangerous tendency to be impulsive. She trembled a little when Jordan kissed her, and devoutly hoped he hadn't noticed.

During the ferry ride back to Seattle, they drank coffee in the snack bar, and when they reached the city, Amanda asked Jordan to stop at a supermarket. She bought chicken, fresh corn and potatoes.

Gershwin greeted them with a mournful meow when they entered Amanda's apartment. Appeasing his pique was easy, though; Jordan simply opened a can of cat food and set it on the floor for him.

Amanda was busy cutting up the chicken and washing the corn, so Jordan wandered back into the living room and used the log left from his last visit to start a fire on the hearth.

"We forgot to decorate your tree," Amanda said when he returned to the kitchenette to lean against the counter, watching her put floured chicken pieces into a hot skillet.

"It'll keep," Jordan answered. When she'd finished putting the chicken on to brown, he took her into his arms. "Mandy, Karen's bringing the girls to Seattle Friday night. They're going to spend two weeks with me."

Amanda was pleased, but a little puzzled that he'd waited until now to mention it. "That's great. I guess you found that out when the kids called."

He nodded.

"Why didn't you tell me?"

Jordan shrugged. "If you recall, we were a little busy after that phone call," he pointed out. "And then I was trying to work out how to ask you to spend next weekend on the island with us."

Amanda broke away long enough to turn the chicken pieces and put the corn on to boil. "I don't think that would be a very good idea, Jordan," she finally said, looking back at him over her shoulder. "After all, we aren't married, and we don't want to confuse the kids."

"How could we confuse them? They're not teenagers, Amanda. They're too small to understand about sex."

Amanda shook her head. "Kids know something is going on, whether they understand what it is or not. They sense emotional undercurrents, Jordan, and I don't want to get off on the wrong foot with them." She turned down the heat under the chicken and covered it with a lid. "Now how about a glass of wine?"

Jordan nodded his assent, but he looked distracted. After uncorking the bottle and pouring a glass for himself and for Amanda, he wandered into the living room.

Amanda followed, perching on the arm of the sofa while he stood at the window, watching the city lights.

"Come on, Jordan," she urged gently. "'Fess up. You're scared, aren't you? When was the last time you were responsible for your kids for two weeks straight?"

There was a hint of anger in his eyes when he turned to look at her. "I've been 'responsible' for them since they were born, Amanda."

"Maybe so," she retorted quietly, "but somebody else did the nitty-gritty stuff—first Becky, then your sister. You don't have any idea how to really take care of your daughters, do you?"

Jordan was offended initially, but then his ire gave way to a sort of indignant resignation. "Okay," he admitted, "you've got me. I wanted you to spend next weekend with us because I need moral support."

Amanda went back to the kitchen for plates and silverware, then began to set the small, round table in the living room.

"You know my phone number," she said. "If you want moral support, you can call me. But you don't need somebody else in the way when you're bonding with your kids, Jordan."

"Bonding? Hell, you've been reading too many pop psychology books."

"You have a right to your opinion," Amanda responded, "but I'm not going to be there to act as a buffer. You're on your own with this one, buddy."

Jordan gave her an irate look, but then his expression softened and he took her in his arms. "Maybe I can't change your mind," he told her huskily, "but I can sure as hell let you know what you'll be missing."

Amanda pushed him away. "The chicken will burn."

Jordan chuckled. "Okay, Mandy, you win. For now."

Twenty minutes later they sat down to a dinner of fried chicken, corn on the cob, mashed potatoes and gravy. Amanda's portable TV set was turned to the evening news, and the ambience of the evening was quietly domestic.

When they were through eating, Amanda began clearing the table, only to have Jordan stop her by slipping his arms around her waist from behind. "Aren't you forgetting something?" he asked, his voice a low rumble as he bent his head to kiss her nape and sent a jagged thrill swirling through her system.

"W-what?" Amanda asked, already a little breathless.

Jordan slid his hands up beneath her shirt to cup the undersides of her breasts. "Dessert," he answered.

Amanda was trembling. "Jordan, the food—"

"The food will still be here when we're through."

"No, it won't," Amanda argued, following her protest with a little moan as Jordan unfastened her bra and rubbed her nipples to attention with the sides of his thumbs. "G-Gershwin will eat it."

His lips were on her nape again. "Who cares?"

Amanda realized that she didn't. She turned in Jordan's embrace and tilted her head back for his kiss.

While taming her mouth, he grasped her hips in his hands and pressed her close, making her feel his size and power.

She was dazed when he drew back, pliant when he steered her toward the bedroom and closed the door behind them.

The small room was shadowy, the bed neatly made. Jordan set Amanda on the edge of the mattress and knelt to slowly untie her shoes and roll down her socks. For a time he caressed her feet, one by one, and Amanda was surprised at the sensual pleasure such a simple act could evoke.

When she was tingling from head to foot, he rose and pulled her shirt off over her head, then smoothed away the bra he'd already opened. He pressed Amanda onto her back to unsnap her jeans and remove them and her panties, and she didn't make a move to stop him. All she could do was sigh.

After the last of her garments was tossed away, Jordan began removing his own clothes. They joined Amanda's in a pile on the floor.

"Jordan," Amanda whispered, entwining her fingers in his hair as he stretched out beside her, "don't make me wait. Please."

He gave her a nibbling kiss. "So impatient," he scolded sleepily, trailing his lips down over her chin to her neck. "Lovemaking takes time, Mandy. Especially if it's good."

Amanda remembered their session in Jordan's living room the day before. It had been fast and ferocious, and if it had been any better, it would have killed her. She moaned as Jordan made a slow, silken circle on her belly with his hand. "I can only stand so much pleasure!" she whimpered in a lame protest.

Jordan chuckled. "We're going to have to raise your tolerance," he said.

Two hours later, when both Jordan and Amanda were showered and dressed and the table had been cleared, he reached for his jacket and shrugged into it. Amanda had to fight back tears when he kissed her, as well as pleas for him to spend the night. On a practical, rational level, she knew they both needed to let things cool down a little so they could get some perspective.

But when she'd closed the door behind Jordan, Amanda

rested her forehead against it for a long moment and bit down hard on her lower lip. It was all she could do not to run out into the hallway and call him back.

Slowly she turned from the door and went about her usual Sunday night routine, choosing the outfits she would wear to work during the coming week, manicuring her nails and watching a mystery program on TV.

The bed was rumpled, and it still smelled of Jordan's cologne and their fevered lovemaking. Forlornly Amanda remade it and crawled under the covers, the small TV she kept in her room turned to her favorite show.

Two minutes after that week's victim had been done in, the telephone rang. Hoping for a call from the real estate agent or from Jordan, Amanda reached for the receiver on her bedside table and answered on the second ring.

"Amanda?"

The voice was Eunice's, and she sounded as though she'd been crying for a week.

Amanda spoke gently to her sister, because they'd always been close. "Hi, kid," she said, for she was the older of the two and Eunice had been "kid" since she was born. "What's the problem?"

"It's Jim," Eunice sobbed.

Now there's a real surprise, Amanda thought ruefully while she waited for her sister to recover herself.

"There's been someone else the whole time," Eunice wept, making a valiant, sniffling attempt to get a hold on herself.

Amanda was painfully reminded of what Madge Brockman had gone through because of her. "Are you sure?" she asked gently.

"She called this afternoon," Eunice said. "She said if Jim wouldn't tell me, she would. He's moved in with her!"

For a moment Amanda knew a pure, white-hot rage entirely directed at her soon-to-be ex-brother-in-law. Since her anger wouldn't help Eunice in any way, she counted to herself until the worst of it had passed. "Honey, this doesn't look like something you can change. And that means you have to accept it."

Eunice was quiet for almost a minute. "I guess you're right," she admitted softly. "I'll try, Amanda."

"I know you will," Amanda replied, wishing she could be nearer to her sister to lend moral support.

"Mom tells me you've met a guy." Eunice snuffled. "That's really great, Mand. What's he like?"

Amanda remembered making love with Jordan on the very bed she was lying in, and a wave of heat rolled over her. She also remembered the photograph of Becky and the white strip of skin on Jordan's left hand ring finger. "He's moderately terrific," she answered demurely.

Eunice laughed, and it was a good sound to hear. "Maybe I can meet him when I come home next week."

"I'd like that," Amanda replied. "And I'm glad you're coming home. How long can you stay?"

"Perhaps forever," Eunice replied, sounding blue again. "Everywhere I turn here, there's another reminder of Jim staring me in the face."

Amanda spoke gently. "Don't misunderstand me, sis, because I'd love for you to live in Seattle again, but I hope you realize you can't run away from your problems. You'll still have to find a way to work them out."

"That might be easier with you and Mom and Bob nearby," Eunice said quietly.

"You know we'll help in any way we can," Amanda assured her.

"Yeah, I know. It means the world to know you're there for me, Mand—you and Mom and Daddy Bob. But listen, I'll get off the line now because I know you're probably trying to watch that murder show you like so much. See you next week."

Amanda smiled. "You just try and avoid it, kid."

After that, the two sisters said their goodbyes and hung up. Amanda, having lost track of her TV show, switched off the set and the lamp on her bedside table and wriggled down between the covers.

How empty the bed seemed without Jordan sprawled out beside her, taking more than his share of the space.

* * *

Two days passed before Amanda saw Jordan again; they met for lunch in a hotel restaurant.

"Did you ever hear from the real estate agent?" Jordan asked, drawing back Amanda's chair for her.

She sank into it, inordinately relieved just to be with him again. She wondered, with a chill, if she wasn't letting herself in for a major bruise to the soul somewhere down the line. "She called me at work yesterday. The down payment is five times what I have in the bank."

Jordan sat down across from her and reached out for her hand, which she willingly gave. "Mandy, I can lend you the money with no problem."

"You must be loaded," Amanda teased, having no intention of accepting, "if you can make an offer like that without even knowing how much is involved."

He grinned one of his melting grins. "I confess—I called the agency and asked."

Amanda shook out her napkin and placed it neatly on her lap. It was time to change the subject. "Who's going to take care of the kids while you're working?" she asked.

"Much to the consternation of Striner and Striner," said Jordan, "I'm taking two weeks off. I figure I'm going to need all my wits about me."

Amanda laughed. "No doubt about that."

Jordan leaned forward in his chair with a look of mock reprimand on his face. "I'll thank you to extend a little sympathy, here, Ms. Scott. You're looking at a man who has no idea how to take care of two little girls."

"They need to eat three times a day, Jordan," Amanda pointed out with teasing patience, "and it's a good idea if they have a bath at night, followed by about eight hours of sleep. Beyond that, they mainly just need to know they're loved."

Jordan was turning his table knife from end to end. "You're sure you won't come out for the weekend?"

"My sister is arriving on Friday night—in pieces, from the sounds of things."

"Ah," Jordan answered as a waiter brought menus and filled their water glasses. "The recipient of *Gathering Up the Pieces*, the pop psychology book of the decade. I'm sorry to hear things haven't improved for her."

Amanda sighed. "They've gone from bad to worse, actually," she replied. "But there's hope. Eunice is intelligent, and she's attractive, too. She'll work through this."

"Maybe she could work through the first part of it—say next Saturday and Sunday—without you?"

Amanda shook her head as she opened her menu. "Don't you ever give up?"

"Never," Jordan replied. "It's my credo—keep bugging them until they give in to shut you up."

Amanda laughed. "Such sage advice."

They made their selections and placed their orders before the conversation continued. Jordan reached out and took Amanda's hand again when the waiter was gone.

"I've missed you a whole lot."

"Then how come you didn't call?"

"I've been in meetings day and night, Amanda. Besides, I figured if I heard your voice, I wouldn't be able to stop myself from walking into your office and taking you on your desk."

Amanda's cheeks burned, but she knew her eyes were sparkling. "Jordan," she protested in a whisper, "this is a public place."

"That's why you're not lying on the table with your skirt up around your waist," Jordan answered with a perfectly straight face.

"You have to be the most arrogant man I've ever met," Amanda told him, but a smile hovered around her mouth. She couldn't very well deny that Jordan could make her do extraordinary things.

The waiter returned with their seafood salads, sparing Jordan from having to answer. His reply probably would have been cocky, anyway, Amanda figured.

The conversation had turned to more conventional subjects, when Madge Brockman suddenly appeared beside the table. There was a look of infinite strain in her face as she assessed Amanda, then Jordan.

Amanda braced herself, having no idea whether to expect a

civil greeting or violent recriminations. "Hello, Mrs. Brockman," she said as Jordan pushed back his chair to stand. "I'd like you to meet Jordan Richards."

"Do sit down," Madge Brockman said when she and Jordan had shaken hands.

Jordan remained standing. "How is your husband?" he asked, knowing Amanda wouldn't dare ask.

"He's recovering," Madge replied with a sigh. "And he's adamant about wanting a divorce."

"I'm sorry," Amanda said softly.

The older woman managed a faulty smile. "I'll get over it, I guess. Well, if you'll excuse me, I'm supposed to meet my attorney, and I see him sitting right over there."

Jordan dropped back into his chair when Mrs. Brockman had walked away. "Are you okay?" he asked.

Amanda pushed her salad away. Even though she'd done it inadvertently, she was partly responsible for destroying Mrs. Brockman's marriage, and the knowledge was shattering. "No," she answered. "I'm not okay."

"It wasn't your fault, Amanda."

There it was again, that strange clairvoyance of his.

"Yes, it was—part of it, at least. I didn't even bother to ask if James was married. And now look what's happening."

Jordan gave a ragged sigh. Apparently his appetite had fled, too, for he set down his fork and sank back in his chair, one hand to his chin.

"The man's marital status wouldn't have made a difference to a lot of women, you know," he remarked. "For instance, you're the first one I've dated who's asked me whether I was married."

"Okay, so infidelity is widespread. So is cocaine addiction. That doesn't make either of them right."

Jordan raised his eyebrows. "I wasn't saying it did, Mandy. My point is, you're being too damn hard on yourself. So you made a mistake. Welcome to the human race."

Amanda met Jordan's gaze. "Were you faithful to Becky?" she asked, having no idea why it was suddenly so important to know. But it was.

"That's none of your damn business," Jordan retorted politely, making a steeple under his chin with his hands, "but I'll answer, anyway. I was true to my wife, and she was true to me."

Amanda had known, in some corner of her heart, that Jordan was a man of his word, and she believed him. "Were you ever tempted?"

"About a thousand times," he replied. "But there's a difference between thinking about something and doing it, Mandy. Now, do you want to ask me about my bank balance or my tax return? Or maybe how I voted in the last election?"

Amanda smiled. "You've made your point, Mr. Richards. I'm being nosy. But I'm glad you were faithful to Becky."

"So am I," Jordan said, as by tacit agreement they rose to go. "When am I going to see you again, Mandy?"

Amanda held off answering until the bill was paid and they were walking down the sidewalk, wending their way through hordes of Christmas shoppers. "When do you want to see me?"

"As soon as possible."

"You could come to dinner tonight."

"Amanda Scott, you have a silver tongue. I'll bring the wine and the food, so don't cook."

Amanda's smile was born deep inside her, and it took its time reaching her mouth. "Seven?"

"Eight," Jordan said as they stopped in front of the Evergreen Hotel. "I have a meeting, and it might run late."

She stood on tiptoe to kiss him briefly. "I'll be waiting, Mr. Richards."

He grinned as he rubbed a tendril of her hair between his fingers. "Good," he answered.

His voice made Amanda's knees quiver beneath her green suede skirt.

When Amanda reached her desk, there was a message waiting for her. In a flash, work—and Jordan—fled her uppermost thoughts. The hospital had called about James, and the matter was urgent.

Amanda's fingers trembled as she reached for the panel of buttons on her telephone. She punched out the numbers written on the message slip and, when an operator answered, asked for the designated extension.

"Intensive Care," a sunny voice said when the call was put through. "This is Betsy Andrews."

Amanda sank into her desk chair, a terrible headache throbbing beneath her temples. "My name is Amanda Scott," she said in a voice that sounded surprisingly crisp and professional. "I received a message asking me to call about Mr. Brockman."

There was a short silence while the nurse checked her records. "Yes. Mr. Brockman isn't doing very well, Ms. Scott. And he's constantly asking for you."

Amanda closed her eyes and rubbed one temple with her fingertips. She'd broken up with James long ago, and had refused his gifts and his requests for a reconciliation. When was it going to be over? "I see."

"His wife has explained the—er—situation to us," the nurse went on, "but Mr. Brockman still insists on seeing you."

"What is his doctor's recommendation?"

"It was his idea that we call you. We all feel that, well, maybe Mr. Brockman would calm down if he could just have a short visit from you."

Amanda glanced at her watch. Her headache was so intense that the numbers blurred. "I could stop by briefly after work." James had won this round. Under the circumstances, there was no way she could refuse to visit him. "That would be about six o'clock."

Betsy Andrews sounded relieved. "I'll be off duty then, but I'll make a note in the record and tell Mr. Brockman you'll be coming in."

"Thank you," Amanda said with a defeated sigh. Once she'd hung up, she reached for the phone again, planning to call Jordan, but her hand fell back to the desk. She was a grown woman, and this was her problem, not Jordan's. She couldn't go running to him every time some difficulty came up.

Pulling open her desk drawer, Amanda took out a bottle of aspirin, shook two tablets into her palm and swallowed them with water from the tap in her bathroom. Then she rolled up her sleeves and did her best to concentrate on her work.

At six-fifteen she approached James's door in the Intensive Care Unit, having gotten directions from a nurse.

He was lying in a room banked with flowers. Tubes led into his nose and the veins in both his hands. He seemed to sense Amanda's arrival and turned to look at her.

She approached the bed. "Hello, James," she said.

"You came," he managed, his voice hoarse and broken.

She nodded, unable for the moment to speak. And not knowing what to say.

"I'm going to die," he told her.

Amanda shook her head, her eyes filling with tears. She didn't love James anymore, but she had once, and it was hard to see him suffer. "No."

His eyes half-closed, he pleaded with her, "Just tell me there's a chance for us, and I'll have a reason not to give up."

Amanda started to tell him there was someone else, that there could never be anything between the two of them again, but something stopped her in the last instant. Some instinct that he really meant to die if she didn't give him hope, and she couldn't just abandon him to death. She bit down on her lower lip, then whispered, "All right, James. Maybe we could—start again."

Chapter 8

Jordan was due to arrive a little more than twenty minutes after Amanda reached her apartment. Gershwin was hungry and petulant, and the boxes containing the fur jacket and the skimpy bikini James had sent were still sitting on the hallway table. Amanda had intended to return them to the department store and ask the clerk to credit James's account, but she hadn't gotten around to it.

Now, without stopping to analyze her motives—certainly she meant to tell Jordan about her promise to James—she stuffed the boxes into the back of her bedroom closet and hastily changed into a silky beige jumpsuit. She had just misted herself with cologne, when the door buzzer sounded.

After drawing a deep breath to steady herself, Amanda dashed through the apartment and opened the door. Jordan was standing in the hallway, a tired grin on his face, a bottle of wine and several bags from a Chinese take-out place in his arms.

Looking at him, Amanda thought of how it would be to have him walk out of her life forever, and promptly lost her courage. She told herself it wasn't the right time to tell him about James.

Smiling shakily, she took the wine and fragrant bags from him and stood on tiptoe to kiss his cheek.

He shrugged out of his overcoat and hung it on the coat tree while Amanda carried the food to the table. She hadn't put out place settings yet, so she hurried back to the kitchenette for plates, silverware, wineglasses and a cork screw.

Jordan looked at her strangely when she returned. "Is something wrong, Mandy?"

Amanda swallowed. *Tell him,* ordered the voice of reason. *Just come right out and tell him you're planning to visit James in the hospital until he's out of danger.* "W-wrong?" she echoed.

"You seem nervous."

Amanda imagined the scenario: herself telling Jordan that she meant to pretend she was still in love with James just until he was stronger, Jordan saying the idea was stupid, getting angry, walking out. Maybe forever. "I'm okay," she lied.

Jordan popped the cork on the wine bottle. "If you say so," he said with a sigh, and they both sat down at the table to consume prawns, fried noodles and chow mein. Their conversation, usually so free and easy, was guarded.

When they were through with dinner, Jordan made Amanda stay at the table, nursing a second glass of wine, while he cleared away the debris of their meal. Returning, he put gentle hands on Amanda's shoulders and began massaging her tense muscles.

"Will you stay tonight?" she asked, holding her breath after the words were out. She needed Jordan desperately, but at the same time she knew guilt would prevent her from enjoying their lovemaking.

Jordan sighed. "You've been through a lot lately, Mandy. I think it would be better if we let things cool off a little."

She turned to look up at him with worried eyes. "Is this the brush-off, Mr. Richards?"

He smiled and bent to kiss her forehead. "No. I just think you need some extra rest." With that, he turned and crossed the room to the entryway. He reached for his overcoat and put it on.

Amanda stood up quickly and went to him. Even though Jordan didn't know what was going on, he sensed something, and he was already distancing himself from her. She had to tell him. "Jordan—"

He interrupted her with a kiss. "Good night, Mandy. I'll talk to you tomorrow."

Amanda tried to call out to him, but the words stopped in her throat. In the end she simply closed the door, locked it and stood there leaning against the panel, wondering how she'd gotten herself into such a mess.

True to his word, Jordan called her the next morning at work, but their conversation was brief because he was busy and so was Amanda. She threw her mind into her job in order to distract herself from the fact that she had, in effect, lied to him. And a chilling instinct told her that deceit was one thing Jordan wouldn't tolerate.

At six-thirty that evening, Amanda walked into James's room in Intensive Care, after first making sure Madge wasn't there. She was wearing jeans and a sweater, and was carrying a bouquet of flowers from the gift shop downstairs.

He smiled thinly when he saw her and extended one hand. "Hello, Amanda."

She took his hand and bent to kiss his forehead. "Hi. How are you feeling today?"

"They're moving me out of the ICU tomorrow," he answered.

But he looked very sick to Amanda. He was gaunt, and his skin still had a ghastly pallor to it.

"That's good."

"You look wonderful."

Amanda averted her eyes for a moment, feeling like a highly paid call girl. What she was doing was all wrong, but how could she turn her back on another human being, allowing him to give up and die? That would be heartless. "Thanks."

James's grip on her hand was remarkably firm. "You're better off without that Richards character," he confided. "He might have made his mark in the business world, but he's really nothing more than an overgrown kid. Killed his own wife with his recklessness, you know.''

Amanda was willing to go only so far with this charade, and listening to James bad-mouth Jordan was beyond the boundary. Somewhat abruptly she changed the subject. ''Is there anything you'd like me to bring you? Magazines or books?''

He shook his head. ''All I want is to know I'm going to get well and see you wear—and not wear—that blue bikini.''

Feeling slightly ill, Amanda nonetheless managed a smile. ''You shouldn't be thinking thoughts like that,'' she scolded. She had to get out of that room or soon she'd be smothered. ''Listen, the nurses made me promise not to stay too long, so I'm going now. But I'll be back after work tomorrow.''

When she would have walked away, James held her fast by the hand. ''I want a kiss first,'' he said, a shrewd expression in his eyes.

Amanda shook her head, unable to grant his request. She smiled brittlely and said in a too-bright voice, ''You're too ill for that.'' Ignoring his obvious disappointment, she squeezed his hand once and then dashed out of the room, calling a hasty farewell over her shoulder.

Only when Amanda was outside in the crisp December air was she able to breathe properly again. She went home, flung her coat onto the couch and took a long, scalding hot shower. No matter how she tried, though, she couldn't wash away the awful feeling that she was selling herself.

In an effort to escape, Amanda telephoned the real estate agency on Vashon Island the next morning to see if the Victorian house had been sold. It hadn't, and even though she had no means of buying it herself, the news lifted her flagging spirits.

She visited James that night, and the next, and he seemed to be improving steadily. He told her repeatedly that she was his only reason for holding on.

By Friday, when Eunice was due to arrive, Amanda was practically a wreck. She had been avoiding Jordan's calls for several days, and she could barely concentrate on her job.

Marion noticed her elder daughter's general dishevelment

when they met at the airport in front of the gate assigned to Eunice's flight. "What on earth is the matter with you?" she demanded. "You have bags under your eyes and you must have lost five pounds since I saw you last week!"

Amanda would have given anything to be able to confide in her mother, but she didn't want to spoil Eunice's homecoming—her sister would need all of Marion's and Bob's support. She shrugged and managed a halfhearted smile. "You know how it is. Falling in love takes a lot out of a person."

Marion's gaze was slightly narrowed and alarmingly shrewd. "You're not fooling me, you know," she said. "But just because I don't have time to drag it out of you now doesn't mean I won't."

Bob was just returning from parking the car, and he smiled and gave Amanda a hug. "You're looking a little peaky," he pointed out good-naturedly.

"She's up to something," Marion informed him just before the passengers from Eunice's flight began pouring out of the gate.

Amanda was the first to reach her brown-eyed, dark-haired sister, and they embraced. Tears stung both their eyes.

After the usual hassles of getting the luggage from the baggage carousel and fighting the traffic out of the airport, they drove back to the family home. Eunice chattered the whole time about how glad she was to be in Seattle again, how miserable she'd been in California, how she wished she'd never met Jim, let alone married him. By the time they reached the quiet residential area where Bob and Marion lived, Eunice had exhausted herself.

She stumbled into the room she and Amanda had once shared and collapsed on one of the twin beds.

Amanda took a seat on the other one. "I'm glad you're back," she said.

Her sister sat up on the bed and began unbuttoning her coat. "I didn't exactly return in triumph, like I thought I would," Eunice observed sadly. "Oh, Amanda, my life is a disaster area."

"I know what you mean," Amanda answered sadly, thinking of the deception she hadn't had the courage to straighten out.

Eunice yawned. "Maybe tomorrow we can put our heads together and figure out how to get ourselves back on track."

With a smile, Amanda opened her sister's suitcase and found a nightgown for her. "Here," she said, tossing the billow of pink chiffon into Eunice's lap. "Get some sleep."

When Eunice had disappeared into the adjoining bathroom, Amanda returned to the kitchen. Her mother was sitting at the table, sipping decaffeinated coffee, and Bob was in the living room, listening to the news.

"How's Eunice?" Marion asked.

Amanda wedged her hands into the front pockets of her worn brown corduroy pants. "She'll be okay once she gets a perspective on things."

"And what about you?"

"I'm in a fix, Mom," Amanda admitted, staring at the darkened window over the kitchen sink. "And I don't know how to get out of it."

Marion went to the counter, poured a cup of coffee from the percolator and brought it back to the table for Amanda. "Sit down and tell me about it."

Amanda sank into the chair. "Some very good things have been happening between Jordan and me," she said, closing her fingers around the cup to warm them. "I never thought I'd meet anybody like him."

Marion smiled. "I feel the same way about Bob."

Amanda touched her mother's hand fondly. "I know."

"So what's the problem?"

"About a week ago," Amanda began reluctantly, "someone from the hospital called and said James was asking for me. He was in the ICU at the time, so I didn't feel I could ignore the whole thing. I went to see him, and while I was there, he told me he'd given up, that he was going to die."

Marion's lips thinned in irritation, but she seemed to know how hard it was for Amanda to keep up her momentum, so she didn't interrupt.

"Essentially, he said I was the only reason he had to go on

living, and if I didn't want him, he was just going to give up. So I've been visiting him and pretending we'll be getting back together again once he's well.''

Marion sighed heavily. ''Amanda.''

''I know it sounds crazy, but I feel guilty enough without being the reason somebody died!''

Marion reached out and covered Amanda's hand with her own. ''I suppose you haven't told Jordan any of this.''

''I'm afraid to. Maybe it would have been all right if I'd mentioned it that very first night after I spoke to James, when Jordan and I were together for dinner, but I couldn't bring myself to do it. I was too afraid he'd make me choose between him and James.''

''I didn't think there was any question of a choice,'' Marion said. ''You're in love with Jordan Richards, whether you know it or not.''

Amanda bit her lower lip for a moment. ''I guess I am.''

''Tell him the truth, Amanda,'' Marion urged. ''Don't put it off for another second. March right over to that phone and call him.''

''I can't,'' Amanda said with a shake of her head. ''It's not something I can say over the telephone, and besides, his little girls will be there. This is their first night together, and I don't want to spoil it.''

''You're going to regret it if you don't straighten this out,'' Marion warned.

''I think it might already be too late,'' Amanda said brokenly, and then she rose from her chair, emptied her coffee into the sink and set the cup down. ''You just concentrate on Eunice, Mom, and don't worry about me.''

Marion shook her head as she got up to see her daughter to the door. ''Talk to Jordan,'' she insisted as Amanda put on her coat and wrapped a colorful knitted scarf around her neck.

Amanda nodded and hurried through the cold night to her car.

The light on her answering machine was blinking when she arrived home, and after brewing herself a cup of tea, she pushed the Play button and sat down at the little table in her living room to listen.

The first call was from James. He'd missed her that night and hoped she'd come to visit in the morning.

Amanda closed her eyes against the prospect, though she knew she would have to do as he asked. Maybe if she used Eunice's visit as an excuse, she could get away after only a half hour or so.

The next message nearly made her spill her tea. "This is Madge Brockman," an angry female voice said, "and I just wanted to tell you that you're not going to get away with this. You took my husband, and I'm going to take something from you." After those bitter words, the woman had hung up with a crash.

Amanda was struggling to compose herself, when yet another voice came on. "Mandy, this is Jordan. I've survived supper, and the kids' baths and story time. I have a new respect for mothers. Call me, will you?" There was a click, and then the machine rewound itself.

Despite the fact that Madge Brockman's call had shaken her to her soul, Amanda reached for the phone and dialed Jordan's number at the island house.

He answered on the second ring.

"Hi, Jordan. It's Amanda."

"Thank God," he replied with a lilt to his voice.

"How are the girls?" She dabbed at her eyes with her sleeve and resisted an impulse to sniffle.

"They're fine. Mandy, are you all right?"

"I—I need to see you. Could I c-come out there?"

Jordan hesitated, then said, "Sure. If you hurry, you can still make the last ferry. Mandy—"

"I'll be there as soon as I can," Amanda broke in, and then she hung up the phone and dashed into her bedroom. She pulled her suitcase out from under the bed and tossed in two pairs of jeans, two sets of clean underwear and two sweaters. Then, after snatching up her toothbrush and makeup bag, she made sure Gershwin had plenty of food and water and hurried out of the apartment.

Several times on the way to West Seattle Amanda's eyes were so full of tears that she nearly had to pull over to the side of the road. But finally she drove on board the ferry and parked.

Safe in the bottom of the enormous boat, she let her forehead rest against the steering wheel and sobbed.

By the time she'd reached Vashon Island and driven to Jordan's house, however, she was beginning to feel a little foolish. She wasn't a child, she told herself sternly, and she couldn't expect Jordan to solve her problems. She might have backed out of the driveway and raced back to the ferry dock if Jordan hadn't come outside to greet her.

He was wearing sneakers, jeans and a Seahawks sweatshirt, and he looked so good to Amanda that she nearly burst into tears again.

Without a word, he opened the door and helped her out, then fetched her suitcase and overnighter from the back seat. Amanda preceded him into the house, wondering what she was going to say.

There was a fire snapping on the hearth, and after setting her luggage down in the entryway, Jordan helped Amanda out of her coat. "Sit down and I'll get you some brandy," he said hoarsely after kissing her on the cheek.

Amanda took a seat on the raised stone hearth of the fireplace, hoping the warmth would take the numb chill out of her soul.

When Jordan sat down next to her and handed her a crystal snifter with brandy glowing golden in the bottom, her heart turned over. She knew she'd waited too long to explain things; she was going to lose him.

"Talk to me, Mandy," he said when she was silent, studying him with miserable eyes.

"I can't," she replied, setting the brandy aside untouched. "Will you just hold me, Jordan? Just for a few minutes?"

Gently he pulled her into his arms and pressed her head to his shoulder. He moved his hand soothingly up and down her back, but he didn't ask any questions or make any demands, and Amanda loved him more than ever for that.

Amanda had just about worked up her courage to tell him

about her promise to James, when a small, curious voice asked, "Who's that, Daddy?"

Amanda started in Jordan's arms, but he held her fast. She turned her head and saw a little dark-haired girl standing a few feet away. She was wearing a pink quilted robe and tiny fluffy slippers to match.

"This is Amanda, Jess. Amanda, my daughter, Jessica."

"Hi," Amanda managed.

"How come you're hugging her?" Jessica wanted to know. "Did she fall down and hurt herself?"

"Sort of," Jordan answered. "Why don't you go back to bed now, honey? You can get to know Amanda better in the morning."

Jessica's smile was so like Becky's that Amanda was shaken by it. "Okay. Good night, Daddy. Good night, Amanda."

When the little girl was gone, Amanda sat there in Jordan's arms, sorely wishing she hadn't intruded. She didn't belong here.

"I shouldn't have come," she said, bolting to her feet.

Jordan pulled her back so that she landed on his lap. "You've missed the last ferry, Mandy," he pointed out. "Besides, I'm not letting you go anywhere in the shape you're in."

Amanda swallowed hard. "I can't sleep with you—not with your daughters in the house."

"I understand that," Jordan replied. "I have a guest room."

Why did he have to be so damned reasonable? Amanda fretted. She didn't deserve his patience or his kindness. "Okay," she said lamely, reaching for her brandy and downing the whole thing practically in one gulp. Maybe that would give her the courage to say what she needed to say.

But it only made her woozy and very nauseous. Jordan lifted her into his arms and carried her to the guest room, where he undressed her like a weary child, put her into one of his pajama tops because she'd forgotten to bring a nightgown and tucked her in.

"Jordan, I made a terrible mistake."

He kissed her forehead. "We'll talk tomorrow," he said. "Go to sleep."

Exhaustion immediately conquered Amanda, and when she awakened, it was morning. Jordan had brought her things to her room. There was a small bathroom adjoining, so she showered, brushed her teeth and put on make-up. When she arrived in the kitchen, wearing jeans and a blue sweater, she felt a hundred percent better than she had the night before.

Jordan was making pancakes on an electric griddle and cooking bacon in the microwave, while his daughters sat at the table, drinking their orange juice and watching him with amusing consternation. While Jessica resembled Becky, the smaller child, Lisa, looked like Jordan. She had his maple-brown hair and hazel eyes, and she smiled broadly when she saw Amanda.

Again, despite her improved mood, Amanda felt like an imposter shoving herself in where she didn't belong. She would have fled to her car if she hadn't known it would only compound her problems.

"Hungry?" Jordan asked, his eyes gentle as he studied Amanda's face.

She nodded, and, seeing that there were four places set at the table, took a chair beside Lisa.

"That's Daddy's chair," Jessica pointed out.

Amanda started to move, but Jordan slapped his hand down on her shoulder and pushed her back.

"It doesn't matter where Amanda sits," he said.

Jessica didn't take offense at the correction, and Amanda reached for the orange juice carton with a trembling hand. She was more than ready to tell Jordan the truth now, but it didn't look as though she was going to get the opportunity. After all, she couldn't just drop an emotional bombshell in front of his daughters.

Jordan's cooking was good, and Amanda managed to put away three pancakes and a couple of strips of bacon even though she couldn't remember the last time she'd been so nervous.

"I think it's about time we decorated that Christmas tree, don't you?" Jordan asked when the meal was over.

The girls gave a rousing cheer and bounded out of their chairs and into the living room.

"You'll have to get dressed first," Jordan called after them. Despite his lack of experience, he seemed to be picking up the fundamentals of active fatherhood rather easily.

"Lisa can't tie her shoes," Jessica confided from the kitchen doorway.

"Then you can do it for her," Jordan replied, beginning to clear the table.

Amanda insisted on helping, and the moment Jordan heard the kids' feet pounding up the stairway, he took her into his arms and gave her a thorough kiss. She melted against him, overpowered, as always, by his strange magic.

"It's very good to have you here, lady," he said in a rumbling whisper. "I just wish I could take you upstairs and spend about two hours making love to you."

Amanda shivered at the prospect. She wished that, too, with all her heart, but once she told Jordan about her visits to James's hospital room and her pretense of rekindling their affair, he probably wouldn't ever want to touch her again.

The idea of never lying in Jordan's arms another night, never feeling the weight of his body or going crazy under the touch of his hands or his mouth, made a hard lump form in her throat.

"Still not ready to talk?" he asked, touching the tip of her nose with a gentle finger.

Amanda shook her head.

"There's time," Jordan said, and he kissed her again, making her throw her arms around his neck in an instinctive plea for more.

"Daddy!" a little voice shouted from upstairs. "I can't find my red shoes!"

Amanda pushed away from Jordan as though he'd struck her, and lifted the back of one hand to her mouth when he turned away to go and help his daughter.

While he was gone, Amanda's bravery completely deserted her. She found her purse and dashed for her car, leaving her luggage behind in Jordan's guest room. He ran outside just as she pulled out of the driveway, but Amanda didn't stop. She put her foot down hard on the accelerator and drove away.

A glance at her watch told her the ferry wouldn't leave for

another twenty minutes, and Amanda was half-afraid Jordan would toss the kids in the car and come chasing after her. Since she couldn't face him, she drove to the café where they'd eaten on a couple of occasions.

After parking her car behind a delivery truck, Amanda went into the restaurant, took a chair as far from the front door as she could and hid behind her menu until Wanda arrived.

"Well, hello there," the pleasant woman boomed. "Where's Jordan?"

"He's—busy. Could I get a cup of coffee?"

Wanda arched one artfully plucked eyebrow, but she didn't ask any more questions. She just brought a cup to Amanda's table and filled it from the pot in her other hand.

"Thanks," Amanda said, wishing she didn't have to give up the menu.

Jordan didn't show up, and Amanda was half disappointed and half relieved. She finished her coffee and went back to the ferry terminal just in time to board the boat.

Because she hoped there would be a message on the answering machine from Jordan and feared there would not, she went to the hospital first, instead of her apartment.

"You're late," James fussed when she walked into his room.

"I'm sorry—" Amanda began.

She'd forgotten what a master James was of the quicksilver change, and the brightness of his smile stunned her. "That's okay," he said generously. "I'm just glad you're here."

Amanda lowered her eyes. She would have given anything to be with Jordan and his children at that moment, helping to decorate the Christmas tree or even listening to a lecture. She regretted giving in to her impulse and running away. "Me, too," she lied.

"Tell me you love me," James said.

Amanda's heart stopped beating. She would have choked on the words if she'd tried to utter them.

For better or worse, Madge Brockman spared her the trouble. "Isn't this sweet?" she asked, sweeping like a storm into the room in a black full-length mink with a matching hat. Her eyes, full of poison, swung to Amanda. "To think I believed you when you said you and James were through."

"Amanda and I are going to be married," James protested, and he raised one hand to his chest.

Amanda was terrified.

"You idiot," Madge growled at him, gesturing wildly with one mink-swathed arm. "She's two-timing you with Jordan Richards!"

"That's a lie!" James shouted.

A nurse burst into the room. "Mr. Brockman, you must be calm!"

Terrified, Amanda backed blindly out into the hallway and ran to the elevator. It seemed to be her day for running away, she thought to herself as she got into her car and sped out of the parking lot.

For a time she just drove around Seattle, following an aimless path, trying to gather her composure. She considered visiting her mother, or one of her friends, but she couldn't, because she knew she'd break down and cry if she tried to explain things to anyone.

Finally Amanda drove back to her apartment building and went in through the rear entrance.

In the bathroom she splashed cold water on her face, washing away the tearstains, but her eyes were still puffy afterward, and her nose was an unglamorous red. It was no real surprise when the door buzzer sounded.

"Jordan or the tiger?" she asked herself with a sort of wounded fancy as she made her way determinedly across the living room and reached for the doorknob.

Chapter 9

Jordan stood in the hallway, holding Amanda's suitcase. He was alone, and his expression was quietly contemptuous.

For the moment Amanda couldn't speak, so she stepped back to let him pass. He set the luggage down with a clatter just inside the entryway and jammed his hands into the pockets of his leather jacket.

"Why the hell did you run off like that?" he demanded.

For a second or so, Amanda swung wildly between relief and dread. She turned away from Jordan, walked to the sofa and sank onto it. "You haven't had a call from Mrs. Brockman?" she asked in a small voice.

Without bothering to take off his jacket—he obviously didn't intend to stay long—Jordan perched on the arm of an easy chair. "James's wife? Why would she call me?"

Amanda swallowed. "I've been visiting James in the hospital," she blurted out. "I told him we could t-take up where we left off."

The color drained from Jordan's face. "What?"

"He said he was going to give up and die—that I was all

he had to live for. So I decided to pretend I still loved him, just until he was strong enough to go on his own."

"And you believed that?" His voice was low, lethal.

"Of course I believed it!" Amanda flared.

"Well, you've been had," Jordan replied coldly.

Amanda stared at him, wounded, her worst suspicions confirmed. "I knew you wouldn't understand, Jordan," she said. "That's why I was afraid to tell you."

"Damn it," he rasped, "don't make excuses. A lie is a lie, Amanda, and there's no room in my life for games like this!"

"It wasn't a game! You didn't see him, hear him..."

Jordan was on his feet again, his hands back in his pockets. "I didn't have to." He walked to the door and stood there for a moment with his back to Amanda. "I could understand your wanting to help," he said in parting. "But I'll never understand why you didn't tell me about it." With that, he opened the door and walked out.

Amanda jumped off the couch and raced to the entryway— she couldn't lose him, she *couldn't*—but at the door she stopped. Jordan had judged her and found her guilty, and he wasn't going to change his mind.

It was over.

Slowly Amanda closed the door. With a concerned meow, Gershwin circled her ankles. "He's gone," she said to the cat, and then she went into the bedroom, found the fur jacket and the skimpy bikini, and returned to her car.

With every mile she drove, Amanda became more certain that Jordan had been right: James had used emotional blackmail to get her to come back to him. She could see now that he'd given a performance every time she'd visited his room; she recalled the shrewd expression in his eyes, the things he'd said about Jordan.

"Fool!" Amanda muttered to herself, flipping on her windshield wipers as a light rain began to fall.

When she reached the hospital, Amanda marched inside, carrying the fur coat over her arm and the bikini in her purse. Some of her resolution faded as she got into the elevator, though. James had a serious heart condition, and for a time he'd been in real danger. Suppose what she meant to say caused him to suffer another attack? Suppose he died and it was her fault?

Amanda approached James's room reluctantly, then stopped when she heard him laughing. "Face it, Richards," he said. "You lose. In another week or two I'll be out of this place. And believe me, Amanda will be more than happy to fly off to Hawaii with me and make sure I recuperate properly."

Her first instinct was to flee, but Amanda couldn't move. She stood frozen in the hallway, resting one hand against the wall.

Jordan said something in response, but Amanda didn't hear what it was—maybe because the thundering of her heart drowned it out.

The scraping of a chair broke Amanda's spell, and she didn't know whether to stay and face Jordan or dodge into the little nook across the hall where a coffee machine stood. In the end she decided she'd done enough running away for a lifetime, and stayed where she was.

When Jordan walked out of James's room, he stopped cold for a moment, but then a weary expression of resignation came over his face.

"I'm going to tell him the truth," she said, her voice hardly more than a whisper.

Jordan shrugged. "It's a little late for that, isn't it?" His eyes dropped to the rich sable jacket draped over her arm. "Merry Christmas, Amanda."

Amanda saw all her hopes going down the drain, and something inside drove her to fight to save them. "Jordan, be reasonable. You know I never meant for things to turn out this way!"

He looked at her for a moment, then walked around her, as he would something objectionable lying on the sidewalk, and strode off down the hall.

Amanda watched him go into the elevator. He looked straight through her as the doors closed.

It was a few moments before she could bring herself to walk into James's room and face him. She no longer feared that her news would cause him another heart attack; now it was her anger she struggled to control.

Finally she was able to force herself through the doorway. She laid the coat at the foot of James's bed without meeting his eyes, then took the bikini from her purse and put it with the coat. When she thought she could manage it without hysterics, she turned to him and said, "You had no right to manipulate me that way."

"Amanda." His voice was a scolding drawl, and he stretched out his hand to her.

She evaded his grasp. "It's over, James. I can't see you anymore."

Surprisingly James smiled at her and let his hand fall to his side. "You might as well come back to me, baby. It's plain enough that Richards is through with you."

Hot rage made Amanda's backbone ramrod straight, but she didn't allow her anger to erupt in a flow of nasty retorts. Clinging to the last of her dignity, she whispered, "Maybe the time I had with Jordan will have to last me a lifetime. But he's the only man I'll ever love." With that, she turned and walked out.

"You'll be back!" James shouted after her. "You'll come begging for my forgiveness! Damn it, Amanda, nobody walks out on me...."

While a nurse rushed into James's room, Amanda went straight on until she got to the elevator. She pushed the button and waited circumspectly for a ride to the main floor, even though her emotions were howling in her spirit like a storm. She wanted to be anywhere but there, anybody besides herself.

She'd hoped Jordan might be lingering somewhere downstairs, or maybe in her section of the parking lot, but there was no sign of him.

Beyond tears, she climbed behind the wheel of her car and started toward the house where she and Eunice had grown up.

She knocked at the door and called out "It's me!" and her mother instantly replied with a cheerful "Come in!"

Bob, it turned out, was putting in some overtime at the aircraft plant where he worked, but Marion and Eunice were wrapping festive presents on the dining room table. Eunice looked a little tired, but other than that she seemed to be in good spirits. Marion was taking her usual delight in the yuletide season, but her face fell when she got a look at her elder daughter.

"Merciful heavens," she sputtered, rushing over and forcing Amanda into a chair. "You're as pale as Marley's ghost! What on earth is the matter?"

Just minutes before, Amanda had been convinced she had no tears left to cry, but now a despondent wail escaped her and tears streamed down her face.

Eunice immediately rushed to her side. "Sis, what is it?" she whispered, near tears herself. She had always cried whenever Amanda did, even if she didn't know what was bothering her sister.

"It's Jordan!" Amanda sobbed. "He's gone—he never wants to see me again...."

"Get her a glass of water," Marion said to Eunice. She rested her hands on Amanda's shoulders, much as Jordan once had, trying to soothe away the terrible tension.

Eunice reappeared moments later, looking stricken, a glass of water in one hand.

"You told him," Marion said as Amanda sipped the cold water.

Eunice dragged up a chair beside her. "Told him what?"

Setting the water down with a thump, Amanda blurted out the whole story—how she'd fallen hopelessly in love with Jordan, how James had hoodwinked her into ruining everything. She ended with an account of the scene in James's hospital room when she'd given back his gifts once and for all.

"What kind of lunkhead is this Jordan," Eunice demanded, "that he doesn't understand something so simple?"

Amanda dragged her sleeve across her eyes, feeling like a five-year-old with both knees skinned raw. Only it was her heart that was hurting. "He's angry because I didn't tell him about it from the first." She paused to sniffle, and her mother produced a handful of tissues in that magical way mothers have. "I tried, I honestly did, but I was so scared of losing him."

"Men," muttered Eunice. "Who needs them?"

"I do," chorused Amanda and Marion. And at that, all three women laughed.

Eunice patted Amanda's shoulder. "Don't worry. After he thinks about it for a while, he'll forgive you."

Amanda shook her head, dabbing at her puffy eyes with a wad of damp tissue. "You don't know Jordan. He's probably never told a lie in his life. He just flat out doesn't understand deception."

"Maybe he's never lied," Marion said briskly, "but he's made mistakes, just like the rest of us. When he calms down, Amanda, he'll call."

Amanda prayed her mother was right, but the hollow feeling in the center of her heart made that seem unlikely.

An hour later, when Amanda announced that she was going home, Eunice grabbed her coat and insisted on riding along. She'd make supper, she said, and the two of them could just hang around the way they had in high school.

"I wasn't planning to stick my head in the oven or anything, if that's what you're worried about," Amanda said with a sad smile as she backed her car out of her parents' driveway.

Eunice grinned. "And singe those gorgeous, golden tresses? I should hope not."

Amanda laughed at the image. "You know what, kid? It's good to have you back."

Her younger sister patted her arm. "I'll be around awhile, I think," she replied. "There's an opening for a computer programmer at the university. I have an interview the day after Christmas."

"There's really no hope of getting back together with Jim, then?" Amanda asked as they wended their way through rainy streets, the windshield wipers beating out a rhythmic accompaniment to their conversation.

Eunice shook her head. "Not when there's somebody else involved," she said.

Amanda nodded. Just the idea of Jordan seeing another woman was more than she could tolerate, even with the relationship in ruins.

After parking the car, Amanda and Eunice dashed through the rain to the store on the corner and bought popcorn, a log for the fireplace, a pound of fresh shrimp and the makings for a salad.

Back at Amanda's apartment, Eunice prepared and cooked the succulent shrimp while Amanda washed and cut up the vegetables.

"You don't even have a Christmas tree," Eunice complained later when she was kneeling on the hearth, lighting the paper-wrapped log.

Amanda shrugged. "I was just planning to skip the whole holiday," she said.

"Knowing Jordan didn't change that?"

"When I was with him, he was all I thought about," Amanda explained. "Same thing when I wasn't with him."

Eunice grinned and got to her feet, dusting her hands off on the legs of her jeans as if she'd just carried wood in from the wilderness like a pioneer. "You could always throw yourself at his feet and beg for forgiveness."

Amanda lifted her chin stubbornly and went to the living room window. "I explained everything to him, and he wouldn't listen."

Rain pattered at the glass and made the people on the sidewalks below hurry along under their colorful umbrellas. Amanda wondered how many of them were happy and how many had broken hearts.

"You shouldn't give up if you really care about the guy," Eunice said softly.

Amanda sighed. "I didn't give up, Eunice," she said. "He did."

At that, the two sisters dropped the subject of Jordan and talked about other Christmases.

Jordan had his own reasons for welcoming the rain, and after he drove on board the ferry to Vashon Island, he stayed in the car, staring bleakly at the empty van ahead of him. He felt hollow and numb, as though all his vitals had shriveled up and disappeared, but he knew the pain would come eventually, and he dreaded it.

After losing Becky, Jordan had made up his mind never to really care about another woman again. That way, he'd reasoned in his naïveté, he'd never have to suffer the way he had after his wife's death.

The trouble was, he'd reckoned without Amanda Scott.

He'd fallen hard for her without ever really being aware of what was happening. Had he told her that he loved her? He couldn't remember.

Maybe things would have been different if he had.

Jordan shook his head. He was being stupid. Telling her he cared wouldn't have prevented her from deceiving him. He drifted into a restless sleep, haunted by dreams of things that might have been, and when the ferry's horn blasted, he was startled. He hadn't been aware of the passing time.

Once the boat docked and his turn came, Jordan drove down the ramp, just as he had a million times before. Rain danced on the pavement, and wet gulls hid out beneath the picnic tables in the park he passed. The world was the same, and yet it was different.

He was alone again.

When he entered the kitchen through the garage door minutes later, he heard the stereo blasting. Taking off his jacket and running a hand through his rumpled hair, he went into the living room.

Jessie and Lisa had dragged their presents out from under the mammoth Christmas tree he and Amanda had chosen together, and piled them up in two teetering stacks. The babysitter, a teenage girl from down the road, was curled up on the couch, chattering into the telephone receiver.

Sighting Jordan, his daughters flung themselves at him with shrieks of glee, and he lifted one in each arm, making the growling sound they loved and pretending to be bent on chewing off their ears.

The baby-sitter, a plain little thing with thick glasses, hung up the telephone and tiptoed over to the stereo to turn it off.

Jordan let the girls down to the floor, took out his wallet and paid the sitter. The moment she was gone, Jessie folded her arms and announced, "Lisa has more presents than I do."

Jordan pretended to be horrified. "No!"

"Count them for yourself," Jessie challenged.

He knelt and began to count. The red-and-silver striped package on the top of Lisa's stack turned out to be the culprit. "This one is for both of you," Jordan said, tapping at the gift tag with his finger. "See? It's says 'Lisa *and* Jessie.'"

Jessie examined the tag studiously and was then satisfied that it was still a just world. "Where did Amanda go?" she asked, looking at him with Becky's eyes. "Why did she run away?"

Jordan had no idea how to explain Amanda's abrupt disappearance. He still didn't understand it completely himself. "She's at her apartment, I guess," he finally answered.

"But why did she runned away?" Lisa asked, rubbing her eye with the back of one dimpled hand.

"She probably went to heaven, like Mommy," Jessie said importantly.

Her innocent words went through Jordan like a lance. Young as they were, these kids were developing a strategy for being left—Mommy went to heaven; Daddy doesn't have time for us; Amanda was just passing through.

Jordan kissed both his girls resoundingly on the forehead. "Amanda's not in heaven," he said, sounding hoarse even to himself. "She's in Seattle. Now put these presents back under the tree before Santa finds out you've been messing around with them and fills your stockings with clam shells."

The telephone rang just as Jordan was rising to his feet, but he didn't lunge for it, even though that was his first instinct. He answered in a leisurely, offhand way, but his heart was pounding.

"Hi, little brother. It's Karen," his sister said warmly. "How are the monkeys getting along?"

Jordan forced himself to chuckle; he felt like weeping with disappointment. So it wasn't Amanda. What would he have said to her if it had been? "Do they always pile their presents in the middle of the living room?" he countered, trying to sound lighthearted.

Karen laughed. "No, that's a new one," she said. "How are you doing, Jord?"

He ran a hand through his hair. "Me? I'm doing great." *For somebody who's just had his insides torn out, that is.*

"No problems with memories?"

Jordan sighed and watched his children as they put their colorful gifts back underneath the tree. It seemed hard to believe there had ever been a time when he found it difficult even to look at them because they reminded him so much of Becky. "I guess I'm over that," he said huskily.

"Sounds to me like things are a little rocky."

Karen had always been perceptive. "It's something else," he said. The pain he'd been expecting was just starting to set in. "Listen, Karen, you and Paul and I have to have a talk about the girls. I want to spend more time with them."

"Took you long enough," Karen responded, her voice gentle.

Jordan remembered how she'd helped him through those dark days after Becky had died; she'd been there for him while he was in the hospital, and later, too. If she'd been in his living room instead of miles away on the peninsula, he'd have told her about Amanda.

"Better late than never," he finally replied.

"Paul and I will be down on Christmas Eve, as planned," Karen went on, probably sensing that Jordan wasn't going to confide anything important over the phone. "Save some room under that tree, because we're bringing a carload of loot, and Becky's parents will send boxes of stuff."

Jordan chuckled and shook his head. "Just what they need," he said, watching the greedy munchkins playing tug-of-war with a box wrapped in shiny blue paper. "See you Christmas Eve, sis."

Karen said a few more words, then hung up.

"I'm hungry," said Lisa as a stain spread slowly through the fabric of her plaid jeans.

"She peed her pants," Jessie pointed out quite unnecessarily.

With a grin, Jordan swept his younger daughter up in his arms and carried her off to the bathroom.

'Twas the night before Christmas, and Amanda Scott was feeling sorry for herself. She sat with her feet up in front of the fire while her mother, stepfather and sister bundled up to go to the midnight service at church.

"No fair peeking in the stockings while we're gone," said Bob with a smile and a shake of his finger.

Marion and Eunice were less understanding. They both looked as though they wanted to shake her.

"Moping around this house won't change anything," Marion scolded.

"Yeah," Eunice agreed, gesturing. "Put on your coat and come with us."

"I'm wearing jeans and a sweatshirt, in case you haven't noticed," Amanda pointed out archly. Bob had on his best suit, and Marion and Eunice were both in new dresses.

"Nobody's going to notice," Marion fussed, and she looked so hopeful that Amanda would change her mind that Amanda relented and pushed herself out of the chair.

Soon, she was settled beside Eunice in the back seat of her parents' car. It was so much like the old days that for a while Amanda was able to pretend her life wasn't in ruins.

"Maybe a little angel will whisper in Jordan's ear and he'll call you," Eunice said in a low voice as Marion and Bob sang carols exuberantly in the front seat.

Amanda gave her sister a look. "And maybe Saint Nicholas will land on our roof tonight in a sleigh drawn by eight tiny reindeer."

"Okay, then," Eunice responded, bristling, "why don't you call him?"

The truth was that Amanda had dialed Jordan's number a hundred times since they'd parted. Once she'd even waited to hear him say hello before hanging up. "Gee, why don't I?" she retorted. "Or better yet, I could plunge headfirst off an overpass. I just *love* pain."

Eunice folded her arms. "Don't be such a poop, Amanda. I'm only trying to help."

"It isn't working," Amanda responded, turning her head to look out at the festive lights trimming roofs and windows and shrubbery.

The church service was soothing, as family traditions often are, and Amanda was feeling a little better when they drove back home. They all sat around the tree, sipping eggnog and listening to carols, and when Bob and Marion finally retired for the night, Eunice dug a package out from under a mountain of gifts and extended it.

Amanda accepted the present, but refused to open it until she had found her gift to Eunice. It was another tradition; as girls, the sisters had always made their exchange just before going to bed.

When Amanda opened her gift, she laughed. It was a copy of *Gathering Up the Pieces*, the same book she'd bought for Eunice.

Eunice was amazed when she opened her package. "I don't believe this," she whispered, a wide smile on her face. She turned back the flyleaf. "And it's autographed. Wow."

"I waited in line for hours to get it signed," Amanda exaggerated. She was remembering meeting Jordan that day, and feeling all the resultant pain.

"Let's go to bed and read ourselves to sleep," Eunice suggested, standing up and switching off the Christmas tree. Its veil of tinsel seemed to whisper a silvery song in the darkness.

"Good idea," Amanda answered.

She was all the way up to chapter three before she finally closed her eyes.

The kids were asleep and so, as far as Jordan knew, were Paul and Karen. He sat up in bed, switched on the lamp and reached for the telephone on the nightstand. The picture of Becky had been moved to a shelf in his study, but he looked at the place where it had stood and said, "Know what, Becky? I've got it bad."

A glance at his watch told him it was after two in the morning. If he called Amanda now, he would be sure to wake her up, but he didn't care. Whatever happened, he had to hear her voice and wish her a merry Christmas.

He punched out the number and waited, nervous as a high school kid. While the call went through, a number of scenarios came to mind—such as James answering with a sleepy "Hello." Or Amanda telling him to go straight to hell.

Instead he got a recorded voice. "Hi. This is Amanda Scott, and I can't come to the phone right now...."

Jordan hung up without leaving a message, switched off the light and lay back on his pillows. She was probably at her parents' place, he told himself.

Or maybe she was in Hawaii, helping James recuperate.

Jordan turned onto his stomach and slammed one fist into the pillow. He knew the lush plains and contours of Amanda's body, and he begrudged them to every other man on earth. They were his to touch, and no one else's.

His groin knotted as he recalled how it was to bury himself in Amanda's depths, to feel her hands moving on his back and the insides of her thighs against his hips. She'd lain beneath him like a temptress, her eyes smoldering, her body rising to meet his, stroke for stroke, her hands curled on the sides of the pillow.

But then, as release approached, she would bite down hard on her lower lip and roll her eyes back, focusing dreamily on nothing at all. A low, keening whimper would escape her as she surrendered completely, breaking past her clamped teeth to become a shameless groan...

Jordan sat bolt upright in bed and switched on the lamp again. He couldn't quite face the prospect of a cold shower, but he was too uncomfortable to stay where he was. He tossed back the covers, reached for his robe and tied it tightly around his waist. The cloth stood out like canvas stretched over a tent pole.

Feeling reasonably certain he wouldn't meet anybody, Jordan slipped out of his room and down the darkened stairs. In the kitchen he poured himself a glass of chocolate milk and carried it back to the living room. There he sat, staring at the silent glimmer of the dark Christmas tree, the bulging shapes of the stockings. The thin light of a winter moon poured in through the smoked-glass windows, making everything look unfamiliar.

"Jordan?" It was Karen's voice, and seconds before she switched on the lights, he grabbed a sofa pillow and laid it on his lap. His plump, pretty sister, bundled in her practical blue chenille robe, looked at him with concern. "Are you all right?"

"No," Jordan answered, tossing back the last of his chocolate milk as though it could give him the same solace as brandy or good whiskey. Since it was safe to set aside the pillow, he did. "Don't ever let anybody tell you it's 'better to have loved and lost, than never to have loved at all,'" he advised, sounding for all the world like a melancholy drunk. "I've done it twice, and I wish to God I'd joined the foreign legion, instead."

Karen sat down next to him. "So you're just going to give up, huh?"

"Yeah," Jordan answered obstinately. He had to change the subject, or risk being smothered in images of Amanda lying in somebody else's bed. "About the kids—"

"You want them back," Karen guessed with a gentle smile. Jordan nodded.

Chapter 10

Amanda sat staring at the bank draft in amazement that dreary Saturday morning in February while a gray rain drizzled at the kitchen windows. "I don't understand," she muttered, glancing from Marion's smiling face to Bob's to Eunice's. "What's this for?"

Bob reached across the table to cover her hand with his. "I guess you could say it's an investment. You've been walking around here for two months looking as though you've lost your last friend, so your mother and I decided you needed a lift. It's enough for the down payment on that old house you wanted, isn't it?"

Amanda swallowed, reading the numbers on the check in disbelief. It was five times the down payment the owner demanded—Amanda still called once a week to see if the house had sold, and had gone to see it twice—and must have represented a major chunk of her parents' savings account. "I can't take this," she said. "You've worked so hard and budgeted so carefully...."

But Bob and Marion presented a united front, and they were

backed up by a beaming Eunice, who was now working full-time at the university and living in her own apartment.

"You have to accept it," Marion said firmly. "We won't take no for an answer."

"But suppose I fail?" Since the breakup with Jordan, Amanda's confidence had taken a decided dip, and everything was more difficult than it should have been.

"You won't," Bob said with certainty. "Now call that real estate woman and make an offer before the place is snapped up by some doctor or lawyer looking for a summer house."

Amanda hesitated only a moment. Hope was fluttering in her heart like a bird rising skyward; for the first time in two months she could see herself as a happy woman. With a shriek of delight, she bolted out of her chair and dashed for the telephone, and Bob and Marion laughed until they had tears in their eyes.

The real estate agent was delighted at Amanda's offer, and offered to bring the papers over to Seattle for her to sign. They agreed to meet Monday morning at Amanda's office in the Evergreen Hotel.

When Amanda was off the phone, she turned to her parents. "I can't believe you're doing this for me—taking such a chance—"

"A person can't expect to win in life if they're afraid to take a risk," Bob said quietly.

Amanda went back to the table and bent to hug each of her parents. "You'll be proud of me," she promised.

"We already are," Marion assured her.

On Monday morning Amanda arrived at work with a carefully typed letter of resignation tucked into her brief-case. In another two weeks she would be rolling up her sleeves and making a start on her dream—or, at least, part of it.

She flipped through the messages on her desk, sorting them in order of importance, and at the same time looked into the future. The house she was buying was hardly more than a mile from Jordan's place. She was bound to meet him on the highway or run into him in the supermarket, and she wondered if she could deal with that.

Even after two months Amanda ached every time she thought of Jordan. Actually encountering him face-to-face might really set her back.

There was a rap at the door, and Mindy stepped in, smiling. "You look pretty cheerful today. What's going on? Did you and Jordan get back together or something?"

Amanda opened her briefcase and took out the letter of resignation, keeping her eyes down to hide the sudden pain the mention of Jordan had caused her. "No," she answered, "but I'll be leaving the Evergreen in a couple of weeks— I'm buying that house I wanted on Vashon Island."

"Wow," Mindy responded. "That's great!"

Amanda lifted her eyes to meet her friend's gaze. "Thanks, Mindy."

Mindy's brow puckered in a frown. "I'll miss you a lot, though."

"And I'll miss you." At that moment the intercom on Amanda's telephone buzzed, and she picked up the receiver as Mindy left the office. "Amanda Scott."

"Ms. Scott, this is Betty Prestwood, Prestwood Real Estate. I'm afraid I've been delayed, so I won't be arriving in the city until around noon. Could we possibly meet at Ivar's for lunch at twelve-fifteen? I'll have the proper papers with me, of course."

Amanda automatically glanced at her calendar, even though she already knew she was free for lunch that day. She probably would have eaten yogurt in her office or gone to the mall with Mindy for fast food. "That will be fine."

After ending that phone call, Amanda went to the executive manager's office suite and handed in her resignation. Mr. Mansfield, a middle-aged man with a bald head and an ulcer, was not pleased that his trusty assistant manager was leaving.

He instructed her to start preliminary interviews for a replacement as soon as possible.

Amanda spent the rest of the morning on the telephone with

various employment agencies in the city, and when it came time to meet Mrs. Prestwood for lunch, she was relieved. It wasn't the food that attracted her, but the prospect of a break.

After exchanging her high heels for sneakers, Amanda walked the six blocks from the hotel to the seafood restaurant on the waterfront. The sun was shining, and the harbor was its usual noisy, busy self.

Mrs. Prestwood, a small, trim woman with carefully coiffed blond hair and tasteful makeup, was waiting by the reservations desk.

She and Amanda shook hands, then followed the hostess to a table by a window.

Just as Amanda was sitting down, she spotted Jordan—it was as though her eyes were magnetized to him. He looked very Wall Street in his three-piece suit as he lunched with two other men and a woman.

Evidently he'd sensed Amanda's stare, for his eyes shifted to her almost instantly.

For a moment the whole restaurant seemed to fall into eerie silence for Amanda; she had the odd sensation of standing on the bottom of the ocean. It was only with enormous effort that she surfaced and forced her gaze to the menu the waitress had handed her. *Don't let him come over here,* she prayed silently. *If he does, I'll fall apart right in front of everybody.*

"Is something wrong?" Betty Prestwood asked pleasantly.

Amanda swallowed and shook her head, but out of the corner of her eye she was watching Jordan.

He had turned his attention back to his companions, especially the woman, who was attractive, in a tweedy sort of way, with her trim suit and her dark hair pulled back into a French twist. She was laughing at something Jordan had said.

Amanda made herself study the menu, even though she couldn't have eaten if her life depended on it. She finally decided on the spinach salad and iced tea, just for show.

Mrs. Prestwood brought out the contracts as soon as the waitress had taken their orders, and Amanda read them through carefully. Lunch had arrived by the time she was done, and in a glance she saw that Jordan and his party were leaving. He was resting his hand lightly on the small of the woman's back, and Amanda felt for all the world like a betrayed wife.

Forcing her eyes back to the contracts, she signed them and handed Mrs. Prestwood a check. Since the owner was financing the sale himself, it was now just a matter of waiting for closing. Amanda could rent the house in the interim if she wished.

She wrote another check, then stabbed a leaf of spinach with her fork. Try as she might, she couldn't lift it to her mouth. Her stomach was roiling angrily, unwilling to accept anything.

She laid the fork down.

"Is everything all right?" Mrs. Prestwood asked, seeming genuinely concerned.

Amanda lied by nodding her head.

"You don't seem very hungry."

Amanda managed a smile. Was Jordan sleeping with that woman? Did she visit him on the island on weekends? "I'm just getting over the flu," she said, which was at least a partial truth. She was probably coming down with it, not getting over it.

Mrs. Prestwood accepted that excuse and finished her lunch in good time. The two women parted outside the restaurant with another handshake, then Amanda started back up the hill to the hotel. By the time she arrived, her head was pounding and there were two people waiting to be interviewed for her job.

She talked to both of them and didn't pass either application on to Mr. Mansfield for his consideration. One had obviously considered herself too good for such a menial position, and the other had an offensive personal manner.

Amanda's headache got progressively worse as the afternoon passed, but she was too busy interviewing to go home to bed, and besides, she couldn't be sure the malady wasn't psychosomatic. She hadn't started feeling really sick until after she'd seen Jordan with that woman in the dress-for-success clothes.

At the end of the day Amanda dragged herself home, fed Gershwin, made herself a bowl of chicken noodle soup and watched the evening news in her favorite bathrobe. By the time she'd been apprised of all the shootings, rapes, drug deals and political scandals of the day, she was thoroughly depressed. She put her empty soup bowl in the sink, took two aspirin and fell into bed.

The next morning she felt really terrible. Her head seemed thick and heavy as a medicine ball, and her chest ached.

Reluctantly she called in sick, took more aspirin and went back to sleep.

A loud knocking at the door awakened her around eleven-thirty, and Amanda rolled out of bed, stumbled into the living room with one hand pressed to her aching head and called, "Who is it?"

"It's me," a feminine voice replied. "Mindy. Let me in—I come bearing gifts."

With a sigh, Amanda undid the chains, twisted the lock and opened the door. "You're taking your life in your hands, coming in here," she warned in a thick voice. "This place is infested with germs."

Mindy's pretty hair was sprinkled with raindrops, and her smile was warm. "I'll risk it," she said, stepping past Amanda with a stack of magazines and a box of something that smelled good. She grimaced as she assessed Amanda's rumpled nightgown and unbrushed hair. "You look like the victim in a horror movie," she observed cheerfully. "Sit down before you fall down."

Amanda dropped into a chair. "What's going on at the office?"

"It's bedlam," Mindy answered, setting the magazines and food down on the table to shrug out of her coat. "Mr. Mansfield is finding out just how valuable you really are." Her voice trailed back from the kitchenette, where she was opening cupboards and drawers. "He's been interviewing all morning, and he's such a bear today, he'll be lucky if anybody wants to work for him."

Amanda sighed. "I should be there."

Mindy returned from the kitchenette and handed Amanda a plate of the fried Chinese noodles she knew she loved. "And spread bubonic plague among your friends and co-workers? Bad idea. Eat this, Amanda."

Amanda took the plate of noodles and dug in with a fork. Although she still had no appetite, she knew her body needed food to recover, and she hadn't had anything to eat since last night's chicken soup. "Thanks."

Mindy glanced at the blank TV screen in amazement. "Do you mean to tell me you have a chance to catch up on all the soaps and you aren't even watching?"

"I'm sick, not on vacation," Amanda pointed out.

Mindy rushed to turn on the set and tune in her favorite. "Lord, will you look at him?" she asked, pointing to a shirtless hero soulfully telling a woman she was the only one for him.

"Don't listen to him," Amanda muttered. "As soon as you make one wrong move, he'll dump you."

"You *have* been watching this show!" Mindy accused.

Amanda shook her head glumly. "I was speaking from the perspective of real life," she said, chewing.

Mindy sighed. "I knew that rascal would be fooling around with Lorinda the minute Jennifer turned her back," she fretted, shaking her finger at the screen.

Amanda chuckled, even though she would have had to feel better just to die, and took another bite of the noodles Mindy had brought. "How do you know so much about the story line when you work every day?"

"I tape it," Mindy answered. Then, somewhat reluctantly, she snapped off the set and turned back to her mission of mercy. "Is there anything you want me to do at the office, Amanda? Or I could shop for you—"

Amanda interrupted with a shake of her head. "It's enough that you came over. That was really nice of you."

Mindy rose from the couch and put her hands on her slim hips. "I know. I'll make a bed for you on the couch so you can watch TV. Mom always did that for me when I was sick, and it never failed to cheer me up."

With that, Mindy disappeared into the bedroom, returning soon afterward with sheets, blankets and pillows. True to her word, she made a place for Amanda on the couch and all but tucked her in when she was settled with her magazines and the controls for the TV.

Before going back to work, she made Amanda a cup of hot tea, put the phone within reach and forced her to take more aspirin.

When Mindy was gone, Amanda got up to lock the door behind her, then padded back to the bed. She was comfortably settled when the telephone rang. A queer feeling quivered in the pit of her stomach as she remembered seeing Jordan in the restaurant the day before, felt again the electricity that passed between them when their eyes met. "Hello?" she said hopefully.

"Hello, Amanda."

The voice didn't belong to Jordan, but to Mrs. Prestwood. Amanda could pick up the keys to her house at the real estate office whenever she was ready.

Amanda promised to be there within the week, and asked Mrs. Prestwood to have telephone service hooked up at the house, along with electricity. Then she hung up and flipped slowly through the magazines, seeing none of the glossy photographs and enticing article titles. She was going to be living on the same island with Jordan, and that was all she could think about.

By the time Amanda recovered enough to return to work, half her notice was up and Mr. Mansfield had selected a replacement. Handing her her final paycheck, which was sizable because there was vacation pay added in, he wished her well. On her last day, he and Mindy and the others held a going away party for her in the hotel's elegant lounge, and Bob, Marion and Eunice attended, too.

That Friday evening, Amanda filled her car with boxes, one of which contained Gershwin, leaving the rest of her things behind for the movers to bring, and boarded the ferry for Vashon Island.

Since it was cold and dark in the bottom of the ship, she decided to venture upstairs to the snack bar for a cup of hot coffee. Just as she arrived, however, she spotted Jordan again. This time he was with his daughters, and the three of them were eating French fries while both girls talked at once.

Amanda's first instinct was to approach them and say hello, but in the end she lost her courage and slipped back out of the snack bar and down the stairs to her car. She sat hunched behind the wheel, waiting for the whistle announcing their arrival at Vashon Island to blast, and feeling miserable. What kind of life was she going to have in her new community if she had to worry about avoiding Jordan?

In those moments Amanda felt terribly alone, and the enormity of the things she'd done—giving up her job and apartment and borrowing such a staggering sum of money from her parents—oppressed her.

Finally the ferry came into port, and Amanda drove her car down the ramp, wondering if Jordan and the girls were in one of the cars ahead, or one behind. She didn't get a glimpse of them, which wasn't surprising, considering how dark it was.

When Amanda arrived at her new old house, the lights were on and Mrs. Prestwood was waiting in the kitchen to present the key, since Amanda had not had a chance to pick it up at the office. The old oil furnace was rumbling beneath the floor, filling the spacious rooms with warmth.

Amanda wandered through the rooms, sipping coffee from the percolator Betty Prestwood had thoughtfully loaned her and dreaming of the things she meant to do. There would be winter parties around the huge fireplace in the front parlor—she would serve mulled wine and spice cake with whipped cream. And in summer, guests could sleep on the screened sun porch if they wanted to, and be lulled into slumber by the quiet rhythm of the tide and the salty whisper of the breezes.

There were seven bedrooms upstairs, but only one bathroom. Amanda made a mental note to call in a plumbing contractor for estimates the next morning. She would have to add at least one more.

Amanda's private room, a small one off the kitchen, looked especially inviting after the long day she'd had. While Gershwin continued to explore the farthest reaches of his new home, she went out to the car to get the cot and sleeping bag she'd borrowed from her stepdad. After a bath upstairs, she crawled onto the cot with a book.

She hadn't read more than a page, when Gershwin suddenly landed in the middle of her stomach with a plop and meow.

Amanda let her book rest against her chin and stroked his silky fur. "Don't worry, Big Guy. We're both going to like it here." The instant the words were out of her mouth, though, she thought of the jolt that seeing Jordan and the girls had caused her, and her throat tightened painfully. "You'd think I'd be over him by now, wouldn't you?" she said when she could speak, her vision so blurred that there seemed to be two Gershwins lying on her stomach instead of one.

"Reoww," Gershwin agreed, before bending his head to lick one of his paws.

"Love is hell," Amanda went on with a sniffle. "Be glad you're neutered."

Gershwin made no comment on that, so Amanda dried her eyes and focused determinedly on her book again.

The next morning brought a storm in off Puget Sound. It slashed at the windows and howled around the corners of the house, and Gershwin kept himself within six inches of Amanda's feet. She left him only to carry in the boxes from the car and drive to the supermarket for food.

Since she'd prepared herself to encounter Jordan, Amanda was both relieved and disappointed when there was no sign of him. She filled her cart with groceries, taking care to buy a can of Gershwin's favorite food to make up for leaving him, and drove back over rain-slickened roads to the house.

The tempest raged all day, but Amanda was fascinated by it, rather than frightened. While Gershwin was sleeping off the feast Amanda had brought him, she put on her slicker and a pair of rubber boots she'd found in the basement and walked down to the beach.

Lightning cracked the sky like a mirror dropped on a hard floor, and the water lashed furiously at the rocky shoreline. Amanda stood with her hands in the pockets of her slicker, watching the spectacle in awe.

When she returned to the house half an hour later, her jeans were wet to her knees despite the rain garb she wore, and her hair was dripping. She felt strangely comforted, though, and when she saw Betty Prestwood's car splashing up the puddle-riddled driveway, she smiled and waved.

The two women dashed onto the enclosed porch together, laughing. Betty was only a few years older than Amanda, and they were getting to be good friends.

"There's an estate sale scheduled for today," Betty said breathlessly when they were in the kitchen and Amanda had handed her a cup of steaming coffee. "I thought you might like to go, since you need so much furniture. It's just on the other side of the island, and we could have lunch out."

Amanda was pleased that Betty had thought of her. Even though she had a surplus of funds, thanks to her own savings and the loan from Bob and Marion, it was going to cost a lot of money to get the bed and breakfast into operation. She needed to furnish the place attractively for a reasonable price. "Sounds great," Amanda said, ruefully comparing her soggy jeans and crumpled flannel shirt to Betty's stylish pink suit. "Just give me a few minutes, and I'll change."

Betty smiled. "Fine. Do you mind if I use the phone? I like to check in with the office periodically."

Amanda gestured toward the wall phone between the sink and stove. "Help yourself. And have some more coffee if you want it. I won't be long."

After finding a pair of black woolen slacks and a burgundy sweater, along with clean underthings and a towel and wash-cloth, Amanda dashed upstairs and took a quick, hot shower. When she was dressed, with her hair blow-dried and a light application of makeup highlighting her features, she hurried downstairs.

Betty was leaning against one of the kitchen counters, sipping coffee. "When are the movers coming?"

"Monday," Amanda answered, pulling on a pair of shoes that would probably be ruined the instant she wore them outside. "But even when all my stuff is here, the place is still going to echo like a cavern."

Betty laughed. "Maybe we can fix that this afternoon."

After saying goodbye to Gershwin, who still hadn't recovered from his stupor, Amanda pulled the ugly rubber boots she'd worn earlier on over her shoes, put on her slicker and followed Betty to her car.

Since the auction was scheduled for one o'clock, they had time for a leisurely lunch. Mercifully Betty suggested a small soup-and-sandwich place in town, rather than the roadside café Amanda knew Jordan frequented.

She ordered a turkey sandwich with bean sprouts, along with a bowl of minestrone, and ate with enthusiasm. She wasn't over Jordan, and she was still weak with lingering traces of the flu, but her appetite was back.

After lunch, she and Betty drove to a secluded house on the opposite side of the island, where folding chairs had been set up under huge pink-and-white striped canopies. Amanda's heart sank when she saw how many people had braved the nasty weather in search of a bargain, but Betty seemed to be taking a positive attitude, so she tried to follow suit.

The articles available for sale were scattered throughout the house—there were pianos and bedroom sets, tea services and bureaus, sets of china boasting imprints like Limoges and Haviland. Embroidered linens were offered, too, along with exquisite lace curtains and grandfather clocks, and wonderful old books that smelled of age and refinement.

Amanda's excitement built, and she crossed her fingers as she and Betty took their places in the horde of metal chairs.

A beautiful old sleigh bed with a matching bureau and armoire came up for sale first, and Amanda, thinking of her seven empty bedrooms, held up her bid card when the auctioneer asked for a modest amount to start the sale rolling.

A man in the back row bid against her, and it was nip and tuck, but Amanda finally won the skirmish with fairly minimal damage to her bank balance.

After that she bought linens, one of the grandfather clocks and a set of English bone china, while Betty purchased a full-length mirror in a cherrywood stand and an old jewelry box. At the end of the sale, Amanda made arrangements for the auction company to deliver her purchases, then wrote out a check.

It was midafternoon by then, and her soup and sandwich were beginning to wear off. Having lost sight of Betty in the crowd, she bought a hot dog with mustard and relish and a diet cola, then sat quietly in one of the folding chairs to eat.

She nearly choked when Jordan walked up, turned the chair in front of hers around and straddled it, his arms draped across the back. His expression was every bit as remote as it had been the last time she'd seen him, and Amanda prayed he couldn't hear her heart thudding against her rib cage.

"What are you doing here?" he asked, his voice insinuating that she was probably up to no good.

Amanda was instantly offended. She swallowed a chunk of her hot dog in a painful lump and replied, "I thought I'd try to steal some of the silverware, or maybe palm an antique broach or two."

He grinned, though the expression didn't quite reach his eyes. "You bought a bedroom set, a grandfather clock and some dishes. Getting married, Ms. Scott, now that Mrs. Brockman is out of the picture?"

It was all Amanda could do not to poke him in the eye with the rest of her hot dog. Obviously he didn't know she'd bought the Victorian house, and she wasn't about to tell him. "It'll be a June wedding," she said evenly. "Would you like to come?"

"I'm busy for the rest of the decade," Jordan answered in a taut voice, his hazel eyes snapping as he rose from the chair and put it back into line with the others. "See you around."

As abruptly as that, he was gone, and Amanda was left to sit there wondering why she'd let him walk away. When Betty returned, bringing along two of her friends to be introduced, Amanda was staring glumly at her unfinished hot dog.

Because Jessie and Lisa were staying with Becky's parents in Bellevue that weekend, Jordan was driving the Porsche. He strode back to it, oblivious to the rain saturating his hair and his shirt, and threw himself behind the wheel, slamming the door behind him.

Damn it all to hell, if Amanda was going to go on as if nothing had happened between them, couldn't she at least stay on her own turf? It drove him crazy, catching glimpses of her in restaurants, and in the midst of crowds waiting to cross streets, and in the next aisle at bookstores.

After slamming his palms against the steering wheel once, he turned the key in the ignition, and the powerful engine surged to life. The decision had been made by the time the conglomeration of striped canopies had disappeared from the rearview mirror; he would go home, change his clothes and spend the rest of the day in Seattle, working.

The plan seemed to be falling into place until an hour later, when he was passing by that Victorian place Amanda had liked so much. The lights were on, and there was a familiar car parked in the driveway.

He met Betty Prestwood's pink Cadillac midway between the highway and the house. She smiled and waved, and Jordan waved back distractedly, noticing for the first time that the For Sale sign was gone from the yard.

He braked the car to a stop and sprinted through the rain to the door, feeling a peculiar mixture of elation and outrage as he hammered at it with one fist.

Chapter 11

Amanda had just changed back into her jeans and a T-shirt when the thunderous knock sounded at the door. Expecting an enthusiastic salesperson, she was taken aback to find Jordan standing on her porch, dripping rainwater and indignation.

"Aren't you going to ask me in?" he demanded.

Amanda stepped back without a word, watching with round eyes as Jordan stomped into the warm kitchen, scowling at her.

"Well?" he prompted, putting his hands on his hips.

He seemed to have a particular scenario in mind, but Amanda couldn't think for the life of her what it would be.

She left him standing there while she went into her bathroom for a dry towel. Handing it to him upon her return, she asked, "Well, what?"

"What are you doing in this house? For that matter, what are you doing on this *island*?" He was drying his hair all the while he spoke, a grudging expression on his face.

Amanda hooked her thumbs in the waistband of her jeans and tilted her head to one side. "I own this house," she replied. "As for why I'm on the island, well—" she paused to shrug and spread her hands "—I guess I just didn't know I was supposed to get your approval before I stepped off the ferry."

Jordan flung the towel across the room, and it caught on the handle of the old-fashioned refrigerator. "Are you married to James?"

She went to the percolator and filled two cups with coffee, one for her and one for Jordan. "No," she answered, turning her head to look back at him over her shoulder. "I explained the situation to you. I was only trying to help James in my own misguided way. Where did you get the idea I meant to marry him?"

Jordan sighed and shoved his hand through damp, tangled hair. "Okay, so my imagination ran away with me. I tried to call you on Christmas Eve, and you weren't home. I had all these pictures in my mind of you lying on some secluded beach in Hawaii, helping James recuperate."

Although she was delighted, even jubilant, to know Jordan had tried to call her, she wasn't about to let on. She brought the coffee cup to him and held it out until he took it. "How would my lying on a secluded beach help James recuperate?"

"With you for a visual aid, a corpse would recuperate," he replied with a sheepish grin. His eyes remained serious. "I've missed you, Mandy."

She felt tears rising in her eyes and lowered her head while she struggled to hold them back. She didn't trust herself to speak.

Jordan took her coffee and set it, with his own, on the counter. "Don't you have any chairs in this place?"

Amanda made herself meet his eyes as she shook her head. "Not yet. The movers will be here on Monday."

He approached her, hooked his index fingers through the belt loops on her jeans and pulled her close. So close that every intimacy they'd ever shared came surging back to her memory at the contact, making her feel light-headed.

"I may have neglected to mention this before," he said in a voice like summer thunder rumbling far in the distance, "but I'm in love with you, and I have a feeling it's a lifetime thing."

Amanda linked her hands behind his neck, reveling in her

closeness to Jordan and the priceless words he'd just said. "Actually, you did neglect to mention that, Mr. Richards."

He tasted her lips, sending a thrill careening through her system. "I apologize abjectly, even though you're guilty of the same oversight."

"Only too true," Amanda whispered, her mouth against his. "I love you, Jordan."

He ran his hands up and down her back, strong and sure and full of the power to set her senses aflame. He pressed his lips to her neck and answered with a teasing growl.

Amanda called upon all her self-control to lean back in his arms. "Jordan, we have things to talk about—things to work out. We can't just take up where we left off."

His fingers were hooked in her belt loops again. "I'll grant you that we have a lot to work through, and it's going to take some time. Why don't we go over to my place and talk?"

With considerable effort, Amanda willed her heart to slow down to a normal beat. She knew what was going to happen—it was inevitable—but she wanted to be sure they were on solid ground first. "We can talk here," she said, and she led him into the giant, empty parlor with its view of the sound. They sat together on a window seat with no cushion, their hands clasped. "I was wrong not to tell you I was seeing James again, Jordan, and I'm sorry."

He touched her lips with an index finger. Outside, beyond the rain-dappled glass, the storm raged on. "Looking back, I guess I wouldn't have been very receptive, anyway. I was feeling pretty possessive."

Amanda rested her head against his damp shoulder, unable to resist his warmth any longer, trembling as he traced a tingling pattern on her nape. "I thought I was going to die when I saw you at Ivar's with that corporation chick."

Jordan laughed and curved his fingers under her chin. "'Corporation chick'? That was Clarissa Robbins. She works in the legal department and is married to one of my best friends."

Amanda felt foolish, but she was also relieved, and she guessed that showed in her face, because Jordan was grinning at her. "You have your girls back," she said. "I saw you on the ferry last night."

Jordan nodded. "They didn't actually move in until a month ago. After all, they were used to living with Paul and Karen, so we just did weekends at first. And they're staying with Becky's parents until tomorrow night."

She tried to lower her head again, but Jordan wouldn't allow it.

"Think you could fall for a guy with two kids, Mandy?" he asked.

"I already have," she answered softly.

Jordan's mouth descended to hers, gentle at first, and then possessive and commanding. By the time he withdrew, Amanda was dazed.

"Show me the bridal suite," he said, rising to his feet and pulling Amanda after him.

She swallowed. "There's no bed in there, Jordan," she explained timidly.

"Where do you sleep?"

His voice was downright hypnotic. In fact, if he'd started undressing her right there in the middle of the parlor, she wouldn't have been able to raise an objection. "In a little room off the kitchen, but—"

"Show me," Jordan interrupted, and she led him back to where she slept.

"That'll never hold up," he said, eyeing the cot Amanda had spent the night on. With an inspired grin, he grabbed up the sleeping bag and pillow. "Now," he went on, grasping her hand again, "let's break in the bridal suite."

Amanda felt color rise in her cheeks, and she averted her eyes before leading the way around to the front of the house and up the stairs.

The best room faced the water and boasted its own fireplace, but it was unfurnished except for a large hooked rug centered in the middle of the floor.

Jordan spread the sleeping bag out on the rug and tossed the pillow carelessly on top of it, then stood watching Amanda with a mingling of humor and hunger in his eyes. "Come here, Mandy," he said with gentle authority.

She approached him shyly, because in some ways everything was new between them.

He slipped his hands beneath her T-shirt, resting them lightly on the sides of her waist; his hands were surprisingly warm.

"I love you, Amanda Scott," he told her firmly. "And in a month or a year or whenever you're ready, I'm going to make you my wife. Any objections?"

Amanda's lips were dry, and she wet them with her tongue. "None at all," she answered, and she drew in a sharp breath and closed her eyes as Jordan slid his hands up her sides to her breasts. With his thumbs he stroked her long-neglected nipples through the lacy fabric of her bra. When they stood erect, he pulled Amanda's T-shirt off over her head and tossed it aside.

"Let me look at you," he said, standing back a little.

Slowly, a little awkwardly, Amanda unhooked her bra and let it drop, revealing her full breasts. She let her hand fall back in ecstatic surrender as Jordan boldly closed his hands over her. When he bent his head and began to suckle at one pulsing nipple, she gave a little cry and entangled her hands in his hair.

He drew on both her breasts, one after the other, until she was half-delirious, and then he dropped to his knees on the sleeping bag and gently took Amanda's shoes from her feet. She started to sink down, needing union with him, but he grasped her hips and held her upright.

She bit down on her lower lip as she felt his finger beneath the waistband of her jeans. The snap gave way, and then the zipper, and then Amanda was bared to him, except for her panties and socks.

Her knees bent of their own accord, and her pelvis shifted forward as Jordan nipped at the hidden mound, all the time rolling one of her socks down. When her feet were bare, he pulled her panties down very slowly, and she kicked them aside impatiently, sure that Jordan would appease her now.

But he wasn't through tormenting her. He massaged the insides of her thighs, carefully avoiding the place that most needed his attention, and then lifted one of her knees and placed it over his shoulder.

Amanda was forced to link her hands behind his neck to keep from falling. "Oh," she whimpered as she realized what a vulnerable position she was in. "Jordan—"

He parted her with his fingers. "What?"

Her answer was cut off, and forced forever into the recesses of her mind when Jordan suddenly took her fully, greedily, into his mouth. She thrust her head back with the proud abandon of a tigress and gave a primitive groan that echoed in the empty room.

Jordan raised one hand to fondle her breast as he consumed her, and the two sensations combined to drive her to the very edge of sanity. She began to plead with him, and tug at the back of his shirt in a fruitless effort to strip him and feel his nakedness under her hands.

He lay back on the floor, bringing Amanda with him, and she rocked wildly in a shameless search for release while he moved his hands in gentle circles on her quivering belly. When he caught both her nipples between his fingers, Amanda's quest ended in a spectacular explosion that wrung a series of hoarse cries from her throat.

She sagged to the floor when it was over, only half-conscious, and Jordan arranged her on the sleeping bag before slowly removing his clothes. When he was naked, he tucked the pillow under her bottom and parted her knees, kneeling between them to tease her.

The back of one hand resting against her mouth, Amanda gave a soft moan. "Jordan—"

"Umm?" He gave her barely an inch of himself, but that was enough to arouse her all over again, to stir the fires he'd just banked. At the same time, he bent to sip at one of her nipples in a leisurely fashion.

Amanda groaned.

"What was that?" Jordan teased, barely pausing in his enjoyment of her breast.

"I want—oh, God, Jordan, please—I need you so much...."

He drew in a ragged breath, and she felt him tremble against the insides of her thighs as he gave her another inch.

She clutched at his arms, trying to pull him to her. "Jordan!" she wailed suddenly in utter desperation, and he gave her just a little more of himself.

Amanda couldn't wait any longer. She'd had release once, it was true, but her every instinct drove her toward complete fulfillment. She needed Jordan's weight, his substance, his force, and she needed it immediately.

With a fierce cry, she thrust her hips upward, taking him all the way inside her, and at that point Jordan's awesome control snapped.

Amanda watched through a haze of passion as he surrendered. Bracing his hands on the rug and arching his back, he withdrew and lunged into her again in a long, violent stroke, leaving no doubt as to the extent of his claim on her.

Triumph came at the peak of a sweet frenzy that tore a rasping shout from Jordan's throat and set Amanda's spirit to spiraling within her. For a few dizzying moments she was sure it would escape and soar off into the cosmos, leaving her body behind forever. The feeling passed, like a fever, and when Jordan fell to her, she was there to receive him.

He kissed her bare shoulder between gasps for air, and finally whispered, "Don't mind me. I'll be fine in a year or two."

Amanda's breath had just returned, and she laughed, moving her hands over his back in a gesture meant both to soothe and to claim. But her eyes were solemn when Jordan lifted his head to study her face a few moments later.

"Do you think it will take a long time for us to get things ironed out, Jordan?"

He kissed her forehead. "Judging by what just happened here, I'd say no."

"Good," she answered.

He traced the outline of her mouth with the tip of one finger. "Will you give me a baby, Mandy?" he asked huskily.

Her heart warmed within her, and seemed to grow larger. "Probably sooner than you think," she replied.

Jordan chuckled and drew her close to him, and they lay together for a long time, recovering. Remembering. Finally, he bent to kiss her once more before rising from her to reach for his clothes. He gave her a long look as she sat up and wrapped her arms around her knees, then sighed. "We've got a lot of talking to do," he said. "Now that there's some chance of concentrating, let's go over to my place and get started."

Amanda nodded and grabbed her jeans and panties. Because her things were scattered all over the rug, she wasn't able to dress as fast as Jordan, and he was brazen enough to watch her put on every garment.

Fifteen minutes later they pulled into his garage. When a blaze was snapping in the living room fireplace, they sat side by side on the floor in front of it, cross-legged and sipping wine.

Amanda started the conversation with a blunt but necessary question. "Are you still in love with Becky?"

Jordan considered her words solemnly and for a long time. "Not in the way you mean," he finally said, his eyes caressing Amanda he watched her reactions. "But I'll always care about her. It's just that I feel a different kind of love for her now. Sort of mellow and quiet and nostalgic."

Amanda nodded, then let her head rest against his shoulder. "In a way, she lives on in Jessie and Lisa."

Jordan sighed, watching the fire. He told her about the accident then, about feeling Becky's arms tighten around his waist in fear just before impact, about the pain, about being in the hospital when her funeral was held. "I felt responsible for her death for a long time," he said, "but I finally realized I was just using that as an excuse to go on mourning forever. Deep down inside, I knew it was really an accident."

Amanda gave him a hug.

"Thanks, Mandy," he said hoarsely.

She sat up straight to look at him. "For what?"

"For coming along when you did, and for being who you are. Until I met you, I didn't think love was an option for me."

The rain began to slacken in its seemingly incessant chatter on the roof and against the windows, and Amanda thought she saw a hint of sunshine glimmering at the edge of a distant cloud. She linked her arm through Jordan's and laid her temple to his shoulder, content just to be close to him.

Jordan intertwined his fingers with Amanda's, and his grip was strong and tight. With his other hand he tapped his wineglass against hers. "Here's to taking chances," he said softly.

The movers arrived on Monday, and so did the furniture Amanda had bought at the estate sale. She called in several plumbers for estimates on extra bathrooms, and that night she and Jordan and the girls sat around her kitchen table, eating chicken from a red-and-white striped bucket.

"I'm glad you didn't go to heaven," Jessie told Amanda, her dark eyes round and earnest.

"Me, too," Lisa put in, nibbling on a drumstick.

Amanda's gaze linked with Jordan's. "I could have sworn I visited there once," she said mysteriously.

Jordan gave her a look. "Dirty pool, lady," he accused.

"Uh-uh, Daddy," Jessie argued. "Amanda doesn't even *have* a pool."

"I stand corrected," Jordan told his daughter, but his eyes were on Amanda.

Tossing a denuded chicken bone onto her plate, Amanda stood up and bent to give greasy, top-of-the-head kisses to both Jessie and Lisa. "Thanks for being glad I'm around, gang," she told the girls in a conspiratorial whisper.

"You're welcome," Jessie replied.

Lisa was busy tilting the bucket to see if there was another drumstick inside.

Jordan watched Amanda with mischievous eyes as she dropped her plate into the trash and then leaned back against the sink with her arms folded.

"I suppose you people think I can't cook," she said.

No one offered a comment except for Gershwin, who came strolling into the kitchen with a cordial meow. The girls were delighted, and instantly abandoned what remained of their dinners to pet him.

When he realized he wasn't going to get any chicken, the

cat wandered out of the room again. Jessie and Lisa were right behind him.

"Come here," Jordan said with just the hint of a grin.

"I've got no willpower at all where you're concerned," Amanda answered, allowing herself to be pulled onto his lap.

"Good. Will you marry me, Mandy?"

She tilted her head to one side. "Yes. But we agreed to wait, give things time—"

"We've had enough time. I love you, and that's never going to change."

Amanda kissed him. "If it's never going to change, then it won't matter if we wait."

He let his forehead fall against her breasts, pretending to be forlorn. "Do you know what it's going to do to me to go home tonight and leave you here?" he muttered.

She rested her chin on the top of his head. "You'll survive," she assured him. "I need a few months to get the business going, Jordan."

He sighed heavily. "Okay," he said with such a tone of martyrdom that Amanda laughed out loud.

Jordan repaid her by sliding a hand up under her shirt and cupping her breast.

Amanda squirmed and uttered a protest, but the steady strokes of his thumb across her nipple raised a fever in her. "We'll just have to be—flexible," she acquiesced with a sigh of supreme longing.

"We're not going to have much time alone together," Jordan warned, continuing his quiet campaign to drive her crazy. "Of course, if we were married, it would be perfectly natural for us to sleep together every night." He'd lifted one side of Amanda's bra so that her bare breast nestled in his hand.

"Jordan," Amanda whispered. "Stop it."

In the parlor, Amanda's television set came on, and the theme song of the girls' favorite sitcom filled the air. "A nuclear war wouldn't distract them from that show," Jordan said sleepily, lifting Amanda's T-shirt and closing his lips brazenly around her nipple.

She knew she should twist away, but the truth was, the most

she could manage was to turn on Jordan's lap so that she could see the parlor doorway clearly. The position provided Jordan with better access to her breast, which he enjoyed without a hint of self-consciousness.

When he'd had enough, he righted her bra, pulled her shirt down and swatted her lightly on the bottom. "Well," he said with an exaggerated yawn, "it's a school night. I'd better take the girls home."

Amanda was indignant. "Jordan Richards, you deliberately got me worked up...."

He grinned and lifted her off his lap. "Yep," he confessed, rising from his chair and wandering idly in the direction of the parlor.

Flushed, Amanda flounced back and forth between the table and the trash can, disposing of the remains of dinner. After that, she wiped the table off in furious motions, and when she carried the dishcloth back to the sink, she realized Jordan was watching her with a twinkle in his eyes.

"In three days we could have a license," he said.

In the parlor, Jessie and Lisa laughed at some event in their favorite program, and the sound lifted Amanda's heart. The children would always be Becky and Jordan's, but she loved them already, and she wanted to be a part of their lives almost as much as she wanted to be a part of their father's.

She walked slowly over to the man she loved and put her arms around his waist. "Okay, Jordan, you win. I want to be with you and the kids too much to wait any longer. But you'll have to be patient with me, because getting a new business off the ground takes a lot of time and energy."

His eyes danced with delight as he lifted one hand for a solemn oath. "I'll be patient if you will," he said.

Amanda bit down on her lower lip, worried. "I don't want to fail at this, Jordan."

He kissed her forehead. "We'll have to work at marriage, Mandy—just like everybody else does. But it'll last, I promise you."

"How can you be so sure?" she asked, watching his face for some sign of reservation or caution.

She saw only confidence and love. "The odds are in our favor," he answered, "and I'm taking the rest on faith."

It was September, and the maples and elms scattered between the evergreens across the road were turning to bright gold. They matched the lumbering yellow school bus that ground to a halt beside the sign that read Amanda's Place.

The bus door opened and Jessie bounded down the steps and leaped to the ground, then turned to catch hold of Lisa's hand and patiently help her down.

Amanda smiled and placed one hand on her distended stomach, watching as her stepdaughters raced toward the house, their school papers fluttering in the autumn breeze.

"I made a house!" Lisa shouted, breathless with excitement as she raced ahead of her sister to meet Amanda on the step.

Amanda bent to properly examine the drawing Lisa had done in the afternoon kindergarten session. A crude square with windows represented the house, and there were four stick figures in front. "Here's me," Lisa said with a sniffle, pointing a pudgy little finger at the smallest form in the picture, "and here's Jessie and Daddy and you. I didn't draw the baby 'cause I don't know what he looks like."

Amanda kissed the child soundly on the forehead. "That's such a good picture that I'm going to put it up in the shop so everybody who comes in can admire it."

Lisa beamed at the prospect, sniffled again and toddled past Amanda and into the warm kitchen.

"How about you?" she asked Jessie, who had waited patiently on the bottom step for her turn. "Did you draw a picture, too?"

"I'm too big for that," Jessie said importantly. "I wrote the whole alphabet."

Putting an arm on the little girl's back, Amanda gently steered her into the kitchen. "Let's see," she said.

Jessie proudly extended the paper. "I already know enough to be in second grade," she said.

Amanda assessed the neatly printed letters marching smartly

across Jessie's paper. "This is certainly one of the nicest papers I've ever seen," she said.

Jessie eyed her shrewdly. "Good enough to be in the shop like Lisa's picture?"

"Absolutely," Amanda replied. To prove her assertion, she strode through the big dining room, now completely furnished, and the large parlor, where Lisa was plunking on the piano, into the shop. Several of her quilts were displayed there, along with the work of many local craftspeople.

Her live-in manager, Millie Delano, was behind the cash register. It had been a slow day, but there were guests scheduled for the weekend, and the quilts and other items had sold extremely well over the summer. Amanda was making a go of her bed and breakfast, although it would be a long time before she got rich.

She held up both Lisa's picture and Jessie's printing for Millie's inspection. The pleasant middle-aged woman smiled broadly as Amanda made places for the papers on the bulletin board behind the counter and pinned them into place.

Jessie, who sometimes worried that her fondness for Amanda made her disloyal to her mother, beamed with pride.

The girls were settled in the kitchen, drinking milk and eating bananas, when Jordan arrived from the city. "Is my family ready to go home?" he asked, poking his head around the door.

Jessie and Lisa, who were always delighted to see him, whether he'd been away five minutes, five hours or five days, flung themselves at him with shrieks of welcome. Amanda, her hands resting on her protruding stomach, stood back, watching. Her eyes brimmed with tears as she thought how lucky she was to have the three of them filling her life with love and confusion and laughter.

After gently freeing himself from his daughters, Jordan walked over to Amanda and laid his hands on either side of her face. With his thumbs he brushed away her tears. "Hi, pregnant lady," he said. A quiet pride made Amanda's heart swell. "Hi," she replied with a soft smile.

He gave her a leisurely kiss, then steered her toward the

door. Her coat was hanging on a wooden peg nearby, and he helped her into it before handing Jessie and Lisa their jackets.

Amanda was struck again by the depth of her love for him when, in his tailored suit, he dropped to one knee to help Lisa with a jammed zipper. She couldn't have asked for a better father for her child than Jordan Richards.

When the hectic family project of preparing dinner was behind them, and Lisa and Jessie had had their baths, their stories and their good-night kisses, Jordan led Amanda into the living room. They sat on the sofa in front of a snapping fire, with their heads touching.

Jordan brought his hand to rest on Amanda's stomach, and when the baby kicked, his eyes were as bright as the flames on the hearth. Amanda couldn't help smiling.

He smoothed back a lock of her hair. "Tired?" he asked.

"Yes." Amanda sighed. "How about you?"

"Beat," Jordan replied. "Personally, I don't see that we have any choice but to go straight to bed."

Amanda laughed and thrust herself off the couch. "Last one there is a rotten egg!" she cried, waddling toward the stairs.

*   *   *   *   *

MARRIAGE ON DEMAND
by Susan Mallery

* * *

To my stepson, Larry.
After a somewhat rocky start,
we seem to have found something wonderful together,
and I'm grateful for that. I wanted to give you
some sage advice about life and living, but hey,
I'm still figuring out this journey, as well.
I'll always be here for you. Much love.

Dear Reader,

When authors talk among themselves, a subject that comes up often is "Books of the Heart." These are stories the authors ache to write but often can't for any number of reasons. Either they are too different, or too long or just too strange. But sometimes writers are lucky enough to have a "book of the heart" published.

Marriage on Demand is one of those books for me. From the moment I first thought of Austin and Rebecca, I knew I had to write their story. Their intense, sensual romance wouldn't get out of my head. Thankfully my wonderful editor at Silhouette loved the book as much as I did and it was originally published in 1995.

The response was immediate. Sales were tremendous, as were the reviews. *Marriage on Demand* won Best Special Edition of the Year from *Romantic Times Magazine*. I've received more mail on this book than on anything else I've written. Perhaps there's a little Rebecca in all of us. Perhaps each of us longs for an Austin of our own.

If you've never read one of my books before, then you've picked one of my best for an introduction. I don't usually read my books after they've been published, but I promise I'll be sitting down with this one. I very much want to spend some more time with characters who are more like old friends than creations of my imagination.

Best,

Susan Mallery

Chapter 1

She'd forgotten how good the devil looked in blue jeans.

Rebecca Chambers stood just inside the garage door, soaking wet. The sound of the storm outside blocked the steady drip-drip from her dress and hair, but she could feel the individual drops collecting on her arms and legs, then falling to the ground. No doubt her mascara had formed perfect half circles under her eyes. She didn't normally wear much makeup, but today she'd taken special pains with her appearance. Her white T-top was silk, and washable, thank goodness. But her loose floral-print jumper was a silk blend that wouldn't survive the drenching. Mud caked her new black flats. She probably looked like something the cat dragged in. Or worse.

She didn't know if God was punishing her for all her ridiculous fantasies, or if the Fates were having a good laugh at her expense. She sighed softly and brushed her wet hair out of her face. Did it matter? For whatever reason, every time she was in the presence of the man in front of her, she made a complete and total fool of herself. She couldn't stop thinking wicked and inappropriate thoughts. They muddled her brain and left her gasping for air and complete sentences. It had been going on for two years. She glanced down at her dripping self and bit back a groan.

Her gaze was drawn away from her bedraggled appearance to the man bent over a car engine and the way he filled his jeans. It wasn't fair, she told herself, staring at the worn denim and the tight rear end that led to illegally long, lean legs. He was going to stand up, turn around and see her. She was going to look like a dripping, homeless rat, and he was going to be gorgeous. He would stare at her with his killer gray eyes and wait for her to speak. If her tongue didn't get tied up in knots, her knees would start shaking. It didn't matter that she was almost thirty years old and a responsible adult.

In the past two years she'd been in the same room with Austin Lucas exactly eleven times. She'd made a fool out of herself twelve times. Once she'd not only knocked over a small table containing the refreshments for the local meeting, but she'd been in such a hurry to escape from his presence that she'd turned without watching where she was going and ran smack into a wall.

She tried not to think about that. Despite the slight chill from her wet clothing and hair, her cheeks were hot with embarrassment. She pressed her hands to her face and wished she had somewhere else to go. But she didn't. He was her only hope. What on earth was he going to say when he saw her?

She glanced frantically around the garage, hoping to find a source of courage. A radio sat on the workbench lining one wall. Soft rock music filled the room. Next to the front left bumper of the car stood a red toolbox on a dingy cart. Nothing very inspiring, although the maleness of the equipment made her feel even more out of place. She was one of three girls and had little experience with guy stuff.

She drew in a deep breath, inhaling the odors of machine oil, wet cement and something that could only be the heady scent of Austin himself. She fought the urge to back up a step. Inside her belly, nerves and expectations joined hands in an uneven dance of hyperawareness. Please, God, why did it have to be him? Around town, women whispered he was as tempting as the devil himself. Heaven knows he tempted her.

She cleared her throat. "Mr. Lucas?"

He chose that moment to drop a wrench and swear loudly. The curses drowned out her words. She opened her mouth to speak again, but he bent down to pick up the tool and his jeans stretched tight across his rear.

Fourteen years ago, Rod Dowell had walked into her sophomore algebra class wearing tennis whites. She'd melted into her school-issue wooden chair and had wondered if she would ever be able to breathe normally again. She finally had, but it had taken almost three years. She'd carried the secret of that crush with her all the way until graduation when she finally found the courage to wish him luck. His brief, "Yeah, you, too," had sent her reeling with excitement.

Now, staring at Austin Lucas, or rather at his long legs and tight, rounded rear end, she could feel her tongue twisting itself into knots and her hands getting sweaty on top of already being damp. It didn't matter that she was far too old for adolescent crushes. It didn't matter that he wouldn't be interested in a woman like her. It didn't matter that she was completely out of her league with him—a peewee ball player trying to compete with a pro. She couldn't resist him, and she couldn't walk away. He was her only hope.

Rebecca squared her shoulders and told herself she had to say something before she shivered to death. She opened her mouth. He spoke before she could.

"How long are you gonna stand there dripping?"

"Not long," she said, her voice shaky. "Another ten minutes or so." She clamped her hand over her mouth, not able to believe she'd actually said that. Her eyes fluttered shut. She wanted to die. She prayed for the cement floor to crack and swallow her whole. The floor didn't budge.

"You can look now," he said, a hint of teasing deepening his already low voice.

Rebecca opened one eye, then the other. Austin stood in front of her, wiping his hands on a dirty rag. He wasn't especially good-looking, she told herself, then wondered why she bothered to lie. It didn't do any good. He wore a faded denim shirt tucked into even more faded jeans. The slashed fabric by his left knee had nothing to do with fashion and everything to do with his life-style. His sleeves had been rolled up to his elbows. The top three buttons of the shirt were undone, exposing just enough chest to threaten her sanity.

Her gaze rose higher past the square jaw and firm mouth—not smiling, of course, for Austin rarely smiled—to hollow cheekbones and a straight nose. His cold gray eyes carefully shuttered all emotions. Thick dark hair had been brushed away from his face. It hung down long enough to scrape the bottom of his collar.

He was handsome as sin. Her gaze flickered to the small gold hoop earring he wore. The delicate circle of gold looked out of place on his totally masculine form. She'd never known a man who wore an earring. The small hoop looked perfect, she thought in defeat. It made her think of pirates and women stolen away for secret pleasures. It made her wonder about his flaunting of convention. It made her think about being in his bed. No doubt she would die of pleasure, but what a way to go. She stiffened her spine and told herself to get a grip. He was just a guy, and the gold hoop was just an earring. Of course Glenwood was a small town and slightly right of the rest of the nation. Men didn't wear earrings here.

But Austin made up his own rules. That was, she acknowledged, part of his appeal. He was the bad boy, the devil in disguise. How could a woman like her be expected to resist that?

"Rebecca?" he said.

The sound of her name on his lips made her toes curl inside her damp, muddy shoes. "Huh?" Eloquent to the last, she thought, fighting back a groan.

"Why are you here?"

She opened her mouth to speak. Nothing came out. She closed it and thought carefully, then tried again. "My car's stuck."

He frowned, his dark eyebrows drawing together. "Okay. Where is your car?"

He was speaking slowly, as if to a half-witted child. She wanted to get indignant and tell him she was perfectly capable of carrying on a conversation. Unfortunately she wasn't. With him she'd never managed more than a sentence or two without some sort of disaster striking. She glanced around the open garage. At least there wasn't anything to break or spill here.

"It's in the driveway," she said, moving out of the room and into the rain. The drenching downpour had slowed somewhat, settling into a steady sprinkle. She felt the drops on her head and shoulders.

He hesitated before stepping out into the open. "Do you want an umbrella?" he asked.

She glanced down at her floral-print dress. It hung loosely, albeit damply, around her body. The long, calf-length skirt was heavy and probably stretching. "I think it's a little late for that, don't you?"

His gaze slipped over her, heating her chilled flesh and sending electric bolts zooming through her blood. When their eyes met, he smiled slowly. "I guess so."

He stepped past her, his worn black cowboy boots squishing in the mud. She stood rooted in place. It wasn't the thick muck that held her so firmly. It was his smile. She'd never seen Austin smile before. Lines had collected by his gray eyes; his teeth had flashed white. The smile had made him look teasingly dangerous, like a wolf pretending to be a lapdog. It had reminded her she was completely out of her element. He was all black leather and five different kinds of sin. She was a babe in the woods, uncomfortable and unwilling to play in the fast lane. He would find her as interesting as flat beer.

She turned on her heel, almost losing her shoe in the process, and started after him. He stood next to her old station wagon. Most of the fake wood paneling had long since cracked and peeled. The side of the car was two-tone, from an accident several years before. The engine had been rebuilt twice, and the vehicle needed new tires.

"You drive this thing?" he asked, staring at it as if he'd never seen anything so pathetic in his life.

"The home owns it," she said. "I don't have a car of my own. There's a bench seat in the back, allowing us to seat five more kids, six if they're small. It's practical."

He glanced at her and raised one eyebrow. She'd never actually seen someone do that. She wanted to see him do it again, but she didn't ask him to. He might not understand.

"Practical or not, it's sure as hell stuck." He walked around the wagon. Each footstep squished in the mud.

His property stood at the far end of Glenwood. He had about ten acres. There was a three-car garage, an oversize, two-story barn and a huge empty house. The house was the reason she'd come calling in the rain.

According to rumors, which she couldn't help but overhear, he was richer than God, had never married and was determined to keep his private life private. Glenwood was too small for him to achieve that. His long-term affairs were well documented by most of the women in town. A stunning redhead driving a white sports car had made biweekly trips through town and down his dusty, unpaved driveway for almost six months. Several times Rebecca had seen her and felt a stab of jealousy. Austin's collection of ladies made men envious and women dream. Rebecca had dreamed, too, even as she'd known it was useless. Austin's women had two things in common: curves and attitude. She glanced down at the wet clothing clinging to her straight, girlish body. She had neither.

He bent over the hood and rocked the car. She watched the muscles bunch in his arms. His shirt was already soaked and clinging to his back and chest. Rain fell on her face and dripped off the end of her nose. In the distance, she heard the rumble of thunder.

"Where are your keys?" he asked.

"In the ignition."

He opened the door and slid into the seat. Within seconds the car started. Dependable as always, she thought, realizing she had a lot in common with the old car. Not very exciting, but they both got the job done.

Austin put it in drive. The wagon rocked forward. He eased on the gas. The wheels spun wildly in the mud. Rebecca jumped back to avoid being sprayed. Her right shoe stuck. She waved her arms in the air to try to maintain her balance. The car engine shut off. She heard squishing footsteps moving toward her but she didn't dare look. She didn't want to see the disgusted or amused expression in his eyes.

She started to go down and was forced to lower her stocking-clad foot into the mud to save herself. The thick cold earth swallowed her up to her ankle.

"Perfect," she muttered.

A warm, strong hand gripped her arm. "You okay?" Austin asked.

She looked up at him. Her dark hair was in the way, so she moved it off of her face. She stared at him, dumbfounded.

Water rolled off his face and onto his chest. Drops slipped down into the open V of his shirt. The cotton clung to him, hugging his tanned skin, outlining his muscles, leaving nothing to her imagination.

She swallowed hard. Where his fingers touched her, she felt individual jolts, as if she'd been hooked up to an electric current. Her breasts swelled inside her damp shirt.

"Rebecca?"

"What? Oh, I'm fine." She glanced down at herself. One foot was in the mud, the other almost as dirty. Her wet and stretched dress flapped in the cold wind. The color from the fabric was bleeding into her white silk T-top. The damp material clung to her chest, outlining her rather pitiful curves. So much for swelling. No one would notice, much less be impressed, she thought, remembering the generous curves of Austin's redhead.

"I think I lost my shoe," she said, pointing to a lump in the mud.

In the distance there was a flash of lightning. "The storm is getting worse," he said. "I can't get the car loose. Kyle's borrowed my truck, and I don't think my car is going to have any better luck in this mud. Come on up to my place and we'll call a tow truck."

"I don't want to be any trouble."

He smiled again. Her heart beat faster inside her chest. "It's a little too late for that."

He released her and bent over to dig through the mud for her shoe. When he'd retrieved the ruined flat, he handed it to her. She took it and stared at the coated leather. It would never be the same again. The fitting end to a lousy week.

He started walking toward an enormous barnlike structure partially concealed by a grove of Chinese maple trees. He didn't bother to look back to see if she followed. She limped along with one shoe on and one shoe off. Thank goodness they were flats. The rain increased its intensity, turning from a steady sprinkle into a downpour again. The temperature seemed to drop considerably, too.

When they reached the brick-bordered cement path, it was easier to keep up with his long-legged stride. Her lone shoe made a squishy noise with each step. Her wet hair flapped in her face. She pulled off her velvet headband and saw it was ruined along with everything else she was wearing. Why hadn't she grabbed an umbrella before she left? No, she thought, shaking her head. That would have required a brain—something she didn't seem to have when it came to Austin.

She glanced at the clipped grass stretching out on both sides of the path, then at the slabs of cement. At anything but the tall, dark and very appealing male specimen right in front of her. It didn't work. Again and again her gaze was drawn back to him.

He walked with an easy loose-hipped grace. His arms swung with each stride. Despite her bedraggled appearance, she couldn't help thinking that if she hurried and caught up with him, their arms might brush and then she—

Stop it! she commanded herself. This was insane. And embarrassing. She was here on a mission and she couldn't forget that. Still, his scent drifted to her and made her think about tangled sheets and bare skin and—

"Oh, my," she whispered, trying to ignore the heat suddenly blossoming in her belly.

"What's wrong?" he asked, stopping and turning toward her.

She almost plowed into him. As it was, she skidded to a stop, the big toe of her one bare foot jabbing painfully into the concrete. "Nothing," she said through gritted teeth, fighting the urge to grab her toe and hop on one foot until the pain faded.

He glanced down at her. She stood five feet eight inches in her stockinged feet. The low shoe gave her a half inch more. She stood eye to eye with a lot of men. Austin topped her by a good seven inches.

"You are the most peculiar woman," he said, then turned away and crossed the last few feet to the door of the barn.

Great, she thought, grumbling. Peculiar. That was romantic. Peculiar. When she wanted to be beautiful, witty, curvaceous, intoxicating. She shrugged. She was never going to be any of those things. Her destiny was to be ordinary. That was the reason Rod Dowell had never noticed her and Austin wouldn't, either. She was the girl next door. Wholesome, innocent, ordinary. Like milk. People took it and her for granted. She wanted to be the dash of cognac at the end of a perfect evening. Instead, she was reserved for pouring over breakfast cereal. It wasn't fair.

Austin cleared his throat. She looked up and saw he was holding open the door, obviously waiting for her to step inside. She ducked in, careful not to slap his legs with the hem of her soggy dress.

The foyer was a small room with no furniture. A big metal door with a window in the top half led to what looked like a large machine shop and laboratory. To the left, stairs curved up to the second floor.

"Up there," he said, pointing to the stairs.

"Up there?" She swallowed.

"Only if you want to get dry."

"Oh. Sure. Thanks."

He lived up there. Alone. Except for the occasional female visitor. Like the redhead.

It wasn't that Rebecca went out of her way to learn things about Austin. She might have a crush on him, but she wasn't completely nuts. Still, people talked, especially about him. No matter how much she tried to slip away or tell herself not to listen, she always heard things, and remembered them.

She gripped the metal railing and started to climb. She could feel the moisture rolling off her and dripping on the stairs. Her footsteps sounded uneven, the clunk of her shoe, the silence of her bare foot.

He was right behind her. She could feel his gaze on her back, heating her. Was he staring at her the way she'd stared at him? Foolish to think he might. He probably barely realized she was female.

At the top of the stairs, she stepped onto a hardwood floor. Her first impression was of space, light and warmth. The living quarters covered the entire loft of the barn. There were no separate rooms; areas flowed into each other.

Eight-foot-high windows added to the feeling of openness in the cavernous room. Two overstuffed couches cordoned off an area to form a living room. Entertainment equipment provided a divider between that room and the kitchen. A king-size bed with—she gulped—a black satin comforter lined up against the opposite wall.

She stared at it, stunned, then grinned. Now she had a new element to add to her fantasies. Black satin. Who would have guessed?

The only walled room was at the far end of the loft. Through the open door she saw the sink and tub of the bathroom. The temperature in the loft was pleasant after the chill of the rain.

A brilliant flash of light cut through the late afternoon. On its heels, thunder boomed, shaking the building. Rebecca jumped and grabbed for the railing. Instead of cold metal, her fingers encountered warm skin.

Before she could pull back, he caught her hand in his. "Are you afraid of the storm?" he asked, his voice quiet after the thunder.

She started shaking. It had very little to do with her body temperature and her damp clothes, and everything to do with his closeness. "A little," she murmured.

Their gazes locked. Gray irises darkened like the coming of night. He gave away nothing, no emotions, no thoughts. It was like staring into the storm itself and only being able to imagine the destruction. His fingers slipped between hers and he tugged her closer to him. Her bare foot rested against the edge of his cowboy boots.

"Don't be afraid." He reached up. With his free hand he brushed the moisture from one cheek.

The tender gesture, so incongruous when compared to his reputation, made her want to snuggle against him.

"I have a lightning rod on the other side of the house. We're perfectly safe."

She blinked. So much for a romantic moment. "Gee, thanks."

"You're welcome. Stay right there, and I'll go get some towels."

"Towels?" she echoed.

He was already walking toward a large armoire on the far side of the bed.

"To dry off. You'll probably want to get out of those wet things. I'll call for a tow truck, but it may take a while."

"You want me to take off my clothes?"

He opened the armoire and pulled out an armful of fluffy towels. "You *are* dripping on my floor."

She glanced down, but the puddle beneath her made little sense. Naked. She was going to be naked in Austin Lucas's house. Her. Little Miss Ordinary was going to spend the afternoon naked with the devil. She didn't know whether to laugh out loud or run for the door.

"Rebecca?"

She stared at him, trying to focus. "Yes?"

"Are you sure you're okay? You didn't fall and hit your head or anything, did you?"

No, I'm just naturally stupid around you, she thought, knowing she could never admit that aloud. "I'm a little tired," she said, then realized it was the truth. This had been the longest and worst week of her life.

He moved from the armoire to a closet concealed in the wall. With a push of his hand, a hidden door swung open. He reached inside and pulled out a white terry-cloth robe, then started walking toward her.

She held her breath. When he was standing in front of her,

he handed her everything. She glanced at the robe. It looked new. As if to confirm her guess, he reached for a sleeve and pulled off a tag dangling from one end.

"A gift from a friend," he said by way of explanation.

A woman friend, who else? She found it hard to believe a guy would give another guy a bathrobe. No, some foolish female had bought this for Austin expecting him to wear it and think of her.

"The bathroom is through there," he said, pointing to the half-open door at the end of the loft. "You look cold. Maybe you should take a hot shower to warm up."

Maybe you could kiss me and warm me up.

Rebecca felt her eyes widen in panic. Oh, please, God, let me not have spoken that thought aloud. She held her breath and waited.

Austin's eyes gave nothing away, and the expression on his face didn't change at all. Slowly she let her breath out. She'd only thought it. Danger. The man was pure danger.

"Thanks for everything," she said. "I didn't mean to be such a bother."

His gaze flickered over her face. "No problem. While you're taking a shower, I'll call for a tow. Then you can tell me what brought you out here in the first place."

She nodded and continued to stare at his face. She wanted to see him smile again, but she couldn't think of anything funny to say.

She felt a little push on her back, as if he was urging her to get on her way. She took one step, then another, heading for the bathroom. This was really happening to her. She was actually in his house. Austin's house. No one would believe this. Of course she wasn't going to tell anyone. Okay, maybe Travis and Elizabeth. She sighed and hugged the towels close to her chest. Maybe not even them. It was all too wonderful, too precious. A dream come true.

As she reached the bathroom door, her memory kicked in. Austin had said he didn't know why she'd come by. In her stupor, she'd forgotten to tell him the reason for her visit. She shook her head.

"I can't believe I didn't tell you why I stopped by," she said, turning back toward the center of the room. "I'm sure you heard that—"

She stopped in midsentence and stared. Austin stood beside the large bed. He'd already stripped off his shirt and was in the process of unbuttoning his wet jeans. As she looked at him, his hands slowed. His chest was bare, gleaming in the dim afternoon light. Her gaze followed the sprinkling of hair on his chest as it arrowed down to the open waistband of his worn jeans. From where she was standing, it didn't look as if he was wearing anything underneath them.

She swallowed hard and tried to speak. Nothing. She urged herself to turn and keep walking toward the bathroom, but her feet wouldn't budge. It would have taken an act of God to move her, and everyone knew Austin Lucas was only the devil.

Chapter 2

Rebecca looked as stunned as a doe caught in headlights and as wet as a drowned rat. Her long dark hair hung in wet curls, draping over her shoulders and dripping onto the floor. She opened her mouth to speak. No sound came out. She tried again, made a squeaking noise, then fled into the bathroom. The door slammed shut behind her.

Austin chuckled. He finished stripping off his wet jeans and tossed them onto the floor. He reached into the closet and pulled out another pair. He'd barely stepped into the first leg when he heard a loud shriek from the bathroom. After dropping his jeans, he sprinted to the door and knocked.

"Rebecca? What happened?"

There was a low moan from the other side of the door.

"Rebecca? Damn it, open up. Did you hurt yourself?"

"No. I just…"

He heard footsteps and the door opened a crack. He could see part of her face and one brown eye. Mascara collected under her lower lashes. Any color on her face had long been washed away. Her dress hung damply from her shoulders. She was a mess. The one eye he could see closed briefly.

"I just saw myself in the mirror. Now I know why you were smiling so much."

The tension left his body. "Oh, that."

Her eye opened. "Yeah, that. I'll just be a minute here, while I try to repair the damage."

"Take your time."

"I'm going to need it," she mumbled.

Her gaze drifted down from his face to his chest, then lower. She blinked and her eye got bigger. At that moment he realized he'd dropped the dry jeans he'd been pulling on. Her gasp was audible.

"I... I... Oh, heaven help me!" The door slammed shut.

Austin shook his head and headed back across the room. He couldn't have been the first naked man she'd ever seen, but she'd been staring as if he was. He slipped into his jeans and buttoned the fly, then grabbed a shirt and shrugged it on. He didn't bother fastening it.

His bare feet slapped against the hardwood floor as he made his way to the kitchen and started coffee. He rummaged around in a bottom cupboard until he found a bottle of whiskey, then poured a half inch into both coffee cups. If nothing else, the liquor would chase away the rest of her chill.

The sound of the storm increased. Bolts of lightning arced across the darkening sky. Rumbles of thunder shook the building. He stared out the window at the rain and the flashes of light. Behind him he could hear the gurgle of the coffeepot and the faint sound of the shower. He tried not to picture the woman standing under the warm spray or the way she would slowly lather her slender body.

He rubbed his hand over his face, but the action did nothing to chase away the tiredness. He'd been tired for days now, but he knew it had nothing to do with the hours he was putting in. Everything was changing and he didn't know how to make it stop.

The coffeepot gave a last hiss and then was silent. Pipes rattled as the shower was turned off. He stepped back and leaned against the kitchen counter, watching the door. He knew she would come out eventually. He also knew exactly how she would look, swimming in his oversize bathrobe. Her skin would be pale, her eyes large and questioning, her hair a damp mantle of silk. She would look at him and blush, then stare at the ground. He would be torn between telling her she was in no mortal danger and wanting to make every one of her ridiculous fantasies come true.

Rebecca Chambers had a crush on him. It had been obvious from their second meeting when she'd managed to spill an entire pitcher of water at dinner one evening. He'd just dropped by to give Travis a message. Rebecca had been there, wearing one of her flowing floral-print dresses. With her loose clothing and headbands holding her curly dark hair off her face, she reminded him of a schoolgirl out of uniform for the day.

He knew she wasn't a girl, but it was easier to think of her that way. Safer. She wasn't for him.

It took another ten minutes, but at last the bathroom door opened a crack. He thought about calling out that he wasn't naked anymore but didn't. She had enough backbone for three warriors; she just hadn't figured it out yet. Besides, he liked teasing her and watching her blush. It was about the only innocent pleasure he had in his life.

One bare foot eased out of the open door. He glanced at the pale skin and trim ankle. His muscles tensed as a familiar heaviness filled his groin. The dim light would make his condition harder for her to discern. Just as well—for both of them. If she kept on blushing around him, her face would be permanently red. If she didn't blush, he would be tempted to do exactly what she'd been thinking about.

She took another step and this time cleared the bathroom door. She looked exactly as he had pictured, all soft and pale, overwhelmed by his robe. She'd rolled up the sleeves a couple of times so they only hung to her knuckles. The knotted belt trailed almost to her knees.

"Do you want some coffee?" he asked, raising a mug.

Her head jerked toward him. She'd washed away the rest of her makeup, and without cosmetics, she looked about seventeen. Her mouth was well shaped, slightly wide and normally tilting up at the corners. Now it twisted down on one side as she nibbled her lower lip.

Her hair fanned out over her shoulders just as he'd pictured it. A flash of heat seared through his belly. For that second he wished she was like the widow in the next town. Jasmine visited him a couple of times a week. She was rich, lonely and bored. They made hot and fast love, seeking mutual release and no commitment. It had been easy to be with her, and easy to let her go. Three months before, they'd decided to end the affair. He didn't miss her, but parts of him missed her body. It would be a mistake to start something like that with Rebecca, even if her slender shape, so different from Jasmine's lushness, taunted him. Rebecca would be long and lean, a wildcat, he suspected. It was the innocence in her eyes that kept him from finding out.

"Coffee would be nice," she said, her voice low and steady. She took a step toward him, then paused.

He turned his back to her and poured the steaming liquid into both mugs. "Cream, sugar?"

"Cream," she said, sounding a little closer.

He grabbed a small carton from the fridge, added a splash then picked up the mug and held it out. She crossed the hardwood floor and took it.

"Thanks. I'm sorry to be such a bother. Dripping all over everything. Thanks for the robe. I'm sure my clothes will dry quickly and then I can be on my way. Except for the car. But you said you'd call for a tow truck. I guess that'll take a little while, what with the weather and all. I really appreciate—"

"Rebecca?" Slowly, so as not to alarm her, he turned toward her and leaned against the counter.

She stopped chattering and glanced at him. Her eyes were dark and wide, her face flushed with embarrassment. "Yes?"

"You're babbling."

The flush deepened. "I know. I'm nervous."

"Don't be." He reached over past her to the phone mounted on the wall. He drew the receiver to his ear and listened to the silence. Grimacing, he set it back in place, then motioned for her to follow him.

"What is it?" she asked, trailing behind him as he headed for the living area.

"Phone's out. Usually happens during bad weather."

"You can't call the tow truck?"

The panic in her voice almost made him smile. Almost. He didn't necessarily like scaring her, even if it wasn't a bad idea. Maybe if she was scared enough she would stop looking at him as if she'd already imagined them together in bed.

He sat in the single chair opposite the sofa and set his mug of coffee on the upturned crate that served as an end table. She slowly lowered herself to the middle of the couch. The oversize cushions threatened to swallow her whole.

"If I don't lose power, they should get the phone working in a couple of hours," he said, reaching over and clicking on a floor lamp.

She clutched the mug tighter. "And if you do lose power?"

"It means the whole line is down, and you'll be stuck here until tomorrow."

Her mouth opened to form a perfect O but she made no sound.

"I promise I don't bite," he said, leaning back in the chair.

"I know." She sighed, sounding disappointed.

Lightning flashed outside the windows, and thunder filled the room. Rebecca flinched at the loud noise, then took a big gulp of coffee. She sucked in a breath, then coughed. "There's liquor in this!"

"So?"

She raised her eyebrows and looked at him as if he'd just suggested they take a naked stroll through the local church. "What do you think you're doing by serving liquor?"

"My mistake. I could have sworn you were over twenty-one. At least twenty-two."

She straightened in her seat and glared at him. The gold tones of the sofa contrasted with the pristine white of the borrowed robe and the dark brilliance of her curly hair. "I'll have you know I'm twenty-nine, but that isn't the point."

"What is?" he asked mildly, his calm voice a contrast to her shrill tones.

"That I…that you…" She drew a deep breath, then sagged back against the cushions. "You could have warned me."

"I thought it might warm you from the inside."

Like electricity seeking a conductor, her gaze sought his mouth. Oh, no. He knew exactly what she was thinking, damn her innocent little hide. He told himself she was a fool. He told himself to ignore her. It didn't help. He could practically taste her. His heartbeat quickened and his blood flowed hotter.

She sipped her coffee, never taking her gaze from him. Most of the time he found her feelings for him faintly amusing. From a distance she was easy to take. But here, in the close confines of his loft, with the storm cutting them off from the rest of the world, it would be far too simple to take her up on her offer.

He eyed her relaxed posture and the way his robe had slipped off one of her knees, baring her calf and part of her thigh. Her skin looked smooth. He knew it would be warm to the touch, soft and supple.

He forced himself to look away and concentrate on the facts. One, she was a friend of Travis and Elizabeth's. He wouldn't hurt either of them for anything, and dallying with Rebecca was bound to upset them. Two, she wasn't his type. At twenty-nine she'd probably been involved with men before, but not men like him. He knew that. There was something about him. He didn't know if it was his money or his desire to stand outside and observe without always participating, but women seemed to find him attractive. The invitations came fast and furious. He was always careful about which ones he accepted. The rules of the game were simple—no emotional involvement, no promises, no commitment. He glanced back at his guest. Rebecca Chambers and those like her played for keeps.

"Austin, I—"

"Don't worry about it, honey. Just tell me why you're here."

Her eyebrows drew together in a delicate frown. She reminded him of a porcelain doll come to life. He would do well to keep thinking of her as off-limits, he told himself as the collar of her robe parted slightly, allowing him a view of her pale throat.

"Because of the fire."

"Fire?" He jerked his thoughts back from their erotic journey and concentrated on what she was saying.

"The one in town a few days ago. I'm sure you heard about it."

"Just that a couple of old buildings burned down." He shrugged. "I've been working hard this week, and I haven't been to town."

"Oh."

She took another sip of her coffee, then set the mug on the table in front of her. As she bent forward, the robe gaped more, allowing him to see down the front. She had a small build, but the shape of her breasts was perfect. Creamy ivory crested in coral. His mouth grew dry. He clenched his hands into fists and wished to hell she would stay upright.

"The children's home burned down."

"What?" He sprang to his feet. "Is everyone all right?"

"We're fine. We were lucky. It was during the day. The older kids were at school and the younger ones were at the park playing. No one was there, so there weren't any injuries. But we lost the whole building. All our supplies, the kids' toys, everything."

"It's gone?" He stalked over to the large window taking up most of one living room wall. He didn't even have to close his eyes to picture the old two-story building. It had been built sometime in the thirties. Most of the bigger rooms had murals. He'd often stood for hours studying those paintings, wondering who the people in the pictures were and what the artists had been thinking as they'd painstakingly worked their art.

He reached the window and braced his hands on the sill. He could feel the chill of the wind and the dampness from the storm. A large bolt of lightning flashed across the sky and the lights in the room flickered.

"Austin?"

"Yeah?"

"Are you all right?"

"What?" He inhaled sharply, as if he could still smell the

odors of stew, old athletic shoes and baby powder. "Yeah. I'm just surprised."

"I didn't know you had a connection with the children's home."

He heard her bare feet on the floor as she walked toward him. He didn't turn around, but continued to stare out in the darkening afternoon and the rain pouring down. "I lived there for a couple of years."

He glanced down at her. She stood next to him, staring up. Her mouth hung open. She closed it slowly and didn't say anything, but he could see the questions in her brown eyes. If he told her the whole story, she'd get all compassionate and misty-eyed. It happened to women all the time. Occasionally he used the story to his advantage, but not today. Not with Rebecca. He didn't want to encourage her. Not because he wasn't interested, but because he was.

"You're an orphan?" she asked, her voice low and sympathetic.

"Not exactly."

"Then why were you in the home?"

He didn't answer. He stared down at her, knowing he was giving her what Jasmine had laughingly called the ice glare. She hadn't been intimidated by it because she hadn't been involved enough to care. Rebecca swallowed hard as his expression became more forbidding. She looked away and folded her hands together in front of her waist.

He felt as if he'd just kicked a kitten and had to fight the urge to apologize. Damn. What was wrong with him? Why was she getting to him? Was it the unexpected desire he felt when he looked at her? Or was it something more ominous? A whisper of envy for the innocence in her face. The knowledge that he had never been that open to the world, not even when he was a child. Life had taught them very different lessons. He'd always known he wasn't like everyone else. He'd accepted that fact, had even been proud of it. Until about a year ago, when he'd awakened to the realization that he would always be alone.

"You don't want to talk about it," she said, brushing a

strand of hair off her face and turning away. Her shoulders slumped.

He swore under his breath. Why did she have to be so easy to read?

"I was transferred there from another home. I was a troublemaker when I was a kid."

She looked back at him and gave him a sweet smile. "That I believe."

"I'd hated where I'd been and I'd planned to hate this place. Then at school I met Travis and his brothers. They sort of changed everything for me."

"I've always wondered how the two of you became friends. You seem so different."

He raised his eyebrows. "In what way?"

She leaned against the wall and tucked her hands in the small of her back. "He's so open and friendly. Always good for a laugh. And you're..." She stopped talking and looked up at him. "What I meant to say is that you're..."

"Yes?" He folded his arms.

Her breathing increased, and with it the rise and fall of her chest. The thick robe parted slightly, exposing her neck and the hollow of her throat. It shouldn't have been provocative, but the sight of her bare skin made him want to move close to her and touch and taste every inch of her body. He shifted so the natural reactions to his thoughts would be less obvious.

"You're different," she said at last. "How exactly *did* you meet Travis?"

"I tried to beat him up."

"What?"

He grinned at the memory. "We were both in the eighth grade. I think I'd been in school about two days and I'd already been in four fights. Travis said something about me being a bully. I turned on him. What I didn't know at the time was that if you mess with one Haynes brother, you mess with all of them. The other three came running, ready to take apart my hide."

"What happened?"

"I was ready to get the—" he glanced at her "—living

daylights out of me, when Travis did the damnedest thing. He took my side against his brothers. They wouldn't fight him. Then the vice principal showed up and they *all* defended me.''

''And you've been friends ever since,'' she said, staring straight ahead with a dreamy expression in her eyes. ''That's a lovely story. Travis must have seen that you were just a scared and lonely little boy.''

Austin was torn between a desire to frighten her back into being afraid of him and surprise that she'd figured out the truth. That was exactly what Travis had seen. Funny, he'd never told anyone that before. But his relationship with Travis and his brothers had been the reason he'd returned to Glenwood. This was the only place he'd ever liked well enough to stay for more than a few months at a time.

''Yeah, well, it was a long time ago.'' He pushed off the windowsill and walked over to a desk in the corner by the stairs. ''What's going on with the children's home? Do you need money?'' He opened the top drawer and pulled out a checkbook. ''Is that why you came to see me?''

''Not exactly.''

He'd picked up a pen, but now he put it down. Rebecca crossed the room and stopped behind the wing chair he'd been sitting in. She rested her hands on the high back and gripped the fabric. The lights flickered again; the sounds of the storm increased. He could hear the rumble of thunder and the pounding of the rain on the windows.

He would have given his soul to see her slip the robe off her shoulders and walk into his arms. The corner of his mouth quirked up. He didn't have a snowball's chance in hell of that happening. She might have a crush on him, but she wasn't about to throw herself at him. Just as well. He would have a hard time refusing that kind of invitation.

He studied her face, the high cheekbones, the wide mouth, and tried to figure out what it was about her that made him want to break all his rules. Some of it was her crush. It was tough not to be flattered when a woman like her acted like a fool in his presence. Normally women fawning over him made him uncomfortable enough to start checking for the closest exit.

But Rebecca was different. Maybe it was because she watched him with such adoration. Ironically it was her high ideals that would keep her safe from him. There was just enough decency left in him not to want to destroy her false image. If Rebecca Chambers knew the truth about him, she would run screaming in the opposite direction.

He was doing her a favor by keeping the truth a secret. He ignored the voice inside that whispered he might not just be doing it for her. That maybe he had something to gain. Maybe her blushes and stammerings and long glances fed some empty, almost dead part of his useless heart.

She raised her hands and grabbed her hair, pulled it back into a ponytail, then released the long curls. She was a fairy-tale princess, he thought, then scoffed at his own fancy. Get real, Lucas, he told himself.

"I need your house," she said, and drew a deep breath as if preparing to deliver a long speech. "Oh, God, I know what you're thinking. It's too much to ask. I *wouldn't* ask you except I've been everywhere else. I have twenty kids sleeping in the school auditorium, but they can't stay there indefinitely. The state has assured me I'll have money to build a new facility, but in the meantime, I'm on my own. Travis suggested I see you. He said there's an empty house on your property that'd be big enough. We wouldn't be a bother."

"Somehow I doubt that."

She took a step closer. Her hands twisted together, the fingers lacing and unlacing. "Oh, Austin, you're my last hope. I've checked around town. The problem is I don't have any money. I have some, but I need to replace food and clothing and toys. People in town have been great, but it's not enough. We'd only need the house for about three months." She grimaced. "Gosh, that sounds so long. I could split the kids up, but I hate to do that. David is just seven. His parents and older sister were killed in a car crash. He's pretty normal, considering what's happened to him. He talks and still does his schoolwork. But he can't seem to make friends. He stands outside all the games the other children play. He watches them. Even when they invite him, he won't join in. It's been six weeks since the accident.''

She rubbed her palms together, then held out her hands pleadingly. "He has relatives, but they're too busy fighting over the estate to care about a seven-year-old boy. The deal they've all worked out is whoever gets control of the money is willing to be stuck with the kid." She shook her head. "*Stuck.* He's sweet and funny and very bright. If I can find a family willing to adopt him, I'll petition the court for custody. In the meantime, we're the only family he has."

He tried not to think about the lost boy, but deep in his chest he felt a familiar ache. "Rebecca, I don't see—"

"Then I have to make you see." Her voice became husky. "Oh, Austin, there are so many children. There are the twins. They've been abandoned by their alcoholic grandmother. And Melanie, she's just f-five." Her voice cracked. "Her uncle... His older brothers had done bad things to him, so he took it out on Melanie. The doctor's aren't sure if she'll ever be able to have children."

He cursed under his breath and stood up. In three strides he was standing directly in front of her. He placed his hands on her shoulders and shook her gently.

"Hush, Rebecca. It's okay. What I started to say is that I don't think it's going to be a problem. You're welcome to the house. For as long as you need it."

She blinked several times and he realized she was fighting tears. Through the thick layer of the robe, he could feel her slender shoulders tremble. There were dark circles under her eyes and lines of weariness around her mouth.

"Really?" she asked.

"Really. Have you been handling all of this alone?"

She nodded. Her head dipped toward her chest. "I haven't hired a new assistant since Elizabeth went on maternity leave." She sniffed, then raised her head. Her smile was a little shaky, but it hit him like a right hook to the jaw. "I can't tell you what this means to us."

He released her and stepped back. Great. He'd just gone up

three points in her estimation. He didn't need to fuel her case of hero worship.

"It's nothing," he said, flicking his hand dismissively. "The house is empty. You'll have to rent some beds and stuff. I'll pick up the tab for that."

When her big eyes got bigger, he grimaced. "I'm not doing this for you, Rebecca," he said bluntly. "I'm doing it for the kids and because the people who ran the home were good to me when I stayed there. This isn't anything but a business deal. I'm paying an old debt. Don't make it more than it is."

Judging by the light in her eyes, he hadn't made his point well enough.

"This is wonderful!" she said. She tugged on the belt around her waist. "I was so afraid of what would happen if you'd said no." She laughed. "I can't tell you how uncomfortable it is sleeping in a cot in the elementary-school auditorium."

"Why have you been staying there?"

"I lost my night supervisor, and I haven't been able to hire someone to replace her. About a month ago, I moved into the home. It was easier."

"You lost everything in the fire, too." It wasn't a question.

"Not everything, exactly. I had some stuff in storage."

He wanted to pull her into his arms and hold her until all the bad things went away. He wanted to hit the stairs running and never look back. "Saint Rebecca," he muttered.

"What?"

"Nothing." He shook his head. "Let me guess. You've been doing this all by yourself. Coordinating where the kids are going to stay temporarily, finding a new place, collecting clothes."

"You sound as if I've done something wrong. The children are my responsibility."

He felt old and tired, and far too cynical to spend time with someone like her. In his ugly little world, very few people went out of their way to do more than they had to. He was as guilty as the rest of them. It was easier to stay detached that way. Easier to forget why he couldn't get involved.

"Did I say something to offend you?" she asked.

He looked at her, at the long dark hair, at her big eyes and the trembling set of her mouth. From the top of her head down to her unpainted toenails, she was alien to him.

He leaned toward her and slipped his hand over her shoulder to the nape of her neck. She stiffened but didn't move. Despite her recent shower, he could smell the sweet scent of her body. It reminded him of vanilla and sunshine, nothing like the musky Oriental fragrances his lovers normally favored.

Her skin was as smooth and warm as he'd imagined. His thumb traced a pattern on her spine, then he curled his fingers into her hair. Her expression held no fear, only faint anticipation and a trusting calm that made him want to bellow with impatience.

"Who the hell are you, Rebecca Chambers?" he asked. "What are you doing in my life?"

"I don't know how to answer that," she whispered.

His other hand reached for the collar of the robe. It would be so easy to grab the thick material and jerk it open, exposing her to his gaze. Would she fight him or submit willingly?

He touched the terry cloth, moving back and forth, but didn't go near her skin.

"Have you ever gotten a ticket?" he asked.

She nodded. "I forgot to put enough change in the meter."

A parking ticket. He almost groaned. "Ever been really stone-face drunk?"

"No."

"Had sex with a stranger?"

She blushed and shook her head. Her eyes never left his. He saw the flash of fear, but it was gone before he could feed it.

"Have you ever, in your entire life, done anything bad?"

Her gaze dropped to his mouth, then to the floor. "No."

He released her and stalked away. Figures.

"Where are you going?" she asked.

"To call the tow truck and get you the hell out of here."

There was a brilliant flash of lightning, followed by a boom of thunder. The building shook as if God had reached down and bumped it. The lights inside flickered once, twice, then exploded into darkness. He stumbled into an end table and swore. If the power was out, the phone lines were down for the night. He was stuck here. And so was she.

Chapter 3

"Are you all right?" Rebecca asked as Austin stumbled in the darkness.

His answer was a mumbled curse.

She stood where he'd left her, in the middle of his living room. Her heart was still pounding in her chest, and her knees felt weak.

He'd touched her. Even thinking about his brief caress sent the blood racing through her veins. His hand on the back of her neck had been hot and hard. He'd stared at her as if he wanted to devour her for dinner, then dish up the remains for breakfast. She wasn't sure she would have refused him.

Even though it was dark and there was no one to see her blush, she covered her cheeks with her palms. How could she think that about him? A crush was one thing, but casual sex with a man she barely knew was something quite different. Oh sure, she'd thought about making love with Austin hundreds of times. But thinking and doing were two different things...weren't they?

Have you ever had sex with a stranger?

He would never know the images his question had evoked.

She'd already seen Austin naked, so it wasn't difficult to picture him aroused. His body had been all that she'd imagined. Before she'd slammed the bathroom door shut, she'd seen his long, powerful legs, the breadth and definition of his chest. Between his thighs she'd seen dark curls and his...his organ!

In all her twenty-nine years, she'd only ever seen one other man naked. Wayne had been blond and built like a bear, all thick limbs and barrel-chested. He'd been an all-American linebacker at college their senior year. Everything about him was so different from Austin's lean grace, and dark, demonic, good looks.

Wayne had been someone she'd laughed with, someone who had grown up with the same rules and goals as she had. Wayne had understood about values, about the importance of other people's feelings. Wayne had been warm and sensitive.

Austin was none of those things. He was a loner. She'd always wondered about his past, but she'd never thought he would have lived in the Glenwood children's home. She'd heard that he'd been wild as a teenager, breaking rules and the law, getting into trouble. Even now he lived up to his reputation. Between his self-made fortune, his gold earring and his women, he flouted the conventions of their small town. He was nothing like Wayne, nothing like herself. So why couldn't she stop thinking about him?

The sun had set behind the clouds, taking away the last of the light. From another part of the loft, drawers were being opened and slammed shut. After several minutes she heard the scratch of a match, then a weak flicker of light danced off the far wall.

"You might as well come into the kitchen," Austin called out. "I don't have enough candles for the whole place. Can you see your way?"

"I'm fine," she said, and wondered if she had the courage to take him up on his less than gracious invitation. She'd hoped he found her at least slightly attractive. But her answers to his questions had pointed out to both of them that she was far from his type. A man with a reputation of being the devil himself wouldn't be interested in a woman like her.

She walked around the wing chair and toward the light. Austin stood by the phone, staring at the receiver. He banged it once against the wall and listened. Then he slammed it back in place.

"The line's out."

"I figured as much," she said.

He planted his hands on his hips and stared at her. "Looks like you're stuck with me for the night."

I don't mind.

She didn't say the words, but she must have thought them pretty loudly because Austin stiffened, raising his head slightly and staring at her. He reminded her of a wildcat catching scent of its prey.

Squat candles sat in saucers around the kitchen and on the butcher-block table. The flames danced in time to a rhythm she could neither feel nor hear. The storm raged around them, but for once she wasn't afraid of the lightning or the thunder. It was as if the rest of the world had ceased to exist. She was alone with this man. Time had disappeared, along with common sense. She had this night. Ignoring the fact that she was naked under his robe and feeling extremely vulnerable, she balled her hands into fists and promised herself not to waste it.

"Are you hungry—"

"Would you like me to fix—"

They spoke at the same time. Austin recovered first. "Are you hungry?"

"A little. I could fix something, if you'd like. Is the stove gas or electric?"

He turned to glance at the range set into a granite counter. "The starters are electric, but the unit is gas."

"No problem. If you have another match, I can start it manually." She spoke briskly and walked over to the refrigerator. After pulling it open, she glanced at the contents. "What sounds good? There are a couple of steaks, some salad, a—"

Something warm brushed the back of her hand. She gasped and jumped back. The refrigerator door slowly swung shut.

Austin stood close enough for her to see the hairs on his chest and the slow thudding pulse at the base of his neck. She had the most incredible urge to plant her mouth there and taste his skin.

She bit down hard on her lower lip to keep from yelping her embarrassment. What on earth was wrong with her? She hadn't had more than a sip of his doctored coffee, so it couldn't be the alcohol. Maybe standing out in the rain had left her brain waterlogged.

"You don't have to cook for me," he said.

"I don't mind. It's the least I can do after all the trouble I've been."

"Far be it from me to interfere with a woman on a mission of mercy." He stepped back and motioned to the refrigerator. "Help yourself."

She worked quickly and efficiently. He directed her when she needed to find a bowl or a pot, and within twenty minutes they were eating dinner.

While she'd been cooking the steak, Austin had set the table and opened a bottle of red wine. She sipped cautiously, not wanting the wine to loosen her tongue. She was already in too much danger of saying something stupid. Heaven knows what would happen if she got drunk!

They chatted about mutual acquaintances in town and the children. She forced herself to concentrate on his words, rather than on the way the candlelight made his skin glow like burnished gold. He'd pulled on a shirt, but hadn't bothered to fasten it. She didn't want to say anything and have him do up the buttons, but it was hard not to stare.

"What about you?" he asked, pouring her another glass of wine. "Why are you taking care of other people's children, instead of having a half dozen of your own?"

"What makes you think I want children?"

He raised one eyebrow. Gosh, she really wanted to know how he managed to do that. The storm had decreased in fury, but the lights hadn't come back on yet. The candlelight slipped shadows across his face, making his expression impossible to read.

"You're the type," he said. "Are you telling me you don't?"

"I do." She pushed her fork around her plate. "It just hasn't worked out that way."

"Still waiting for Mr. Right?"

For the first time that day, she could meet his gaze without thinking anything improper. She shook her head. "Not exactly. Mr. Right died."

He'd raised the wineglass to his lips, but now he set it down untasted. "I'm sorry."

"Thank you. It's been a while, so I've recovered. I'll never forget him, of course. Wayne was—" she smiled "—nothing like you."

"I'm not surprised." His expression was unreadable.

"I don't mean that in a bad way."

"I never thought you did."

She wasn't sure if he was angry or simply making conversation. It was easier to assume the latter. "Wayne and I met in college. He was bright, funny. He looked like a big blond bear, but he was sweet and gentle. We got engaged, but I wanted to put off the wedding until I had my masters degree. We'd set the date and everything, but three months before the wedding, he was in a bad car accident. A year later he died."

"Must have been hard on you."

A polite remark most people made. Funny, but she had the feeling Austin really meant it. "It was. About a year and a half after I lost him, I moved here. Like I said, I'll never forget him, but it's getting easier."

Most of the time. Without wanting to she remembered the way Wayne had looked in his hospital room and the expression on his face when the doctor had told him he would never walk again, would never do all the physical things he'd so loved. She remembered his pain when the doctor had gently explained he would never be "a man" again. Wayne hadn't been able to meet her eyes. He'd never cried in her presence, but she'd shed enough tears for the both of them.

It was her greatest regret, she acknowledged to herself. She would have married Wayne, anyway, and had that last year together, but he didn't want to. He told her he wouldn't saddle her with someone who was less than a man. He'd sounded so bitter that she'd never brought up the subject again. But it had lingered in that hospital room like an unwelcome third party. He'd never said the words, but she knew he blamed her.

It was her fault. She'd been the one to hold back. While they'd dated and been engaged, they'd played and loved like any young couple, but they'd put off going all the way until they were married. Because she'd asked him to. There had been so many wonderfully sensual things to do together that she hadn't minded not consummating their love. Until it was too late and she'd found out their love would never be expressed in the ultimate act of sharing. She would never marry the man she loved, never carry his child.

All the years they'd spent together, she'd guarded her virginity, ready to give it as the most precious gift a bride could bring her husband. In the end, Wayne had died hating her for keeping herself from him. Her innocence had mocked him, reminding him of what he'd lost, of what he could never have again. It mocked her, as well. She was an anachronism. A twenty-nine-year-old virgin who had saved herself. For what? Her "gift" was a reminder of all she'd lost. It no longer had meaning. She wanted it disposed of and forgotten.

"Rebecca?"

"Hmm?" She glanced up and saw Austin staring at her. She blinked several times. "I'm sorry. I was just thinking."

"About Wayne?"

She sighed. "Yes. It's difficult losing someone like that. There were so many unresolved issues. I wanted to explain it all to him, but he wouldn't listen. I can't blame him. It was my fault."

She stopped talking and realized Austin didn't have a clue what she was going on about. He nodded encouragingly, giving her permission to continue, but she couldn't. What was she supposed to say? *Gee, Austin, I'm really upset because my late fiancé and I never went all the way. I'm a twenty-nine-year-old virgin and I'm sick of it. Want to help me out?*

Her line of thinking should have shocked her. It didn't. Which meant she was in more trouble than she'd thought.

She didn't know how long she'd been quiet, but suddenly

she became aware of a tension in the room. It was a subtle vibration that seemed to reach deep inside of her, warming her from the inside out, causing her pulse to quicken and her skin to tingle.

She glanced across the table and saw Austin watching her. His gray eyes glowed in the candlelight. His irises were the color of the storm. Stubble darkened his cheeks and jaw, shadowing the lines of his face, making him look more dangerous. He inhaled deeply. The slight movement caused his earring to catch the light. The gold glinted sharply, once again making her think of pirates and treasure, of captured women and forbidden love.

It was becoming difficult to breathe. She told herself it was just a foolish reaction to being in the same room with the object of her crush. Maybe it was because she'd been thinking about and missing Wayne. Or it could have been the result of her exhaustion. Since the fire, she hadn't had a decent night's sleep or a moment's rest. When she hadn't been scouting for supplies, she'd been figuring out a way to approach Austin about borrowing his house. She still found it hard to believe he'd said yes. He didn't have to. A lot of people would have turned her away, citing problems with noise, potential destruction or insurance.

So many people nicknamed him the devil, but he'd been very nice to her. In fact—

"Stop looking at me like that," he growled.

She stiffened, startled by the anger in his voice. "Like what?"

"Like I'm some damn noble prince riding in on a white horse. I'm not anybody's idea of a hero, and if you think I am, then you're worse than a fool."

He drained the last of the wine into his glass, then slammed down the bottle. "The storm is already almost over," he said, glaring at her. "In the morning the road will be dry enough for you to drive out of here. If not, I'll dig out the damn car myself."

"You swear a lot," she said without thinking.

"You don't swear enough."

"I don't swear at all."

He grimaced. "That's my point. We have nothing in common. I like my women experienced and easy. You're not either."

She was too shocked to blush. She stared at him. "Wh-what are you talking about?"

He leaned over the table far enough to grab a handful of her hair. He wrapped it around his hand twice and then pulled her close, until their mouths were millimeters apart.

"You know exactly what I'm talking about, Rebecca. Believe me, I, of all people, understand the appeal of what's forbidden. But I'm one man you shouldn't try to tame. I'm not interested."

She flinched as if he'd slapped her. Before she could control herself, her eyes filled with tears. Her face grew hot, then cold. She tried to pull away, but he held her firmly in his grasp.

"Damn it all to hell," he muttered. "I'm not trying to hurt you. You're not my type. More important, I'm not yours. I'm no Wayne whatever-his-name-was who helped little old ladies cross the street. I'm a selfish bastard. And I do mean bastard, lady. In every sense of the word."

She studied his mouth as he spoke, feeling the sweet puffs of his breath on her face. He was being cruel in a good way. She was sure in time she would be grateful. For now she just wanted to crawl under the table and die. Or have him kiss her. Despite his taunting words, her body was reacting to his closeness. She wanted to scream in frustration. She was too old to have a crush on a man.

She drew in a deep breath and gathered what little dignity and strength she had left. "Austin, I'm sorry if I offended you. I didn't—"

She never got to finish her sentence. He pulled on her hair, dragging her that last millimeter so that their lips touched. Mouth to mouth, he held her in place, not moving, not breathing, just touching gently, firmly, erotically.

Involuntarily her eyes fluttered shut. Heat poured through her as if someone had doused her with sun-warmed rain. Her toes curled and her fingers gripped the edge of the table. When she thought she would go mad from the bliss, he moved his head slightly, brushing her lips. More heat, fiery heat, flared between them. She gasped for breath. His tongue reached out and touched the tip of hers. Before she could melt in place, he released her and rose to his feet.

She sank back in the chair and listened to the thundering of her heart. Her hands were shaking, her breasts felt inflamed, that secret place between her thighs throbbed painfully. She didn't dare look at him. What if he hadn't felt the same reaction?

She caught her breath. What if he had?

Without saying a word, Austin stood up and stalked across the room. He opened the armoire and pulled out a pale garment, then walked back to her.

"Here," he said, tossing it to her.

She grabbed the item, then stared at it. A man's T-shirt, she thought. But what—

"It should be big enough for you to wear to bed."

She stared at him.

He cursed again. "Alone. Damn it, Rebecca, stop it. It's late. You're tired. You take the bed. I'll sleep on the couch. In the morning you'll be out of here, and we'll pretend this never happened."

She didn't point out that it was still quite early. She was too curious about what the "this" they were to pretend never happened was. What had happened between them? A brief kiss? Or something she hadn't realized? She drew her eyebrows together and wished she were a little more experienced at the whole man-woman thing.

"I don't want to go to bed yet," she finally blurted.

"No one is asking your opinion," he said sharply. "You're reacting to the situation and probably to the trauma of the fire earlier this week. It doesn't have anything to do with me, and I'm not going to be responsible for your regrets come morning. I might be a bastard, but I'm not a complete jerk."

Now she was really confused. She dropped the T-shirt on the table and rose to her feet. After tightening the belt of her robe, she shoved her hands into the deep pockets and looked at him. "I don't know what you're talking about. One minute we're having a nice conversation about our lives and the next you're kissing me, then sending me to bed."

He circled around the table until he was standing in front of her. They stood close enough for her to feel the heat of his body. She supposed she should have been nervous or afraid, but she wasn't. Despite what everyone said, deep inside, Austin Lucas was a nice man. Only someone nice would donate his house to needy orphans. How was she supposed to resist him?

"I'm not your damned fiancé," he said, his eyes flashing like the storm.

"I know."

"That's my point. You want me because I'm different, and dangerous. You want me to help you forget. You want me to be the exciting bad thing in your life. You want me in your bed."

She couldn't have been more shocked if he'd slapped her. How had he guessed? Had she been that obvious?

"I—I don't want you," she stammered, knowing she was blushing and praying the candlelight was faint enough that he wouldn't see the color flaring in her cheeks. All her confidence disappeared like smoke in the wind. She turned to leave, but he grabbed her arm and held her in place.

"Did you hope I wouldn't see what you were thinking?" he asked, his voice low and husky.

She moaned softly, shame joining embarrassment.

"Did you imagine I couldn't read the fantasies, Rebecca, that I didn't notice you staring at me, wanting to touch me, wanting me to touch you?"

It was worse than her dream about showing up naked at church. She felt as if someone had stripped her bare and was now mocking the pitiful being she was inside. Her soul felt raw, scourged by the sharp edge of his words. She had to get out, run away and hide. He was laughing at her. Making fun of her. She wanted to die.

"I'm sorry," she whispered, trying to turn away. Tears threatened. She blinked them back, but it wasn't enough. One rolled onto her cheek. "Just let me go. I'll never bother you again."

He released her arm, but before she could step away, he placed his hands on her shoulders and drew her close.

"Damn you, Rebecca Chambers, don't cry. I warned you I was a bastard. Why couldn't you have listened? I'm not trying to hurt your feelings. I want you to understand that I'm nothing like the man you think I am. There's nothing good in me. Forget me. Find another Wayne and have babies."

His gentle words washed over her, easing some of her exposed rawness inside. His body was warm and hard, offering shelter and comfort. She sniffed back her tears until he touched her hair. The tender stroking of his palm on her head was more than she could stand.

Her sob caught her by surprise. Her whole body shook. "I'm sorry," she said, trying to get control. "I—I'm not usually like this. I think it might be the f-fire and everything."

"I know. It's okay. You cry as much as you want."

She didn't want to cry at all, but she couldn't seem to help herself. His strong arms wrapped around her, holding her safely in his embrace. His heartbeat was steady against her cheek. She cried for all she'd lost, for the children's fears and her own. She whispered her concerns, about lying alone at night and wondering how she was supposed to keep it all together. She confessed that the responsibility scared her sometimes, but she kept on because there was no one else.

When the sobs had faded to sniffles, she became aware of the fact that her mouth rested against the bare skin of his chest. He was damp from her tears, yet still warm and smelling faintly musky. Through the thickness of her robe—his robe—she could feel the length of his legs, but little else save his heat. His hands moved up and down her back with long, comforting strokes. His chin rested on her head and he spoke quietly to soothe her.

"You must think I'm a fool," she said, knowing she should pull away, but not wanting to.

"No. I think you're very special. I'm sorry I said anything.

I didn't want to hurt you. I was trying to make you see that I'm not anyone's idea of a fantasy lover.''

"I don't want a fantasy."

His hands grew still.

She raised her head until she could stare at him. "You're right, Austin. I do—" she searched for the right word "—think you're attractive, partially because you're nothing like Wayne. But I don't have a romantic fantasy about you. I don't know you well enough to be picturing home and hearth." She swallowed hard. He'd apologized to her, but she was the one who'd started the whole thing. "I'm sorry if I embarrassed you. If I'd known you could tell what I was thinking, I would have thought about something else."

His gray eyes flickered with some emotion she couldn't read. His mouth twisted into a wry smile. "I wasn't complaining," he said. "I was trying to explain why I was turning you down. I won't deal with your regrets."

"And if I promise not to have any?" she asked without thinking.

"Rebecca." His voice was a low growl. She felt it vibrate in her own chest and realized her breasts were plastered against him. She thought about pulling away, but didn't. A wave of courage surprised her. She might never have this chance again.

In a way he was perfect for her. As he'd pointed out, he wasn't interested in a relationship. She'd already figured that one out on her own. He was wild and experienced. She would never choose to fall in love with someone like him. Which was what made him so safe. She was a twenty-nine-year-old virgin, and she needed a man to fix that. She'd recently started dating, but had always broken things off before they got serious. She didn't want to have to explain about her condition. She'd tried twice and both men had stared at her as if she were a two-headed snake. Being a virgin at her age said something about a person, and she didn't like what it said about her. She'd been saving herself for Wayne and then he was gone. Her gift had no meaning, save a painful one. It reminded her of what she'd kept from him. She wanted it done away with.

Who better to help her out than Austin? Heaven knew she'd

had enough fantasies that being in bed with him would almost be familiar.

"I'm serious," she said, drawing in a deep breath and sliding her hands up his arms to his shoulders. She could feel the rock-hard strength of his muscles. "Maybe if we make love, I'll get over my crush and leave you alone."

"That doesn't say a whole lot about my skills in bed," he muttered.

She was afraid he would be repulsed by the idea and turn away, but he didn't. His hands resumed their stroking of her back, but this time they moved lower, sliding over the curve of her derriere.

"No regrets," she said. "No dreams about white picket fences. No fantasies about a future together, I promise."

His gaze locked on hers. She couldn't read his emotions. It was like staring into a bottomless pool or jumping off a cliff into a cloud. She didn't know how far down she would go. Would he catch her, or let her fall and shatter?

He brought his hands around to her face and cupped her cheeks, then lowered his head toward hers.

She drew a breath in anticipation of their kiss. His mouth brushed hers, slowly, carefully, as if she were the most fragile of creatures. Back and forth, back and forth. Her fingers curled slightly as she gripped his shoulders. Her knees began to tremble.

He pulled back. Their gazes met and for the first time she could read something in his eyes. Desire. It dilated his pupils so much the gray got lost in a sea of need. Until that moment, she'd wondered if she was setting herself up again. Had he toyed with her, making her confess her wants, knowing he shared none of them?

Now she knew the truth. He shared the trembling, the heat. Her confidence returned and with it the sense of rightness about her decision. Austin Lucas might be the devil, but she trusted him not to hurt her. She smiled slightly. So much for being logical. For the first time in her life, she was going on instinct.

"No regrets? You promise?" he asked.

She knew this was completely insane, but it felt right. Wayne was gone. She needed to get on with her life. Austin was the perfect solution. Plus, she would finally find out if her fantasies had come close to the real thing. She smiled. "Yes."

It was as if her single word gave him the permission he'd been waiting for. Before she knew what was happening, he buried his hands in her hair, holding her head still. His fingers flexed against her scalp, sending tingling sensations down her spine.

His mouth angled over hers, searing her with hot, fast kisses. He devoured her, sucking her bottom lip, nibbling on her top. He touched his tongue to the corners of her mouth, then swept across the closed seam, urging her to part for him.

She opened to admit him, her breath already quickening with anticipation. In and around, over and under. Hot, wet, seeking. He plunged inside like a marauding warrior, ready to take that which he'd won. Then he retreated, playing with her, touching, stroking, tasting, discovering every inch of her tender mouth, making her pant with longing.

His hands moved down from her head to her neck. His thumbs traced a line from her chin to the hollow of her throat. His fingers left small warm brands on her sensitized skin.

She clung to him, her anchor in the storm, her source of strength. Mindless half phrases passed through her consciousness. It had never been like this. Not with those men she'd dated, not with Wayne. Before, the buildup had been slow, gentle kisses, a natural progression from kissing to petting. It had been quiet and lovely.

Not frantic like this. Her body was too hot, quivering with need and heat. Her breasts ached. Her nipples pressed against the terry cloth, throbbing for his touch. Between her legs an answering echo pulsed in time with her thundering heartbeat.

His mouth left hers and moved along her jaw to her ear where he whispered that she was beautiful. His tongue traced the shape of her ear. His teeth nibbled on her lobe. Ribbons of heat and desire rippled down her body, making her legs shake and threaten to buckle.

She slipped her hands down his chest and across to the bare strip of skin exposed by his open shirt. He was warm to her touch, smooth except for the crinkling hair. Muscles bunched under her fingers. She moved to his waist and drew her palms up slowly, then across his broadness. He answered with a quick intake of air.

She felt his hand at the tie of the robe. With one tug, it was free. He grabbed the collar, then drew it apart and down her arms. She was naked before him.

The cool air of the room surprised her. Without thinking, she brought her hands up to cover her breasts. As always, their small size embarrassed her.

Austin stared into her eyes. "Has there been anyone since Wayne?"

The intensity of his gaze made it impossible to lie. Not that she would have, anyway. "Just a few dates."

"So you haven't made love with anyone in the past couple of years?"

She swallowed. "No." She hadn't made love with anyone, ever, but he hadn't asked that.

"Do you want to change your mind? We don't have to do this."

"I want to." She needed to. Not just because it would rid her of her pesky virginity, but because her body was on fire for this man. She had to feel him on her, in her. She had to know what it was like to be with him in the most intimate way possible.

"Then why do you hide yourself from me?"

She glanced down at her hands covering her breasts. "I'm not like her."

He frowned. "Who?"

"I don't know her name. She's pretty, with red hair. She used to come out here a couple of times a week." Rebecca bit down on her lower lip and wondered why she was trying to explain this. "I wasn't spying on you or anything, but people in town talk and it's hard not to listen when they just happen to mention it and—" She clamped her mouth shut.

"You think you're too small," he said bluntly.

She nodded.

His slow grin surprised her.

"What's so funny?"

"Your old boyfriend did a lousy job, Rebecca. You are a beautiful woman, perfect in every way. Long, lean, with just enough curves to drive a man wild."

Her spirits lifted slightly. "Really?"

"Yes."

"Well, that makes me feel better. I've always been worried that, you know, I was too little on top. I— What are you doing?"

He bent over and picked her up in his arms. She squealed and wrapped her arms around his neck. With only the flickering candles to guide him, he walked to the bed and set her in the middle of the black satin comforter. The slick fabric was cool against her heated skin. Before she could slip away to one side, he placed his hands on either side of her waist.

"You're just right on top. Trust me, I know." His smile faded. "I don't have any protection with me, but I had a blood test for my life insurance a couple of months ago," he said. "It came back clean. I haven't been with anyone else since."

She stared at him. What on earth? Oh! That. He waited patiently. "Ah, yeah, me, too. I mean, I'm okay. You know." How could there be a problem? She'd never been intimate before.

"So you're safe then?"

Safe? Of course she was safe. She couldn't possibly have any sexually transmitted disease because she'd never had the sex required to do the transmitting. "Yes."

"Good." He shrugged out of his shirt.

When he stood up and started unfastening his jeans, she told herself to look away. But she didn't. She'd already seen him naked. It had been thrilling, and she wanted to see him again.

But he didn't look exactly the same. When he pushed his jeans past his hips, his arousal sprang free. He was a lot larger than she anticipated, hard and ready. Despite the flicker of fear that raced through her, she was glad. At least she knew he wanted her, too.

Without speaking, he lay down beside her. There wasn't enough light from the candles for her to be able to see his expression, but she felt his warmth. He leaned over her, trapping her arms between them. He raised up, pulled her arms free and drew them around his neck. Then he bent down and kissed her.

The touch of his lips was electric. Hot, sparking sensations shot through her body, clear to her toes. Her fingers curled into his hair and she felt the silky brown strands slipping against her skin.

He moved his mouth slowly, as if he had all the time in the world. As if nothing existed but them and the night and the storm. She supposed she should be nervous and appalled at her own behavior. She would be. Later. For now there was only this man.

He raised his head and smiled at her. She smiled back. Bare legs brushed. Shivers raced from each point of contact and collected in her breasts and between her thighs. Anticipation made her muscles contract.

He moved his chest back and forth. His sprinkling of hair tickled her breasts and made her nipples pucker. Then he bent his head lower and took one hardened tip in his mouth.

She sucked in her breath on a gasp. His lips caressed the taut point. His tongue traced erotic circles over and over again. He reached for her other breast, cupping her small curves, stroking the sensitive skin, tweaking her nipple into a tight bead.

She felt his hardness against her thigh. She longed to touch him but didn't have the courage. Instead, she stroked his back and sides, reaching down to cup his rear, squeezing the firm, muscled flesh.

She touched his shoulders, then his long hair. Warm to cool. His scent invaded her. Her index finger traced his ear and the gold hoop.

He moved his mouth to her other breast, exchanging fingers for tongue and vice versa. Her heart rate increased and the pulse between her thighs grew more insistent. Her arms fell to her sides. She grasped at the satin comforter and held on. It had been too long. Her breasts were too sensitive. Just the feel of his hot breath, his tongue flicking over the nipples, making the tight points higher and tauter, sent her flying toward ecstasy. Her last conscious thought was that her fantasies about making love hadn't even come close to the sensual magic of this moment.

Austin raised his head and looked at Rebecca's face. Her eyelids closed and her mouth parted as she drew in more and more air. He felt her quivering response as he suckled her.

He slipped his hand lower, across the smooth skin of her flat belly to the dark curls below. Heat radiated from her. It would be so easy to bury himself inside her waiting warmth and just explode. However, as hard as he was, that explosion would occur in about three thrusts. Hardly enough to satisfy her. He wanted to feel her body ripple with satisfaction and watch her eyes slowly return to focus. He wanted to learn every inch of her. Only then would he take his own pleasure.

His finger sought and found her tight opening. He traced the entrance to paradise, making his stomach tighten in anticipation as her body thrust toward him.

The night made her pale skin glow as if iridescent. Despite his best intentions, his need throbbed heavily. Just looking at her and thinking about what he wanted to do was enough to send him close to the edge. He forced himself back.

He drew her nipple deeper into his mouth. At the same time, he sought out the tiny point of her pleasure. He touched it with the tip of his finger. She jumped. Slowly, carefully, he caressed that place, over and around, moving faster and lighter.

Her body quivered, her hips shifted beneath his hand, making it easy to find the rhythm that pleased her. He'd planned to bring her close, then take his time tending to every part of her before finally sending her over the edge. But when her breathing suddenly quickened and her muscles tensed, he knew he couldn't stop.

He raised up on one elbow so he could watch her face. Her eyes opened, but she stared at him without seeing. Her pelvis thrust in time with his movements. Soft moans escaped her lips.

He could feel her tension and the promise of her release. His finger moved more quickly now. She spoke his name and was suddenly still. He rubbed her sweet spot once, twice, forcing her into the fiery explosion. He urged her on, touching gently, keeping pace with her, until she relaxed against his touch.

He looked at her. Perspiration coated her chest. She gasped for breath. Slowly her eyes focused on him. Another spasm caught her and her entire body trembled. It was the sexiest thing he'd ever seen in his life. He had to have her now.

He rose to his knees and positioned himself against her slick opening. She smiled welcomingly.

"Finally," she whispered.

He closed his eyes as he eased himself inside. So damn tight and wet. He held on to her legs, struggling for control. He wanted to let go right away, but he didn't. He couldn't.

He was less than halfway in when he felt resistance. His mind tried to focus but his body wouldn't let him. His need was overpowering. He flexed his hips and pressed on. The barrier resisted, then gave way. Against his palms, the muscles in her legs stiffened.

He stared down at her. Realization dawned and, with it, a sense of disbelief. Rebecca Chambers had been a virgin.

Chapter 4

Austin tried to gather enough self-control to pull back. The flash of anger helped. What the hell kind of trick was she pulling, anyway?

Rebecca's eyes opened and their gazes locked. He wasn't sure what he'd expected to see there, but it wasn't contentment and relief.

"Don't stop," she whispered, and flexed her hips.

The unexpected movement sent him farther inside her. Involuntarily he arched into the pleasure.

"Damn you," he muttered, digging his fingers into her thighs. "If you think I…"

She drew her knees back toward her chest, exposing herself to his gaze, making it easier for him to go deeper. Around his engorged organ her muscles rippled with an aftershock of her recent release. He sucked in his breath, fighting for control.

"Please," she whispered. She raised her hands to his arms and gently stroked his skin. "Don't stop."

She moved her hips again. The awkward, inexperienced movement should have sent him running in the opposite direction. Unfortunately the throbbing between his legs had other plans. Pressure built rapidly. He gritted his teeth and sucked in his breath, then exhaled and gave up the war. The damage had already been done. It couldn't get any worse.

He bent over her, placing his hands on either side of her shoulders. After pulling almost all the way out, he thrust in deeply. She arched toward him, her pelvis tilting in an exaggerated movement.

"Not so much," he whispered, kissing her neck and ear. "It's more of a rocking motion."

She changed her rhythm instantly and about sent him over the edge. He knew he was ready to explode inside her.

He reached down and took one of her nipples into his mouth, sucking deeply. Her breath caught in her throat. She breathed his name. He raised his head until their eyes met. A smile curved her mouth. And then he couldn't focus on her anymore. Inside him, the pressure and need built. He straightened, kneeling between her thighs, thrusting quickly, holding her hips. He tried to think about hanging on, giving her the time to catch up with him, then the thought disappeared into the fire that engulfed him. Heat built as the vortex of sensation grew.

In the back of his mind, a voice whispered he might be hurting her, and he tried to hold back. Then she reached forward and cupped his buttocks, pulling him closer.

The explosion ripped him apart from the inside. Pleasure sucked at his breath and turned his muscles into quivering stone. Scattered pieces of his psyche remained suspended for a single heartbeat, before reassembling.

Sanity returned and, with it, the ability to move. Austin stayed where he was but slowly opened his eyes.

Rebecca stared up at him. Her face was flushed, her full mouth smiling faintly. There was nothing mocking about her expression, or predatory. But she'd come to his bed a virgin. What the hell was going on?

"You probably want an explanation," she said, turning away from his gaze.

"Probably," he agreed.

The blush started just above her small, perfect breasts and climbed quickly up her neck to her cheeks.

"I didn't lie to you," she said, her voice soft and laced with embarrassment.

"You left out a pretty big detail." He probed his emotions and was surprised to discover he wasn't angry. Confused, a little panicked perhaps, but not outraged. Unless of course she had planned this.

He drew his eyebrows together and glared down at her. "If you thought you were going to try and trap me—"

"I didn't," she said quickly, turning her head toward him and meeting his gaze. "Far from it. I…" She swallowed and the blush got deeper.

"Yes?" He rested his hands on her knees, liking the feel of her soft, naked skin under his palms. He supposed if he was any kind of a gentleman, he would pull out of her so that she could cover herself with the sheet. Fortunately for him, he wasn't a gentleman, so he didn't have to worry about her embarrassment. He wanted to keep her off guard. After what had just happened, he was damn well going to get the truth out of her, regardless of how low he had to stoop to get it. Besides, being this close to her was exciting him again.

"I didn't tell you I was a virgin because I knew if *you* knew, you wouldn't make love to me." She spoke very quickly, as if forcing the words past a constricted throat. "Don't be mad at me, please? I sort of picked you on purpose. Because of your reputation and all. I thought if anyone could fix my problem, you could. Maybe you should be flattered."

She ended her speech with a tentative smile. He kept his face stern and her smile died quickly, leaving her mouth trembling and vulnerable. He had to fight the urge to bend down and gather her into his arms. The need to hold her close and comfort her was almost as overwhelming as the need that had pushed him to take her virginity.

"Not good enough, Rebecca," he said, deliberately making his voice cold.

She shivered and crossed her arms over her bare chest. "You're angry at me." It wasn't a question, so he didn't answer. "I suppose I understand why. I guess a man doesn't like to be burdened with a woman's virginity without at least having some kind of warning.''

That got him where he lived. He was about to pull back and let her cover herself with the sheet when she reached out one of her slender pale hands and touched his thigh. Instantly heat seared him, going directly from the point of contact on his leg to his groin. Blood flooded him, causing him to fill and stretch her. Her brown eyes widened.

''Austin?''

He muttered a curse and started to shift away.

She grabbed his wrist and held on. ''Don't go yet. I have to tell you I'm glad it was you. I know it's silly, but you made me feel safe and wonderful. I want to thank you for that.''

He shook his head. ''This is the craziest thing that's ever happened to me.''

Her smile returned full force. ''I doubt that. You must always have women throwing themselves at you. I can't be the first one who's succeeded in seducing you.''

Despite his confusion and the anger that could flare to life at anytime, he grinned at her. ''You did *not* seduce me.''

Her hips flexed, drawing him closer. ''Sure I did.''

''Rebecca,'' he growled, ''don't toy with me.''

''Then don't be angry. Oh, Austin, I know this isn't what you planned, but it was perfect for me. You made my first time wonderful. I'll treasure this always. I didn't come here to trap you, and I didn't mean to lie. If you knew what it's been like being a twenty-nine-year-old virgin… I told a couple of men I'd been dating and they stared at me like I was crazy. They couldn't get away from me fast enough.''

''Then they were fools.''

Her blush had faded, but now it returned. ''Thank you.''

He stared down at her, at her naked, slender body, so pale against the black satin comforter, at her hair fanning out around her shoulders. Her mouth was slightly swollen from his kisses, her skin flushed with faint embarrassment. Despite the warmth of the room, or perhaps because of their intriguingly intimate position, her nipples were hard, two coral-colored, tempting peaks.

He ran his hands down her bare thighs toward her center, then drew back before touching her soft, protective curls. "I'm not the answer to your prayers, Rebecca. I'm no hero."

"You're wrong about that, but I know what you mean. I'm not looking for a commitment. I just want to forget about my past, and my virginity was the last reminder. I'd saved it for Wayne and he's been gone a long time. I wanted *it* gone, too. Please don't make a big deal out of this. I won't."

"I want to believe that."

She raised herself up on one elbow and drew an X over her left breast. "Cross my heart. I'm not involved. I know you're not, either. You've had so many women that in two weeks you won't even remember my name."

Her smile was too much to resist. He bent forward and pressed his mouth to hers. She still tasted sweet. That surprised him. He pulled back and studied her face. The air of innocence continued to cling to her, as if it had nothing to do with the loss of her maidenhead. He grimaced at the old-fashioned phrase. What was wrong with him? So she'd been a virgin. So he'd been the one to change that. So what? It didn't *mean* anything.

"I'll probably remember you for at least a month," he said, trying to match her light tone.

"I'm not going to get all weird on you, Austin." She traced his face, her touch warm and soft against his skin. "I know you're completely out of my league."

He was only five years older than she was, but suddenly he felt like a debauched old man. Her sweetness mocked his black soul, her quick, easy smiles hurt his tired eyes. He'd seen too much, done too much, lived too long in the dark. She was right—he was out of her league, but not in the way she imagined.

He felt her hand slip from his jaw to his neck and then lower. She rocked her hips slightly, urging him to take advantage of their position and his aroused state.

He couldn't. He swallowed and tasted the bitterness of regret on his tongue. When he started to pull out, she murmured a protest. He silenced her with a quick kiss. "You'll be sore enough in the morning," he said quietly.

He went into the kitchen. Candlelight danced against the walls and ceiling, weaving erotic patterns that made him want to forget what he'd just done. But he couldn't.

Deep inside the darkest, blackest part of him, a primal rage swelled. It wasn't directed at Rebecca, but at the cosmos and fates that had drawn them together. His muscles tensed. Sound vibrated in his throat, but he swallowed the words because they had no meaning. He fought the sexual thoughts that flooded him and the urge to claim this woman again.

The primitive reaction, the desire to proclaim her as his own, shocked him. He'd spent most of his adult life fighting against his primal nature and the sudden confrontation with that animalistic side of him was unexpected. Was it about bedding a virgin or bedding Rebecca? A shudder racked his body. He didn't want to know.

"Austin, are you okay?" she called from across the room.

He cleared his throat. "I'm fine." He banished those thoughts to a small place in his mind and turned his back on them.

He returned to the bed, knelt beside her and brushed the hair from her face. "How do you feel?"

"Wonderful."

"Sore?"

She shifted, then grimaced. "Maybe a little."

Her pale body looked so slender and fragile on his big mattress. He wanted to take back all they'd done together and forever erase it from both their memories. At the same time, he wanted to take her again. He didn't. Instead, he slipped under the covers beside her. The storm had passed, but the electricity stayed off. She snuggled against him, her body feminine and warm. He thought about pushing her away, then told himself it was a little too much like closing the barn door after the horse was long gone. So when she rested her arm on his chest, he pulled her close, slipping one leg between hers.

"Thank you again," she said, resting her head on his shoulder. "Now I'm just like everyone else. Normal."

"What are you going to do with your newfound freedom? Start seducing unsuspecting men?"

She giggled softly. Her breasts gently brushed his side and her breath fanned his face. He tightened his arm around her back and rested his cheek against her hair.

"No. I'm not the seducing type. I would like to find someone and get married. Have a few kids."

"Maybe you'll meet another Wayne."

She stiffened slightly, then relaxed. "I don't want another Wayne. I could never love anyone the way I loved him."

He hadn't expected her words to affect him, but they did. Occasionally he was reminded of his solitary existence. Most of the time it didn't bother him; he even preferred life that way. But sometimes, like tonight, the words crept past his barriers and entered his soul. Sometimes he felt regrets for what he'd lost and a sense of longing for what he would never have. If only things had been different.

Austin grimaced, then called himself a fool. It hadn't been different, and he'd given up on wishes a long time ago. They didn't make any difference, anyway.

Rebecca snuggled closer and sighed. "Are you still mad at me?"

"I was never mad."

"Good." She leaned over and kissed his cheek, then settled down with her head on his shoulder. "Night, Austin."

"Good night, Rebecca."

Within seconds she was asleep. He listened to the sound of her breathing. He would like to think his expert lovemaking had worn her out, but he had a feeling her exhaustion was more about the stress caused by the fire than anything else.

He tried to turn away from her, but even in her sleep she clung to him, seeking out his warmth, holding on to him with her arms and legs. He fought against the desire her presence evoked. His body betrayed him, hardening into throbbing need. It would be easy to roll her over and take her again. She probably wouldn't mind. But he couldn't.

Rebecca Chambers had been a virgin. He shook his head, unable to believe it even now. She'd been right. He wouldn't have made love with her if he'd known the truth. Not because he was afraid of hurting her, but because it implied a gift he didn't want to have. She'd promised to walk away from him and not look back. Was that possible? She'd sworn she had no emotional connection to him.

He shifted slightly, pulling her closer and gently rubbing her back with his hand. She slept on.

He couldn't argue with her logic. He wasn't relationship material. He didn't want a wife and didn't know the first thing about being a husband. As long as they were both able to walk away, there wouldn't be a problem. Besides, he wouldn't ever have to see her again.

He closed his eyes, then opened them suddenly. Of course he was going to have to see her again. She was moving into his house with her orphans. A premonition of danger filled him. He tried to fight the feeling, but it was too strong.

She'd promised to walk away and not look back, but it wasn't going to be that easy. As he stared into the darkness he wondered what kind of a price he would pay for this night.

Rebecca awoke to bright sunshine and the smell of coffee. She stretched against the soft sheets and opened her eyes.

This wasn't the children's home. This wasn't even the school auditorium where she'd spent the past few nights. She glanced around the unfamiliar loft, then gasped.

She was in Austin's bed.

She stared down at the wide mattress, at the decadent black satin comforter, then rubbed her fingers against the expensive sheets. Without thinking, she started laughing.

"I guess this means you're awake. How'd you sleep?"

The low masculine voice cut through her amusement. Rebecca glanced up at Austin, who was leaning against the kitchen counter. With the sunlight behind him, she couldn't read his expression, but his body proclaimed him wickedly male, in jeans and a worn sweatshirt pushed up to the elbows.

"I slept great," she said. "How about you?"

"Not bad."

She couldn't believe they were having this mundane conversation, especially after what had happened last night. He continued to stare at her. She didn't know whether to dive under the covers and hide, or toss the sheets and blankets aside and boldly offer herself up again.

He took the decision away from her by turning toward the counter. "Coffee will be ready in about two minutes if you want to wash up first."

"Okay." She reached for the robe he'd draped across the foot of the bed and slipped it on. When she stood up an aching soreness between her legs reminded her of their lovemaking. As if she needed reminding.

Once in the bathroom, she quickly checked her reflection in the mirror, searching for any changes. Her face looked the same, if a little pale. There was no visual proof of the difference in her body, but she felt the relief clear down to her bones. She wasn't a virgin anymore. Thank goodness. And Austin, she thought, giggling softly.

As she washed her face and brushed her teeth, she reveled in the sensual memories. He'd made everything perfect, bringing her exquisite pleasure, and ridding her of the reminder of her failure with Wayne. It was as if someone had lifted a great weight from her shoulders. She was free.

She wanted to do it again. She paused in the act of rinsing out her mouth. Would he want to? She'd read in an article in a woman's magazine that men liked to have sex early in the morning. Something about their hormones peaking. She knew it was shameful, but she would very much like to have him in bed with her again. Last night everything had been so new, she hadn't had a chance to pay attention to what was happening. Plus, it had been kind of dark and she hadn't been able to see much.

She reached for a towel and wiped her mouth, then grinned. She felt wicked and very much alive.

There was a window overlooking the back of his property. She looked out and saw the ground had dried. No doubt she would be able to drive her car right out. She turned toward her clothes hanging on the shower door. The dress and blouse were dry, as well. She thought about putting them on, but decided to wait. If she did manage to entice Austin back to bed, the robe would be less cumbersome than her dress.

Humming happily under her breath, she left the bathroom and headed for the kitchen. Austin stood where she'd left him, leaning against the counter. He'd set two cups on the table. She reached for the one lightened with cream and smiled.

"Good morning."

Instead of responding, he looked at her. Something dark and frightening flickered in his gray eyes, then he blinked and his expression was devoid of any emotion. Sometime while she'd slept he'd showered and shaved. His jaw was clean, his hair damp and brushed away from his face. She thought about him moving her clothes out of the way and then putting them back. Had he thought about her as he'd touched her things?

This morning his mouth was pulled into a straight line, but she remembered last night when he'd smiled at her in bed. They'd been naked then, touching. She'd been scared but willing, wanting him to be the one with her, in her. She took a sip of coffee and waited for him to speak.

The silence stretched between them. Her good mood began to fade. "You're angry again," she said, wishing he would stop staring at her as if he hated her.

"No. Concerned."

"Why? I promised not to have any regrets or second thoughts and I don't."

A muscle tightened in his jaw. He turned away. She gripped the mug to keep it from slipping out of her hand. He wasn't worried about her. Her second thoughts weren't the problem. *His* were.

"Oh, no." She set the mug on the table and stared at her feet. The floor was shiny with the morning sun reflecting off the polished wood. "You thought it was awful. You're sorry we did it."

"It wasn't awful," he said, his voice low and controlled.

"But you are sorry." She risked glancing at him. He stared out the big kitchen window. The stiff set of his back and shoulders spoke volumes. "Is it because I was a virgin?"

He nodded slowly.

"Why? It's no big deal. I'm the only one it affected and I wanted it gone. You did me a really big favor. I'm grateful."

He glanced at her and raised one dark eyebrow. "Grateful? I doubt that."

"Oh, Austin, it's the nineties. Don't get all macho on me. I have no claim on you. You made my first time terrific and I'll always be pleased about that. Everything went just the way I wanted it to. Can't you believe that? Is this some weird guy thing?"

"I guess it must be."

She wasn't sure, but she thought she saw a slight smile threatening at the corners of his mouth. "If you really want to believe it meant something or was some kind of gift, then consider it an early Christmas present."

"One I can't take back."

It might hurt to hear the truth, but she had to know. "Do you want to?"

He stepped close to her. She was glad she'd put her coffee cup down, because when he touched her face, she gathered enough courage to place her hands on his shoulders. His kiss was soft and fleeting. When he would have pulled back, she raised herself on tiptoe and clung to him. Their breaths mingled; his heat warmed her. The pressure of his large hands caressing her back made her lean nearer and offer herself to him.

When he reached for the collar of her robe, she held her breath. In the bright morning light, she could see his face, the desire in his eyes. His black hair gleamed. She touched the damp strands, their coolness contrasting with his heat. His worn sweatshirt was soft against her fingers, his muscles hard. Long legs brushed hers.

As he lowered his head to her neck, her heartbeat increased. Her blood raced faster and hotter, her knees trembled. She told herself it was just her crush. It was just sex and the desire to experience it all again. It wasn't him. Austin Lucas wasn't the sort of man a woman willingly fell in love with. He wasn't the marrying kind. He was sin and seduction, sex and surrender—not commitment.

He nibbled along her jaw, then pushed the robe aside and licked her collarbone. When she moaned, he raised his head and looked at her.

She wondered if he could still read her mind. Yesterday he'd known exactly what she was thinking. She tried to hide her thoughts, then realized it was pointless. Besides, Austin already knew the truth about himself. He didn't want a woman to fall in love with him. Thank goodness her feelings were just an adolescent crush. Getting involved with him would be dangerous to her well-being. Better for her to remember her own limitations.

He reached up and cupped her face, then tenderly touched her mouth with his. He moved his lips back and forth, creating a lethargy that stole her strength, leaving her clinging to him. He whispered that she was beautiful. For a moment she allowed herself the fantasy that this was real. But the thought was too fantastic to imagine. He didn't want a woman like her in his life permanently. He didn't want anyone.

Did he ever get lonely?

The question surprised her. She must have instinctively stiffened when she thought it because he glanced at her and smiled. "What's got you looking so serious?" he asked.

"I was just thinking about you." At his frown she was quick to assure him. "Not in a good way." She paused. "I didn't mean that exactly. Of course I was thinking nice things, but not that nice. That is—"

He silenced her with a quick kiss. "I know what you're saying." He stepped back and drew her robe around her securely, then tightened the belt.

"What are you doing?" she asked.

"Covering up the temptation."

"Oh." She was disappointed. "Why?"

"Because it's safer for both of us. I'm going to order the furniture for the children tomorrow. When do you want it delivered?"

She allowed herself to be distracted by his question, mostly because she was on shaky ground. Had he stopped kissing her because of what she'd been thinking, or didn't he want her anymore? She could ask, but the truth was she didn't want to know.

She sat down at the table and sipped her coffee. There was a blank pad of paper and a pen. "May I?" she asked, pointing at them.

"Help yourself." He took the seat opposite.

"I'd like to look at the place this morning, then I can give you an idea of a delivery date."

"The house probably needs painting and cleaning."

She brushed her hair out of her face. "I've got plenty of volunteers." She made a few notes.

They discussed the logistics of getting everything done. When her list was two pages long, she looked up at him. "Any special rules?"

He shrugged. "I can't think of any except I want the kids kept away from the barn. There's lots of electronic equipment in there and some tools that could hurt them. I'll keep it locked when I'm not downstairs, but it would be better if they avoided the area."

"I can do that." She scribbled another note. With Austin's generous help, it was all coming together. "So between the— Why are you staring at me like that?"

He didn't answer. His gray eyes bore into hers. She'd seen him angry before, laughing, sarcastic and distant, but none of those emotions had prepared her for the darkness she saw flooding his irises. "Austin?"

He blinked as if coming out of a trance. "Did you plan last night?" he asked abruptly.

"Plan it? I don't understand."

"Figures. When I asked you if it was safe for us to make love, what was I talking about?"

She gripped her pen tightly in her hands. This was so embarrassing. "About, you know, sexually transmitted diseases. I've never been tested or anything, but you don't have to worry. There can't be a problem. I've never been with anyone else."

He flinched as if she'd slapped him. "That's not what I meant. When I asked if you were safe I was talking about birth control."

She felt her mouth open, but she couldn't speak. Birth control? Oh, no. She stared at him, at those fathomless gray eyes, at his unreadable expression, and thanked the Lord she didn't have a clue as to what he was thinking. She didn't want to know. Birth control. It had never crossed her mind.

Without thinking, she touched her stomach through the robe. It felt exactly the same. Panic flared, but she fought it down. She closed her mouth.

"There's no need to worry," she said. "It was just one time. There's no possible way I could get pregnant."

Chapter 5

Austin bent over the engine of his Mercedes, but he couldn't block out the sounds behind him. Straightening slowly, he reached for a rag and cleaned his hands. After tossing it down, he looked toward the slight valley through the grove of trees.

A large, empty house stood alone in a patch of sunshine. Grass stretched out fifty feet in each direction before blending into cultivated forest. Normally the house stood silently, a solid reminder of his achievements. He'd told the Realtor that he was buying the property because the barn and loft were perfect for his needs. What he'd never mentioned to anyone, what he'd barely admitted to himself, was that he'd bought it because of the house. The three-story building could easily hold all the kids from the children's home. It was a big old Victorian mansion, with more rooms than he'd bothered to count, two staircases and a master suite that could house a family of four.

He'd never spent a single night there. It was enough that he owned it. When he doubted himself, when he believed the lies his mother had told him as a child, when the foretelling of his future came back to haunt him, he walked to the top of the grassy knoll in front of the garage and stared at the empty, silent house. The big structure was his medal of honor, his proof that they'd all been wrong. He hadn't ended up a criminal in prison. He'd made it out. He might still be a bastard, but he was also his own man. He'd made his way.

Today, however, when he walked to the top of the knoll and looked down, the house was alive with activity. Volunteers had parked their cars near the front lawn. Children played in a side yard. He could hear their laughter and shrieks. Bits of conversations drifted to him. He caught a word, part of a sentence. It looked like half the town had turned out to help Rebecca get his house ready for the children.

Just two days ago she'd been naked in his bed, stirring softly in the bright morning light. Then she'd driven out of his life and he hadn't seen her since. He'd been half expecting her to show up and ask him to help. It was his house, after all. But she hadn't.

He watched as a little girl in bright pink pants and white T-shirt toddled toward the trees. Before he could start walking toward her, an older child, a boy of seven or eight, saw what she was doing and ran to grab her hand. He pulled her away from the trees and back into the center of the game they'd been playing.

Something tender and wistful caused Austin's throat to tighten. As soon as he recognized it, he banished the feeling. He was getting old and stupid, he told himself. Who was he trying to kid? He had no room in his life for children, or a woman, for that matter. He wanted his relationships on his terms. Casual sex, minimal conversation. Nothing long-term. Nothing else was safe. Rebecca was smart enough to know that about him. That's why she'd left without looking back. As she'd so bluntly put it, he'd done her a favor. They were both realistic enough to look at that night for what it was. No ties, no questions about feelings or love.

Love. He shook his head. Love was an illusion. Something men said to get women into bed and something women used to trap men, then steal their money. He didn't want any of that in his life. He didn't even want a relationship. God help him, that was all he needed. Some clingy female cluttering up his space.

He was about to head back to his garage when a shiny new minivan pulled up in front of the Victorian house. Travis Haynes, the local sheriff, stepped out, then hurried around to assist his very beautiful, very pregnant wife down.

Austin told himself it was rude to stare, but he couldn't look away. He'd known Travis since they'd been eighth-graders in junior high. Elizabeth was the first woman his friend had ever found happiness with. They practically glowed when they were together. Travis had taken a lot of teasing from his brothers and from Austin when he'd fallen for Elizabeth. Austin wondered how much of their good-natured ribbing had been generated by envy.

As Austin watched, Travis hurried off, then returned quickly with a chair. He placed it in the shade and made sure Elizabeth was settled before going off to help the others. Another car pulled up behind the van. Kyle, Travis's youngest brother, got out and went to greet his sister-in-law. They talked briefly, then laughed. The sound of their amusement floated to him, taunting the silence around him and making him want to walk over and join them. He knew Kyle and Elizabeth would welcome him. There was certainly enough work for an extra volunteer.

He took a single step toward the house, then stopped and turned back to the garage. With a shake of his head, he banished all thoughts of the people working close by. He didn't need them. He didn't need anyone. He'd always been solitary. It was safer that way—easier to hide the truth from everyone. It wasn't as if he was lonely.

He made a few adjustments on the car engine. The Mercedes required a lot of work, but it was worth it. Like the house, he'd bought it because of what it represented. He didn't care what other people thought of his wealth—he flaunted his possessions for his ghosts. When the mocking voices from the past rose up to smother him, he silenced them with a list of accomplishments.

Sometimes he stared at his investment statements, unable to believe the balances in his accounts. He knew he'd been lucky.

His ability to predict trends, to visualize a substance and then chemically engineer it, had earned him independence and a fortune. For whatever reason, God had reached down and touched his brain, allowing him to work his magic in his lab. Several large aerospace firms and the military had tried to buy out his patents, but he would only lease them, holding on to them for the future. He wasn't sure why. Certainly not for his children. He didn't have any.

Unless Rebecca was pregnant.

Austin straightened slowly. He'd done his best not to think about her. Hell, he'd even considered finding someone else to be his regular bed partner, but he couldn't seem to stir up any interest. For a brief moment he allowed himself to fantasize about the possibilities if Rebecca had been different. If she'd been experienced and willing to get involved with something unemotional and temporary.

"Yeah, right," he muttered, leaning against the side of his car. He had a bad feeling that if she was that type of woman, he wouldn't have wanted her in the first place.

He swore. He'd just admitted he wanted her at all. What was wrong with him? He couldn't be interested in a woman like her. She was the marrying kind. She'd been a virgin at twenty-nine. He wasn't sure he'd ever met a virgin over the age of eighteen before. Most of them were smart enough to stay clear of him. But not Rebecca. No, she'd come calling, practically throwing herself at him. Thinking her sexy thoughts and then staring at him with those big brown eyes. How was he supposed to resist that? It wasn't his fault.

He drew in a deep breath and let it out slowly. He was going to have to talk to her eventually. Find out if she was pregnant.

Pregnant. The thought made his blood run cold. Please, God, anything but that. He couldn't bring a child, his child, into the world. He knew what would happen—the same thing that had happened to him. No one deserved that kind of life.

When the horrors from his past threatened, he ignored them. In a few days he would go to the house and they would have a rational conversation. Like two adults. He was probably worrying about nothing. After all, they'd only done it once. What were the odds of her getting pregnant?

Before he could figure them out, a small sound distracted him. He turned toward the noise and saw a young boy standing on the driveway in front of the garage. He wore clean jeans with a blue T-shirt and scuffed athletic shoes. White-blond hair hung down to his eyes. The boy didn't say anything, just stood slightly outside the garage, looking in.

"Hi," Austin said.

The boy looked up. The tilt of his head caused his bangs to fall to the side, exposing big blue eyes. All morning Austin had heard the laughter and excited screams of the children as they played. The not unpleasant sounds had reminded him of his time in the Glenwood children's home. However, the child in front of him didn't look as if he'd participated in any of the games. His expression was wary and sad, far too old for a seven-or eight-year-old boy.

When the child didn't return his greeting, Austin tried again. "What's your name?"

"David."

"I'm Austin." He held out his hand. The boy stared at him, then slowly moved into the garage. They shook solemnly. Austin gave him a quick smile, but the child didn't respond. His face was pale, as if he hadn't spent any time in the sun with the other children.

Something tugged at Austin's memory. David. Had Rebecca mentioned the boy when she'd explained why she needed the house? Was he the one who'd lost his parents and sister?

"Am I in trouble?" the boy asked, his voice low and quiet.

"For what?"

"Rebecca said we weren't suppose to come up here and bother you. I was just lookin'. I'll go back now."

Austin recalled the rest of the boy's story. He had relatives fighting over his parents' estate, but no one wanted him. Austin knew what it was like to be cast aside. As long as he lived he would never forget his own mother's angry words as she'd dumped him on another relative or friend.

Without trying, he remembered being in her old Mustang.

She always made him ride in the back seat, as far away from her as possible. They'd pulled up in front of the house of one of his uncles. He'd tried to fade back into the dark upholstery so she would forget he was there with her, but it hadn't been enough. He could still hear the silence after she'd turned off the car's engine, then the strike of the match as she'd drawn it across the matchbook. He inhaled the acrid smell of sulphur and the scent of her cigarette. She'd half turned toward him then, her hazel eyes staring at him, loathing oozing from her as visible as sweat.

"Uncle Fred said he'd keep you for a few weeks. I've got to get a job. You're just too damn expensive, Austin. Stop eating so much. And don't get your clothes dirty. You're a pain in the neck, kid. When I run out of relatives willing to take you in, I'm gonna dump you completely. So don't screw this up, you hear?"

Her hair had been the same color as his, black as midnight. Even then, at five or six, he'd thought her beautiful. And very cruel. He'd loved her and hated her with equal intensity. By the time he was eleven, she'd beaten and starved all the love out of him. When she'd finally made good on her promise to put him in a children's home, he'd almost been relieved.

He fought off the memory, mentally flinging it away from him, hating the weakness that allowed him to remember or give a damn. When he refocused on the garage, the boy was already turning away, prepared to go back alone to the new children's home.

"Do you like cars?" Austin asked.

David stopped in his tracks, then slowly looked back. "I used to. My family died in a car crash."

He spoke matter-of-factly. Austin was appalled. The boy must have heard adults saying the words over and over again for him to deliver them without emotion.

"Are you afraid of them now?" he asked.

David's mouth twisted as he thought about the question. "No. I don't think so. I wasn't there when it happened. I was spending the night with Randy. His mom let me stay with them until I came here."

Austin tried to imagine what the boy had been through. First he'd lost his entire family. Then, he had relatives who didn't want him, only his money. Finally he'd found some kind of peace at the children's home and the damn building had burned down. It was too much for anyone, let alone a seven-year-old.

Austin dropped to a crouch. He was close enough to touch the child, but he didn't. He remembered his own distaste when strangers had tried to cuddle him. That kind of affection had to be earned.

"Why'd you come up here, David?" he asked, careful to keep his voice low and friendly.

The boy shrugged. "Rebecca said you had a bunch of tools and stuff. I used to make things. You know, with my dad. I helped him make a bookcase once. He let me put on the varnish." David's thin chest puffed up with pride. For a second Austin thought he might smile, but his mouth remained straight.

"Maybe we can work on something together," Austin offered without thinking. He instantly wanted to call the words back. He didn't have the time or inclination to get involved with some kid. Besides, the problems with the estate would be settled and David would be moving on.

But he needn't have worried. David nodded, but didn't look enthused, as if too many people had made promises and then not followed through.

Austin rose to his feet. "We'd better get you back to the house before everyone realizes you're missing."

"They won't notice until dinner. Rebecca does a head count then. But I'll go back." David glanced up at him, as if searching his face for something. Before Austin could speak, he turned and started walking away.

"David."

The boy paused.

"I'll walk you back."

He looked surprised. "Really?"

"Sure. I don't want you getting lost."

David glanced through the trees toward the house, then back at him. "I can see everyone. I won't get lost."

Again Austin dropped to a crouch. This time he placed his hand on the boy's shoulder. He met his troubled gaze. "I was making a joke. I know you won't get lost. I'll feel better if I walk you back. Is that okay?"

David's white-blond eyebrows drew together. "I guess." He glanced at the hand on his shoulder. Austin thought he might pull away. He could feel the boy's bones through the thin material of his T-shirt. But David didn't step back, and Austin wondered if he'd misjudged the child. Maybe he wanted to be held and hugged. His parents had probably touched him. He might miss the contact. Unlike Austin, whose only regular physical closeness with his mother had been the back of her hand across his face.

Austin squeezed gently, then stood up. As they walked toward the other children, he tried to make conversation. "What do you think of the house?"

"It's big. I like the yard. There's no swings, though. At the other place there were swings."

"What else do you like to do?"

David shrugged but didn't answer. Before Austin could think of another question, he heard someone calling his name.

He looked up and saw Kyle jogging toward him. A deputy sheriff, Kyle was the youngest and tallest of the Haynes brothers—about six-two—with the Haynes-family dark, curly hair and good looks. He was a good kid who had a way with women. As Kyle came to a halt in front of him, Austin grinned.

"What's so funny?" Kyle asked. A lock of hair flopped onto his forehead. He brushed it out of the way with a familiar, impatient gesture.

"I was just thinking of you as a kid, but you're not anymore, are you?"

"Nah. I'll be thirty next year. Practically over the hill."

"Time to settle down and raise a family." Austin made the observation mockingly.

Kyle planted his hands on his hips and glared at his friend. "Yeah, sure. I'll find the right woman and get married right after I figure out the answer to world peace. Why are you just now showing up here? It's nearly two o'clock."

Austin glanced at David who was openly listening to their conversation. "This young man came to visit me. I'm bringing him back."

Kyle grinned and grabbed Austin's arm. "I don't think so," he said, hauling his friend toward the house. "You're going to help me paint."

Austin glanced at Kyle's jeans and shirt, for the first time noticing they were covered with flecks of white. "I don't have the time."

"Bull—" Kyle glanced at the boy. "Uh, make that I don't believe you. You're the one who donated this house in the first place, so it's your fault we all had to come and do work. The way I see it, you don't have a choice about helping."

"I don't, do I?" Austin allowed himself to be pulled toward the front steps. He glanced behind and saw David standing uncertainly on the lawn. He pulled free of Kyle's grip and turned to the boy. "Looks like they're going to force me to paint. You want to help?"

David stared up at him, his big eyes wide and blue. He wanted to believe him, Austin could tell. He wanted to participate and have fun, but he was afraid. Austin felt as if someone had reached inside his chest and crushed his heart. He knew exactly what David was thinking because he'd been there. The boy took a step closer.

"Looks like you've made a friend," Kyle said. "I didn't know you liked kids."

David froze. Hope fled his expression. "My aunts and uncles don't like kids, either." His voice sounded wary and far too old.

Austin told himself it would be easier just to walk away. David wasn't his problem. Rebecca or one of the other volunteers would take care of him. If they noticed one small boy standing on the sidelines. How would David grow up? Would he withdraw more into himself, or would he lash out, funneling his hurt into anger and rage, becoming a bully, hurting others before they hurt him?

Austin shrugged. "Kids are okay," he said, knowing if he

made more of it he would be lying and David would know. "But if I have to paint, I wouldn't mind some help."

David swallowed hard. "Okay," he said, trying his best to sound casual, but unable to hide the eagerness in his voice. He ran up the stairs and waited by the open front door.

Austin glanced at Kyle. His friend grinned. "Isn't this interesting."

Austin gave him the ice glare. "Don't say a word," he growled.

Kyle's grin got bigger. "Who me? Never."

Two hours later, they'd almost finished painting a small bedroom. Austin glanced at the floor, then at the boy standing next to him. There was more paint on the newspaper covering the carpet and on David than on the walls, but the job was getting done. While Austin worked the roller, David carefully painted the baseboards and outlined the window. Austin would finish up around the glass later.

He listened to the sounds of conversation in the other rooms. They'd only run into a few people as they'd come into the house and been assigned a room to paint. No one had said anything about his joining in uninvited or the fact that David was going to help. He wondered what Rebecca would make of the whole thing, but so far he hadn't seen her.

"My room was blue," David said as he bent over the door. Austin had taken it off the hinges and laid it over two sawhorses. The boy worked slowly and carefully, making his brush strokes all go in the same direction. If he glopped paint up occasionally, Austin didn't think whoever was going to stay in this room would mind too much.

"You must miss it," Austin said.

"A lot. Sometimes when I first wake up in the morning, I forget. When I open my eyes, I can't remember where I am." David bit down on his lower lip.

Austin panicked at the thought of having to deal with tears. He didn't mind the kid helping him, or their talking about the boy's past, but he wasn't equipped to deal with any kind of pain.

"You got enough paint, there, sport?"

Momentarily distracted, David glanced down at the small tray Austin had given him. "I think I need a little more."

"Coming right up." He dropped the roller into the pan and bent over the paint can.

"Well, what have we got here? Two strong, handsome men painting a room. Be still my heart."

Austin didn't have to turn around to recognize that voice. He knew the owner intimately. Without having to close his eyes, he could see Rebecca stretched out naked, her pale body contrasting with his black satin comforter. Her dark hair fanning out over her shoulders, her eyes two parts welcoming and one part scared. He could taste her and feel her, and damn it all to hell, he was getting hard.

He picked up the paint can and held it in front of himself while he tried to think mundane, nonsexual thoughts. "Hello, Rebecca."

"Austin, what a surprise."

Her smile was as sweet as he remembered. Despite the fact that everyone at the house was cleaning or painting, she wore a dress. Some floral-print gauzy thing that fluttered around her knees and left her arms bare. The thin fabric brushed over her slender curves, hiding rather than accentuating, but he didn't need to see them to remember how they'd felt in his hands and mouth. That train of thought wasn't helping his condition, so he forced himself to study her face instead.

Her only concessions to the cleanup was that she'd pulled her hair back into a braid and wasn't wearing a scrap of makeup. Her gaze met his bravely, then ducked away. She seemed calm and in control, but he could see the blush on her cheeks.

"What brings you here?" he asked, pouring paint into David's tray.

"I heard you were helping us. I confess I thought Kyle was joking, but I see he wasn't." They were standing closer now. The small room got smaller. She had to tilt her head back to meet his gaze. "I'm so pleased you decided to come over. I'd wanted to ask, but I didn't want to intrude."

"Kyle shanghaied me into it."

"I see." She turned to David. "It was good of you to pitch in. Are you doing that door all by yourself?"

For the first time since he'd met him, David smiled. Then he nodded vigorously. "I did the baseboards, too."

Rebecca glanced around at his handiwork. "I'm very impressed. I told everyone this morning that you children didn't have to work if you didn't want to. You're the only one who's helped us." She bent down and fluffed his bangs, then kissed his cheek. "Thank you, sweetie."

David mumbled something under his breath and ducked his head.

Rebecca took the brush from his hand and put it on the tray. "There's lemonade and cookies on the lawn. Why don't you take a break and have a snack? When you're done, I'm sure Austin would like you to bring him a glass of lemonade."

David looked up at him. "That would be great, sport," Austin said.

"Okay. I won't be long." The boy ran out of the room.

Rebecca straightened and stared at her hands. She had paint on her thumb and forefinger. "I really appreciate your taking the time to work with him." She rubbed at the paint while she spoke.

"No problem. He found his way up to my garage. I was walking him back when Kyle insisted I help with the painting."

"Oh, no. I told everyone to stay away from you. I'll remind them again after dinner."

"I didn't mind."

She looked up at him then, her brown eyes wide with surprise. "Really?"

"Yeah, well, David's no bother."

"Oh, Austin."

He almost groaned aloud. That damned look was back in her eyes. The one that said she thought of him as a knight on a white charger. Women. He thought his behavior the other night would have chased away all her foolish illusions.

It was the wrong thing to think about, because it made him remember her in his bed and how his body had felt next to her.

It also made him remember that she'd been a virgin and that they hadn't used birth control.

"Rebecca, we have to talk."

She rubbed at the paint one more time, then dropped her arms to her sides. "I know. But not now, okay? There are lots of people around and I don't want them overhearing this."

"Fine. We can do it later, but soon."

"I'm sure there's no problem."

He wished she was right. Life was rarely that simple. He set the paint can on the floor and picked up the roller. He turned his back to her and started on the wall. "I'll finish this room before I leave."

"Oh, you don't have to run off." She'd moved closer. Even with the windows open paint fumes filled the house. Despite their acrid aroma, he could still smell the faint scent of her body. Vanilla. Why did she have to smell like vanilla? "There's going to be a potluck dinner in a couple of hours. You're welcome to join us."

"No, thanks." He felt her moving closer. If she touched him he would be lost.

"But I— Oh, David, you're back already."

"I brung you lemonade, Austin."

He glanced down at the boy. "I appreciate this." He took the glass and downed it in four long swallows. "That was great," he said, handing it back.

David looked from him to the empty glass, then giggled. Austin smiled. He made the mistake of raising his gaze to Rebecca's. The starry-eyed stare was back. He clamped his lips together and tried not to swear in front of the kid.

"Are you staying for dinner, Austin?" David asked. "They're already setting up the tables. There's a big barbecue and corn on the cob and everything."

"I don't think I can…"

David clutched the glass tightly in his small hands. "You can sit by me."

Austin studied the youngster. Two hours ago the boy had stood outside his garage, all solemn and far too clean for a normal seven-year-old on a spring Saturday. Now he was smiling, not a lot but still smiling, and covered with paint. He looked…better. Happier. Austin knew he was a bastard through to his soul, but he couldn't deliberately hurt the kid.

"Sure, I'll sit by you," he said, knowing this was going to make Rebecca want to canonize him. When he got her alone, he'd make sure she understood he was absolutely the last person in the world to qualify for sainthood. If she could read his mind and know that all he wanted was her naked, in his bed, legs spread and her woman's place wet and hot, she would change her mind real quick. Only he wasn't going to tell her what he was thinking. The way his luck had been running, she would want to act out his fantasy.

David grinned, then handed Rebecca the glass and started painting the door again.

Rebecca leaned close to Austin. Too close. "Looks like you've made a friend."

They were the same words Kyle had spoken, but this time he didn't mind them as much. "Maybe. He's a good kid."

She stared into his eyes. He tried not to read her emotions. After a moment she smiled. "See you at dinner."

"Yeah, sure."

She turned to leave, pausing only to ruffle David's hair. The boy looked up, seeming to like the physical contact.

They worked for another hour and finished the room, then made their way to the cleanup station in the empty utility room. An older man was taking the dirty brushes and sending people to wash at one of the various bathrooms in the house.

"What have we got here?" the man asked. "Two fine workers by the looks of things. The bathroom by the front of the house should be empty by now, if you two gents don't mind sharing."

"We don't mind," David said, before Austin could answer.

As they turned away, the boy reached up and took his hand. Austin almost stumbled from surprise. He glanced down at David, seeing the child's hope and an expectation of rejection. His fingers were small and warm, sticky with paint. Austin squeezed them gently, then headed for the bathroom. As the boy chattered about the upcoming meal, Austin told himself the sudden tightness in his throat was from the paint fumes and nothing else.

Chapter 6

It was nearly eight in the evening when the last carload of volunteers pulled out of the makeshift parking lot and headed down the dirt driveway toward town. The setting sun caught the slightly rusted front fender of the old station wagon parked by the trees and reflected a single beam toward the wide front porch. Rebecca closed the front door of the mansion and dropped the key into her dress pocket, then moved to the stairs and took a seat next to Austin.

"That's the last of them," she said as she settled herself on the wooden step. He shifted to make room for her. She wanted to tell him not to bother, that she wouldn't mind if their arms brushed, but she figured he might not want to know about that. After all, two mornings ago he hadn't taken her up on her subtle offer to make love again. She didn't think it was because he hadn't read the intent in her eyes. Austin might have a few flaws, but stupidity wasn't one of them.

"You had a lot of people out here helping," he said.

His voice was low and controlled. She liked the sound of it, of him. When he spoke, she wanted to stretch like a cat napping in sunlight. Her body grew warm, her mind lethargic. It would be easy to start purring. She bit her lower lip to keep from smiling.

"Everyone has been very helpful," she agreed. She drew her knees up to her chest and wrapped her arms around them. The full skirt of her dress fell past her shoes. She stared out at the vast expanse of green lawn and the grove of trees beyond. The sun had slipped lower, until most of it was hidden behind the leafy branches. The slight breeze still carried on it the warmth of the day. Despite her bare arms, she felt no chill.

Without wanting to, she turned toward Austin. His profile fascinated her—the straight nose, the well-formed lips. Her gaze moved slightly to the right and she saw his gold-hoop earring. It was silly how that tiny piece of jewelry got to her. She supposed it was because this was Glenwood and men didn't wear earrings. Somehow it made Austin appear even more wicked. And tempting and—

"What did you say?" she asked, realizing he was speaking to her.

"I asked when you thought the painting and cleaning would be finished. The furniture is ready to be delivered anytime."

"Oh." She thought for a moment. "There are only two more rooms to paint, and they're pretty small. The kitchen has been scrubbed from top to bottom, so I'd guess by noon tomorrow. Is that all right?"

He looked at her. Pure gray eyes met and held her own. She wanted to see desire and affection lurking there. Of course she saw nothing of the sort. Austin kept his feelings carefully concealed. It was part of his charm, she admitted to herself. The mystery about him. Why was it women were instinctively drawn to men who were bad for them? It didn't make sense. Thank goodness her feelings for him was only a crush that would fade with time. Any woman who actually fell for Austin was destined for heartbreak.

"I'll call the man in the morning and have him bring everything somewhere between noon and two."

"That would be great. Thanks." She smiled slightly. "I know you don't want to hear this, but I really appreciate everything you've done for the children. First loaning me the house, then paying for the furniture. And you were terrific with David today. He had a great time with you. Since the accident he's been withdrawn and…'' She stopped talking when he groaned low in his throat and rose to his feet. ''What's wrong?''

''Stop looking at me like that,'' he commanded, pacing in front of the steps.

''Like what?''

''Like I'm some damn nice guy.''

''But you are. Austin, you've proved it over and over. Face it, there's no way a man who opens his house to orphans can be all bad.''

He swore under his breath. She pretended not to hear the word or notice the way he was rubbing his temple, as if he had a headache.

''Besides,'' she continued, ''there are worse things than being a nice guy.''

He stood in front of her, his legs spread slightly, his boot-clad feet firmly planted on the walkway. Flecks of paint had spattered his worn jeans and red polo shirt. ''I am not, and I have never been, nice.''

She shrugged, fighting a smile. ''If you say so.''

''I do.''

The last rays of sunlight caught his long hair, making it shine. There was no hint of other colors in the dark strands, no red or brown, just pure black. Broad shoulders tapered to a narrow waist and hips. He was tall, strong and good-looking. A predator with a gentle streak that he didn't want to acknowledge. She didn't mind. Knowing it was there was enough.

When the intensity of his gaze started to make her nervous, she glanced around at the wide porch. It was big enough for a small dance to be held there. Everything about the house was oversize. It was a stunning home, but empty.

''Why did you buy this place?'' she asked.

He looked up past her to the wide windows and the peaked roof. ''Because I could.''

That didn't make any sense. ''Do you ever plan to live here?''

He shrugged. "I'm not sure. I like the loft. It's convenient and more my style."

"Then the house is just for show?"

He dropped his gaze to her face. "Exactly."

She wondered who he was showing it to. Judging from the lack of furniture and the dust on the floors, he hadn't spent any time in the mansion at all. So he hadn't bought it to impress women. Obviously he hadn't been inside the house for years.

"I'll do my best to keep the kids under control," she said. "They can be really hard on a place. You've been so generous. I don't want to repay that with broken windows and crayon drawings on the walls."

He moved to the stairs and took his seat next to her again. "Don't worry about it. I've already told you—I'm doing this because when I showed up at the home, the people there were good to me. I owe them. I wasn't the easiest kid in the world."

She turned her head toward him. "Gee, why doesn't that surprise me?"

He smiled slightly. "I guess it's pretty obvious I've never been a model citizen."

"You're not so bad." She released her knees and straightened up. "You didn't have to help out today, but I'm glad you did. I never thought David would enjoy spending time with a man. I'll make sure someone can work on a project with him in the future."

"He's a good kid."

Rebecca rested her elbows on her knees and dropped her chin to her palms. "The whole problem with his family makes me crazy. I can't believe his relatives don't want him. He's smart, funny, well behaved. What's not to like? I just don't understand people like that."

"How can you be in your business and still be so damned innocent?"

Austin's angry tone caused her to draw away from him. "What are you talking about?"

He gestured widely. "You work with these kids every day. You know about the abuse and neglect. Adults who use children for their perverted sexual pleasure. Parents who abandon their flesh and blood. Hunger, drugs, crime, they all prey on the young. You have to know about it, and see it. Why do you still believe in happy endings?''

''I'm not Pollyanna.''

''You're damn close.''

''I know bad things happen to children. But good things happen, too. Orphans find new families. Sick kids get better. Okay, so some don't find complete happiness, but I believe in doing everything I can to help. Why do you want to make that sound like such a crime?''

His mouth twisted at one corner. He shifted until his back pressed against the pillar at the top of the stairs and he was facing her. One long leg stretched out behind her back. The other bent at the knee with his foot resting on the second step. The toe of his cowboy boot was hidden by the hem of her skirt.

''You're trying to empty the ocean with a teaspoon.''

''At least I'm trying. What are you doing to make it better?''

''Saint Rebecca.''

Usually she was able to control her temper. The little things that annoyed most people rarely got to her. But Austin's cynical view of the world rubbed her the wrong way. ''So what's your story? Why do you insist on seeing everything from the worst possible angle? I know you were in the children's home when you were a kid. Is it that you didn't get adopted? Do you think the system failed?''

He raised one eyebrow. ''I couldn't have been adopted. My parents were both still alive.''

''Then why were you there?''

She blurted out the question without thinking, then wanted to call it back. The sun had fallen behind the trees, leaving them in shadow. The cries of the night creatures began softly, building in sound and intensity with each passing minute. The smell of earth and grass, the coming cool of evening, reminded her that she was alone with Austin. Isolated with a man she didn't really know. They'd been intimate with each other. She knew a little about his body, his touch and his kisses, but almost nothing about his soul. He played the villain to hide a softer side. That she believed. But why he felt he had to conceal his gentleness she didn't know.

Something deep inside, some voice she'd learned to listen to, whispered that it was better she didn't understand him. She knew instinctively that learning the truth about Austin would be deadly. Not because the information would scare her away but because it would be too easy for her crush to blossom into something more dangerous. A woman would be a fool to care about a man like him. She knew that as surely as she knew the sun would rise tomorrow. Everything about him and his life-style screamed that he was destined to break hearts. Hers was already so fragile she wouldn't survive if it shattered again.

"You really want to know why I was at the home?" he asked, his voice deceptively lazy as if he didn't care about her answer. But her time with the children had taught her to look past the obvious. The sudden stiffness in his shoulders, the watchful expression in his eyes warned her that her answer carried some significance.

She didn't want to know. She would regret hearing his story. Yet the side of her that he mocked, the instinct to heal, was too powerful to be ignored. "Tell me, please."

"My mother wasn't much interested in raising a kid. She used to dump me with relatives while she went off and had a life. Eventually she ran out of family, so she left me on the steps of an orphanage up by Sacramento. When I turned out to be more than they could handle, they sent me here."

He spoke the words casually, as if they told a story about someone else. The urge to reach for him and hold him close almost overwhelmed her, but she forced herself to stay where she was.

"How old were you?" she asked.

"Ten or eleven. She came by every few months to take a couple of pictures of me." His mouth twisted. "She needed proof that I was alive to keep her meal ticket going."

"I don't understand."

He'd been looking out into the night, but now he turned his dark gaze on her. His eyes bore into her, as if he were searching down into her soul. She felt cold suddenly, although the temperature hadn't changed. She folded her arms over her chest and shivered.

"Blackmail." He let the single word hang alone for several seconds. "My father was—" he shook his head "—is a successful politician in Washington. Married, two kids, conservative constituency. He made the mistake of having an affair with my mother back when he was a nobody. She got pregnant and decided he was her meal ticket."

"She used you for blackmail, then left you in an orphanage?"

"No big deal."

No big deal? Who was he kidding? Rebecca stared at him, trying to absorb what he'd told her. How could any mother treat her child like that?

"I don't know what to say," she murmured. "It must have been awful for you."

"I got by."

She remembered Austin's care when he'd worked with David that afternoon. No wonder he'd handled the boy so well. He knew what it was like to lose everything. "You know what David's feeling," she said. "That's why he likes you so much."

"You're making it more than it was. I let the kid help me paint the room. Nothing more. I'm not like you, Rebecca. I don't believe the world's worth saving."

"That must make your life very lonely. How do you stand it?"

He glared at her. "I think I liked you better when you were spilling things and couldn't get out more than a sentence without blushing."

"I didn't know you liked me at all," she blurted without thinking.

"I don't generally sleep with women I dislike."

"But I seduced you. It wasn't your choice."

He leaned forward until they were close enough for her to feel the heat of his body. Excitement licked up her spine. "How the hell can you still be so innocent?" he asked.

"Honey, you never had a prayer of seducing me. If I hadn't been interested, we wouldn't have done it."

She wrinkled her nose. "Big talk now that it's behind us. You keep your interpretation of what happened and I'll keep mine."

She studied the lines of his face. Stubble shadowed his jaw. The twilight pulled the color from his features, making his eyes look dark and mysterious. A waste of time. He didn't need any help to be more appealing. There was something too magnetic about him already. If only she could figure out what it was. She knew it was something about the way he was always alone. Maybe he challenged women on a primal level. Maybe females were instinctively drawn to a solitary male, wanting to bring him into the circle of intimacy.

"Now what are you plotting?" he asked. He moved a little closer. For a moment she thought he might kiss her. Anticipation made her body hum.

"I was wondering if you are ever lonely," she said without thinking, then could have cheerfully slapped herself.

Predictably Austin withdrew, pulling back until he was leaning against the pillar. He folded his arms over his chest. "Save it for the children. I don't need you trying to get inside to save me, Rebecca. Even if you had a prayer of getting the job done, I'm not interested in being saved. I like my world just the way it is."

"All right." She stretched her legs out in front of her, resting her heels on the lowest step, and folded her hands in her lap.

"Why don't I trust you?" he asked. "That was too easy."

"*I'm* not the difficult one. I'm straightforward, open, honest. You're the brooder. You can make fun of me all you want, but I'd like to point out that I'm a tiny bit closer to normal than you."

His gaze flickered over her face. A smile pulled at his firm mouth, but it wasn't humorous. "Let me guess. You're one of four kids?"

"Three."

"All girls."

She clutched her knees again, pulling them close to her body. "How'd you know that?"

His smile turned genuine. "Because you're such a girl yourself."

"What does that mean?"

"Look at you. You wear dresses all the time. Floral lacy things. You probably don't own a pair of jeans."

"It's hardly a crime."

"You were never a tomboy." He spoke with the confidence of a man who knows women. She wasn't sure if that was good or bad.

"You're right. I never wanted to play rough with the boys. I liked being a girl, and I like being a woman. I like doing female things. Cooking, being with the children."

"Don't defend yourself. I was making an observation, not a criticism."

His good humor had returned. Apparently he'd put her question out of his mind, but she hadn't. Did Austin get lonely? Did he really plan to spend the rest of his life living in his loft by himself? She couldn't understand that. All her life she'd wanted a husband and family. Back in high school and college, she'd studied hard because she'd wanted a career, but she'd always known that wouldn't be enough for her. She needed people around her. She needed a family. She liked the rhythm of life, births, holidays, the passing of the years. Sometimes her heart felt so full of love she thought it might burst open. She wanted a man in her bed, the same man, night after night. She wanted to feel her child growing inside her, then watch that child change from an infant to a toddler, from a teenager to an adult. She wanted to give her child the love-filled life she'd had when she'd been growing up.

She looked up at Austin. He was staring into the distance, his dark eyebrows drawing together in a faint frown. He was good-looking enough to make her weak with longing. There was just enough of a bad boy inside him to push her past reason. But he wasn't the one. She knew that. She needed someone like herself. Someone who believed in family values and shared her philosophy of life. She needed a man, not the temptation of the devil in disguise.

Funny that the devil had been the one to save her. Finally she felt like every other woman. Without the albatross of her virginity hanging around her neck, she was free to start looking for someone to share her life with.

Not someone like Wayne, she thought firmly. She'd loved him with all her heart, but it had been a young love. She would never know if it would have lasted through the changes maturation brought. She wanted to believe it would have, but she wasn't sure.

"We have to talk about it, Rebecca," Austin said at last, breaking the silence between them.

She knew exactly what he was referring to. "I'm not pregnant. I didn't try to trick you into anything. Why can't you let it go?"

"Because my luck isn't that good. When's your period due?"

She opened her mouth to answer, then closed it as color flooded her cheeks. She'd been doing so well with him, too. But with one simple question he left her embarrassed and gasping like a fish.

She ducked her head. "Ten days," she mumbled.

"The home pregnancy kits I looked at said you could check within three days of being late."

She stood up. "I can't believe we're talking about this. I'm *not* pregnant. We only did it once. What are the odds?"

"As long as there's a chance you are, we have to talk about it."

He rose to his feet, towering over her. She refused to be intimidated. "No, we don't. If I'm pregnant, which I'm not, then it's my problem. I don't want or need your help."

He grabbed her shoulders. "Damn it, Rebecca, I'm not going to be responsible for bringing a bastard into this world."

She shook herself free of his grasp. "It's not up to you. If I'm wrong, then I'm keeping this child and you can't make me choose otherwise."

He flinched as if she'd slapped him. Some emotion tightened

his mouth briefly. "That's not what I meant," he said, his voice low and strained. "I can't…" He shook his head. "Thirteen days, then. Let me know either way."

He hurried down the stairs and toward the grove of trees that separated the house from the two-story barn. She moved to the edge of the porch. "Austin, wait."

He didn't stop, didn't even slow down. His long legs carried him farther and farther away, and then he was lost to the night.

Squeals of laughter carried across the bright green lawn. Rebecca smiled at the sounds, then sank back into the comfortable lawn chair that had been a gift from the hardware store in town. Tall, leafy trees provided shade from the afternoon sun, but the kids didn't seem to mind the June heat.

"I could get used to this," Elizabeth said from the chair next to hers. Rebecca's friend sipped on her icy glass of lemonade, then held the tumbler to her flushed face. "I've finally found a comfortable position. Do you think I could take this chair home with me and sleep in it?"

Rebecca laughed. "Go ahead. You need your rest." She glanced at her friend's rounded belly, stretching the front of her maternity blouse. The pale peach fabric set off Elizabeth's faint tan and brown hair. Even with her stomach sticking out and her ankles swollen, she looked beautiful. There was a contentment in her eyes Rebecca envied.

Elizabeth smiled at her. "I can't believe I have almost a month left. I feel like I'm going to go at any moment. I keep asking the doctor if she could have made a mistake and she just gives me that knowing grin of hers. It makes me crazy."

"It'll be worth it," Rebecca promised. She raised herself into a sitting position, then swung her feet over the side of the chaise longue so that she was facing the other woman. "Soon you'll have a new baby. You must be excited."

"I am. But it's been so long since I had Mandy, I'd forgotten nine months felt more like nine years."

A loud burst of laughter caught Rebecca's attention. About ten of the children were playing a complicated game on the front lawn. They raced around, laughing and yelling to each other. Yesterday had been the last day of school, and to the children, summer stretched endlessly in front of them.

"They seem to have recovered from the shock of the fire," Rebecca said.

"Thanks to your hard work."

Rebecca shrugged. "Just doing my job. It's really the volunteers who deserve the credit. All the cleaning and painting. Plus Austin donating the house. We'd still be sweltering in the school auditorium if it wasn't for him."

Elizabeth grinned at her. "So how is it living so close to him? Are you getting over your crush or is it getting worse?"

"I haven't figured that out yet." Rebecca set her glass on the ground. "He's not exactly how I imagined him to be."

"Better or worse?"

She thought about her last conversation with Austin. She didn't know what to make of all that he'd told her. The horror of his past, the way he wouldn't admit to being a nice guy, his patience with David, his insistence on being a loner.

"Maybe both," she answered.

"That's definitive. By the way, I never got a chance to ask you before. What happened the night of the storm? Rumor has it you spent the night at his place. That couldn't possibly be true, could it?"

Rebecca saw the teasing look in her friend's eyes. Elizabeth was one of her closest friends. She trusted her completely. It would be a relief to tell someone what had happened. She opened her mouth to speak, but no words came. Rebecca tried again, then shocked herself and Elizabeth when she burst into tears.

"Rebecca?" Elizabeth scrambled into a sitting position as quickly as her distended belly would allow. "What's wrong?"

"Oh, n-nothing." Rebecca buried her face in her hands, trying to stop the flow of tears. She felt like a fool. "I d-don't know why I'm acting like this. I did spend the night with Austin and I'm really h-happy about it."

"I can tell." She felt the other woman's cool hands on her bare forearms. "Hush, honey. You're going to be fine. Take deep breaths."

Rebecca tried to inhale deeply. Her shoulders were shaking and her throat felt raw. "I'm overreacting, I think."

"I would guess so."

Rebecca looked up and glared at her friend. "You're not helping."

"I don't know what's wrong. How can I say the right thing if I'm completely in the dark?"

Rebecca sniffed. "I guess that makes sense." She straightened and wiped the back of her hand across her face. Elizabeth looked at her with growing concern. "I'm fine," she assured her. "Really."

"So what happened?"

"I—" She clamped her mouth shut. How was she going to say this delicately? "Austin was— He told me that—"

Elizabeth raised her eyebrows until they touched her bangs. "Yes?"

"We had sex."

"Oh, my." Elizabeth stared at her for several seconds, then started chuckling.

Rebecca glared at her. "You're not supposed to laugh. It isn't funny."

"Yes, it is. You've had a crush on him for years, then the first time the two of you are alone, you sleep together." She grinned broadly. "Little Rebecca, I would never have suspected that of you. How was it?"

Rebecca straightened her shoulders. "I can't believe you asked me that." She brushed away the last trace of her tears, then looked down and smoothed the front of her pale blue sundress.

"And?" Elizabeth asked.

Rebecca sighed. "It was wonderful. If you repeat that, I'll deny every word."

"My lips are sealed." Elizabeth leaned forward and squeezed her arm again. "Are you okay? The way you said it, I assume there wasn't any talk about having a relationship."

"Austin doesn't do relationships." She thought about all they'd discussed. She couldn't tell anyone about his concerns that she might be pregnant. She and Elizabeth were close, but even she didn't know about the whole virginity issue. "I'll admit that our night together didn't lessen the intensity of my crush, although I can hold a conversation with him now without making a complete fool of myself."

"That's progress." Elizabeth reached for her glass and took a sip, then tucked a loose strand of hair behind her ear. "What happens now?"

"I don't know. I still like him, but I've realized I don't know anything about him. He's always so apart from everything. He was generous in giving me use of this house and paying for the furniture. I think he's a nice guy, although he hates it when I tell him that."

Elizabeth tried to stand up. She leaned forward and pressed her hands on her thighs, but she couldn't get any leverage. Rebecca stood up and held out both hands. When her friend took them, she pulled her to her feet.

"Thanks." Elizabeth smoothed her short-sleeved, peach top over her belly and grimaced. "I look like a whale."

"You look beautiful."

"Thanks for lying. It makes me feel better." She rubbed the small of her back and stepped from between the chairs. "For what it's worth, I don't think any man likes to be called nice. It upsets their macho self-identity."

"I'll keep that in mind."

Elizabeth shaded her eyes against the afternoon sun. "Travis should be here any minute to pick me up. I'm going to grab my daughter and get out of your way. Call me if you want to talk."

"I will."

They hugged, then Elizabeth headed for the house. Rebecca lingered by the chaise longues, not wanting to leave her shady spot. She had tons of paperwork to fill out, but the thought of locking herself in her small office was too depressing. She felt restless and out of sorts. She didn't want to admit it, but she had the horrible feeling it was because she wanted to see Austin. He was just on the other side of the trees. It would be easy enough to stroll over there, but so far she hadn't come up with an excuse to go find him.

A low, rumbling sound broke through her musings. She turned toward the noise and saw a large truck turning the corner and moving onto the driveway. The heavy vehicle lurched forward slowly, rocking and swaying as it rolled over the uneven dirt road. The children outside stopped playing and came to gather around her.

"What do you think it is?" one of the boys asked.

"I don't know," she answered. "We haven't ordered anything that big."

The truck came to a stop about ten feet in front of the lawn. A burly man with gray hair jumped out of the driver's side, while a younger man stayed in the cab.

"I'm looking for Rebecca Chambers," the driver said, waving a piece of paper. "I got a delivery here."

"What is it?"

He peered at the sheet. "A playground set with extra swings."

"Let me guess. It was purchased by Austin Lucas."

"Yup. Where do you want it?"

Before she could answer, the children broke into cheers. One of her assistants, Mary, came out of the house to see what was going on. Rebecca explained about the equipment and asked her to show the men to the side yard. She watched the children lead the way.

Why was he doing this? He, who claimed to have no feelings about anyone, who had told her more than once he was a complete bastard, had bought playground equipment for the children. What was going on?

She took one last look at the kids, but they were too busy to notice her. Mary would keep an eye on them, she told herself, turning on her heel and heading through the trees.

Before she'd made it halfway through the grove she admitted she was using this as an excuse to see him. Before she'd made it out of the grove she'd admitted she didn't care if it was an excuse. She had to see him if only to have him yell at her. It didn't matter what happened when they were together. It had been less than a week since she'd seen him, and she missed him.

She shook her head as she marched past the garage and up the cement and brick pathway. If she was the swearing sort of person, she'd be saying something creative right now, but she wasn't. She balled her hands into fists and called herself a fool. At least that had a ring of truth.

At the door to the barn, she paused long enough to make sure her headband was in place and her dress smooth. Then she pulled open the outer door and stepped into the foyer. Before she could lose her courage, she grabbed hold of the door to the laboratory and yanked it open, then stepped inside.

She wasn't sure what she'd expected. Perhaps loud screeches from metal machines and smoke circling on the floor. She knew he invented something to do with heat-resistant substances but wasn't exactly sure what.

The long lab was surprisingly quiet. Computers hummed, as did the air-conditioning unit that kept the room a comfortable temperature. There were long tables against the walls, and shelves filled with equipment. The intimidating machines reminded her that Austin was both highly intelligent and incredibly rich. Obviously she was in over her head. What had she been thinking of, having a crush on him? He would never want someone like her in his life. He would want someone like him. A scientist maybe, or a doctor.

She looked around and wondered if she should just leave. It might be easier for both of them. Before she could duck outside, she heard a clunk, then footsteps. Austin came around one of the big computers. He wore jeans and a long-sleeved white shirt rolled up to his elbows. As he walked toward her, he pulled goggles off his head. When he spotted her, he stopped and stared.

"Rebecca. What are you doing here?"

She'd tried to prepare a rational speech. At the sight of him, it fled her brain. She felt as stupid and incapable of intelligent conversation as she had when she'd stood dripping in his garage.

She opened her mouth to thank him for the playground equipment, but those weren't the words that came out.

"If you want me to stop thinking about you, about that night, then why are you being so nice?'' she asked without taking a breath. ''Just stop it. Did you have to give the kids your house? Did you have to send over furniture? And now this. Playground equipment. How am I supposed to resist that? How am I supposed to put you behind me and date someone else? You're messing up my life, here, Austin. I don't want to get involved with you. You certainly don't want to get involved with me. I know you don't want me or anything, so please, don't do this anymore. I can't take it.''

She stopped talking and waited for him to yell at her. She couldn't believe what she'd said. Her only saving grace was that it was the truth.

''Damn it, Rebecca, you think I don't know that?''

She stared at him stunned. ''Wh-what did you say?''

''Do you think I like this thing between us? I don't. I hate it.'' He tossed the protective goggles on the desk and moved closer to her. ''I'll stop being nice if you'll stop haunting me.''

''I don't—''

She never got to finish her sentence and tell him she didn't understand. He stopped directly in front of her and placed his hands on her shoulders, then hauled her hard against him. Even if she'd wanted to protest, she couldn't have. He tilted his head slightly and brought his mouth down to hers.

Chapter 7

Austin hoped Rebecca would bolt or slap him, anything to keep him from the madness that possessed him. She did neither. When he touched his lips to hers, she moaned softly and brought her hands up to his shoulders. Her slender body pressed against his.

She tasted as sweet as he remembered and she smelled of vanilla. When he brushed his mouth back and forth over hers, she parted for him, calling him into her. He told himself to back off, that she was more kinds of trouble than he could handle. He didn't know what it was about her that got to him. It could have been her innocence or that damn crush. He had a bad feeling that he was having one last fling with the world before shutting himself down completely. Who could say?

None of it made sense. Not her reaction to him, nor the way he couldn't stop thinking about her.

He slipped one hand under her hair behind her neck. She was warm and smooth to his touch. He threaded his fingers through her long, silken strands, wondering how they'd feel on his thighs, forming an erotic curtain as she took him in her mouth.

He groaned low in his throat at the thought, deepened the kiss and ground his hips against hers. She answered by pulling him closer still, gripping his shoulders and whimpering against his assault.

He knew it was a mistake, that he was playing with fire, but he didn't give a damn. He brought his other hand down from her throat to her breasts. He brushed across her slight curves, feeling the taut nipples through the layer of her clothes. She gasped at the contact. Her sundress had a long row of impossibly small buttons down the front. As he opened them one by one, he kissed the line of her jaw, then moved lower, planting more kisses down the side of her throat.

She held on to him as if she had no strength left. Her body trembled against his. When he'd unfastened the buttons down to her waist, he nudged her backward until she was against the desk. He shifted her so she sat on the raised surface. Only then did he look at her face.

Her flushed skin made her eyes look bigger. She met his gaze with an unfocused stare. Knowing he was ten kinds of fool and possibly the biggest slime ever to walk the earth, he took her headband off and tossed it behind her onto the desk. With one quick jerk, he pulled her dress down her arms. She wasn't wearing a bra.

He stepped back and looked at her. The long, flowing fabric was soft and romantic. Her hair fanned over her shoulders, partially concealing her naked breasts. She was the picture of seductive innocence and he wanted to take her right there, plunging deep inside over and over again until they were both shaken and exhausted.

She read his mind. Slowly her eyes focused on his face. Her gaze dropped lower, stopping at the obvious proof of his desire. Her welcoming smile ate away at his fading self-control.

"Yes," she whispered, tossing her hair back over her shoulders and baring herself to him.

"Damn you, woman," he growled, then swooped down on her.

He kissed her neck, her ears, her eyelids. He plunged his hands into her hair, holding her immobile. When he kissed her, he was violent, searching her mouth, biting her lips. He whispered exactly what he wanted to do to her, what he wanted her to do to him, in the most graphic of terms. As he licked her ears, he explained exactly how he would feel in her mouth, and then what she would feel when he did that to her. Even as his body got harder, aching with the need to take her, he waited for his actions and words to scare her off. He monitored her gasps of pleasure and surprise and waited for her to push him away in disgust.

She didn't. When he bent over to take one of her hardened nipples in his mouth, she breathed his name and pulled his head closer. When that wasn't enough, she parted her legs and pressed her damp center against him. His half-formed plan had backfired. She wasn't afraid of him—he was turning her on. Austin cupped her breasts in his hands and buried his face in her hair. He hadn't planned on making love with her on his desk, but why not? It wasn't as if she was still a virgin.

But she had been. They hadn't used birth control and he didn't have anything with him now. It was unlikely she did, either. She might already be pregnant with his child. What the hell was he thinking of?

He tore himself away from her and walked over to a workbench by the front door. He leaned against it, not wanting to look at her, not able to look away. She stared at him, obviously as stunned by the passion between them as he had been. She touched her fingers to her swollen mouth.

"Austin?"

The air-conditioning clicked off, leaving only the hum of the computers. In the quiet of the large room, their breathing was audible. He tried to tune out the sound, along with the faint echo of his name. He did his best to ignore the pressure of his erection and the heat boiling his blood.

"How do you do that?" she asked, her voice quiet in the stillness. "You make every part of me tingle as if I've never really been alive before."

"Stop," he commanded. "Stop before you say something you'll regret."

She surprised him by smiling. "I have no regrets. Not about

you, about what we did last week, or even about this." She waved her hand in front of her body, then glanced down. Her dress pooled at her waist, the short sleeves hung on her forearms. She was bare to his gaze, but didn't seem embarrassed. Casually she pulled up her dress and began to fasten the buttons. Her smile deepened. "Okay, I'll admit to one regret. That you stopped."

He pushed off the workbench and stalked toward her. "Don't play with me, Rebecca. You don't have the armor to survive in this league. If you don't watch your step, you're going to find yourself falling hard and getting hurt. I'm not interested in your gentle dreams of children and white picket fences. If you get in my way I'll take what you're offering, and when I'm done I'll walk away without looking back."

She finished fastening her buttons, then searched behind her for her headband. After securing it, she looked up at him. "Are you trying to convince me or yourself?"

He took two steps and closed the gap between them. Leaning forward, he gripped her shoulders. There was nothing passionate or gentle about his touch. He squeezed harder, not caring that he might mark her.

"Grow up," he growled. "Look around you. I'm not salvageable. Find someone else, someone like you. Someone who hasn't seen this world in all its ugliness. Someone who can still believe in happy endings."

Her brown eyes burned with conviction. "You believe. You just don't want to admit it." He knew he had to be hurting her, but she didn't flinch or try to pull away. "I'm not afraid of you, Austin Lucas. I know the truth."

"Bull. I told you I was placed in the Glenwood home when I was thirteen, but I didn't tell you when I left, did I?"

She shook her head.

"I stole a car when I was fifteen. The police caught me ten miles the other side of the Oregon boarder. I served my time in a juvenile facility until I was eighteen and they cut me loose."

"So? A lot of people make mistakes when they're kids. It doesn't mean anything."

He let her go and stepped back. Not because he was pleased with what she'd said, but because his level of frustration had increased his temper to a point where she was in danger.

"Listen to me," he said, his voice low and controlled. "Listen to what I'm telling you. I'm not a nice guy. There's no profit in being nice. I want to live my life by my rules. I've never been married because I don't see the point. I've had women in my life. Lots of women, but no serious relationship. Ever. Because I don't want one. I'm not interested in having one with anyone, including you. The sex was great, I'll admit that. But that's all it was—sex. Go home. Find yourself someone who wants to get married and have babies. Stop trying to fix me."

Rebecca stared at him without saying anything. Her big brown eyes searched his face as if he held the answers to her questions. He wanted to tell her he wasn't good for anything, but he doubted it would matter. Maybe he'd convinced her and maybe he hadn't. Either way, he wanted her gone from his lab, his property and his life. He wouldn't make her leave the house; he'd already given his word that the children could stay there. But he was going to make damn sure that they stopped running into each other. Every time he saw her he thought about their night together. Worse, he wanted to repeat it. Even knowing she was innocent and he was the wrong man to get involved with someone like her. Even knowing she had the power to rip him apart and leave him bleeding. Even knowing she might be the only one brave enough or stupid enough to keep trying to get inside. He wouldn't risk it. He'd learned that lesson too well.

She lowered her gaze, then nodded as if coming to a decision. "All right," she said, her voice steady. "I understand what you're saying. Just answer me one question. Why did you buy the playground set for the children?"

He was glad she wasn't looking at him just then. It made it easier to lie.

The truth would only hurt his case. Buying the playground equipment had been an impulse when he'd driven to Stockton a couple of days ago. He'd seen it from across the street and had made time to go into the store. The sturdy jungle gym had reminded him of the fun he'd had with Travis and his brothers all those years ago. He'd bought it because those memories were among his best, and because the equipment had made him remember how having friends in his life had made everything easier. But that was only part of the reason. He'd bought the equipment because little David had missed playing on the swings.

Without trying to he could see the pain in the young boy's eyes. The pain of loss and abandonment. He'd once felt like that, when his mother had dumped him on some unknown relative's doorstep. He'd stood on the porch and watched her drive away. At seven he'd been confused, half hoping she would come back and get him, half praying he would never have to see her again. He'd loved and hated his mother with equal intensity. Until he'd grown up enough only to hate.

He didn't want that for David. He wasn't willing to get involved with the kid, but swings were no big deal. No child should have to survive without knowing some kind gesture.

But the lie was cleaner. He shoved his hands into his jeans pockets. "I needed the tax deduction."

Rebecca raised her head. "You expect me to believe that? You could have simply written a check. It would have required a lot less effort."

"If you don't like my answer, maybe I should just take it back."

"Tough talk. I don't buy it."

He shrugged. "Believe what you want."

She slid off the table onto the floor and brushed at the front of her skirt. "I can't win with you. You're always trying to make our conversations about something else. I'd hoped we could at least be friends, but you obviously don't want that. And I know I'm not enough like your other women to entice you to, well…" Her voice trailed off as a faint blush stained her cheeks. She started toward the door.

"Wait." He grabbed her arm as she walked past him. Her skin was warm to the touch. Instantly his body reacted to her closeness. He dropped her arm and tried to ignore the pressure in his groin. "You just invited me into your bed."

"I..." She swallowed, then raised her chin slightly. "I wasn't going to ask you for any kind of commitment. I just thought that since you were between women, and we'd already done that and it was very nice, that we might, you know." She managed to get out her entire speech without looking away from him.

She was offering him exactly what he wanted. Hot sex, no ties. Yeah, right. He studied her face. The wide eyes, the full mouth, trembling slightly at the corners. Long curly hair tumbled over her shoulders. The warm weather and her time in the sun had turned her pale skin the faint color of honey. She stood before him, a virtual innocent. She'd saved herself for twenty-nine years and now she wanted to be his mistress.

"Why?" he asked.

She cleared her throat. "I could use the experience."

Terrific. She wanted a tutor. The hell of it was he wanted to say yes. "Explain one thing to me. If you were so in love with Wayne, why were you still a virgin when he died?"

"I made a mistake," she said softly. Clasping her hands together in front of her, she stared off into the distance. "I convinced him to wait. I thought coming to him a virgin on our wedding night would really be special. A magical moment. Something wonderfully traditional in a world overwhelmed by change." She looked up at him and smiled sadly. "It probably sounds stupid to you."

"Actually it doesn't."

"You don't have to humor me, Austin. I know the truth now. Wayne never pressured me, but I knew what he was thinking. I guess every guy would think the same thing. We did other things, but never that. I was proud of myself, thrilled about my precious gift."

Bitterness tainted her words, sharpening her tone. She swayed slightly and he thought about moving closer and offering comfort. He didn't. Even if she wanted him to hold her, he would only hurt her in the end. He shoved his hands deeper into his pockets and curled his fingers into his palms.

"Wayne was hit by a car while he was out jogging," she said. "He was paralyzed from the waist down. It was about three months before the wedding. I still wanted to get married, but he wouldn't. He told me he wouldn't saddle me with someone who was less than a man."

"He couldn't...?"

She shook her head, then dropped her chin to her chest. "He died hating me for that. I told him it didn't matter to me, but I could see the truth in his eyes. Every day he saw me, I was a reminder of all he'd lost. But I was too much of a coward to let him go. I was there, with him, every day until he died. It took almost a year. They said complications, but I think he lost the will to live."

Austin exhaled a breath slowly. That night when he'd first realized what he'd done to Rebecca, he'd been shocked and unsettled. He'd never been with a virgin. He'd told himself it didn't make any difference. He hadn't believed it then and he didn't believe it now. Maybe it was cultural or part of a man's genetic makeup, but bedding her had been different from bedding all the other women he'd known.

"If it meant so much, why me?" he asked. "Why not wait until you were ready to marry someone else?"

She moved toward the door, then stopped and looked back at him. "Once Wayne was gone it didn't matter anymore. I wanted it gone. You were the perfect candidate. I knew you'd never want anything permanent. Besides, I found out nobody thought of my virginity as a gift."

He had, he realized, surprised that her words slipped past his defenses and lodged themselves deep inside. He felt a small sting, knowing she'd used him. Maybe it was fair that she had, even if he'd always done his best not to use women, seeking those who shared his rule and staying away from the innocents. Until Rebecca. He'd unknowingly crossed the line.

No, he told himself. That wasn't true. Even if he hadn't known how inexperienced she was, he'd been sure she wasn't like his usual bedmates. Her crush had intrigued him, her sweetness had lulled him into forgetting his own rules.

"You took a chance," he said. "I could have hurt you."

"Oh, Austin, give it up. You'd never deliberately hurt me."

"What have I done to earn that kind of faith? You don't strike me as a fool."

"You don't strike me as the bad guy. I guess we're even." She reached for the handle and pulled it. The door swung open. "You win. I'm leaving. You've made it clear you don't want to be my friend or my lover. I guess that leaves us neighbors and nothing else. Goodbye, Austin."

He let her go because it was easier than explaining why she should stay, and because, for once, it was the right thing to do. He'd hurt her. It was inevitable. She didn't understand why he wouldn't bed her, even though she'd made the offer on what she thought were his terms. He'd warned her that he was a complete bastard, but she hadn't believed him.

He headed back into the lab, hoping to bury himself in his work and forget about her. He laughed harshly. Not a prayer of that. For the next few days he would do nothing *but* think about her, until he knew whether or not she was pregnant.

What if she was? What if she carried a child? His child.

He didn't know. He didn't want to think about her growing big with his baby or bringing a life into this world. He would kill before he would subject anyone to the torture of how he'd been raised. If nothing else, those years with his mother had taught him that children need love, stability and normal parents.

But he was the wrong person to provide any of those things. Rebecca would be a good mother, he acknowledged. Leading with her heart was what she did best. The smartest thing for him would be to forget it and not get involved. Unfortunately he didn't have a choice.

She'd thrown herself at him and he'd turned her down. After almost a week that still hurt. Rebecca sat on the cushions in front of the bay window of her bedroom and stared out at the grove of trees that separated the large house from Austin's loft. From her second-story window she could see part of his roof and a bit of one wall. Not very exciting, she admitted sadly. Yet looking at that corner of his barn thrilled her. She could close her eyes and picture him sleeping in that big bed, imagine the black satin comforter covering part of his body, but leaving bare an arm or leg.

She drew in a deep breath and sighed. She was hopeless. Despite everything that had happened between them, she was still wasting her time on fantasies. Hadn't she figured out that he wasn't interested? She'd made it very clear that she was willing to have a "sex only" relationship with him. No emotional commitment, no ties. And he'd said no.

She buried her face in her hands, fighting the wave of embarrassment that washed through her. Why had she done it? In the heat of the moment, when she'd felt his hands on her body, she hadn't been able to think at all. The wonder of being that close to him had overwhelmed her, and she'd known that it would be worth any price to keep him in her life. Even the price of being his mistress.

She raised her head slightly and glanced down at the plain cotton nightgown she wore. It covered her from shoulders to calves, draping loosely over her slight curves. It wasn't the least bit seductive. She didn't own silk underwear or paint her nails or wear exotic perfume. She still got excited about Christmas, and sometimes, on Saturday morning, she watched cartoons with the kids. No wonder Austin had turned her down. She wasn't really mistress material.

He'd told her to find someone like herself or Wayne and settle down. She'd told herself exactly the same thing. Only she couldn't seem to summon up any interest in dating. A couple of men had called during the past week, but she'd turned them down. She wanted to be with Austin or no one at all. The thought should have horrified her. After all, it was time for her crush to start fading. It hadn't. She had a feeling it wasn't ever going to.

The more she'd gotten to know Austin, the more she liked him. The more she saw the side of himself he tried to keep concealed, the more she wanted to know his secrets and discover the real man behind the facade. She'd seen flashes of tenderness, and a gentle spirit. It would be a tough fight getting him to open up, but she had a feeling the rewards would last a lifetime.

She was a fool to dream. He wasn't for her. She should simply walk away and do her best to forget. But it was too late even for that.

Her gaze moved across the room to the open door to the bathroom. On the counter sat a small cup. The pink plus on the bottom made forgetting Austin all but impossible. She was pregnant.

For a few minutes she toyed with the idea of not telling him, then dismissed it. First of all, it wasn't her way to conceal the truth. She wouldn't be able to sleep if she was that dishonest. Second, on a purely practical level, he would find out the truth when she started to show. In a town as small as Glenwood, an unwed mother, even one who was almost thirty, was going to cause some talk.

Okay, she was going to tell Austin, but what was she going to say? She remembered what he'd said about his own father, how his mother had used him for blackmail. She shuddered. Austin was rich. Would he worry about that with her? Not that he would care if anyone knew he had a child, but did he think she would try to get money out of him?

Rebecca stood up slowly and stretched. She would have to tell him right off that she wasn't interested in his fortune. She'd always wanted children. This isn't exactly how she'd pictured everything happening, but the baby was a gift from God. She was a little shocked, but happy. It was all going to work out. Somehow. If he wanted to help out, she would accept the offer, but she wasn't going to trap him.

A baby. She touched her hand to her still-flat belly. It didn't feel real. A life was growing inside her, a child she and Austin had made in that moment of love.

She took a step toward her closet, then stopped. No, not love, she reminded herself. It had been about sex and nothing else. Austin didn't believe in love and she wasn't in love with him. She might be a fool, but she wasn't crazy. Falling in love with Austin was a guarantee of heartbreak. She liked him a lot, enjoyed his company, thought he was a great guy. That wasn't love.

When she had dressed, she went downstairs to help with the

children's breakfast. After that she tackled the mounting paperwork in her office, but it was hard to concentrate. She kept trying to figure out what she was going to say to Austin and wondering how he would react.

Finally, when she couldn't stand not knowing, she called out to Mary that she was going for a walk, then left the house and headed through the trees to Austin's barn. On her way she passed the open garage. Voices stopped her, and she paused to investigate.

His Mercedes sat in the center of the garage, next to a large four-wheel-drive truck. There was a hall leading to another room. That's where the voices came from.

"Austin?" she called.

"We're in here."

We? Rebecca swallowed hard. Who was with him? A woman? She hesitated, wishing she'd taken the time to put on some makeup. All she'd done was wash her face and brush her hair, then pull on one of her favorite sundresses. She glanced down at the pale, floral-print fabric. Skinny straps held up the bodice. The dress showed off her slight tan and made her feel wonderfully feminine. She'd known she would need a boost of confidence when she faced Austin. Of course she'd just assumed they would be alone.

Stiffening her spine for courage, she walked across the garage and stepped into the workshop. It was a huge open room with big windows and a long workbench down the center. Toolboxes and saws and stacks of lumber had been pushed against the walls. At one end of the bench sat Austin and David. Between them was a small wooden box.

David grinned at her. "We're making a birdhouse. Austin's gonna let me paint it."

For once the shadows had been chased from the child's eyes. His color was good, his contentment genuine.

Austin cleared his throat. "I sort of reached a dead end in my research and thought I'd take a break. David was here, so we decided to build something together."

She stared at him for several seconds before she was able to put a name to the expression she saw lurking in his gray eyes.

Embarrassment. She suppressed a smile. Austin was embarrassed at being caught working with the boy. They'd obviously been having a great time together. What was the big deal? Why couldn't Austin admit he liked the kid?

Men. She would never understand them.

"I think it's terrific," she said, moving closer and studying their project. "It's going to be very nice. Where are you going to hang it?"

"Outside my window," David said. He pointed to the metal loop at the top of the roof. "Austin said we can hang a hook under the eaves and I'll be able to see who comes to live in my house."

"Pretty neat." She ruffled the boy's blond hair. He looked up at her and smiled. The poignancy of his expression made her want to weep. If it'd been her choice, she would adopt David in a minute. As a single woman, she would have problems with his relatives. They'd mentioned they were willing to let him go to a family, but abandoning him to a single parent would look bad, even to their selfish minds. Besides, she already had a child of her own to worry about.

Instantly all her concerns about Austin and how he would react returned to swamp her. She glanced at him and saw he was watching her. Could he see her guilt? Had he guessed? She sent up a quick prayer to God to please transport her somewhere else, but He wasn't listening. She sighed. He probably *was* listening, but figured she had to go ahead and face the ramifications of what she'd done.

She squared her shoulders. Not for a minute did she regret making love with Austin. She didn't even regret being pregnant. It was telling Austin about it that was giving her pause.

She crouched down in front of David and smiled at him. "I have to talk to Austin, honey. Would you mind finishing the birdhouse another time?"

David leaned forward and gave her a hug. "I'll go to the house and ask Mary for a snack."

"You do that."

He turned toward Austin. "Can I come back tomorrow?"

Austin looked uncomfortable, then nodded. "Sure, sport."

David threw his arms around him and squeezed tight. Austin sat in his chair, frozen. He made no move to hug the boy back, although Rebecca thought she saw a flicker of affection in his eyes. David released him and scampered out of the room. She heard his running footsteps on the concrete in the garage, then there was quiet.

They were alone.

She stood up, edged back from the table and started to walk around the workshop, investigating the tools and supplies.

"What's up?" Austin asked. He remained seated at the workbench and bent over the birdhouse.

His not looking at her made it easier, she told herself, even as she wondered how he could be so casual. Of course he couldn't know why she was coming to see him. But it had been exactly thirteen days. Had he guessed? Maybe he didn't care.

She sighed. What was she supposed to say? She thought of several opening lines and discarded them all. Why was this so hard? All she had to say was *Austin, I'm pregnant.* No big deal.

She stood staring at a red toolbox and opened her mouth to speak. "It doesn't mean anything." That wasn't right. She tried again. "It doesn't have to mean anything to you if you don't want it to. It means a lot to me. Of course, why wouldn't it? I just don't want you to think it's about money. Yours. I don't want it or feel that a claim is necessary. It doesn't have to be disruptive. I guess you can ignore the whole thing."

"Rebecca? What the hell are you talking about?"

She turned to face him. He'd risen to his feet and loomed over her. Six feet four inches of confused male.

"I have a great job," she said. "Lots of support, friends, a decent income. I don't have my own place, but I'll be getting one as soon as the new home for the children is built. I think it would be a mistake for me to move out while they're in temporary quarters."

"I still don't know what this has to do with anything." His gray eyes locked on hers. He wasn't smiling. He wasn't doing anything but waiting and watching. It was unnerving, like trying to take a test with the teacher breathing down her neck. "Just say it."

"I'm pregnant."

Nothing about his expression changed. His mouth stayed in a straight line. His eyes continued to hold hers. Not by a twitch of a muscle did he give away what he was thinking. She waited, clasping her hands in front of her waist, nibbling on her bottom lip. The silence stretched between them until the room vibrated from the tension. Would he blame her? Did he understand that she hadn't done this on purpose? She'd never really seen Austin angry. Would he frighten her? She knew he wouldn't hurt her, but fear could be pretty upsetting.

She tried to think of something intelligent to say. Nothing came to mind. Just when she became convinced he was never going to say anything at all, he spoke. She'd spent the morning planning her response to any number of things he might say. She thought she'd planned for every contingency. She'd missed one.

"Rebecca," he said, his voice low but clearly audible, "will you marry me?"

Chapter 8

Rebecca might have been beautiful and gentle, and terrific with kids, but she was an amateur when it came to hiding her feelings.

Austin watched her carefully, monitoring what she was thinking. Shock widened her eyes and drew the color from her skin. Her lips parted, but she didn't speak. Her fingers twisted together. She looked as stunned as when she'd turned around and seen him undressing that night in his loft. But she didn't recoil. That was something.

She was going to refuse, of course. He expected her to. Why would a woman like her want to marry a guy like him? After what he'd told her the last time they'd been together, he was surprised she'd come this close to him again. No doubt her sense of right and wrong had convinced her he should know about the baby.

Baby. He swore under his breath and stared at her stomach. He couldn't believe it. They were going to have a child together. Whether she wanted to or not, they were going to get married. No child of his was going to be born a bastard.

"You want to marry me?" she asked softly.

"Yes."

She held out her hands in front of her, palms up. "Why?"

"Because of the baby."

"This is the nineties, Austin. You don't have to marry a woman just because you got her pregnant. I would have thought you'd be the last person to care about convention."

"I don't care what other people think. This is between you and me. I want us to get married. I want my child to have a name."

There. He'd said it. He watched as understanding dawned in her eyes. He'd told her a little about his childhood and what had happened to him. Being the compassionate type, she would melt inside. It was a dirty trick, but he didn't care. He would do whatever was necessary to protect his child from the horrors of the world. Even if he had to lie, cheat and steal. He trusted no one. Not Rebecca, not even himself.

"I thought you'd be angry," she said shyly. "You're acting very calm about the whole thing. Did you guess?"

"No, but I'm not surprised. Life has a way of holding me responsible for my actions. I didn't think this time would be any different."

"That's not very romantic." She tossed her hair over her shoulders, leaving her face bare to his gaze.

"I know. I'm sorry. This isn't about moonlight and roses, but the proposal is genuine."

"If we get married, I'll be your wife."

"I know."

"But I don't love you."

For the first time since she'd made her announcement, he relaxed enough to smile. "I know. I don't want you to love me. I want to give the baby a name and a home. Nothing else. I know this isn't what you'd planned. Maybe you would have found another Wayne. Maybe you wouldn't have. You're still emotionally connected with him. When you're ready to let go of him and move on, we'll work something out. Being married doesn't have to change our lives all that much."

She drew her eyebrows together, as if she was mulling over his argument. "I don't..." She paused, then tried a different tack. "I do care about you, Austin, but marriage, gosh, that's so huge. It's really not necessary. I can take care of the child fine on my own. He or she can have your last name. I don't mind that."

He took a step toward her, closing the distance between them. When she tilted her head back so she could meet his gaze, he gently touched her cheek. Her soft skin burned him clear down to the black hole of his heart. "That's not good enough. I've got a lot of flaws, but running away from my responsibilities isn't one of them. You were the inexperienced one. I should have known better than to assume the birth control was taken care of. I didn't know you were a virgin, but I could tell you hadn't been around. Your pregnancy is my fault. I was too caught up with wanting to get you into bed to think the thing through. Now there's a baby to consider. I won't walk away from that."

"If I remember correctly, *I* was the one making all the offers. You resisted me, almost to the end." She smiled up at him, her expression teasing.

"Rebecca Chambers, I wanted you from the first time I saw you two years ago."

"Really?"

He nodded.

"Then why didn't you say anything? Ask me out?" Her smile broadened. "Although I probably would have expired right on the spot. The shock would have been too much."

"I would never have asked you out. You're not my type."

He was being honest with her. He wondered if it would scare her away. But Rebecca was strong, even if she didn't believe it about herself. He'd always suspected there was a core of steel inside her. She proved it now by not taking offense at something that was obvious to both of them.

"If I'm not your type now, I'd better learn how to be," she said. "After all, we are having a child together. Even if we don't get married, there are going to be a lot of joint decisions." She shrugged. "The list is endless. I don't even know where to start. What kind of parents are we going to be, Austin? I don't know the first thing about being a mother."

"You're with kids all the time. You'll be fine."

"I don't know." She wrinkled her nose. "I think it's going to be different when the child is ours. That is, if you plan to be part of your child's life."

Your child. He dropped his hand to his side as a coldness swept over him. She was worried about being a mother when she had years of experience being with children. How the hell was he supposed to be any kind of a father? He'd met his own father once about twelve years ago. The brief meeting had been hostile, with the older man threatening to have Austin arrested for trespassing if he ever dared bother him again.

Could he risk it? Could he allow himself to get involved with a baby, try to guide a young child, a teenager? What did he know about growing up? His life had been a collection of different homes and relatives, of knowing he didn't fit in and wasn't wanted. He had nothing to offer a child. He didn't know the first thing about being a father.

He turned away.

"Austin, wait." He felt her slender hand on his back. "Don't be afraid. I know you don't have a lot of experience with kids, but you'd be a great father. Look at how you are with David."

He shook off her touch and walked to the far side of the workshop. What did she know? Could she smell the fear, taste it, as he could? Was she able to see into the blackness and know the truth about him? Dear God, not that. No one could ever know. He barely acknowledged the truth himself.

They were so different, he and Rebecca. She came from a warm, loving home. Her parents were still married to each other. Her only act of defiance against all the rules had been sleeping with him. The irony caught him off guard. He was the only bad thing in her life, and she was his only act of decency. Of course he'd screwed that up royally by sleeping with her.

Why couldn't she have married Wayne and left him the hell alone? Wayne would have been a great father. He had probably been born to the job.

A little voice whispered that Wayne was gone and he was here. Rebecca wasn't carrying the other man's child. She wasn't Wayne's fiancée anymore. None of it helped. He was still jealous of a dead guy. Stupid, but true.

"I don't care if I know what I'm doing or not," he said, turning back to look at her. She stood where he'd left her. Waiting. How long would she wait, hoping for a miracle? Would he see that hope fade slowly, day after day, or would it die quickly? He couldn't lie to himself. If he convinced Rebecca to marry him she would believe in him, in them. She would want it all. He could offer her nothing but his name and his money. Eventually she would figure out it wasn't enough. But she would stay because of the child, and that was all that mattered.

"I'll do my best," he said. "I want us to get married and give our child a home."

"Why should I?" she asked. "I don't need to get married to have the baby. You don't need to get married to give this child your name. Why is getting married so important?" She folded her arms over her chest and tapped one foot.

He hadn't expected that kind of an argument. "I could take care of you," he said, not sure what she was looking for. "There's plenty of money. You wouldn't have to work if you didn't want to. What are you going to do when you're eight or nine months along? I can provide health care, arrange for a nanny, even a nurse. It's hard raising a child on your own. Believe me, my mother made sure I knew how hard. It would be easier if you had someone to help." *Most of all, I don't want my child to be a bastard.* But he couldn't bring himself to say that. Rebecca already knew about that part of his life.

"How practical," she said. "All the advantages are mine. What do you get out of it?"

I get to know my kid's okay. He didn't say that, either. "That's not important. Isn't it enough that I want to do this?"

"No." She walked toward him. When they were less than a foot apart, she placed her hands on his chest. "I'm not always a practical person. What if I want to marry for love?"

"I thought you loved Wayne."

Slowly she shook her head. "Wayne was the love of my youth. I'll never know what would have become of that. But he's gone. I've let him go. What if I want to hold out for love and passion? What if I want the fairy tale?''

His chest burned where she touched him. He could feel the heat circling through him. He could show her passion in a hot minute, but he suspected that wasn't all she was talking about. It wasn't just about sex. It was that something more. He'd seen it occasionally lurking in the eyes of a few of his lovers. Even though they'd known the rules of the game, sometimes they'd stared at him and he'd seen their hopeful expressions. He knew what they wanted, and he was confident he didn't have it to give.

''I don't know any fairy tales,'' he said. ''I don't believe in love.''

She didn't flinch or back away, and he was again reminded of her subtle strength. ''Do you believe in anything? Do you at least like me, Austin?''

''Yeah. I like you.''

''Tell me why.''

Slowly he reached up and touched her hair. The long curly strands slipped against his finger. Raw silk, he thought. He could tell her that her hair was the most beautiful thing he'd ever seen and touched. But he didn't. He dropped his hands to her shoulders and his gaze to her breasts. He could tell her that she had driven him past reason in bed, that he couldn't stop thinking about her, of being with her, in her, touching her in wildly sensual ways she would never have imagined. But he didn't. His gaze moved back to her mouth and he could hear her voice, the sound of her laughter. He could tell her that he could listen to her talk for all eternity. Her beliefs, her innocence, her faith, all delighted and shamed him. He could tell her that she made him hope, even though hope was painful. But he didn't. He found a truth because she deserved one, but it was a safe truth.

''I like you because you think of the children first,'' he said.

She tilted her head slightly and pursed her lips together. ''Okay. I guess I buy that. Kiss me.''

''What?''

''Kiss me. I mean a real kiss. Kiss me like you want me.''

Finally, something he could handle. As he bent his head closer to hers, he thought it was a strange request, then realized he didn't care. He'd spent the past several days remembering the last time he'd kissed her. It was definitely something he wanted to do again.

As always the first brush of her lips made him realize how warm and tender she was. She raised her hands to his face, holding him close to her. He tried to be gentle, moving softly against her mouth, but she wouldn't let him. She raised herself on tiptoe, and angled her head. Then her tongue pushed past his, invading his mouth, sending fire racing in all directions.

She sucked on his lower lip and murmured his name. Her hands slipped from his face to his shoulders, then down his back. Slender fingers reached for, then gripped, his rear. Involuntarily he tilted his pelvis forward, pressing his manhood against her belly. A minute ago, he hadn't thought of making love with her. Now his body was hard and ready.

Her tongue continued to play against his. He chased hers back so he could taste her sweetness. His hands roamed her torso, tracing the line of her spine, then circling around to cup her breasts.

He raised his head long enough to glance at the workbench. It was plenty long and wide, although it wouldn't be that comfortable. Of course, Rebecca could be on the top. Then he could cushion her from the wooden surface.

Before he could voice his opinion on the matter, her hand moved from his rear to his hip, across the front of his jeans to the length of his desire. She cupped him lightly. He sucked in a breath and arched against her, wishing there wasn't anything between his heated flesh and her palm. He wanted her like he'd never wanted another woman.

The thought was like being doused with cold water. His desire didn't fade, but his rational mind had a chance to take hold. He dropped one of his hands over hers. After squeezing gently, teasing himself with the potential release, he drew her fingers away. This wasn't supposed to be about him at all. This was supposed to be about the baby and convincing Rebecca to marry him.

He stared down at her, at the passion darkening her eyes. Her mouth was damp from his kisses, her face flushed. He could see the hard points of her nipples though the fabric of her dress.

"That was some kiss," she said, her voice throaty. "I like you, too, Austin. Does that surprise you?"

It did, but he just shrugged. He lowered his arms to his sides. She kept one of her hands on his waist. He hated that he liked the feel of her touching him.

"I like that you're good to me and the children. I like how you are with David. You want to think the worst of yourself. I'm not sure why."

It was because he knew the truth. But he couldn't explain that to her. He hoped she never had a reason to find out.

"I don't love you," she went on, "but I respect you."

It was enough, he told himself. Better, in fact. Anyone who cared about him too much would end up finding out he wasn't worth the trouble.

"And I will marry you."

He told himself that the emotion filling him was relief and that he pulled her into his arms to thank her and not to keep her from reading his expression.

"You won't regret it," he said, burying his face in her sweet-smelling hair. "I'm not Wayne or anything like him, but I'll do my best to be a decent father and husband." The words sounded foreign. What did they mean? Could he do it? He was going to have to try.

"I'm not looking for a replacement for Wayne." She pushed him back until she could see his face. "Believe me, I don't need another relationship like that. I want to marry you. For the baby, even for me a little, I think, and because of who you are."

He knew that if she really knew him, she would turn away in disgust. He could tell her, but she wouldn't believe it. "I'll do everything I can to keep you from regretting your decision."

She giggled. "That sounds ominous. This is going to be hard on both of us. How about if we both promise to try to make it work? Isn't that better?"

"Sure."

"So when's the, uh, wedding?" She blushed as she asked the question, ducking her head as if she expected him to get angry.

"How about in a couple of weeks? That'll give you time to hire someone to take your place at the home."

She stared at him as if he'd suggested she eat a live chicken. "Take my place? You expect me to quit my job?"

"No." He brushed a strand of hair off her face. "You'd mentioned you were going to be hiring someone to take over nights. Once you're married, we'll be living together. So you'll be sleeping here. With me."

"Oh, my." She bit her lower lip. "I hadn't thought of that."

"Did you assume we'd live apart?" For some reason the thought annoyed him, though he tried not to let on.

"No. Not really. I guess I didn't think about it at all. I just sort of figured we'd get married, but everything else would go on the same. I'm concerned about the children being alone at night."

"They won't be alone. Someone else will be with them."

"But after the fire, they need me."

"Why? Aren't they usually asleep? They probably won't even know you're gone."

He watched as compassion warred with the common sense of his argument. "But *I'll* know. I have to think about them."

He touched her chin, forcing her to meet his gaze. Sunlight filtered in from a window in the far wall, highlighting her features. He thought about the first time he'd seen her. It had been at some meeting about raising money for a new park. She'd made part of the presentation. In her flowing floral dresses, with her long hair and luminous skin, she'd reminded him of a stunning piece of art. Some perfect porcelain figurine, breathed to life by a tender wind.

Get real, he told himself. He had no time for fanciful thoughts. She was a woman, nothing else. But she sure was beautiful.

"You have to think about the baby," he said. "You can't

keep running around using up all your time and energy. There's more than just you to consider.''

"I hadn't thought of that," she admitted. "Okay. I'll hire someone. If there's a problem I'll be close enough to go right over. Two weeks, then."

He nodded.

"Can we invite Travis and Elizabeth?" she asked.

"We can invite anyone you'd like. If you have family or other friends."

Rebecca shook her head and stepped away from him. "I don't think so. Let's keep this private. Travis and Elizabeth are enough for me."

He remembered then that she was one of three girls. Had he destroyed her dreams of a big wedding complete with a team of bridesmaids and an orchestra to play the first waltz? What other dreams was he going to cost her?

"Maybe we could get married in the afternoon, then go out with them for an early dinner," she said.

"Fine."

But he wasn't thinking about the wedding. He was promising himself with an intensity he normally avoided that he would do anything, go to any lengths, to make Rebecca happy. Not because she might love him. God help him, that was the last thing he needed or wanted. But because she'd agreed to marry him. Because she was having his child. And because she was the only decent thing in his otherwise empty life.

Chapter 9

The bride's dressing room in the back of the old Glenwood Christian church was big enough to accommodate a formal wedding party, including a bride in a gown with a cathedral train and a host of bridesmaids. Rebecca felt a little lost standing there alone. Her tea-length ivory gown didn't require petticoats or extra space. It hung straight from her shoulders and was fitted to just below the waist where it flared out, ending a few inches below her knees.

She turned around slowly, wondering if the ghosts of past brides would be friendly and wish her happiness, or if they would mock her solitary state. Maybe she'd made a mistake by not inviting some friends from town to be with her. It had been an impulsive decision made when Austin had told her to invite whoever she liked. As she listened to the silence and felt the presence of the ghosts, she finally admitted why.

She was afraid he wasn't going to be there.

In her heart of hearts she fully expected to walk up the center aisle of the church by herself and find the minister standing alone. It would be easier for her if only one or two people were witness to her humiliation.

Even as she tried to talk herself out of her negative thoughts, that insistent voice way back in her head whispered she was going to be abandoned at the altar. Austin would change his mind. He didn't really want to marry her. A man like him didn't want a woman like her. He could have anyone. Someone beautiful and talented, witty and comfortable in sophisticated surroundings. They would travel the world together, maybe on a yacht. Drink champagne and eat caviar. She'd never even seen caviar and, frankly, preferred it that way. Why would anyone want to eat salty fish eggs?

A sob caught in her throat, but she trapped it there. She wasn't going to give into the emotions raging inside her. She couldn't. If she started to cry, she might never stop. Then where would she be?

She glanced down at her watch. The slim, gold timepiece had been a graduation gift from her parents. She'd already written the telegram she was going to send them, informing them about the wedding. They would be shocked, but in time they would understand. She'd promised to bring her new husband home to meet them for Christmas. Of course if there wasn't going to be a wedding, then she wouldn't have to worry about her folks' reaction. See, she thought, there was good news in even the worst of circumstances.

She crossed the large, empty room and sat in front of the vanity. On the table in front of her was a floral headpiece, a bouquet and a small jeweler's box. She picked up the headpiece. Small, delicate ivory orchids formed a fragrant circle. She looked straight ahead and met her own apprehensive gaze in the mirror.

Her eyes were big, wide with nerves. Make that terror, she thought, trying to lighten her mood. Her smile was tentative at best, and quivering at the corners. She brushed her hair away from her face. She'd debated whether or not to wear it up, but in the end had decided that loose would be easiest. She'd been shaking since dawn and never would have been able to pin it properly.

She set the circle of flowers on her head and secured it in place. Long ivory ribbons fell down her back. She wore pearl earrings she'd had since she was sixteen. They'd been her grandmother's. Something old, she thought, touching them. The something new was her dress. She'd sewn a tiny blue ribbon into the lining of her right shoe. She glanced down at the satin-and-lace pumps. They matched the dress and had cost far too much, but they were beautiful. Even staring at them made her feel better about everything. She supposed she'd been foolish to indulge, but it was her wedding day. She owed it to herself to wear something special. For Austin. If he showed up.

Her heartbeat, which had finally slowed to normal, picked up again. Her hands grew cold and damp, and her stomach tied itself in knots.

"Please God, let him be there."

She'd whispered that prayer a thousand times through the long night and morning. Maybe it would help, but she doubted it. Since she'd accepted Austin's proposal, she'd been besieged by doubts. He would have been, as well. She was here today because she'd given her word and because it was best for the baby. And maybe, just maybe, because being married to Austin Lucas was her ultimate fantasy. It was crazy, but she couldn't ignore the thrill of excitement that rippled through her every time she thought about walking into his loft, knowing that she was his wife and that they would be spending the rest of their lives together. Not to mention the weakness that invaded her knees every time she reminded herself they would be sharing a bed. But he didn't have those fantasies. He was marrying her because of the baby. He could easily have changed his mind.

Before the doubts could overwhelm her again, the door to the bride's room opened. She looked up, expecting to see the minister's wife telling her it was time. Instead, Elizabeth stepped inside.

"Rebecca? Mrs. Johnson said you were in here. I got your note. What's going on?" Elizabeth blinked several times. The room was dimly lighted, compared to the bright sunshine of the June afternoon. She stared at her friend. As her eyes adjusted, she drew in a sharp breath. "Oh, my God. You're getting married!"

Rebecca rose to her feet and crossed the room. "Don't be angry," she said, touching Elizabeth's arm. "I really need your help. I'm not sure I can make it through on my own."

Elizabeth studied the flowers in her hair, then dropped her gaze to the lace dress. "Oh, my God. You're getting married."

Rebecca smiled. "You just said that."

"I can't believe it. When you called last week and asked Travis and I to be here, you mentioned a committee meeting. When you said to dress up because we were going out to dinner afterward, I never suspected this. I'm supposed to be your closest friend. I think I *should* be upset you never let on."

"Don't be." Rebecca led her over to a small love seat opposite the vanity. When they were sitting next to each other, she rested her hands on her knees and stared at the ground. "I was afraid to tell you. I didn't want anyone to know. But I couldn't go through this alone. For what it's worth, Austin wanted to let you both know right away. It was my idea to keep it a secret."

"You're marrying Austin Lucas?"

Rebecca raised her head and looked at her friend. "Am I crazy?"

"Maybe. This is all so sudden. Less than a month ago you were upset because you'd spent the night with him. Now you're—" Elizabeth gasped. "You're pregnant."

Rebecca nodded.

"Oh, my. This is one for the record books." Elizabeth patted her own rounded belly. "Enjoy the view of your feet while you still have it. Married and pregnant, all within a month. Are you sure this is what you want?"

"Yes. No. Oh, I don't know. Is it?" Rebecca twisted her hands together. "I'm terrified about all of this. I'm marrying a man I don't know that well, whom I don't love. But I like him. I respect him. We both want the baby. I think he'll be a good father. I think he needs me in his life, although he'd rather eat glass than admit it. Is it enough? Am I making a mistake?"

"Oh, honey. You should have told me. You shouldn't have to go through this alone."

Elizabeth put her arm around her shoulders and pulled her

close. Rebecca absorbed her friend's warmth and support. "I was afraid to."

"Why? After what happened to me with my first husband, I'm the last person in the world to judge anyone. You know that."

Rebecca swallowed hard. "I almost didn't tell you at all. I was afraid he wouldn't show up. I thought it was better to face that by myself. But then, I couldn't get married without you being here."

Elizabeth drew back. "You were afraid Austin would leave you at the altar? Just standing there alone?"

Rebecca nodded miserably.

"Then you really don't understand your husband-to-be at all, do you? I know Austin is difficult at times, and mysterious. But he has a strong sense of honor. He's here. I saw him. He's a little pale under his tan, but he looks determined."

Rebecca let out a deep breath. "Thanks for telling me. I was panicked, wondering what I was going to do."

Elizabeth leaned forward and took both her friend's hands. She squeezed them and smiled. "You don't have to do this if you don't want to. Travis and I have half a dozen bedrooms that aren't being used. You're welcome to come live with us for as long as you want. We'd love to have you. Besides, you can see firsthand what you'll be getting into when you have your baby." She glanced down and patted her belly. "Assuming I *ever* have mine. I feel like I've been pregnant for years."

Rebecca studied her friend's kind face. Elizabeth had an impish smile. Love of life and laughter radiated from her almond-shaped eyes. She wore her brown hair pulled back in a French braid. Her skin glowed. Even the awkward shape of her body couldn't detract from her loveliness. She'd always been pretty, but loving Travis had made her beautiful. The love she'd been afraid to risk again had been returned to her tenfold. Her generous offer, given from the heart, made Rebecca's eyes dampen.

She stared at their clasped hands. Elizabeth's diamond ring winked back at her. Her friend was married, with one child, another on the way and many responsibilities. Yet she'd made the time and room for Rebecca.

"Thank you for inviting me to stay with you," she said. She sniffed and tried to smile. "You're probably going to think I'm crazy, but I want to marry him. Part of it is because of the baby, but not all of it. I know I would have been fine on my own. But our child deserves to know both of us, don't you think?"

"I can't decide for you," Elizabeth said. "You have to do what feels right for you and the baby. Is this what you want?"

"Yes. It is. *He* is. Not just because I'm pregnant. I like him. I think he's nice, no matter that he tries to tell me otherwise."

"Could you love him?"

"Yes." Rebecca spoke without thinking. At first she wanted to call the words back, but in the end she didn't. "It's scary, but I think I could. I've been wondering about my crush on him. Do you think my heart was trying to tell me something for the past two years but I wasn't ready to listen?"

"It's possible. Stranger things have happened." Elizabeth squeezed her hands, then released her. "But be careful, okay? Austin is a loner. He's never gotten involved like this before. I don't want to see you hurt."

"I don't think I get a choice in the matter." Rebecca stood up and forced herself to smile. "How do I look?"

"Stunning. Where did you find that dress?"

"I went to a shop in Stockton. I hope Austin likes it."

There was a tap on the door. Mrs. Johnson, the minister's wife, stuck her head into the room. "We're about to start the wedding, dearie. Are you ready?"

Rebecca nodded.

"Give me a minute to get to the organ. When you hear the music, you can go ahead and start up the aisle."

"Wait," Rebecca called before the older woman could leave. She grabbed Elizabeth's hand and pulled her to her feet. She was glad she'd invited her friend to be with her. "I have a matron of honor." She looked up at Elizabeth. "If you wouldn't mind. I'd prefer not to stand up there by myself."

"You won't be by yourself, you silly. Austin will be there."

Elizabeth glanced down at her blue dress. It was simple, with short sleeves and a draped front that flowed over her extended belly. "I'm not dressed for a wedding, but I wouldn't miss it for the world. Thank you for asking. I'm honored."

Rebecca stepped close and they hugged. She held on, absorbing her friend's strength and quiet confidence. Then she stepped back and smiled at Mrs. Johnson. "We're ready."

"Good. I'll play something pretty for your friend. Then, when she's reached the front, I'll start the wedding march. Good luck." The door closed quietly.

Elizabeth laughed. "I'm suddenly nervous. This is ridiculous."

Rebecca walked over to the table and picked up her bouquet. The scent of ivory roses and tiger lilies mingled with her perfume. She studied the arrangement, then pulled out one of the lilies.

"Here. Matrons of honor should have flowers."

Elizabeth took the blossom, then studied her. "Do you have everything? Something old and all that?"

"I'm missing the borrowed something. Do you have a tissue?"

"I can do better than that." Elizabeth unsnapped a gold bracelet from around her wrist. "Travis gave me this when I told him I was pregnant. It's a gift of love and promise. It'll bring you luck today." She slipped the bracelet on Rebecca's wrist and fastened it.

Outside the room, soft organ music began.

"I think that's my cue," Elizabeth said. "Are you all right?"

"I'm fine. See you at the altar."

Elizabeth gave her a quick kiss on the cheek. "Austin is going to be there. I promise. You'll be fine." She started out the door, then turned back. "Believe in the love, Rebecca. It can work miracles."

When she was alone, Rebecca took one last look in the mirror. She stared at her reflection, hoping to find a hint as to whether or not she was making the right decision. She couldn't find any answers.

She studied her dress. The simple lines were so different from the beaded gown she'd ordered for her wedding with Wayne. Everything was different from the wedding she'd planned with Wayne. There was no church full of guests, no four-tiered cake, no family, no honeymoon in Hawaii. She'd played it safe and lost all her dreams. Now she was making new plans. They were different, but they could be just as satisfying if she let them.

Elizabeth had asked if she could love Austin. Could she? She thought she might if she could get through to him. Seeing him with David had helped her believe love might be possible. She'd seen proof he was a warm, caring man. He kept that part of himself hidden. In time she would find out why. For now it was enough to know it existed.

The music changed, becoming the familiar chords of the wedding march. Rebecca clutched her flowers more tightly in her suddenly damp hands. She grabbed the ring box from the vanity, then walked to the door, opened it and stepped out into the hallway.

The music was louder here. She made her way to the back entrance of the church. Wide double doors stood open. The sound poured over her, making her want to cry. She was getting married, alone, in an empty church, away from her friends and family. She wanted to call everything off. She wanted to sit down and sob her heart out. Instead, she took the first step into the sanctuary.

She stared past the rows of empty pews, past the stained-glass windows that filtered the afternoon sunlight, past Mrs. Johnson sitting behind the massive organ off to one side. Her gaze swept across the altar and settled on four people standing at the front of the center aisle.

She recognized Elizabeth, who smiled encouragingly, and the minister, then Travis, as best man. Swallowing her fear, she allowed her gaze to settle on the man she would marry.

He was there. Relief made her weak, but she forced herself to keep walking. Slowly, step after step, moving closer.

Austin faced the rear of the church, looking at her steadily. Nothing in his face or cool gray eyes gave away what he was thinking. She didn't care. It was enough that he was there and waiting.

Halfway up the aisle she faltered. She made the fatal mistake of allowing her gaze to dip below his face. He wore a charcoal-gray suit. Her steps slowed. At that moment she realized she'd only ever seen him in jeans. There was so much about her husband she didn't know. What kind of man was he? How would he treat her? What did he dream about, wish for? Where were his scars? Would he ever trust her, care for her? Would they grow old together?

She stopped in the center of the aisle. The music swept around her, but she couldn't move. This was insane. What had she been thinking of? From the corner of her eye she saw Elizabeth take a step toward her. Austin didn't move. Their eyes locked.

He spoke her name. Oh, his lips didn't move and there wasn't any sound, but she heard him. He didn't force her to come toward him. Instead, he held back, giving her the choice. She knew he wanted her to choose him. She could feel his thoughts as if they were her own. Then he smiled and her doubts faded. She took a step, then another. Effortlessly she reached the end of the aisle. Austin never once took his gaze from her face. When she was next to him, he held out his hand, palm up. She gave Elizabeth her bouquet and the tiny box containing his ring, and placed her fingers on his. As one they turned toward the minister.

"Dearly beloved, we are gathered here in the sight of God and this company..."

The minister spoke the familiar words, but she scarcely heard them. Rebecca could think of nothing but the man beside her. The heat and scent of his body swept around her, circling her in a cocoon of safety. She darted a quick glance at him, taking in his appearance.

Under his suit jacket he wore an ivory shirt, the exact color of her dress. His conservative blue-and-gray tie reminded her of a banker, but then she glanced up and saw the minister frowning at Austin's earring. She wanted to giggle. She liked his earring because it made her think of pirates, stolen women and forbidden love. She liked it because it was a part of him.

"Do you, Austin Lucas, take this woman to be your lawfully wedded wife?"

Austin repeated the vows slowly, carefully, as if each word was a promise. When it was her turn, her voice shook. Then she risked looking up at him.

"I do," she said.

He smiled. His smiles were rare jewels to be treasured. This one reached deep inside her, clear to her heart, and made her feel welcome. She smiled back. He squeezed her fingers and the last of her fears fled.

They were marrying because of a baby. Couples had been doing that since the dawn of time. Children were an affirmation of the future. A gift of joy. She looked at her soon-to-be husband and saw the questions in his eyes. He was wondering, too. They had much to learn about each other, but the discovery could be wonderful.

She sent up a prayer of thanks that she had made the right decision, that the feelings she had inside would blossom into love. She prayed that their child would be healthy and grow strong under their care.

Please, God, let me be enough to heal him, she thought. *And let him want to love me back.*

"The ring, please," the minister said.

Austin reached into his right jacket pocket and pulled out a ring. Rebecca stared at him with surprise. Of course he'd bought her a ring. She'd even bought him one. But she hadn't thought about it until this moment.

A thrill shot through her. What would it look like? What had he picked for her? She bit her lip as he brought the sparkling band to her hand, then slid it onto her finger. She froze, staring.

A circle of diamonds winked up at her. Pear-shaped stones nestled against each other, forming a pattern of brilliance. The ring was much heavier than the small quarter-carat solitaire Wayne had bought her all those years ago. Much more expensive. Austin could have bought a luxury car with the money he'd spent on this ring.

He was rich. She'd forgotten about that. It shouldn't make a difference, but it did. She sent up a prayer that Austin would know she hadn't married him for his money.

"It fits," he said, leaning forward and speaking softly in her ear.

"It's beautiful."

"I'm glad you like it."

She met his gaze and saw that he'd been nervous about her reaction. That tiny sign of insecurity made her relax again. She tilted her hand so the diamonds caught the light.

"I never imagined having anything this exquisite."

The pride that flashed in his eyes told her she'd said the right thing. It was going to be all right, she told herself.

"Is there a ring for the groom?" Mr. Johnson asked.

"No," Austin said.

Rebecca blinked. "Oh. I bought you one. Don't you want it?"

The minister stared at them as if they were insane. "You didn't discuss this ahead of time?"

She shook her head. "It doesn't matter, Austin. I don't want you to be uncomfortable." She tried to keep the disappointment out of her voice. It had never occurred to her that he wouldn't want to wear a ring. Of course many men didn't, and he worked a lot in the lab. She supposed it would get in his way.

"I didn't think you'd bother," Austin said. "I'd like to wear your ring."

"Really?"

He nodded.

She took the box Elizabeth held and removed the gold band. She'd spent the better part of an afternoon picking out this ring. It had been the same day she'd gone to buy her dress. The plain gold bands had been too plain, but anything with a stone hadn't seemed like Austin. She'd finally found what she wanted in a small store tucked on a side street. The heavy gold was engraved with a pattern that gave it a look of elegance. She'd been able to picture it on Austin's hand.

Now, as she repeated the words and slid it onto his finger,

she was glad she'd bought it. She'd guessed at the size, but it fit perfectly. She glanced up at him and smiled.

"Thank you," he said. His eyes darkened with something she dared to identify as affection.

Her toes curled inside her satin pumps. They were going to make it. She knew that now. Her last prayer of the day was one of thanks.

Travis poured champagne into his glass. "I guess I don't have to tell you that this comes as a surprise."

"No," Austin agreed. "You don't."

He glanced around the private room he'd reserved in the back of the Country Inn restaurant. The minimum for parties was twelve, but he'd convinced the manager to make an exception. The order for several bottles of expensive imported champagne had helped. It was warm for June, but the dimly lighted room was cool. Lush ferns hung from the hooks in the bare-beam ceiling. The table had been set with fine china and crystal. Tasteful paintings graced the wall.

He hoped Rebecca was happy with the location. She'd been the one who'd wanted the dinner party. He'd offered to host something larger, with more of her friends, but she'd declined. Just as she'd declined his offer of a honeymoon. She'd said she couldn't be away from the children that long. To be honest, he was relieved. The last thing he needed was to spend time with her in a romantic location. It was going to be hard enough living together in the loft. At least there he'd been able to remodel the floor plan to make it more workable.

He looked up and realized Travis was staring at him patiently. "I'm sorry. What did you say?"

"I asked if you were going to tell me what was going on. I didn't even know you and Rebecca were dating."

As soon as the four of them had arrived, Rebecca and Elizabeth had ducked into the ladies' room. The two men were alone. Travis was the best friend Austin had ever had. Twenty-one years ago, Travis had stood up for Austin against his own brothers. A bond had been formed that day, one that had never been broken. There was a lot about Austin's life that Travis didn't know, but Austin had done his best not to lie.

"Rebecca didn't want to tell anyone until it was done. She asked me to keep quiet, so I did."

"But this is all so sudden. You'd always said you weren't interested in getting married." Travis leaned back in his chair. "Don't get me wrong. I'm happy for you. Rebecca and I have been close friends ever since she moved to town. I don't think you could have made a better choice. But why the rush and secrecy?"

Austin smiled slightly. "Come on, Trav, you're smarter than that. Why does any couple get married in a hurry?"

His friend frowned. "Elizabeth and I didn't want to wait because we were in love and because we couldn't live together during the engagement. Mandy is very impressionable. Something tells me that's not why you two did this." He frowned, thinking. Suddenly he straightened in the chair. "Holy— She's pregnant?"

Austin nodded. He hadn't been sure what his friend's reaction would be. Although he'd been bothered by Rebecca's request not to tell anyone about the wedding, in a way it had made things easier for him. He'd thought people might talk. That didn't bother him. He was used to that kind of attention. It came with his reputation. But Rebecca was different. She'd never done anything bad in her whole innocent life. No. She'd done one thing—she'd slept with him.

"Hot damn." Travis pounded him on the back. "Congratulations. That's terrific." He grinned and leaned close. "Scared?"

Austin smiled. "Terrified."

"Tell me about it. These women think it's so easy to be a father, but I'll tell you, it keeps me up nights." He shrugged. "I guess all we can do is our best. I know one thing for sure. I'm going to do a better job than my old man."

Austin wanted to say the same, but he didn't know what kind of father his old man had been. He'd been absent. Austin had only met him once in his life, and it had been ugly. He shook off the thought, not wanting to break the mood with unpleasantness from the past.

There was a noise by the door. Elizabeth entered with Rebecca following her. Both he and Travis rose and held out chairs for the women.

Rebecca paused before sitting down. Their eyes met. Makeup accentuated her brown irises, and high cheekbones. Her hair flowed around her shoulders and tumbled down her back in erotic disarray. A circle of small white flowers sat on her head. The ivory lace dress, the flowers, the tentative smile, all made her look like a sacrificial virgin.

Technically Rebecca wasn't a virgin anymore, but the air of innocence still clung to her. He wondered if it always would.

He stood behind her chair until she was seated. She rested her bouquet on the table between her and Travis. Austin sat on her right. Her left hand lay on the table, the diamonds in her ring gleaming in the candlelight.

He smiled slightly, remembering the stunned look on her face when she'd seen the ring. The wide-eyed stare had convinced him more than any words that she hadn't married him for his money. He would have sworn an oath that, until that moment, she'd forgotten he was wealthy.

He glanced from her hand to his own. The engraved gold band fit perfectly. He'd been surprised, as well, but pleased. Her gesture had erased some of the bitterness he felt about the day.

He glanced around the small table set for four and imagined what it could have been. He'd offered her a party for all her friends; he'd offered her a big wedding. She'd wanted no part of either. She hadn't told a soul about the baby or the wedding. He'd finally figured out why: she was ashamed of him.

Before he could say anything to her, Travis stood up and raised his glass. "I'd like to propose a toast. To the happy couple. May you be blessed with a lifetime of joy and love."

Elizabeth raised her glass. "Hear, hear."

Rebecca smiled. Austin waited, but she didn't drink. Then he noticed Elizabeth put her glass down untouched. Travis took a sip and smiled. "Smooth, Lucas. Only the best."

He glanced at Rebecca. She caught his eye and read his confusion. She leaned toward him. A strand of hair slipped off her shoulder and brushed against the back of his hand. A shiver raced up his arm.

"It's the alcohol," she whispered. "Neither of us can drink because we're pregnant. It's not good for the baby."

Understanding dawned. "Sorry, I should have thought of that."

"It's okay."

He motioned to a waiter standing by the door and ordered sparkling mineral water for the women. Soon the first course was served and everyone started chatting.

When the meal was finished and they were waiting for dessert, Austin glanced over and saw Rebecca staring at her hand. Travis and Elizabeth were talking to each other in low tones.

"What is it?" he asked, searching her face.

"I'm in shock, I think." She smiled.

He noted the shadows under her eyes. "Have you been sleeping?"

"Not very well," she admitted. "There's been a lot to do to get ready for the wedding and everything. I was up late packing."

He frowned. "I could have done that for you today."

She surprised him by blushing. "No, I wanted everything done so that when we got back to, uh, your place my things would already be there. Silly, huh?"

She bit her lower lip and looked anxious, as if she expected him to be annoyed. "No. I understand." But in truth he didn't. She'd been the one keeping the whole thing a secret. Why was she bent on getting moved into his place so quickly? He'd half expected her to tell him she wouldn't be moving in for a few days. He would have let her stay with the children for about a week, then he would have moved her over himself. It looked like that wasn't going to be a problem.

He told himself it didn't matter what she thought of him or the wedding. The important thing was that they were married and his child wasn't going to be a bastard. It was enough. Or it should have been. But he couldn't shake the feeling of inadequacy. Damn. He was thirty-four years old, respected in his field, successful, kind to animals, relatively thoughtful. Women in town whispered about him. He should have been a catch. So why had Rebecca kept the wedding a secret? Why didn't she want anyone to come and witness the ceremony? Why had she refused a big party? And why did he have to care so damn much? He should be happy. He didn't want her getting too emotionally involved with him. She obviously wasn't. Everything was going his way. In fact, he told himself, it couldn't be better.

Austin was quiet all through dessert and their goodbyes to Travis and Elizabeth. Rebecca wondered what she'd said to upset him. She didn't think it was because she wouldn't drink the champagne. He wouldn't want her risking the baby's health. So what was it?

He held open the passenger door of the Mercedes. She'd had Mary drop her off that morning, so her car, or rather the home's car, was back where it belonged. She'd made arrangements to have her things moved over to Austin's during the ceremony. Everything was all set. She glanced down at her ring. She should be as happy as could be. So why did she feel like crying?

"In a few months, as soon as the children have settled into their new place, we'll move to the big house," Austin said as he fastened his seat belt. "There'll be more room for you and the child."

"Are you moving with us, or are you going to stay in the loft?"

He'd already placed the key in the ignition, but now he turned to look at her. "I'd planned to move with you. Would you rather that I didn't?"

She blinked to hold back the sudden burning in her eyes. They'd been married less than three hours and already they were talking like strangers. "No, of course not."

"Then why did you ask?"

"Because of the way you phrased your statement. You said there would be more room for me and the child. As if you weren't going to be there."

He raised his hand, as if he was going to touch her. She leaned closer, but then he lowered his arm to his side and rested his fingers on the edge of his seat.

"I'm committed to this marriage," he said, not meeting her gaze. "I'm going to do the best I can to be a good husband and father. If you'll let me know what you expect of me, I'll do my best to oblige."

Hardly a romantic declaration, she thought grimly. But this was Austin, and he'd never pretended to be marrying her for love.

"I don't really have any expectations," she said. Although a little hand-holding and touching would be nice. But she couldn't say that to him. Couldn't he just know what she was feeling?

He rested his left hand on the top of the steering wheel. It was close to seven in the evening, and the sun was still up. Light glinted off the gold band on his finger. He was her husband. She was supposed to be able to say anything to him. Unfortunately it wasn't going to be that easy.

"I've opened accounts for you at all the major stores in the area," he said. "I know you lost a lot of your things in the fire. Feel free to buy whatever you want. We now have a joint checking account. I have someone who comes in and does the cleaning and I think we should keep her. I don't like that car you drive. In the next day or so, I want to buy you a new one. Maybe a minivan. Let me know your schedule and we'll pick a time that's convenient."

He continued with his list, explaining about life insurance, medical insurance and stock options. She felt more like a newly hired employee than a wife.

"Austin, stop. Why are you telling me all this?"

Finally he looked at her. She tried to read the expression in his unfathomable gray eyes, but his feelings were too deeply buried. "We're married. You're my responsibility."

"You make me sound like a puppy rather than a woman. Or a life partner. I know these aren't the best of circumstances, but if we try, I think it can work. I like you. You've said you like me, too. Please don't destroy everything we've built so far by talking about checking accounts and insurance. Tell me you're excited about the baby. Tell me you're terrified of picking out china patterns and don't want to change your flatware. Give me a hint that this wedding isn't the worst thing that's ever happened to you.''

Before she could blink it back, a single tear rolled down her cheek. Austin sucked in his breath, then used his thumb to brush away the drop.

"Damn it, Rebecca, don't you dare cry. You're the one with the regrets, not me.''

"Regrets? What are you talking about?''

"Don't pretend. I know what you've been thinking. You're embarrassed by this whole thing. Frankly I'm surprised you agreed to marry me at all.''

He faced front and reached for the key. Before he could turn it, she grabbed his wrist. "Austin, wait. I'm not embarrassed to be marrying you. Why would you think that? I confess I'm a little apprehensive about making the marriage work, but that's about me. I'm not like those other women you've had. I'm not beautiful and smart and experienced. I don't know how to please a man or look good in an evening gown. I'm not who you would have chosen. I know that. But you agreed because of the baby. If anyone is embarrassed, it should be you.''

He leaned back in his seat. "So why didn't you want people to know about the pregnancy and the wedding?''

She mumbled her reply.

He turned sharply and grabbed her shoulders. "What did you say?''

She flicked her hair back behind her shoulders. The evening sun hit him directly on the side of his face, highlighting the black in his hair and reflecting off his earring. He'd shaved recently; she could tell by his smooth jaw. The ivory shirt and tie, the conservative cut of his suit, were all out of character for the Austin Lucas she knew. He'd done it for her, so she would be more comfortable. And then he'd thought she was embarrassed to be marrying him.

Shame washed over her, shame and a growing awareness of how she'd misjudged this man. She'd had a crush on him, tempted him into bed so that she could be rid of her virginity. Never once did she give a thought to what her action meant to him. She'd used him sexually, the way men have used women for centuries. That wasn't right. She'd taken away his choices, married him and given him nothing in return.

"Oh, Austin, I'm so sorry," she whispered, and threw herself in his arms.

He held her close. She squeezed her eyes shut and tried not to cry. After a moment she got her emotions under control, but she didn't pull back. She liked the feel of his hard chest against her breasts and the way his large hands held her securely against him. He murmured soft words of concern, promising he would make her world right. But his was the world that needed fixing.

"I wasn't ashamed of you," she said softly, inhaling the masculine scent of his body. "I was ashamed of myself. I couldn't bear to think that people were saying I'd trapped you. I was afraid you'd get so upset at the talk that you'd change your mind. I thought you wouldn't show up."

There. She'd said it. Admitted her ugly truth and exposed the blackness of her deed.

He cupped her face and eased her back until he could see her. "Is that all?"

"All? It's horrible. Slimy. You must be disgusted." She closed her eyes and waited for his anger.

"You can look," he said, his voice low and teasing.

She opened her eyes. He smiled.

"You're not angry."

"You're right. It's okay to be scared, Rebecca. I'm scared, too."

"I never would have thought that."

"I'm just a man. No more, no less."

A good man, but she knew better than to say that aloud. He would flinch and probably withdraw.

"Okay," she said. "Let's not mess up this way again. No more wondering what the other person is thinking. Next time, ask me. And I'll do the same. Deal?"

She held out her hand. He glanced at it. "Deal." But instead of shaking, he leaned over and kissed her. It was a brief brush of lips, nothing more. But she experienced a reaction clear down to her belly.

He straightened in his seat. "Let's go home."

Home. She leaned back and relaxed. Everything was going to work out. She smiled lazily, thinking of the coming night. It had been almost a month since they'd made love. Not a day had gone by without her thinking about it, about him and how he'd made her feel. She wanted to experience his lovemaking again, only this time she wanted to be more a part of what they were doing, rather than just lying there. She closed her eyes and tried to remember exactly what Austin had done to her body so she could do those things to him.

But the recent activity and sleepless nights caught up with her. She must have dozed because the next thing she knew, they were parked in front of the barn and Austin was opening her door.

"Wake up, sleepyhead," he said, reaching over to unfasten her seat belt.

"Did I fall asleep? I'm sorry."

"It's all right. You're tired. Can you get out of the car?"

"Of course I can. I'm not an invalid."

She swung her legs around and stood up. But before she could take a step, Austin leaned over and swept her up in his arms.

"Put me down," she demanded.

"No. You need to be in bed. You're exhausted."

"Oh, I'm not that tired," she said, quickly giving up the fight and snuggling close to him. She wrapped her arms around his neck as he entered the barn and started up the stairs.

She sighed. It was so romantic. He was carrying her over the threshold and to their bed. Her body began to heat up at the thought of making love with him. She eyed his tie and wondered if she could pull it free or if she was going to have to figure out the knot. She wove her fingers through his hair, loving the feel of the silky strands. Her forehead rested on his shoulder. She turned her head toward his neck, ready to press her lips to his skin, when he came to a stop.

"Here we are." He slowly allowed her legs to touch the floor.

When she was standing, she kept one arm around him and smiled. "I can't believe I'm here," she said, reaching for his suit jacket. "It's all been a blur, but I think I'll remember this part." She tugged at the lapels, pulling the fabric over his shoulders.

He stepped back. "Rebecca, no."

"What?"

He placed his hands on her shoulders and turned her to face the room. She hadn't been in the loft since that first night, but she remembered every square inch of his home.

There had been a change. At the far end of the loft a room had been closed off. She saw the tall walls and the open door. Through it she could see the foot of a bed. Her gaze flew to the king-size bed sitting where it had before. Two beds?

"Austin? What's going on?"

"I knew you'd want the privacy. Some space of your own."

She clutched her hands together in front of her waist. "Separate bedrooms?"

"Yes. With your pregnancy and all. I thought it would be best."

Best for whom? She took a step back and bumped into the railing. Grabbing the wooden support, she stared at the walls that enclosed her solitary space. He wanted them to sleep apart. All her dreams for a sexual relationship, all her hopes for the future, vanished in the blink of an eye. No, they didn't vanish. They'd never existed in the first place.

"This is what you want?" she asked.

When he didn't answer, she looked at him. He was staring past her, gazing at something she couldn't see. He twisted his wedding band around and around, as if it was uncomfortable. It probably was.

She'd been fooling herself. He'd never wanted a real marriage at all.

She took a deep breath, determined to make one more try. "Austin, I'm your wife."

"I know," he said, and started for the stairs. "I've thought this through. It's for the best. For both of us."

Chapter 10

Austin stood at the front window of the loft. From here he could see over the trees to the big house where the children were staying. He could see past that to the other side where a larger grove of trees separated his property from his nearest neighbor's. At night the stars glowed from the heavens and moonlight cast eerie shadows across the land. He knew. He'd spent each of the past seven nights staring out this window, listening to the silence and wondering how badly he'd messed everything up.

This morning was different. Voices filled the air. He drew his gaze from the horizon back down to the activity in front of the barn. Rebecca stood in front of the new Volvo station wagon he'd bought her two days before. Several volunteers were loading the vehicle under her careful supervision. At one point she turned toward the barn and glanced up. He knew she could see him standing in the window, but he didn't move back. Their eyes met. He wondered what she was thinking. She didn't smile or wave. She simply stared for a moment, then went back to what she was doing.

He hadn't seen her smile at him since the wedding. He had no one to blame but himself.

It would be easy enough to go downstairs and join in. Knowing Rebecca as he did, he was confident she wouldn't object. His helping might even go a long way to bridging the distance that had grown between them. If nothing else, she could use the help. The state had come through with the money to rebuild the children's home, but it would take a while to get the funding in place. In the meantime, the original lot had been cleared and a construction company had given them a break on the cost. Rebecca had met with the town council and together they had decided to earmark the annual Fourth of July carnival proceeds for the construction project. Austin had offered to pick up the tab until they received the state funding, but Rebecca had refused. He wondered if she would have agreed if he'd made the offer before the wedding. Before she'd seen that he'd arranged for them to sleep in separate rooms.

He continued to stare out the window. Rebecca was gesturing now, motioning to a box. A young man picked it up effortlessly and slipped it into the back of her station wagon. As she smiled her thanks, a shaft of sunlight caught her hair. The silky colors glowed brown, dark blond and red, rippling and changing with each movement of her head. Her skin had turned the color of honey. By the end of summer she would be brown, and there would be freckles on her nose. She would also be showing.

News of their marriage had swept through the small town of Glenwood. He'd deliberately avoided leaving his property for the past week. He'd known what everyone was saying. Rebecca had also stayed close, but he had a feeling it was more out of convenience rather than a fear of gossip. As innocent as she was, she wasn't expecting people to talk. He had to warn her before she left for the carnival.

Travis and Elizabeth had been discreet, only mentioning the wedding and not the pregnancy. Time enough for tongues to wag over that tidbit. He didn't care what people said about him; Rebecca was another matter. If she thought talk was rampant about their marriage, wait until people started counting backward from the baby's birth. He clenched his hands into fists and vowed to protect her. Then he released his fingers and called himself a fool.

Who was he kidding? The person he should protect Rebecca from was himself.

He'd hurt her by closing off a separate bedroom. He'd seen the flash of pain on her face when he'd first brought her here, and he'd heard it in her voice every day since. He'd hoped to do his best by her, but he might have known he would get it wrong. He'd never been around married people. He didn't know what being married meant. He only knew he had to keep Rebecca and the baby safe. If that meant making her unhappy, so be it.

Except he'd promised to be a good husband to her. He'd vowed to care for her for the rest of their lives. He hadn't even been able to accomplish that for a single day.

Maybe he should have paid more attention to the married couples he'd known when he was a kid. He frowned and raised his head to stare over the treetops. That wouldn't have helped, he reminded himself. He'd never had a close friend until Travis, and Travis's folks had been bitterly unhappy. Travis's father had made a habit of playing around, spending all his free time pursuing other women and ignoring his family. Not much of a role model there. Austin had no desire to be unfaithful to Rebecca. All he really wanted was to be with her in the most intimate of ways.

He turned slowly and glanced across the loft to the partitioned-off room. Maybe it had been a bad idea to build the second bedroom without asking her first. Given half a chance, he would jump at the opportunity to have her in his bed. But Rebecca was pregnant. A man was supposed to keep his animal nature to himself at times like these. It was hard enough being in the same house, hearing her footsteps, smelling the sweet scent of her body so close as she passed him in the kitchen. Having her in the same bed would be hell.

He massaged his temples. All this would have been easier if he hadn't seen the happiness in her eyes when he'd first carried her upstairs. She'd touched him and he'd thought he might explode right there. He'd wanted to take her to his bed, tell her that the separate room was for the baby. She would never have known it was a lie. But he couldn't. For once he was going to do the right thing and treat her as she deserved to be treated. It would be better for both of them.

So why did the right thing feel so wrong?

He turned back to the window, but everyone was gone. Then he heard the front door opening and the sound of footsteps on the stairs. Her tread was slow. Was it because she didn't want to face him? He was so damn confused about everything. He'd always known he didn't have a prayer of making a marriage work. That was why he'd always avoided commitment. He was bad at it. All he wanted was to make Rebecca happy. It had only been a week and they were both miserable. Would the kindest act be to let her go?

In his soul he knew the answer was yes, but his heart begged for mercy. Before he could make up his mind what to do, Rebecca reached the top of the stairs. She stepped onto the loft floor and crossed to where he stood by the window.

"The car is all loaded," she said, standing close enough to tempt, close enough to touch, but not touching. Did she torture him on purpose? He wanted to think she did. It would make it easier to dislike her. But he knew better. A kind and giving spirit governed her every action. If she thought her presence in his life caused him pain, she would leave him to the silence.

"Austin? What's wrong?"

He was surprised she knew to ask. Was she getting better at reading him, or was he getting worse at concealing his feelings?

He looked at her. She wore her hair loose. It fell down her back and moved in counterpoint to the graceful movements of her body. When most women would have worn shorts on such a warm summer's day, she was in a sundress with a full skirt. The peach material brought out the color in her eyes and cheeks. She wore something on her lashes and lips, but no other makeup. Her neck and wrists were bare, as were her hands, save for her wedding ring.

Without thinking he took her left hand in his. Slender fingers, strong yet feminine, curled around his. He studied the sparkle of the ring, liking the way it looked on her. As he'd wanted their first night together, he'd marked her as his. He'd claimed the woman, if not her body. He would make it be enough.

"What are you thinking about?" she asked.

He raised his gaze to hers. So many questions flashed through her eyes. He confused her. She tried to understand him and his moods. She tried so damn hard at everything. Had he even once made it easy?

"I was remembering our first night together."

"Why?"

He shrugged. "I was remembering how innocent you looked dripping on my floor and how I could read everything you were thinking."

She flushed and ducked her head. "You must have thought I was a real dweeb."

"I thought you were beautiful and very tempting."

"You regret that night, don't you?"

He released her hand and cupped her chin. Slowly he lifted her head until their eyes met. He owed her, so for once he would tell her the truth. "I regret the loss of your virginity and that I got you pregnant. I don't regret the baby."

"I don't understand."

"You should have saved yourself for someone you loved."

"You don't believe in love."

He smiled slightly. "You do."

"Okay. That sort of makes sense, but how can you be sorry you got me pregnant and not regret the baby?"

"I took away your choice, but the child is something special. I never thought I'd have that chance."

Her eyes misted over. He told himself it was an emotional reaction that had everything to do with hormones and nothing to do with him. He had a feeling he was lying, but he couldn't accept any other truth right now. He was already having enough trouble sleeping at night.

Her lips parted slightly. He could see her white teeth and the tip of her tongue. It would be so easy to bend forward and cover her mouth with his. Too easy. He drew back.

"You're leaving for the carnival?" he asked.

She nodded.

He folded his arms over his chest. "You need to be prepared for the talk."

"Oh. You mean people whispering that I trapped you into marriage? I probably deserve it."

He thought he'd taken care of her concerns about having "trapped" him, but obviously he hadn't. He wanted to assure her that was the last thing he was worried about. He couldn't. Then she would take heart and think there was a chance of making it work. She would only get hurt more. He had to keep her away from him for as long as possible. Better for her to leave because he was a heartless bastard than for her to stay and find out the truth. Her leaving then would destroy what was left of him.

"I doubt they'll have time to even think about that," he said, trying to keep his voice casual. "I have a certain reputation in town."

She smiled, some of the worry leaving her eyes. "I know."

"People are going to speculate about why I chose you."

"But I'm pregnant. Why else?"

"Travis and Elizabeth haven't told anyone. Unless you've been spreading the news, all anyone is going to have is news of the wedding. Nothing else. I just want you to be prepared for some unpleasant questions."

She glanced down at herself. After smoothing the front of her dress and brushing her hair off her shoulders, she looked up at him. Before he could step back, she closed the distance between them and touched his earring.

She was close enough that he could see the smoothness of her skin and feel her sweet breath on his face. Her smile made him want to pull her hard against him and hold her until the rest of the world faded like a bad memory.

"You mean they'll want to know why the town bad boy hooked up with innocent little Rebecca Chambers?"

"Exactly. Except it's Rebecca Lucas now."

"Is it?" she asked, her smile fading. "I suppose technically I *am* your wife." She dropped her hand and turned away. "All right, Austin. Thanks for the warning. I'll be on my guard against the gossip. I'd better leave. I'd hate the carnival to start without me."

"Rebecca, I'm sorry," he said, feeling her pain, but not knowing what to do about it. "I wish——"

"Don't," she said. When she reached the stairs, she looked at him. "I don't want to talk about it today. The sun is shining, the weather is warm. There's too much fun waiting to be had for us to talk about this now." She tilted her head slightly. "What are you going to do today?"

He stood stiffly, trying to act casual. He didn't want her to go, but he had no right to ask her to stay. "I have a couple of experiments I've been working on."

"Oh. All right. I'll probably be late." She hesitated, one foot on the stairs, the other on the hardwood floor. She opened her mouth and closed it, then muttered something that sounded surprisingly like "damn." Only Rebecca never swore.

"Do you want to come with me?" she asked quickly. "You don't have to, of course. I just thought it *is* the Fourth of July and I hate to think of you here by yourself. It's not just that. I'd like us to be together and——" She clamped her mouth shut. "Forget it. It was a dumb idea."

He shouldn't go. The more time he spent with her, the harder it was to turn away from her at night. The more they were together, the more he hurt her and the closer he came to his own self-destruction. Besides, he hated carnivals.

She started down the stairs. He tried to look away, but he could see the slump of her shoulders.

"Rebecca," he called before he could stop himself.

She paused. Before he could think of a nice way to say no, she held out her hand. She didn't speak; she didn't have to. The pull of her offer was as powerful as the tide. He moved toward her, a single wave being drawn away from the safety of the shore and back into the welcoming depths of the ocean.

It was just one day, he reminded himself. She *was* his wife. It was his duty to be with her. His acceptance had nothing to do with the warm feeling of contentment that began inside of him, growing large enough to start filling the black hole of his soul.

Rebecca waited while Austin dropped off the last of the supplies she'd brought. He wouldn't even let her carry the paper bag filled with napkins.

"I'm pregnant, not dying," she said, planting her hands on her hips and trying to glare at him. It didn't work. All he had to do was raise one eyebrow in that way of his and she melted like a snow cone in the early July heat.

"Stop arguing," he said pleasantly. "The quicker you leave me alone to finish this, the quicker I'll be done and we can go get some of the cotton candy you've been eyeing."

He picked up a heavy box containing canned goods for the cooking booth. His muscles flexed underneath his cream polo shirt. She watched the shifting in his arms and back, and felt herself grow weak at the knees. No matter how he'd rejected her, despite the long talks she'd had with herself as she'd lain alone in her solitary, cold bed, he got to her. He always had. She had a feeling he always would.

When the last box was on the counter of the booth, Austin turned to her. "Anything else?"

She shook her head. "We're done." She glanced at the workers inside, already starting on the chili. "I'll be back in a couple of hours to spell someone."

Mary glanced up, her gray hair curling around her face. "Don't worry about me. I plan to spend my day right here. I'm sure some of the youngsters would like a break. But first you go have some fun. You've been working too hard. Austin, I expect you to show your bride a good time."

Rebecca held her breath, worried he wouldn't appreciate the older woman's good-natured interference. He surprised her by smiling and tipping an imaginary hat. "Yes, ma'am. I'll do just that." He glanced at Rebecca. "All right, bride, where do you want to go first?"

"There," she said, pointing to the cotton-candy kiosk set up by the tallest of the roller coasters.

As they crossed over to the stand, he frowned slightly. "Are you sure it's safe for you to eat?"

"I'm fine," she said, taking her place in line. "I haven't had a moment's morning sickness. I feel great."

She had a few symptoms of pregnancy, but she didn't want to go into detail now. Her breasts seemed a little bigger to her, and they were tender. She got tired in the middle of the afternoon. Part of her wanted to share her small discoveries with him; part of her didn't want to find out he didn't care. It was easier to hold it all inside and wait until she knew for sure.

Around them crowds of people surged in different directions. Teenagers lined up for the wild rides. Adults tried their skills at several games. Pies, cakes, jams and preserves, along with photographs, quilts and farm animals were being judged in the two main pavilions. Tonight a local country band would provide entertainment. A dance floor was being set up around seven, with fireworks to follow at dusk.

How long would Austin want to stay? Would he dance with her in the moonlight or would he find an excuse to avoid her?

Before she could decide, the ten-year-old in front of her paid for his cotton candy and it was her turn. She pointed to one of the sugary treats. Before she could slip her purse off her shoulder to pay, Austin passed the man a bill.

"Thank you," she said, faintly surprised.

"My pleasure. Is that your lunch?"

"Yes, but I had an extra serving of vegetables last night, and I promise to behave at dinner." She pinched off a wisp of the pink floss and stuck it in her mouth. "So there."

He shook his head. "You're awful."

"I know. Isn't it great?"

Without thinking she swirled a thin length of the candy around her index finger and offered it to him. Their eyes met. Her good humor faded as she steeled herself to be rejected yet again.

His gray eyes darkened with an emotion she couldn't identify. For a moment she thought it might be pain, but that wasn't right. Why would her simple gesture hurt him? She studied the handsome lines of his face, the hollow cheeks, the firm jaw and straight mouth, and wondered why it had to be him. Why couldn't she have fallen for someone less complicated?

The sounds of the carnival—the screams from the people on the rides, the call of the barkers, the excited conversations disappeared. The world seemed to stop and tilt slightly until she wasn't sure she could maintain her balance. The wisp of cotton candy trembled in the warm afternoon breeze.

Then Austin leaned forward and took the treat in his mouth. His warm lips closed around her finger, his tongue swept her skin clean. Tingling rippled through her, from her hand clear down to that secret place that ached for him.

His eyes held her captive. Slowly, as if he feared she would run away, he raised his hand to her face. He cupped her chin, touching her reverently. She wanted to weep at his gentleness. He brushed her hair back, smoothing it over and over again. Her gaze dropped to his mouth and she silently begged him to kiss her.

Their bodies didn't move, yet they strained toward each other. Her heart ached. Sexually her body was ready to be taken by him, but even stronger than that was the flood of tenderness. She wanted to hold and be held, to protect and be protected, to find refuge and to provide a haven. She wanted him to let her in enough for her to fall in love with him.

Impulsively she decided to tell him.

"Austin, I—"

"Well, well. I'd heard the rumors, but I hadn't thought they could be true."

Austin dropped his arm to his side as if he'd been scalded. He turned toward the voice. Rebecca looked, as well, then wished she hadn't. It was the redhead. The one in the fancy car who had driven to Austin's house twice a week for months.

"Jasmine," he said. "What are you doing here?"

The woman smiled, revealing even, white teeth and not one wrinkle in her classically beautiful face. Rebecca stared at her perfectly made-up eyes, at the coral-colored lipstick, then lower at the knit shirt clinging to large, well-shaped breasts. Her confidence nose-dived into her shoes and whimpered.

"I'm doing my bit for the children's home." Jasmine turned

her attention to Rebecca. "This must be your lovely wife. Such a pleasure to meet you."

"Thanks," Rebecca mumbled, trying not to notice that the other woman's eyes were an enchanting color of green. Not boring brown, but green. Cat's eyes. Everything about Jasmine screamed sophistication, from her designer sandals to her tailored shorts. Rebecca tried not to remember she'd recently bought her sundress on sale for less than twenty dollars. Or the fact that her underwear was cotton. She told herself it didn't matter that her breasts were smaller than pumpkin seeds and that she was still holding a half-eaten stick of cotton candy.

She realized the other woman was staring pointedly at her left hand. "May I?" she asked.

Rebecca raised her fingers to chest level.

Jasmine studied the ring. "It's beautiful. Austin, you always had exquisite taste. I wish you both every happiness."

The words all sounded right, but Rebecca could see Jasmine staring at Austin as if she'd been without food for a week and he was her favorite dish.

"Thank you," Austin said. He glanced at Rebecca. "Shall we go?"

Her battered ego took solace from the fact that he didn't seem inclined to linger in the presence of his former lover. Maybe he was trying to avoid being tempted by what he could no longer have, she thought glumly.

She said goodbye and they left. Rebecca was proud of herself for not turning around to see if the other woman was watching them, and soon they were swallowed up by the crowd.

"It's over between us," Austin said, his low voice carrying to her, despite the cacophony around them.

She stumbled. As quickly as that? He'd never even given their marriage a chance. Her stomach lurched and she dropped the rest of the cotton candy into a nearby trash can. "If you say so."

Austin stopped walking and turned to her. "You sound as if you don't believe me. I assure you I took my wedding vows seriously. I have no intention of straying."

She exhaled a sigh of relief. "You're telling me it's over between you and Jasmine."

"Of course. What did you think?"

It was too silly to explain to him. Why had she been so quick to jump to conclusions? Because Austin wasn't acting like her husband. Had she been so different? she wondered suddenly. Had she acted like his wife?

"I appreciate your telling me that," she said. Maybe he was waiting for her to set the tone in their marriage. Before giving herself a chance to change her mind, she slipped an arm though his. "What do you want to do first?"

The sun beat down. It was already in the eighties. Despite that, she felt a chill as Austin stiffened. Would he pull back? She didn't want him to. Just as she was about to lose hope, he relaxed.

"How about checking out the pavilions? It'll be cooler inside."

She nodded. They walked across the carnival grounds, ducking around running children and talking about the fund-raiser.

One little boy barreled right into Austin's jean-clad legs. Austin grabbed his shoulder with his free hand. "Go a little slower, okay?"

The boy nodded, grinned, then took off, running just as hard as he had before. Austin shook his head. "Kids."

"Oh, I would guess you were just as much of a terror when you were a kid."

"Probably," he agreed. "I never spent a lot of time at places like this, but I would have found a way to get into trouble."

"Your mom didn't bring you to local fairs?" she asked.

He shook his head. He started to pull away from her. Without thinking, she grabbed his hand. "Austin, don't. We can talk about something else if you'd rather."

They'd reached the entrance to the first pavilion. There was a short line. When they paused to wait their turn, she thought he might tug away.

"Please," she whispered, knowing she was leaving herself open to heartbreak.

He shuddered and she wondered what he was thinking. Then

he slipped his fingers between hers and squeezed gently. "My mother couldn't be bothered taking me anywhere, except away from her," he said, not meeting her gaze. "It's not that it bothers me to talk about it so much as there's nothing to say about her. She spent her time looking for a rich man to support her. When it was going well, she left me alone. When it wasn't she used me to blackmail my father."

Rebecca could feel his pain. She wanted to say something comforting, but suspected he wouldn't accept it. Instead, she held on to his hand. "That would be hard for any kid to take. Do you ever see her?"

The line moved forward and they entered the building. It had a partition down the center, and both walls were covered with photographs. It was cooler inside, and people spoke with hushed voices.

"No," he said quietly. "After college I went to work for a research-and-development company and made my first big breakthrough with heat resistant material. I won an award, including a cash payment. There was a write-up in the paper and it got picked up by a wire service. About two weeks later my mother showed up at my door wanting her cut of the money."

The fingers gripping hers tightened. She could see the tension in his shoulders and back. His jaw thrust forward. His hurt and shame were as tangible as the building around them.

"It's the last time I ever saw her."

"I'm glad you threw her out," Rebecca said fiercely, knowing she would be happy to tell his mother what a horrible, evil person she was to have mistreated her child. How could anyone dare to wound a young boy, then have the nerve to approach the man and expect something for her abuse?

"I didn't send her away," he said, pulling his fingers free of Rebecca's. He tucked his hands into his pockets and rocked back on his heels. "I gave her the money."

He turned toward the closest photograph and stared as if the sunset on a farm was the most interesting picture he'd ever seen.

The empathetic side of her was almost overwhelmed by the waves of pain radiating out from him. He'd let his mother use him. Why? She closed her eyes. Because the small boy inside still needed a mother's love.

Oh, Austin, she broke you into so many pieces. Could he be mended? Was she strong enough to help? Was she strong enough to walk away? She didn't have either answer.

"It's getting late," he said, still studying the photograph. "We'd better get you back to the booth."

She nodded, unable to speak.

They didn't talk as they made their way through the crowds. The sun was hotter now. Rebecca felt perspiration on her back. She was grateful to duck under the awning around her booth. Mary was serving up chili. One of the teenage helpers smiled gratefully when offered a break.

"Don't work too hard," Austin said, his voice impersonal. They hadn't talked since his confession. Rebecca wanted to get through to him, but she didn't know the right words. She wasn't even sure there were any.

"Rebecca, look what I got!" David came running up, carrying a small red bear. "I won it at the ring toss. All by myself."

"Good for you." She bent over his prize. "It's wonderful. I've never won anything. You must be very talented." She brushed his hair out of his face. "Are you thirsty? There's soda in that cooler." She nodded toward the white box in the back. David left the bear in her care and ran off.

"How's he doing?" Austin asked.

"He's fine. I've spoken with the family lawyer, but he doesn't have any good news. David's relatives are talking about putting him up for adoption. Even with the promise of his inheritance, none of them want him." She shook her head. "I don't understand people sometimes. How can they be so awful?"

Austin surprised her by bending over the rope cordoning off the booth and kissing her fiercely on the mouth. "Don't ever stop expecting the best of people. Promise?"

She touched her hand to her lips. "Sure."

David reappeared with a soda. "Austin! I didn't know you were here, too. Did you see my bear?"

"It's great." He crouched down and smiled at the boy. "You want to go on a ride with me?"

The boy yelped with excitement. "Yeah! Wow! That's great. Rebecca, we're going on rides."

"I heard." She didn't dare look at Austin. Her eyes were misty, and she knew he would tell her to quit making him into a hero. He would remind her that he was just a bastard, not a nice guy at all.

"We'll be back in a couple of hours."

"Perfect," she said, watching them walk away.

"Rebecca, you're pretty enough to be a decoration, but we need another pair of hands here to serve the chili," Mary called.

Rebecca laughed, then reached for one of the big aprons lying across a table in the back of the booth. "I'm coming." Still watching David and Austin out of the corner of her eye, she made her way up to the front and started taking orders.

Two hours later, she was ready for a break. Mary, one of the few people who knew about her pregnancy, insisted she get off her feet.

"I'm too hot to protest," Rebecca said as she was ushered to a folding chair in the shade of an elm tree behind the booth. She'd barely taken her first sip from her glass of water when Austin and David came around the corner.

They were both laughing. David's action-figure T-shirt was definitely dirtier than she remembered. There was a new stain on the front that looked suspiciously like chocolate ice cream. Austin's eyes had lost their troubled expression. When the boy saw her and called out, Austin glanced in her direction. For once, his smile was easy and welcoming.

"Did you have fun?" she asked as David crawled into her lap.

"Yup. We went on a roller coaster and the Ferris wheel twice."

Austin dropped to the ground beside her chair and leaned against the trunk of the tree. "I'm glad I didn't eat more of your cotton candy. My stomach isn't that young anymore."

Rebecca leaned close to David and ruffled his hair. "How old is your stomach?"

The boy laughed at the question. His blue eyes crinkled with delight. "It's as old as me. Seven." He held up the appropriate number of fingers.

She smiled back and glanced at her husband. But Austin wasn't laughing. He was looking at her with the oddest expression. As if he saw something he wanted more than life itself, but couldn't have. For a second she thought he was aroused, but then she saw the bleakness in his eyes and the straight line of his mouth.

She wanted to ask what was wrong. He wouldn't tell her, though. He would deny there was a problem. What was it? Envy? She bit down on her lower lip. For what?

"My bear liked the rides, too," David said, holding up the small stuffed animal.

"Did he?" she asked, paying only half attention to the conversation.

David nodded. "He had fun today. Like me."

"Like you?" Rebecca cupped the boy's face in her hands. "I can tell you had fun. You have dirty cheeks and ice cream on your shirt." She dropped a kiss on his nose. David giggled.

She glanced at Austin. Unabashed longing swept across his face. For her? No. It wasn't like that.

Understanding dawned. To test her theory, she casually rested one hand on David's back and used the other to brush his hair out of his face. Austin looked away as if it had become too much to bear.

It was the touching that got to him, she thought sadly. Not the sexual contact between a man and a woman, but the loving contact between friends, between an adult and a child, between a mother and her son. She remembered all she knew of his early life and suspected no one had ever taken the time to hold him. He was hungry for physical human contact. Excitement gripped her. Had she just found the way to reach her husband?

"Rebecca!"

A familiar voice called her name. She looked up and saw Travis hurrying toward her. Elizabeth followed more slowly.

Rebecca set David on the ground and stood up. Travis was pale, his breathing rapid. "What's wrong?" she asked.

Elizabeth smiled. "My handsome prince is falling apart." She winced, then drew in a deep breath. "Finally, after being two weeks late, I think it's time."

"Oh, God, what can I do to help?" Rebecca asked.

Elizabeth took her husband's arm. "Would the two of you mind coming with us to the hospital? I think Travis is going to need someone to hold his hand."

Chapter 11

The waiting room at the hospital was painted a cheerful shade of yellow. Sofas and chairs lined the area. A TV blared from one corner. On a table sat a collection of parenting magazines.

Rebecca smiled as she watched Austin and Kyle pace the floor. Austin was as unreadable as ever, although she thought she saw tension in the set of his shoulders and the line of his mouth. Kyle didn't bother to hide his feelings. He was almost as pale as Travis had been when he'd gone in with Elizabeth.

When Rebecca had first moved to Glenwood, Travis had given her the rush. She'd been ready for a relationship, but within ten minutes of their first date they'd both admitted to a distinct lack of chemistry between them. Instead of lovers, they'd become close friends. She'd seen firsthand the trail of broken hearts left by the Haynes boys and their good buddy Austin. Funny to think such a short time later that both Travis and Austin were married men. At least in Travis's case, it had been a bond formed by love.

"Do you think she's going to be all right?" Kyle asked as he paced in front of her. He still wore his khaki deputy's uniform. His hair was rumpled from his constantly running his fingers through the curls.

"Elizabeth said she had Mandy in about eight hours with no trouble. A second child is supposed to be easier than the first. She'll be fine." She patted his arm.

He gave her an absent smile, then continued his path across the room and back. When Austin stalked by her, she stepped in front of him.

"How are you holding up?" she asked.

He shrugged. "Better than him," he said, jerking his thumb at Kyle. "I hope Jordan and Craig get here soon and calm him down. His brothers always did a better job of that than I could."

"So you're not worried at all?"

His gray eyes held hers. "About Elizabeth? No."

The unspoken comment was that he was worried about her. She bit back a smile, not ready to let him know that his concern pleased her. She glanced around the empty waiting room. It was time to test her theory about Austin's behavior earlier at the carnival. Did he secretly long for the comfort of a woman's touch? What if she'd misjudged the entire incident with David, and Austin turned away from her? She reminded herself that they were already sleeping in separate rooms. It couldn't get much worse.

"I'd like something to drink," she said, placing her fingertips on his forearm. "I saw a soda machine in the hallway. Will you please come with me?"

"Sure." He glanced at Kyle, still pacing. "Want something to drink?"

"Scotch?" the deputy asked hopefully.

"Sorry."

Kyle shook his head. "I'll just stay here in case there's any news."

Rebecca led the way to the double glass doors that opened onto the hallway. Even in the maternity ward, hospital smells overwhelmed everything. The combination of antiseptic and the lunch that had been served several hours before made her wrinkle her nose.

When they reached the soda machine, Austin fished several coins out of his pocket. He handed them to her. "Can you drink anything here?" he asked.

"Sure." She studied the displayed labels. "I have to avoid caffeine, but that's all." She dropped in the coins, then bent over and collected the cold can. When she handed Austin the remaining change, he chose a drink for himself, then they started back toward the waiting room.

A mother, her baby in her arms, was being wheeled down the hallway. Rebecca stepped to one side to let her pass. When Austin moved next to her, she took advantage of their closeness to take a small step back, bringing her shoulder in contact with his chest.

Instantly heat flared between them. She told herself to ignore her sexual urges. She was conducting an important emotional experiment.

After the woman had been wheeled past, Rebecca waited before moving. Austin didn't slide away. That was good. When she couldn't think of an excuse not to start walking, she kept her pace slow, making sure their arms brushed. At the entrance to the waiting room, Austin held the door open for her. She had to struggle to keep from grinning. He wasn't avoiding her, even though she'd spent the past fifteen minutes practically glued to his side. She dared to be hopeful.

Kyle looked up as they entered.

"Any news?" she asked.

He shook his head. "Do you really think Elizabeth is going to be okay? What if something happens to her? Jeez, Travis can't lose her now. He's the only one of us to find somebody worth keeping."

"Kyle, you're overreacting," Rebecca said. "Women have babies all the time. Elizabeth is young and healthy, and she's already had one child. There's no reason to be afraid."

The door opened and a strange man stumbled in. His pale features were drawn. He looked as if he hadn't slept or shaved in three days.

When he saw the other people in the room, he smiled weakly. "My wife and I just had a boy. Almost eight pounds."

He sank onto one of the chairs and shuddered. "Oh, God, I don't know how we got through it. The pain kept coming. I don't know how she stood it. I told her to scream, but she wouldn't. I tried to help. I tried to remind her about her breathing." He dropped his head into his hands. "It was horrible. I just wanted to run. It's not like in the movies, ya know? How can I ever face her again?"

Rebecca watched the rest of the color drain from Kyle's face. Even Austin looked a little shaken. She walked over to the man. "How's your wife now?"

"Fine." He looked up at her. His eyes were bloodshot. "Her folks are with her, and everyone is happy. Like it never happened. Not me. I'll carry this to my grave." He lurched to his feet. "I'd better go check on her." He glanced around at the three of them and smiled vaguely. "Good luck." The door swung shut behind him.

Kyle dropped onto the nearest chair. "Elizabeth is going to die."

"No, she's not," Rebecca said briskly. "Men. You're less than useless. Try to keep a positive outlook, Kyle. If something was wrong, we'd have been told."

"If there was time," he said morosely.

She crossed to Austin and smiled up at him. "I give up."

Austin didn't look much better than Kyle. "Aren't you worried?"

"A little," she said. "But childbirth is a normal part of a woman's life. Elizabeth will be fine."

Before he could answer, she wrapped her arms around his waist and leaned against him. She forced herself to relax as she waited to be pushed away. Austin stood immobile for so long she thought he might not even be aware of what she was doing. Then he brought his arms up and encircled her body, holding her close. She breathed a sigh of contentment. Looks like her idea had been dead-on. He needed the touching he'd been deprived of so many years before. He needed to know he was loved, not just desired.

"I didn't mean about Elizabeth," he said, resting his chin

on her head. "Are you scared for yourself? When it's your time?"

"I try not to think about it," she admitted. "Sometimes it's frightening to think about going through labor. I don't deal all that well with pain. Then I think about having a baby, and I know it will be worth it in the end. Birth is a natural part of the cycle of nature. I want children, and this is how I'm going to get them."

"I wouldn't want anything to happen to you."

Her heart fluttered. That statement was the closest Austin had ever come to admitting he cared.

"I feel responsible for the pregnancy," he continued. "Bad enough that your life has been turned around without anything else making it worse."

Okay, so that wasn't exactly the romantic declaration she'd been hoping for, but it was enough.

The door behind them opened. They both turned and saw Travis come in. He was still dressed in green scrubs. The color had returned to his face, and he was grinning like a fool.

Rebecca smiled at him. "Well?"

His gaze swept the room. "Where are my other brothers? Or couldn't they get away?"

"Right behind you," came the gruff response. "Nice of you to wait until we got here."

Jordan and Craig entered the waiting room. Craig, a cop in Sacramento, was still in uniform. Jordan, the black sheep and only fire fighter in four generations of policemen, was wearing jeans and a T-shirt.

Travis turned and held out his arms. The two tall men moved into his embrace. Kyle crossed the room to be included. The four Haynes brothers clung to each other, communicating silently what they could not put into words. Rebecca felt a lump forming in her throat. When she had her child, her sisters would come up to be with her, as would her parents. The warmth and support of her family would allow her to get through whatever she had to.

She turned to Austin, ready to share the moment. He stood stiffly, his hands balled into fists at his sides. The stark pain was back in his eyes. His expression of longing tore at her. In that instant, when she saw down into the empty, hungry part of his soul, she realized he'd spent his entire life on the outside looking in. Although he'd made friends with Travis and his brothers, not once had he been pulled inside the circle of closeness.

Slowly, cautiously, so as not to startle him, she placed her hand on his back. He relaxed slightly, but didn't acknowledge her presence. Still, it was enough that she could be with him and that she knew the truth about him. Tonight she would take the next step in her campaign.

Travis looked up and saw Austin standing beside her. He broke free of his brothers and walked over. He held out his right hand. When Austin took it, Travis shook once, then jerked him into his embrace. Rebecca had to swallow back her tears.

"You never told us, Travis," she said, sniffing. "What did you have?"

He released Austin and grinned at Rebecca. Bending down, he kissed her on both cheeks. "A girl."

"What?" Craig stared at his brother. "Did you say a girl?"

Kyle raised his eyebrows and placed his hands on his hips. "That's not possible. There hasn't been a girl born into this family in four generations."

"There is now," Travis said, grinning like a proud papa. "She's as beautiful as her mother."

Craig shook his head. "A girl. I have three boys. Dad had four boys. He's one of six boys. So how did you get a girl?"

Travis puffed out his chest. "Just lucky, I guess."

"I think it's because you were in love," Rebecca said.

Craig stared at her as if she'd grown another head. Kyle laughed out loud. Only Jordan didn't smile. "I think she's right," he said.

While all the Haynes brothers looked very similar with their dark, curly hair and handsome features, Jordan was the loner. As Rebecca met his gaze, she realized he'd always been the one most like Austin. Although Travis was her husband's closest friend, Jordan shared his inclination to stand outside the circle and look in. He was the quiet one, the rebel the other brothers never ceased teasing about becoming a fire fighter, instead of a cop.

The other brothers gathered around Travis and started slapping him on the back. She looked up at Austin. "Maybe we should go look at the baby."

He nodded and placed his hand on the small of her back. Before they could leave, Jordan stopped them. "I never got to congratulate you," he said, looking at Austin. "You got lucky. Don't let her get away."

"I won't," Austin answered.

Rebecca wanted to believe his comment meant something, but she was sure he was just being polite. Then Jordan turned to her. "I hope you're happy," he said, his tone sincere. Then he touched her face with his fingers and bent to kiss her. The brush of his lips was quick and warm, and overwhelmingly sad. In that split second of connection, she felt his emptiness. Startled, she tried to read his expression. Like Austin, Jordan Haynes had learned to hide what he was thinking.

"Maybe you should find someone of your own," she said, drawing her eyebrows together.

"Unlikely," he replied, and walked back to his brothers.

She stared after him. What *was* Jordan's story? He was the best-looking of the brothers and all of them were easy on the eye. If the stories were true, he'd always been the quiet one. What had happened to make him withdraw?

As they approached the nursery, she shook off thoughts of Jordan. As much as she liked all the Haynes brothers, right now her husband required her full attention.

They stopped in front of the glass wall separating the nursery from the hallway. "They're so small," she said. A black-haired infant directly in front of them waved a fist in the air and made sucking motions.

"Oh, my." Her breath caught in her throat.

Back in the waiting room, with Kyle and Austin so nervous, she'd been able to handle the thought of having a baby. She wasn't showing, she didn't feel sick, and she'd only missed one period. Although she knew in her head she was pregnant, she didn't really feel any different. Even the conversation about going through labor hadn't affected her.

But now, staring at these tiny infants, she felt the heavy responsibility settle on her shoulders. This wasn't an intellectual discussion about some event far off in the future. This was real. She was actually going to have a baby.

A nurse walked into the nursery. "Which one would you like to see?" she asked.

"Baby Haynes," Rebecca said. "She was just born."

"Let me see if she's cleaned up." The nurse disappeared into a back room. Seconds later she returned, a tiny child nestled in her arms. She moved to the glass partition and brushed the pink-and-ivory blanket away from the baby's face.

The little girl, so small and red-faced, opened her big eyes and blinked fuzzily. Her mouth was the shape of a tiny rosebud. Even with her blotchy skin and wisps of light brown hair, she was beautiful.

"Oh, Austin, isn't she wonderful?"

When he didn't answer, Rebecca glanced at him. He was staring at the infant as if she was the most precious thing he'd ever seen. Rebecca felt her eyes start to burn. She blinked to hold back the tears. Then Austin reached for her hand. His fingers slipped between hers and he squeezed.

Together they watched the newborn snuggle deeper into the blankets and fall asleep. Rebecca didn't bother to brush away the tears, not even when Austin put his arm around her and pulled her close. When his free hand touched her still-flat belly, she smiled with contentment. They were going to have a child. Pray God they found their way together and were able to give their baby the warm, loving home every child deserved.

Austin picked up the television remote control and started hunting through the channels. From his place on the sofa he could see Rebecca cooking in the kitchen. After they'd left the hospital, they'd talked about going back to the carnival, but Rebecca had admitted to being tired. He certainly didn't need to spend any more time in the crowds, avoiding gossip and old lovers. So they'd come home.

The news show couldn't hold his interest. He glanced up and watched his wife move from the stove to the counter and back. His wife. He'd never planned to say those words. He'd never thought he would get involved, get married or have a child. It had happened so quickly. He hadn't lied that morning when he'd told Rebecca that while he might regret getting her pregnant, he didn't regret the child.

But it scared the hell out of him. He grimaced, remembering the man who had come into the waiting area and talked about the torture his wife had gone through to have their child. He could still see the horror in his eyes and hear the fear in his voice.

Austin hit the remote again and switched from the news to a baseball game. As much as he wanted a child, he would give his life to keep anything from happening to Rebecca. He couldn't bear knowing he'd hurt her by their living arrangements; he would never survive if he knew the pregnancy would do her harm.

They were going to have a child. He leaned back on the sofa and tried to absorb the words. They'd had little meaning until he'd seen Travis's daughter. She'd been so tiny. How did anyone take care of something that small? How was he supposed to know what a baby needed or wanted?

"It'll be about ten more minutes until dinner," Rebecca called.

"Fine. Do you want me to set the table?"

She looked up and smiled. "Already done."

She'd taken her shoes off when they'd come upstairs. Her hair was pulled back in a loose braid, with a few wisps floating around her face. Her dark eyes flared with life and contentment. From the first moment he'd seen her, he'd thought she was beautiful inside and out. Time had convinced him his initial assessment was correct. Rebecca was one of those rare souls who truly believed there was good in the world. She didn't use sarcasm in her speech. She thought the best of everyone until proved otherwise, sometimes even after seeing proof that person had no good side.

God knows why, but she thought he was worth saving. It

didn't matter what he told her about his past or how much he unintentionally hurt her. She continued to believe he had a heart of gold. Today he'd seen that damn light back in her eyes when he'd taken David on a few rides. Why did she have to make a big deal about it? The kid had been alone. Anyone would have done the same thing. Besides, he'd had time to kill until Rebecca was done with her volunteering.

But she didn't see it that way at all. She'd looked up at him, her eyes glowing with pride, her heart on her sleeve. He'd felt like slime. The sharp pain in his chest had been one part joy, two parts fear. Because it was too easy. It was just a matter of time until this whole thing blew up in his face. The second he started to need her and depend on her, he would lose her.

The problem was, he admitted to himself, it was already too late. Even though they slept apart, he couldn't imagine the place without her. The whisper of her perfume kept him awake long after she'd fallen asleep. The sound of her laughter echoed in his lab, taunting him throughout the day. Needing her would make him vulnerable. Not needing her would snuff out the light in her eyes.

With a certainty that crawled over him like the cool, smooth belly of a snake, he knew he had to let her go. Let her go, or hold on for all he was worth. And he couldn't do that. Ever. Holding on, caring, meant exposing himself. Once his dark secret came to light, he would crumple and blow away on the wind. Then she would know the truth. That inside there was nothing worth loving. The black hole of his soul sucked in all the light and let none escape.

But his arms ached to hold her close. Not just to make love, but to be near her, touching her, being touched by her. All afternoon she'd been next to him, brushing against his body, resting her hand on his arm. Little touches. They'd been a balm to his wounds. He'd horded the memories, storing them to feed on in the long winter to come.

He would let her go because it was the ultimate act of kindness. To bind her to him was unconscionable. A woman like her shouldn't be tied to a bastard like himself.

She hummed under her breath. The sweet sound called to

him. He glanced at her face, at her slender body, at her still-flat stomach, and knew he had to let her go before it was too late. Once their child was born, he would never be able to survive losing her.

His gaze returned to her face. Their eyes met. Rebecca studied him as if she knew exactly what he'd been thinking and didn't like it one bit. Before he could turn away, she slid the pan off the flame, turned off the stove and walked over to him.

"I don't think so," she said.

"What are you talking about?"

"Whatever you're planning. You've already made enough rules without asking for my input. I suppose it's my own fault for letting you. I should have spoken up right away. After all, we're partners in this marriage. Don't you agree, Austin?"

There was a light in her eyes he'd never seen before. The strength he'd always admired seemed to steel her spine as she got closer.

"Yeah, right," he mumbled, not sure what she was talking about. He reached for the remote and punched off the TV.

"They've been your rules, put in place for your convenience. That's about to change." She knelt on the soft next to him, then slid one knee over his thighs so that she was straddling him. Raising her hands high, she unfastened her braid. When her hair was loose, she brought her forehead down to touch his. The dark, curly strands provided a curtain of privacy.

"It's time for new rules. *My* rules." She shifted her weight from knee to knee, then sank onto his lap. Her panties rested against his crotch, her hands touched his shoulders. "Rule number one. More touching." She pressed her breasts against his chest. "Lots more touching."

He told himself to pull away. He knew this was a mistake. One of them was bound to get hurt. But he couldn't move. Her slim arms were like bands of steel. Or maybe he just wanted them to be. Maybe he was tired of pushing her away and hiding from the things she made him feel.

She bent closer and brushed his lips with hers. Instantly fire flared between them. Heat rolled through his body, settling in his groin. By the time she'd leaned forward and nibbled on his ear, he was already hard.

"Oh, Austin, I'm your wife," she whispered, dragging her mouth back to his. "Don't keep shutting me out."

The second kiss wasn't quite as fleeting. She pressed against him, moving slightly. The soft pressure taunted him. Of their own accord, his hands slid up her calves to her thighs. He slipped under her full skirt and touched her warm, bare skin. She shivered against him.

"Don't resist me," she said softly, then swept her tongue across his lips.

He moaned low in his throat. His mouth opened. Slowly, so slowly he thought he might go mad, she pushed her tongue inside. Tentatively tasting, savoring each moment as if it was precious.

He brought his hands up her legs, feeling her muscles tense and release as he held her hips, then slipped back to cup her rear.

She wrapped her arms around his neck and breathed his name, then angled her head and plunged into his mouth again. Her kiss changed from searching to demanding. When he responded, she bit down lightly.

"Stop being a jerk," she said, pulling back and glaring at him. "I mean it. We didn't get married under the best of circumstances. I'll admit that. But so what? We can still make it work between us. But we both have to try." Her brown eyes searched his. "I can't do it by myself. You have to let me in. Just a little. I know you don't want to expose your feelings. That's okay. But you have to give me something to work with."

His hands stilled on her body. "I don't know if I can."

"Try. Today at the hospital when we saw Elizabeth and Travis's baby, I knew we weren't pretending anymore. This is very real. We have to be ready to provide a home for our child."

Or end it now, he thought grimly, knowing he didn't have a hope in hell of letting her walk out that door tonight. It wasn't just because he was hard and ready and the dampness of her panties told him she was just as willing. It was because if he pushed her away he would hurt her, and right now he wasn't strong enough to face that. And, a small voice reminded him, if he sent her away, there would be no one to hold him and care for him....

"I know you have secrets," she said. He stared at her, wondering when she'd learned to read his mind. She went on as if she hadn't noticed. "You don't have to share them with me. What's more important is that we make this marriage work. That we respect each other. That we work on building a bond between us."

He touched her face, then ran his fingers through her long hair. The bond she spoke about was already in place. He could feel the silken ties wrapping around his heart and squeezing. She didn't know what she was asking. It was too late. It had been too late for years. Didn't she know that everything he loved or tried to love had been destroyed?

He'd desperately loved his mother and she'd returned those feelings with abandonment and betrayal. He'd wanted to know his father, but the old man had threatened to put him in prison if he ever approached him again. Even when he was just fifteen and he'd loved this town and his friends more than anything in his life, he'd managed to screw it all up by stealing a car. Just because he knew it wasn't going to last. Rather than wait for the pain, he'd created it himself so he could meet it on his own terms.

He didn't want to mess up with Rebecca, but it was inevitable. Somehow, sometime, he would say the unforgivable, lash out in fear and destroy the bond she sought to weave between them.

"Austin," she said, cupping his face in her hands, "it's not supposed to hurt that much. I'm sorry."

"It doesn't matter."

"Of course it does. You matter to me. Very much." She traced his nose, his mouth, then the line of his jaw. Last of all, she touched his earring and smiled. The tenderness in her gaze made him flinch. "I don't need you to love me back," she said softly. "Just let me in enough to love you."

Desire to believe battled with panic and fear. Panic and fear won. He gripped her waist and lifted her away from him. When he was free, he sprang to his feet and retreated to the far side of the room.

"Don't," he said hoarsely. "Don't love me." His muscles were tight, his arms rigid at his sides. His chest tightened and it was hard to breathe. "I'll save you the effort of even trying. It won't work, you know. I'm not worth the trouble. Never have been. Now get the hell out of here."

Chapter 12

Rebecca rose to her feet slowly, fearful that if she moved too quickly he would bolt. He stood alone on the far side of the room, fighting his feelings. Their eyes met. His anguish was so deep, so gut wrenching, she thought she might break in two just watching him. She raised her hand, as if she could touch him from across the distance of the room.

"No," he growled, and turned away.

He stared out the window at the twilight as if it held the answers to his suffering. He stood in the same place he did each time she left the loft. He always watched her go. Sometimes, when she reached the grove of trees that separated the barn and garage from the main house, she turned back and saw him staring down at her. The sadness in his expression was what had made her come back night after night, even knowing he had shut her out of his bed and his heart.

"I'm not worth the trouble," he said.

He'd spoken the words with the certainty of someone who had heard them a thousand times before. No doubt he had his mother to thank for that. A woman who would dump her child on relatives, then abandon him in a children's home, would easily express her displeasure by telling her son he wasn't worth the trouble.

Often during the busy workday at the home, harried adults would discuss whether or not a child was worth saving. Should they bother to solicit for adoption, knowing most couples wouldn't want to take on that kind of responsibility? She constantly warned her staff that the children overheard more than everyone thought, that they remembered and passed on the bitter judgments. How many times had Austin heard himself discussed? She knew enough about his past to guess the phrases they would have used. Troublemaker. Bully. Antisocial. Unredeemable.

Words tossed around by professionals who sometimes forgot words could be the harshest blows of all. Like the children now in her care, he had been cast aside, unwanted.

He'd proved them all wrong. His accomplishments and generous spirit had long since convinced her of that. He'd fought his way out, forged a new path and stood as a testament to the power of determination. Despite the odds against him, despite his lack of emotional support, despite the deepest, most tragic scar of all. The belief that he wasn't worth the trouble.

She studied the breadth of his shoulders, the strong musculature of his back. Jeans hugged narrow hips and outlined powerful thighs. He wasn't a child anymore. He'd long ago left that part of him behind. He was a man, with a man's sensibilities. She'd been a fool to think she could heal him with a couple of pats on the arm. She might never be able to heal him.

But he was her husband; she had to try.

She'd asked him to open up enough to let her love him. As with the children she provided for, she couldn't make him an empty promise. Not if she wanted him to learn to trust her. She would only get one chance, if that. She couldn't make a mistake.

She shook her head at her earlier belief that she'd found her way in by figuring out he hungered for physical contact. So what? Of course he did. Most victims of abuse did. It wasn't the key; it was a symptom. She would have to risk everything to get through to him.

She studied the set of his head, so proud. Her gaze dropped to her left hand and the diamond ring that proclaimed her as his wife. From the very first moment she'd stood dripping on Austin's garage floor several weeks ago, he'd come through for her. Offering her refuge from the storm, giving his house to the children, warning her away from him, even when she'd wanted nothing more than to have him make love to her.

Later, when he'd given the playground equipment to the children and then married her because she was pregnant, he'd been supportive, giving, generous and kind. He was her husband. She hoped she would be able to give back as much to him.

She took a step closer to him. He stiffened, but didn't move. Another step, then another, until she stood directly behind him. Not touching, not doing anything to send him running, she breathed in the scent of him and searched for the right words.

"I still remember the first time we met," she said softly. "I don't remember anything about what committee meeting it was, but I can see the room." She closed her eyes. "You were wearing a white shirt, rolled up to your elbows, jeans and boots. I was new in town. I walked in and you were the first person I saw. I couldn't move. I couldn't even breathe. When the lady at the desk asked me my name, I couldn't answer her. I felt like I was thirteen and meeting a rock star."

She opened her eyes and stared at the weave of his polo shirt. In front of him through the window, she could see the darkening sky. There was a light on in the living area and an overhead lamp on in the kitchen, but their illumination didn't reach as far as the window. Shadows crept in around them, cocooning them in the protective cloak of night.

"You wore an earring," she continued, smiling at the memory. "I'd never known a man who wore an earring before. You were forbidding and dangerous, and I couldn't stop thinking about you. That night I don't think I slept at all, remembering the meeting. Hearing your voice in my head gave me the shivers."

She drew in a deep breath. His silence unnerved her. She wanted to poke him in the side and make sure he was awake. She smiled slightly. Of course he was awake. But couldn't he say something and make this a little easier?

"You made me feel alive inside," she went on, "as if I'd been missing out on the best part of life and suddenly it was available to me." She paused to collect her thoughts. Now came the hard part. "The first time I met Wayne, I knew he was the man I was going to marry. There was no flash of lightning, no sense of danger, just a rightness, as if I'd met the other half of myself." Interesting how both men had provided her with a sense of completion. She'd never thought of that before.

Despite her declaration, Austin didn't move. She said, "I was with a friend of mine at a pep rally. We were both freshmen. My friend was this skinny little guy, one of those nerdy science types who was always getting beaten up. That day was no exception. Two tough guys grabbed him. I was screaming for someone to help, and then there he was. Wayne waded into the trouble, punched out both the bullies and rescued my friend."

Austin turned and looked at her. In the darkness, she couldn't read the expression in his eyes. "A real hero," he said, his voice cold.

Then she remembered how he'd told her about his first meeting with Travis. How he'd been the bully, picking on everyone. The fights covered the pain, she thought with a flash of insight. She should have seen that before. It made perfect sense.

They were standing so close his breath fanned her face. If she stood on tiptoe she could kiss him. It would be a mistake to do that now, she told herself. He wasn't ready. If the truth be told neither was she.

"He was a hero to me," she said softly. "When he'd done away with the other two guys, we introduced ourselves. He offered to walk me to my next class, and that was it. From that moment on, we were together."

"A touching story. Thanks for telling me."

She ignored his sarcasm. "I have a point here. Marrying

Wayne was logical. There was never another choice. We dated, we fell in love, we got engaged. There weren't any tests along the way. The only fight we ever had was about me wanting to save myself for marriage and wanting to put off the wedding until I had my master's degree. Being a normal male in his twenties, Wayne was frustrated by my stubbornness.'' She shrugged, suddenly embarrassed to be discussing something so intimate.

Despite the darkness she stared into his eyes, hoping to see a glimmer of what he was thinking. His gray irises gave nothing away. Was he bored, angry, hurt—what? She couldn't tell.

"Yes, well, after the accident everything changed."

"You've told me this part, Rebecca. You wanted to get married. He didn't. He died hating you. So what?"

She told herself he was being cruel on purpose. It didn't help. Rather than let him see he'd gotten to her, she lowered her gaze. Her eyes widened. His hands hung at his side, balled into tight fists. She could see the strain around his knuckles. He wasn't quite as disinterested as he wanted her to believe. The small sign gave her hope.

"The 'so what' is that I didn't try hard enough. What I realized later was that I should have forced the issue of marriage. I believe Wayne wanted me to prove that I loved him by making the arrangements, anyway, and risking his rejection. I never did."

She placed her palm on his chest, in the center, close to his heart. He didn't move away. The steady thudding gave her courage. "I'll always care about Wayne—he was my first love. I'll carry those feelings with me always. I'll also always know that I failed him in the end. Not because I stayed a virgin. That was my choice. If I'd known what would happen, of course I would have wanted us to make love. But I couldn't know that ahead of time. Given the same set of circumstances, I still would have wanted to save myself for the marriage bed."

"You belong in a different time, Rebecca Chambers," Austin said gruffly. "You're out of step with the rest of the world."

"I don't think so. And it's Rebecca Lucas, Austin. I'm your wife." He didn't answer so she went on, "All my choices have been easy ones. I've never had to look inside myself and search out the difficult solutions. Until you. I never believed I was very strong. The fire taught me differently. I survived that. I took care of the children. I'm not dismissing the help I was given, but I was the one responsible and I did it.''

He swore under his breath, then reached up and placed his hand on the side of her neck. ''You've always been pure steel. I've known that from the start.''

''That sounds like the beginning of a goodbye.'' When he started to speak, she touched a finger to his mouth. ''No. Not yet. I'm not done. I went into this relationship with my eyes open. I knew exactly who and what you were that first day I came here, dripping on your floor.''

He jerked his hand away, as if her gentleness burned him. ''You never knew. You still don't know. You see what you want to see, not the truth.''

''How do we know you're not the one with the cloudy vision?''

Before he could speak the sky behind him burst into a thousand sparks of color. Seconds later, a muffled *boom* shook the building. He turned, pulling her with him, so they both faced out the window.

Fireworks from the main park in town were clearly visible above the trees. Reds, greens, blues and whites exploded, washing away the brilliance of the stars. Their beauty hurt her eyes.

''This is what you see,'' he said, pointing to the display. ''This is what you imagine me to be. You're wrong.'' There was a moment of calm before the show continued. He gestured to the black, smoky night. ''This is reality, Rebecca. There's no magic, nothing noble here. Just the absence of light.''

''Oh, please.'' She moved in front of him and grabbed his shirtfront. ''I came into this fully aware of what I was doing. I chose to stay here and invite you into my bed. I wanted to be here, with you. I still want to be with you. You didn't force me or coerce me. When I found out I was pregnant, I chose to marry you. I *want* to be your wife.'' She wished she were big enough to shake him, but that wasn't possible. She settled for wrinkling his shirt. ''I'm making a permanent commitment to you. I'm willing to work through all the hard stuff, the boring parts, the past, the future and everything in between. I know you think you're not worth the trouble. You're wrong. You are. Let me inside, Austin. Trust me so I can learn to love you. Let me give you what you've always wanted."

He started to back away. The fireworks cast colored shadows on his face, making him seem otherworldly, as if he really were the devil. She hung on tighter.

"No!" she cried. "I won't lose you. Not now. Trust me, please. Just a little. You're a good and decent man. Kind, generous, sensitive. Even loving, if you'd give yourself a chance."

His eyes bore into hers. Silence crackled around them, broken only by the booms of the fireworks. He took her hands in his and pulled them from his shirt.

"You lead with your chin," he said. "It's a good way to get it busted."

"You'd never hit a woman," she said confidently.

"It's a metaphor."

"To hell with metaphors."

He raised his eyebrows. "What did you say?"

"Oh, Austin, I'm not interested in metaphors and analogies anymore. Let's just deal with us. Can you trust me even a little?"

He didn't even pause before answering. "No."

She felt as if he'd slapped her, but she plunged on. She'd made her commitment; there was no turning back. "I'll make you trust me. I'll prove myself a thousand times if necessary. I'm not going to leave you or hurt you or betray you. I'm going to be here for the next fifty years. Maybe longer if I keep my looks."

He smiled faintly. "You will."

"Believe me."

The smile faded. "I can't."

"Then believe this."

She rested one hand on his shoulder and reached the other to the back of his neck, pulling him down toward her. She raised herself up to kiss him. When he would have resisted, she breathed his name.

He relaxed enough to let her kiss him, but he didn't respond. His mouth stayed closed, his lips didn't move and his arms hung at his sides.

She exhaled her frustration. "Just once give in, would you? Why do you have to be so stubborn?" She tried to think of a way to get through to him. Something deep inside her whispered that if she could get back into his bed, she would have a better chance of making things work. Of course there was a chance the voice doing the whispering belonged to the parts of her he'd awakened with his masterful touch. Which meant her desire was more selfish than she liked.

She glared up at him, loving the way the evening stubble shadowed the lines of his jaw, causing him to look even more forbidding. "Why do you have to make everything so difficult?" she asked in frustration. "I'm already pregnant. What's the worst that could happen now?"

The worst was that he would start to believe, Austin thought, fighting against the will of his body and his soul. Only his mind stood firmly on the other side, watching as if from a distance. The cold logic that made him successful in his chosen field reminded him that his relationship with Rebecca was doomed to failure. By keeping his distance as much as possible, he would minimize the risk.

But she wouldn't want to hear that. Not from him, not now. "You'll be the death of me, Rebecca," he said.

"No." Her smile was sweet and pure. "I'll be your salvation."

"I'm long past saving. If you had any sense, you would have already figured that out."

She opened her mouth to protest. He didn't let her. Before she could make a sound, he raised his hands to her hair and slid his fingers through the silky strands. Gently he tilted her head toward him. A brilliant rocket burst in the sky, showering them with red light, turning her eyes the color of velvet and her skin the sweetest cream.

He lowered his head until his mouth was almost touching hers. Their breaths mingled. "Why do you haunt me?"

"Because I'm your destiny, Austin Lucas. You can't escape me."

She was right, he thought sadly. She was his destiny, but he wasn't hers. She belonged to a gentle man, someone who would cherish her innocence and giving spirit. Not Wayne, not even himself. Somewhere a stranger waited to claim his lady-love. But not tonight, he told himself fiercely. Tonight she was his.

He tugged on her hair, pulling her head back farther, exposing her neck. Bending over her, he kissed the skin beneath her ear, then moved lower to the hollow of her throat. He tasted her, licking and nibbling, enjoying her soft moans of pleasure. She trembled in his embrace and he was lost.

The madness overtook him, wiping out all thoughts of walking away. She clutched at his shoulders and chest, the diamonds in her ring catching the faint light from the kitchen and living room. The flash of brilliance reminded him that she was his wife. He had to claim her or die.

Releasing her hair, he slipped one arm under her legs and the other under her back. He swept her up in his arms simply because he could. She clung to him, burying her face in his shoulder. With quick kisses she traced the line of his collar, then tasted the place where his stubble gave way to smooth skin. She whispered his name, taming him for the moment, and exhaled her satisfaction.

As he crossed the living room, he glanced into her face. Her eyes were clear and trusting. She didn't fear him or their joining. Had he been a different kind of man, he might have read the flickering light as affection, perhaps even love, but he didn't want to know that. It would only make things more difficult later. He would take her to his bed, mark her, claim her, because she wanted him. That desire had taken away his ability to choose. He would pay any price, suffer any pain to have this night and as many nights as she would grant him before leaving. He would hold back the shattered bits of his heart, knowing they were an unworthy offering, and resist the need to pray for a miracle. As he'd said, he was long past saving.

He saw the open door to her bedroom, but he didn't take

her there. Instead, he stopped in front of the king-size bed covered with the black satin comforter. How many nights had he lain awake remembering how she'd looked naked in his bed? He wanted her there again, only this time, instead of burning in the presence of a memory, he would feel her body against his.

Slowly he lowered her to her feet. She stared up at him, patiently waiting for him to lead the way. Her trust mocked his weakness. She was strong, fearless. It never occurred to her that the price for this moment would be high. She'd confessed to him the secrets of her life, of her soul, in an attempt to make him understand. He understood completely; it just didn't change anything. She lived by rules he didn't understand. He envied her simplistic belief.

Then she smiled at him. "You are too handsome by far," she said, touching his cheek. "I think that was my downfall. That and your earring."

He took her hand and kissed her palm. Her eyes widened as he licked the tips of her fingers. Her breathing quickened instantly.

She was such an innocent. She'd only been with a man once in her life. He hadn't known then, hadn't taken the time to seduce her. Regret swept through him, convincing him that this time had to be different. He returned her smile. At last they were treading in territory he knew something about.

He kissed the back of the hand he held, then urged her to sit on the side of the bed. When she was seated, he knelt before her. Once again he slipped his hands through her hair, but gently this time. Teasing, instead of punishing.

"Rebecca," he whispered.

She blinked sleepily. "I love how you say my name."

"Rebecca," he whispered again, lower this time, sensually. "Beautiful Rebecca. Relax. Trust me."

"I do."

The echo of her wedding vow caught him low in the belly. He fought not to flinch. He wanted it all to be real, but it was just an illusion. The woman before him would disappear as the fireworks had done, leaving behind the smoke of his existence and nothing else.

He wove his fingers through her hair, moving lower, dividing it into two sections. He drew her hair over her shoulders, baring her back. His fingers found the zipper of her dress and lowered it. Most of the time she didn't wear a bra, but today he could feel the thin strap in back. He unfastened it, as well, but made no move to take off her clothing.

He leaned close and kissed her cheek. Soft kisses. Lightly he moved over her face, her eyes, her nose, finally her mouth. Brief brushes, lip to lip, never lingering, teasing her into wanting more. She reached for his shoulders. He drew back with her hands in his. Turning them palms up, he rubbed his thumbs around and around, circling her skin, heating it. Then he brought her palms to his mouth. He sucked the most center spots, making her straighten with surprise, then gave his attention to each of her fingers, drawing them into his mouth, tasting the salty length, nibbling on the sensitized tips, before withdrawing and allowing the warm night air to continue his work.

The floor was hard beneath his knees, but he didn't notice any discomfort except that between his legs. His hardness grew with each moment he spent with her. In time he would take his release and it would be all the better for waiting. In time. This was for her.

He released her hands, then drew her to her feet. As she rose, her dress stayed in place. Still on his knees, he hugged her close, burying his face on her flat belly. He breathed in the scent of her, savoring the lingering fragrances of the carnival, the sunshine, the heat, and myriad other smells that would forever mark this day in his memory.

He lowered his hands to her knees, then drew them up under her dress and along her thighs. When he reached her hips, he raised his head and looked up at her.

"Pull up your dress," he said quietly.

His hands held her in place. A shudder rippled her body, then she reached for her skirt. Inch by inch the flowing fabric slid up her legs, exposing her shapely thighs. When the fabric was bunched around her waist, he leaned forward and pressed his lips to her belly, just above the elastic of her panties.

The room was silent around them, except for the faint sounds from outdoors and the rapid cadence of her breathing. With his index fingers, he tugged her panties down a few inches. He turned his head so his stubbled cheeks brushed her sensitive skin. Her breath caught. Back and forth he moved, teasing her in an erotic dance of sensation. Her legs began to tremble. He searched for her belly button and traced the small circle with his tongue. Her muscles rippled in reaction.

Slowly, so slowly he could hear her mentally screaming at him to hurry, he lowered her panties to her ankles. Supporting her at her hips, he held her steady as she stepped out of them.

He turned his attention to the dark curls at the apex of her thighs. Here the heat was more intense, her scent more captivating. Gently, carefully, he brought his mouth to her. She stiffened in shock, then her legs started trembling harder, as if she was having trouble standing. His own need pulsed painfully against the fly of his jeans. He brought his hands down from her hips to her woman's place and used his fingers to part the curls.

When her most sensitive spot was exposed, he touched it with the tip of his tongue. He didn't move, he just held the contact. She tasted of the forbidden, of sweet sin and promise. She gasped his name. He brought his mouth to her and suckled her. She grabbed for his shoulders, letting the dress fall over him, cushioning him in darkness. Her knees buckled and he caught her as she fell.

Her dress slipped off one shoulder, exposing her bra and part of one breast. As he stood up and drew her to her feet, her dress slipped down to her waist. Without his urging, she pushed the garment over her hips and to the floor. Her bra followed.

This time she didn't cover herself. She sat on the side of the bed, then slid onto the comforter. Her gaze was glazed with passion, but underneath, he felt the trust. It should have scared the hell out of him. It should have, but it didn't.

He tugged his shirt out of his pants, pulled it over his head and tossed it aside. Then he moved onto the bed and knelt

between her legs. The night hid the subtleties of her body from
him. He reached to the nightstand and flicked on the light.

"What are you doing?" she asked, blinking in the sudden
glare.

"I want to see everything."

"Why?"

He smiled. "Looking at you turns me on."

"Really?" She sounded surprised. "But you've seen it before. After those other women, how can I be very exciting?"

He would have laughed except he knew the question was
genuine. "Look at me," he said.

"I am."

He shook his head. "Not in the face."

She apparently hadn't forgotten how to blush, he thought,
trying not to grin. She lowered her gaze to his midsection, then
dropped it to the place where his hardness strained against his
jeans.

"I think you're plenty exciting," he said.

She smiled slowly, that sensual smile that spoke of a female's power over a male. When she reached to touch him, he
grabbed her wrists and pinned them above her head. She didn't
struggle. Her surrender was absolute.

"Do you want me to let you go?" he asked, eyeing her full
mouth and needing to kiss it.

"Never," she said.

She wrapped her legs around his hips and drew him closer.
Her wet core brushed against the rough fabric of his jeans.
Pleasure made her arch her head back. When she opened her
mouth to draw in a breath, he covered her lips with his and
plundered her softness.

This time there was nothing gentle about his possession. His
tongue swept inside her mouth, claiming her, daring her to fight
back. The strength he'd always believed in caused her to accept
the dare and duel with him. Tongues circled against each other,
sending electric impulses through his body. He grew hotter,
harder, more ready, as the pressure in his groin built.

He drew his head down her neck and bit her tender skin.
She gasped. Suddenly he had to touch her, all of her. He re-

leased her wrists and covered her breasts. Already taut nipples scraped his palm. Although she didn't know about it, he had a secret stash of books on pregnancy in his lab. While she was at the house, he would read chapters, preparing for his child's birth. He remembered now that most pregnant women had extra-sensitive breasts, so he was careful when he stroked her curves. And he licked gently when he drew the hard points into his mouth.

She clutched at his shoulders, digging her fingers into his skin. Her hips continued to rock against his. She was bringing herself pleasure. He wondered if she knew. He grinned against her breasts. Somehow he doubted it. She was too easily embarrassed to take control in bed. In time she would be the tiger. His organ flexed at the thought.

He straightened and looked at her. The bedside lamp exposed the flush on her face and chest. Teeth marks faded on her shoulders and neck. Her nipples stood at attention, begging for his touch. He glanced down to where her curls pressed against his jeans. When he moved back, he could see the wet spot she'd left on him.

Her hands clutched at the comforter. He took them in his and brought them to her center. "Open for me," he said, placing her fingers on either side of her most secret place.

She swallowed hard and complied.

He rested his hands on her knees and pushed them back toward her chest and out slightly. He could see her most womanly place, feel the heat. She was ready for him, and he was more than ready for her, but it wasn't time. He wanted to hear her cries of pleasure first. He wanted to drive all thoughts from her mind and leave her empty of anything save ecstasy.

He lowered himself on the bed and nipped the back of her thigh. She jumped, then giggled. With his index finger, he traced a line from her tiny point of pleasure to the place that would send him to paradise. She shivered and whispered his name.

He planned to taunt her with her release, to build slowly and make her shake with need. She would cry out, scream and shatter, all for him.

But when he touched her with his tongue he couldn't think about anything but her. Thoughts of technique, of skill, disappeared. He'd been with other women, but that disappeared, as well. His chest and throat tightened as he tasted her sweetness. There was a connection between them, between their bodies. He would bring her pleasure, exquisite pleasure, but honestly. Because he wanted to, rather than because he had something to prove.

So he listened to her breathing, felt the urging pressure of her fingers on his face, shoulders and in his hair. When he could have paused, playing the game, he kept his rhythm steady. And when she asked him to stop, he did, raising his head until their eyes met.

"Be in me," she said. "Make love to me."

His hands shook as he unfastened his jeans. It was insane, he told himself. This was no big deal. He'd done it countless times before. Still he trembled as he undid the last button. His knees threatened to give out when he bent down to pull off his pants. It wasn't the need making him weak; it was the woman. Rebecca. Perhaps in his heart he'd always known what would happen. Perhaps that was why he'd avoided her bed until now.

When he returned to kneel before her, she reached for him to guide him inside. Her touch was tentative but loving, and almost his undoing. Her heat swallowed him, her muscles caressed him. The light of love in her eyes blinded him.

He looked away because he was a creature of the shadows. He plunged in deeply, wondering if she was his greatest sin or, as she had promised, his only hope of redemption. He had meant to shatter her, but he was the one who was shattering.

Her hips moved in time with his, her hands pulled him closer. He couldn't hold back, even though he knew she wasn't ready for their final ascent. He slipped his hand down her leg and dipped his thumb into her moistness. When he found her most sensitive spot, he circled in time with her thrusts, touching lightly, quickly, urging her over the edge.

His performance was juvenile at best, his technique laughable. Another time he would analyze what was wrong with him. This moment it was enough to match her rapid breathing, to gaze at her face, watching her eyes flutter closed as she arched her head back. He held on to his control until her muscles contracted around him, milking his hardness, sending him into oblivion. He plunged deeper and deeper still, holding her hips and hoarsely calling out her name.

When they had found their way under the covers, she snuggled against him.

"I'm not going back into that room," she said, then yawned. "I don't care what you say. We're going to make love every single night and you can't do anything to keep it from happening."

He had a bad feeling she was right. "What about the other room? Do you want me to take the walls down?" he asked.

"No." She rested her head on his shoulder and sighed. "The baby can stay there." Her fingers trailed across his chest, then she tucked them under her chin and closed her eyes. "I'm never going to leave you," she said quietly. "No matter what. You'll see. I'll make you see...."

Her voice trailed off as she fell asleep. Austin lay on his back and stared up at the ceiling. He could hear the regular sound of her breathing. Something had happened to him tonight, something that scared the hell out of him.

Through a combination of events he didn't understand, she'd gotten through to him. She'd found a way past the barriers and reached into the blackness to leave a small light. Its flame burned inside him. He could feel it. In time the blackness would swallow it whole, leaving him once again without hope. It would be worse, though, for the promise she'd given him. Because as surely as he knew that flame would die, he knew she would leave. She thought she'd learned his deepest secret, but she was wrong. There was something else, something far worse than she imagined. And when she knew the truth, she would leave as the others had left. Once again, he would be alone.

Chapter 13

"Okay, the glue should have dried on the wing," Austin said, stretching across the workbench and picking up the white piece of plastic. "Looks like we're ready to paint. Where'd we put the brushes, sport?"

David slid off his chair and collected a brown paper bag from the corner. "They're still in here. We never unpacked 'em." When he handed Austin the sack, he glanced longingly at the wing of the plane. "What color are you gonna paint it?"

"I'm not the one doing the painting. You are."

David stared up at him, his big blue eyes wide with excitement. A grin split his face. "Golly. That's cool." The smile faded. "What if I mess up?"

Austin recognized the sudden distress and silently cursed the circumstances that had made the boy fearful. David wasn't stupid. He knew what his relatives fought over. No doubt he'd figured out that even the promise of his parents' substantial estate wasn't enough to make any of his relatives willing to take him. In the month since the carnival, he'd gone from a bright, inquisitive child to a fearful one. He questioned every move he made, did his best to behave perfectly, as if finding the right behavior would make someone want him.

Austin knew what that kind of pain was like. He wanted to tell David it would get better in time, but it wouldn't. All that would happen was that he would cease to care. He would lie awake in the night and refuse to admit he was bleeding on the inside.

Austin spread out a sheet of newspaper and set the wing in the middle. After opening the pattern so the boy could see what colors were supposed to go where, he uncapped the first small container and handed him a brush.

David worked slowly and carefully, trying to copy the pattern exactly. Austin wanted to tell him it was no big deal if he went outside the lines. He was a kid; he should have fun. But he didn't speak. Partly because he knew David wouldn't understand and partly because he didn't want the kid to care any more than he already did.

Since the carnival, David had been a regular visitor to his workshop. At first Austin had resented the interruptions. He needed to concentrate on his work. In time he'd grown to expect the soft squeak of the door opening, then the hushed footsteps as David stepped inside. He let the boy continue to visit because Rebecca had mentioned that he was still not joining in with the other children. He stood on the outside, watching them play, but never entering the circle. Austin knew all about that, too.

David dipped his brush in the paint and drew a straight line along the edge of the wing.

"Great job," Austin said. "This is going to be the best plane anyone has ever seen."

David smiled up at him. "Will it be done by next Tuesday?"

"It can be. Why? What happens next Tuesday?"

"It's my birthday. I'm going to be eight."

"So you want the plane ready for your party?" All the children had parties on their birthday. He knew. Rebecca was always roping him into taking care of the balloons. He and the helium-tank dealer were spending far too much time together.

David nodded. "My uncle Bob said he might come for my birthday. I want to show him what I can do."

His hopeful expression tore at Austin's heart. He wanted to pull the boy close and protect him against the bastards of this world. He shook his head. Austin was one of them. Would he also protect the child from himself? He had no answer. He only knew it tore him up inside to see David so eager and know he was bound to be disappointed.

"Sure, we'll have the plane ready by then," Austin promised.

David bent over the wing. "Are you coming to my party?"

"I don't know, sport. I have to give a presentation in Kansas on Monday. I don't think I'll be back in time."

"But you *have* to be there, Austin. You're the one I want there the most. More than Uncle Bob."

Even as the child's words warmed him, he fought against the urge to run. He didn't mind spending time with David, but he didn't want to get too involved. "I'll try," was all he promised.

David nodded, but his shoulders slumped and he stopped being quite as careful with the paint. Austin stared at him and swore silently. He was messing up again, this time with an innocent child. The problem was he was as wrong for the kid as he was for Rebecca. This was turning into a disaster.

They continued to work in silence. Finally Austin couldn't stand it anymore. "Why don't we finish this up tomorrow?" he said.

Instantly David put down the brush and started cleaning up. Austin stared at him, not sure what to say or do to make things better. Should he even bother to try?

Footsteps in the garage drew his attention. He looked up, recognizing the sound of his wife.

"Are you two hiding out in here again?" she asked as she came in from the garage. "What is it about hammering and sawing that's so interesting?"

David looked up and returned her smile, but he didn't answer. Austin knew she was smart enough to figure out something was wrong. He steeled himself for her questions. But she didn't ask any. Instead, she crouched down beside the boy and draped her arm around his shoulders.

"What have you been doing?" she asked.

"Working on the plane."

"Show me, please. Is this the wing?"

David nodded.

"Did you paint it yourself? It's a very good job."

Slowly her questions drew him out until he was once again chatting animatedly. While David explained what they'd done and their plans for the plane, Rebecca kept her arm around him and used her free hand to brush the hair from his eyes and touch his face. Constant contact and reassurance. Austin recognized her technique; she used it on him.

In the past month, she'd kept her word. She hadn't gone back to the bedroom he'd built for her. Every night she'd shared his bed. Every night they'd made love. As much as he'd tried, he'd never been able to reclaim his distance. He could only be with her, in her, and feel the moment.

He leaned back in his chair and studied the woman he had married. She wore her thick hair pulled back in a ponytail. The August heat made everyone irritable, but Rebecca looked calm and cool in a loose white dress. The waist was set low, around her hips, and the skirt flowed out around her knees. It wasn't see-through or low cut. Except for the fact that it was sleeveless, there was nothing sexy about the dress.

Yet looking at her now got to him. It made him want her. She didn't even have to touch him. If he closed his eyes he was able to see her as she'd been last night, on top of him, riding him like a pagan queen. As he'd suspected, she had a wild streak of passion far beyond what she'd known about herself. She was flagrant and daring in bed, yet every morning she looked at him with the calm, loving eyes of a Madonna.

Here, in the confines of his workroom, with her safely occupied by David, he could admit the truth. He adored being with her, next to her, inside her making love. More than that, he lived for the sound of her voice, the way she walked, her innocence, her belief in him, the light in her face when she smiled at him. He admired everything about her. But he refused to love her. That final step of faith was beyond him. It always would be. He couldn't trust her. Even more, he couldn't trust himself. Something would happen and she would leave. Not loving her was the only thing that would keep him alive in the aftermath.

Rebecca stood up, drawing his attention back to her. "It's almost lunchtime, David. Why don't you head on back?"

The boy slid out of the chair and obediently headed for the door.

"You want to finish this tomorrow?" Austin called after him.

David shrugged.

"I thought you wanted it done in time for your party?"

David stopped by the doorway and looked back. Disappointment filled his blue eyes. "It doesn't matter now," he said, then left.

Austin grimaced.

"What was that all about?" Rebecca asked, taking the boy's seat and picking up the wing.

"He told me he wanted to have the plane done by next week so he could have it at the party. I guess he changed his mind."

"Why?"

He had a suspicion, but if he was right, it meant that he'd started to matter to the child. That was dangerous for both of them.

It wasn't about him, he assured himself. David wouldn't notice if he was at the party or not. "I'm not sure," he said, then realized he'd just lied to her for the first time.

She set the wing down, then leaned forward and placed her hand on his arm. "I really appreciate your taking the time to work with him. It means a lot to him."

"No big deal." He'd kept his voice gruff on purpose. At the unfriendly tone, he saw Rebecca frown. He knew he confused her. She kept trying to get close to him and he kept backing away. He wanted to tell her it was a mistake to keep trying, but he couldn't. For some stupid reason he needed her to try, even though it was useless. In the back of his mind, he kept waiting for a miracle. There wasn't going to be one. He was long past believing in anything good happening. But he couldn't shake a sense of expectation.

His gaze dropped to her stomach. There was the barest hint of rounding in her belly. He could feel it when they were together at night. He ached at the thought of having a child. It filled him with wonder. At the same time he prayed she would leave him before their baby was born. He couldn't survive losing them both.

"You're not listening to me," she said impatiently.

"I'm sorry. What were you saying?"

She shook her head. "No. Tell me what you were thinking. You had the oddest look on your face."

He couldn't lie to her again. "I was thinking that you make me very happy."

Her smile was slow and sweet, filled with promise. "Do I? I try. It's important to me. Well, of course it is. I mean, I'm your wife. Every wife wants her husband to be happy. Well, not every wife. Some wives might hate their husbands, especially if they're getting a divorce. I'm not saying I want to get—"

"Rebecca?"

She clamped her mouth shut. Faint color stained her cheeks. Her eyes held his, then slipped away. "Yes?"

"You're babbling."

"I know. I was embarrassed by your compliment. Thank you. I'm glad I make you happy." She bit her lower lip. "You make me happy, too."

"Do I?" The thought surprised him. "How?"

"There's that thing you did last night." Her grin was teasing.

He was surprised to find himself feeling a twinge of hurt at her words. He didn't want their relationship to be just about sex. Which was insane, he told himself. He was the one so damn set on keeping her out of his life.

"You make me happy by being with me," she went on. "By helping me and supporting me, by holding me. And mostly by talking to me like I'm an intelligent person."

"You are."

"A lot of guys hate that."

He leaned forward and brushed her lips with his. "A lot of guys are wimps."

She giggled and tilted her head so their foreheads touched. "I'm worried about David," she said.

He straightened. Great. So she'd figured out he'd hurt the child. He tried to think of a defense, then realized he didn't have one. He deserved whatever she was about to say.

"He's been talking about one of his uncles coming to his birthday party," she said.

"He mentioned it."

"The uncle isn't going to show up. He hasn't called or anything, but I've been working with this family for three months now. They don't want anything to do with David. I don't understand them. They make me crazy." She stared at her lap and twisted her ring. "You…"

He braced himself. He told himself he could handle any criticism she might make. He'd always known he wasn't perfect.

"You…" She took a deep breath. "This is so hard."

"Just spit it out."

"I don't spit," she said, giving him a quick smile. Her mouth twisted. "I thought maybe we could adopt him."

He stared at her, sure he couldn't have heard her correctly. "You want the two of us to adopt David?"

She nodded. "I know it's asking a lot. We're still trying to put the marriage together. I'm pregnant. This is the worst possible time. But he needs us, Austin. We would be good for him. And I've seen you working with him. I know you care about him."

"No." He stood up and glared at her. "You want me to be some kid's father?" He laughed harshly. "Hell, lady, you should have been here about twenty minutes ago. I nearly sent the kid into tears because I told him I couldn't make his birthday party."

"But you're going to be in Kansas next week. It's a business trip. That's hardly your fault."

"I could get back if I wanted to. The point is I don't give a damn about some kid's party. I don't care about him or any of those other children. I don't want to adopt him. That's final. Do you understand?'' He stopped when he realized he was yelling. He closed his eyes briefly and struggled for control. ''Rebecca, I'm sorry.''

''No,'' she said, standing. ''You're not. You're still fighting all this, aren't you?''

He didn't answer.

She sighed. ''I know it's only been a month, but I thought I was making a difference.''

He thought she was, too, but it was too dangerous to admit that.

''I love you, Austin.''

He stared at her, the words hanging between them. He couldn't speak.

''I've loved you for a long time,'' she continued. ''I thought it was about my crush, or sex, but it's not. I love you. Flaws and all. Even knowing you might never be able to love me back. I suppose I'm a little crazy. I can't help believing in you.''

''Don't,'' he whispered, backing away from her. ''Don't love me. Don't believe. I won't let you.''

''Austin, wait.''

But it was too late. He stalked out of the room and toward the barn. Instead of entering the building, he walked around it, heading into the trees. He had to be alone. He couldn't let her find him. What if she was able to convince him to believe? No, it couldn't happen. He wouldn't let it.

Adopt David. She was crazy. He would end up destroying the child, just as he'd destroyed everything he loved. What about his own child? What about Rebecca? He didn't want her to love him.

He trekked through the woods, his thoughts going around and around. Nothing was real. Nothing made sense.

The sound of laughter caught his attention. He turned toward the sound. He'd come through the trees to the section that separated the barn and garage from the main house. He could see children playing on the grass. The playground set he'd purchased gleamed in the bright August sun. There were ten or so children, from very young to preteen. They were having fun running around and calling out in the pattern of some intricate game.

He stood outside the circle watching as he always had, as David did. Even as a young boy he'd never fit in. Going from place to place, being dumped where he was never wanted, wondering if his mother would come back for him, praying she wouldn't, praying she would. How confused he'd been. A lonely child. No one had taken the time to know him. Until that day in junior high when Travis had seen past the bully to the scared boy inside. Until Rebecca had believed enough to love him.

He leaned against one of the trees and fought the emotions welling up inside him. He knew what she wanted. A single step of faith. It was so damn hard. But if he didn't take it, he would lose her. He wanted to reach out. He wanted to trust.

Then he remembered even if he did reach out, she would leave, anyway. He would find the one way to drive her from him. As he had with everything he'd ever cared about.

He would never be Wayne—a good, decent man. He would always be the dark loner. In time she would figure that out, as would David. It was better to stay outside the circle. Safer for all of them.

Rebecca tied off the last balloon and attached the ribbon tail. "I miss Austin," she said, staring at the bouquet of balloons she'd spent most of the morning finishing. Streamers flowed down from the high ceiling in the house's giant family room. Most of the furniture had been moved out to clear space for games, although two tables had been pushed against the far wall. One was for the cake and ice cream, the other for presents.

"It is difficult when your husband goes away, leaving you to take care of decorations all by yourself," Elizabeth said, then laughed.

"Okay, I'll admit I miss him for more than his balloon-blowing-up technique, but right now that's most on my mind."

"When does he come back?"

"This afternoon. His plane gets in early enough for him to make it to the party, but I'm not sure he will."

Elizabeth stood up and stretched. Except for her full breasts straining against her T-shirt, she didn't look as if she'd had a baby just a month before.

"I thought Austin liked David," she said.

"He does. It's just difficult to explain." Rebecca grabbed three balloons and walked them to the corner of the table. She bent over and began tying them to the leg. The bright decorations floated in the air. "He's concerned about getting too involved with David, then having him leave when this whole mess with his family is settled."

"Rebecca." Elizabeth joined her. "You'd mentioned something about wanting to adopt David. Did you talk to Austin about that?"

Rebecca secured the knot and straightened. "He doesn't want to."

"I'm sorry."

"It's for the best." She tried to smile, but had a feeling it came out shaky. "At least that's what I keep telling myself. Oh, Elizabeth, I'm so afraid. What if I've made a terrible mistake? I keep trying with Austin. I'm just not sure I'm getting through to him."

"You are." Her friend patted her arm. Her eyes darkened with concern and encouragement. "I know it's hard now, but you have to keep plugging away. Remember what Travis went through with me? He was ready to get married and I didn't even want to see him again. He had to give me time and room to come to my senses. You have to do the same. It's worth it in the end, I promise."

Rebecca glanced down at her wedding band. "But we're already married. I feel as if we've done this whole thing backwards. First we make love, then I get pregnant, then we get married and now we're getting to know each other. I think even a strong relationship would have trouble with that sequence of events, let alone one that's brand-new."

Elizabeth leaned forward and hugged her. She smelled of baby powder. The sweet scent made Rebecca want to cry.

"Give yourself a break. So it's not going perfectly, but it is better, isn't it?"

Rebecca shrugged. "Sometimes I think so. Sometimes I feel like I'm banging my head against the wall."

"You're stronger than any old wall. For what it's worth, I think Austin is desperate to love someone. He just doesn't know how. Show him the way. Keep believing. If not just for yourself, then for your child." Elizabeth glanced at her stomach and grimaced. "I can't stand the fact that you aren't even bloated."

"I am." Rebecca smoothed the front of her dress tight across her midsection. "See?"

Elizabeth snorted in disgust. "I think I'm going to hate you through this pregnancy. You'll probably gain all of fifteen pounds, never get puffy and look perfect two days after giving birth. I'm still fighting to *lose* fifteen pounds and I've been dieting for almost five weeks."

Rebecca grinned. "They must all be in your chest because you look great."

Elizabeth glanced down at the front of her blouse. "Travis is kind of excited about that part. I haven't told him most of it will go away when I stop breast-feeding. I hate to disappoint him." She glanced at her watch. "Speaking of Travis, I've got to run. Little Julia is going to be hungry in about a half hour, and that's one activity Travis can't do for me." She leaned over and kissed Rebecca's cheek. "Hang in there. Keep believing. And if you ever need a break, there's always a room waiting for you at our place."

"Thanks."

Rebecca watched her friend leave, then turned back to the decorations. She was determined to make the party special for David. It was his first one without his family. She'd put the word out in town, and she knew enough about the community of Glenwood to know the people would come through for the little boy. If only Austin would do the same. It would mean so much to David.

She collected another three balloons for the far side of the table. It wasn't all for the child, she admitted. She needed Austin to show up for David because it would give *her* hope for their future. But deep in her bones, she prepared herself to be disappointed. She was beginning to wonder if her husband was ever going to change.

By two-thirty, the party was in full swing. Several people from town had come by to drop off presents for David. The table was stacked high with packages. Some of the children in the home had made him gifts, others had used their candy money to buy something small. Sounds of conversation and laughter filled the room. Despite the hot August afternoon, a lot of the children were outside playing, although the adults stayed in where it was cooler.

Rebecca glanced out the rear bay window and saw David in the center of the activity. For once, he wasn't standing on the outside watching. She breathed a sigh of relief. At least that was going right. Now if only Austin would show up. For the hundredth time in twenty minutes, she checked the door to the family room. Nothing. Then she heard a commotion toward the front of the house. She hurried out, telling herself she was foolish to hope.

As she rounded the corner into the hallway, she saw Kyle setting a large cake on a table by the front door.

"Beware handsome men carrying gifts," he said when he saw her.

"Thanks for getting the cake," she said, trying to keep the disappointment from her voice.

Even so, Kyle must have heard something. He walked over to her and put his arm around her. Brown eyes, as dark as midnight, met her own. He squeezed her hard against him. "You're disappointed because I'm not wearing shorts." He motioned to his jeans. "I know it's difficult for you. You probably spent most of last night dreaming about seeing my legs this afternoon. But in your condition—" he patted her stomach "—I thought the excitement would be too much. I didn't want to be responsible for you fainting away at my feet."

She swatted his arm and stepped out of his embrace. "You have some nerve."

He winked. "Ain't it terrific? Makes you realize you married the wrong man, huh?"

She planted her hands on her hips. "If you ever thought any woman really cared about you, you'd run in the opposite direction."

Kyle's grin faded, leaving him looking devastatingly handsome and just a little lost. "Maybe not."

Rebecca refused to be sucked into a conversation with him. "You always say that when you're between women. Then when you get involved with someone, you can't wait to dump her before she dumps you. What is it about you Haynes men, anyway?"

For a second she thought he might answer her seriously. But that went against Kyle's sense of fun. He bent down and grabbed her around the waist, then raised her in the air and twirled around. "Because us Haynes boys are too good-looking. No one can stand it. That's why you had to marry that sorry dog Austin, instead of me."

"Put me down, you savage."

He lowered her to the floor. "Can you handle the cake? I've got a present for David."

"Sure." She picked up the cake and carried it to the family room. When she set it on the table, she saw David had come inside.

"How are you doing?" she asked him, then straightened his party hat. "Having fun?"

He nodded, but didn't smile. She knew he was missing his family, but he was being a good sport. She gave him a quick hug. "Kyle is here. He's bringing you a present."

"Is Austin home yet?"

"No, honey. He hadn't arrived when I checked an hour ago. He might have had to take a later flight," she said, then told herself it was stupid to lie for Austin. He wouldn't care that she was trying to make him look better to the boy, and it wasn't like her not to tell the truth. Austin would have left a message if he'd taken a later flight. He always told her where he was going to be. No, he was probably already home. He could come to the party if he wanted to.

"Where's the birthday boy?" Kyle asked as he came into the family room. He was holding an impossibly large present. "Someone left this for him in my car." He glanced around. "Rebecca, do you see David?"

David smiled. "I'm right here," he said, crossing to stand directly in front of Kyle.

"Where?" Kyle looked on both sides of him, over his head, then turned and looked behind him. "David? Where is that little guy?"

David giggled. "Kyle, I'm right in front of you."

Kyle looked down. "Oh, there you are. You know you shouldn't hide on your birthday. People might think you didn't want presents." He lowered himself to his knees and placed the huge box on the floor. "Happy birthday, David. This is from me and Jordan."

"Wow!" David plopped down next to him and tore at the wrapping paper. "Thanks. What is it?" He pulled off the large sheet covering the top and stared at the picture of an elaborate train set. "Oh, Kyle! This is so great. Rebecca, look. It's a train!"

She bent down and studied the picture. "It's wonderful." She glanced at Kyle. "It's going to take a lot of work to put it together."

Kyle grinned. "I'm off for the rest of the day. I have tools and stuff in my car. I thought we could work on it tonight after everyone is gone."

"You sound as excited as David."

He shrugged. "Hey, birthdays are for everyone. Glad you like it, David."

The boy gave him a wide grin. "Thanks." The front door opened and closed. He looked up expectantly. One of the men from the town council came into the room. David looked down at the box and bit his lip. Rebecca's heart went out to him. He was waiting for Austin. She said a quick prayer that he wouldn't have to wait very long.

Chapter 14

By the time all the presents had been opened and the cake served, David had given up trying to pretend. Rebecca watched him standing on the edge of a game, observing but not joining in. Several of the children invited him, but he stood stubbornly alone, waiting for the one person who wouldn't come.

He'd asked her once about his uncle. When she'd said she hadn't heard from him, he didn't seem too surprised. Austin was another matter. Over the past couple of months, Austin had become important to the boy. Rebecca fought her anger, knowing it would accomplish nothing. Her husband was acting true to form. She shouldn't be surprised, but she was. She'd hoped he would change.

A loud truck engine broke through her musings. She turned toward the sound. The children stopped their game to watch the large vehicle make its way across the dirt road. Her stomach clenched tightly. She had a bad feeling she knew what this was about.

Two men got out of the cab. "We're looking for a little boy named David," one of them said.

David stepped forward. "I'm David."

The taller of the two jean-clad men grinned. "Happy birthday, son. Someone sent you ponies to ride."

A cheer went up from the children and they all rushed toward the truck. David stood rooted in place. Rebecca walked over to his and put her hand on his shoulder.

"Here." The man thrust out a card. "Let me get 'em unloaded and you can have the first ride."

David turned the card over and over in his small hands. She squeezed him and fought her tears. When he opened the card and read the message, she already knew who had sent the gift.

"They're from Austin," he said, confirming her guess. "He says he's sorry he had to miss the party."

The men led eight ponies from the back of the truck and lined them up. "You ready?" the taller man said, approaching David. "We've got a special pony for you."

Rebecca felt his body stiffen. "I don't want to ride any dumb pony," he said, and threw down the card. He turned and ran toward the house. She took a step toward him, then stopped. He needed some time alone. She would give him a few minutes, then see how he was doing.

"Is there a problem, ma'am?" the man asked.

She shook her head. "He's thrilled about the ponies. It's just he thought someone important to him was going to come to the party and he didn't. Go ahead and start with the other children."

She watched the first kids being placed on the back of the docile animals. Oh, Austin, she thought. You really blew it this time.

She looked back at the house, then at the woods separating this property from the barn. Quickly making up her mind, she called out to Mary that she would be gone for a few minutes, then she headed through the trees toward the loft.

As she passed the garage, she glanced inside. Austin's Mercedes and truck were parked next to the new wagon. He *was* home. She cursed him under her breath, then felt embarrassed by her own use of swear words. That man was a bad influence on all of them, she thought, making her way to the barn and opening the front door.

"Austin Lucas, what do you think you're doing?" she called as she marched up the stairs.

"Rebecca?"

When she reached the second floor, she could see him standing by the bed unpacking. He turned to face her. "What's wrong?"

She laughed harshly and planted her hands on her hips. "You're asking me what's wrong? Typical. You create a problem, then you don't want to deal with it."

He put the jeans he was holding on the bed, then shoved his hands into his pockets. "What are you talking about?"

"David."

He frowned. "Look, I'm tired. There was a thunderstorm last night. I didn't get any sleep. I had to get up early to catch my flight and I just got in. I thought about what happened before and I sent him a present. It should be arriving at any time."

"It's already here."

"So what's the problem? Are you telling me David doesn't want to ride a pony on his birthday?"

"Yes. That's exactly what I'm telling you." She shook her head. "Why can't you see what's right in front of you? It's not the gift. He's got plenty of presents. This is his first birthday without his family. He's lonely and scared about the future. You're the one person who's gotten through to him. He doesn't care about any ponies. He wants to see you. He wants to hear you wish him happy birthday and give him a hug. He wants to know you care."

Austin turned back to the bed and dumped the remaining contents out of his suitcase. "What makes you think I care?" he asked, zipping up the sides.

"You make me want to scream," she said, holding her arms out in front of her. "Why are you so stubborn? What is so terrible about admitting to having any gentle feelings? It won't hurt, I promise. He's just a small boy. He needs you."

"I'm tired," he said coldly, and walked to the closet concealed in the wall.

She stepped closer to the bed. "Damn you, Austin, don't

you dare turn away from me. Who did it? Who beat it out of you? Who made you think you had to be hard to survive? Why isn't it okay to care? Why isn't it okay to love someone?''

He slammed the door shut and glared at her. ''Love is a myth, just a line men use to trap women into sex and women use to trap men into marriage. It doesn't mean a damn thing. It never has.''

There was a darkness in his gray eyes, a determination she hadn't seen before. It was as if he'd found a way to shut the door in her face, and he was never going to open it again.

He didn't believe anymore—if he ever had. Not in David's feelings for him, or hers. Her promise of love had meant nothing to him.

''Then that's it,'' she said. ''You're not going to come see him.''

''No.''

They stood staring at each other, poised like characters in a play. She prayed for a sign that she hadn't made the worst mistake of her life. God chose not to oblige.

An iciness settled over her, freezing her blood and opening a crevice in her soul. It didn't matter what she'd said or how she'd tried to convince him of her feelings and her commitment. He didn't care. He didn't believe. He was and always had been a stranger. She'd created a facade and put it over the real man. It had all been make-believe.

Without saying another word she walked away, down the stairs and out into the bright August afternoon. The heat of the sun should have warmed her, but she didn't feel anything except cold.

What had she done? What was she going to do? A part of her said to keep trying, but her heart whispered it had always been too late.

It was dusk when Austin made his way over to the house. He hadn't seen Rebecca since she'd stormed out of the barn. He couldn't blame her. He'd been a real jerk. The funny part was he'd done it on purpose.

When he came out of the grove of trees, he looked around.

The children had long since gone inside. He looked down at the shoebox-size package in his hand. This was his real present. If David still wanted it.

He stared at the big house knowing he didn't have the courage to walk up there and knock on the door. He couldn't face Rebecca right now. Not knowing what she thought of him.

He started to turn back when a flash of color caught his eye. He stepped to the left and saw David sitting alone under a tree in the backyard. His red shorts and red-and-white shirt looked much the worse for wear. Stains covered the fabric, grass, punch and something that looked like chocolate cake.

So the kid had had a great birthday, he told himself. David probably hadn't even noticed he hadn't shown up.

Yeah, right, he thought, wondering when he'd stooped low enough to start lying to himself.

He walked around the house to the backyard. David was staring at the ground. The slump of his shoulders hit Austin in the gut. He'd stayed away out of fear. Because he wasn't man enough to face a little boy. He deserved to be shot.

"Happy birthday," he said quietly.

David snapped his head up. His blue eyes widened, then he scrambled to his feet and raced across the lawn. "Austin!" he yelled, holding out his arms.

Austin dropped the package, bent down to gather the boy close to him, then pulled him up to his chest. "Hey, sport, how's it going?"

David wrapped his thin legs around Austin's waist and buried his head in his shoulder. "You came. You really came."

"It's your birthday, isn't it? I wouldn't want to miss that for anything."

The boy clung tighter, hanging on as if he never wanted to let go. Austin absorbed the slight weight, wondering why he'd worried it would be a burden. Then David raised his head and looked at him. "I was scared you'd be too busy." His lower lip trembled. "My uncle Bob couldn't come. I didn't miss him like I missed you." He sniffed. "And my parents. I tried really hard not to miss them. But kept 'membering." He choked on a sob. "I want my mommy and daddy."

Tears poured down his face. Austin wrapped his arms around the boy and held him closer. With one hand, he stroked his back, then his head. "It's okay to cry, David," he said, his own voice a little froggy. "I understand."

Hell, who better? He knew exactly what it was like to be left alone on birthdays and other holidays. His mother had done it to him countless times. Once he'd gathered his courage together and the next time he'd seen her after his birthday, he'd asked her if she'd remembered he'd turned nine. She'd looked back at him and snapped, "No. And I didn't get you a damn present, either, so shut up about it."

That was twenty-six years ago and the words still had the power to hurt him.

The child's sobs tore at his heart, reminding him of all the times he hadn't let himself cry. Crying was weak. It let his mother know she'd won. Silence had been his only victory.

Still holding David, he crouched down and picked up the present, then made his way over to the tree where the boy had been sitting. Austin lowered himself to the ground and arranged David on his lap. The sobs had lessened, but not let up completely. Austin continued to hold him, murmuring occasional words of comfort, wishing he knew what else to do.

Rebecca wanted to adopt this boy and bring him into their family. He was probably better off in the home. At least there he was around adults who knew what they were doing. They weren't as broken and flawed inside. They wouldn't thoughtlessly wound him.

Austin leaned his head against the tree and studied the sky. Could he learn to be a father? Did he want to? Was his desire to have Rebecca walk away and take the baby with her just a way for him to cover his feelings of inadequacy?

He shook his head. He was right not to get involved. Look at how he'd hurt David today. This was just one event in a child's life. There were thousands, and he had the potential to screw up every single one of them. He couldn't risk it. It wasn't fair to any kid.

David's sobs faded to sniffles. "Austin, are you mad at me?"

"No, why?"

"'Cause you didn't come to my party before. Did I mess up the airplane bad?"

"No. You did a wonderful job. I'm proud of you."

David sighed and leaned against him. "So you're not mad?"

Austin swallowed hard. Even though Rebecca had told him what David was feeling, he hadn't wanted to believe her. Now he knew the truth. He could walk away from this boy, leaving him with the same type of wounds his mother had inflicted on him, or he could speak the words and start the healing. The former was all he knew how to do. The latter left *him* open to pain.

But David was only a little boy.

"I was never mad," Austin said slowly, staring out into the night. "Sometimes I don't want to know that people care about me. It's hard for me to let people like me. When they do it makes me uncomfortable."

"'Cause you don't like 'em back," David said, his voice very small.

"No!" Austin looked down and cupped the boy's chin in one of his hands. "No. Because I *do* like you back. It scares me."

"Why?"

It sounded too dumb for words, yet of anyone, David would understand. "I'm always afraid if I care about people too much, they'll go away."

David nodded. "Like my mom and dad."

"Yes. But if you don't care, no one ever loves you. You don't get to love anyone back. You spend your life alone. It's safe, but it's not right."

"You're not alone, Austin," David said with the confidence of youth. "You've got Rebecca."

He wasn't so sure anymore. But that wasn't for the boy to worry about. "I'm sorry I missed your party. I didn't mean to hurt you."

David smiled up at him. "I understand. I'm glad you came now." He thought for a minute. "Oh, thanks for the ponies."

Austin remembered the package he'd brought over with him.

He reached around the tree and held it out. "This is for you. Happy birthday."

David grinned and tore at the wrappings. When he raised the lid on the box, he stared at the rows of woodworking tools. "Golly, look at this."

"They're scaled down so they'll be easier to work with," Austin said, absorbing the boy's wide smile and the light in his eyes. "You'll have to be careful, though, and only use them with supervision. We never did finish that birdhouse. I thought you might want to bring them over tomorrow and we'll get to work."

David reached up and flung his arms around Austin's neck. He squeezed hard. "I love you," he whispered. "I knew you'd remember me. I knew you wouldn't forget."

"I'll never forget," Austin promised.

"When I'm gone, will you write me?"

Austin pulled him back and stared at him. "What are you talking about?"

David shrugged and stared at his new tools. "I was in the hallway the other night and I heard Mary tellin' someone that my family is going to send me to a boarding school. I don't know where." He looked up hopefully. "Will you write?"

"Yes," Austin promised. He touched the boy's face, his hair, then finally pulled him against his chest and held on. "I'll write."

David chattered about his party and all the presents he'd received. His voice got slower and slower, until he fell asleep. Austin continued to hold him, to listen to his soft breathing. It was happening again. The family would send David to a school and forget about him. They would abandon him until it came time to move him somewhere else. He would never be wanted, never have a home, never know what it was like to be loved.

It was already starting. David had so easily resigned himself to his fate. Austin raised his gaze to the heavens and silently screamed at a world that would allow this tragedy to occur again.

It was close to midnight when he made his way back to the barn. He'd delivered David to bed, then spent an hour with

Kyle setting up the train set. If the other man had noticed his lack of conversation, he had never let on.

Austin climbed the stairs quietly, thinking Rebecca might be asleep. When he reached the loft, he saw her sitting in the living room. A lamp shone from the corner, but other than that it was dark.

"You were gone when I got back," she said.

"I went to see David." He sat across from her in the wing chair. She was curled up in a corner of the sofa. The large cushions looked as if they could swallow her whole. "We talked about my missing his party. I guess we made up."

"I'm glad."

He leaned forward and rested his elbows on his knees, lacing his fingers together. "He said that his family wants to send him to a boarding school."

"I know."

"Is that why you want to adopt him?"

"I wanted *us* to adopt him," she said, "because I thought we could give him a warm and loving home. I knew about their plans. Given the choice between being shuffled between unwilling relatives and the stable environment of a boarding school, the school comes out ahead in my book."

"I agree."

"Finally. We're in accord about something."

He hated the bitterness in her voice. "I'm sorry, Rebecca."

She pulled her knees closer to her chest. "Are you? About what?"

"About everything."

"That's nice and general. It's clean, tidy, covers everything without your having to admit to any wrong. I'm impressed."

"Don't be sarcastic," he said, staring at her.

"Why? I'm trying to speak to you on your level. I thought you'd appreciate it."

"Don't be like me."

"Be careful, Austin," she said, tossing her head. Her hair settled around her shoulders. "Someone might make the mistake of believing you actually cared. You wouldn't want that to happen. It would be a calamity. The earth might have to open up and swallow us whole.''

He rose to his feet. "Stop it."

"Why? Aren't I being the perfect, loving little wife anymore? Do you miss her? I have news for you, pal. This is what it's like living with you. Nothing matters, not feelings or people. It's all just a game. You hide, then try to destroy anyone who is stupid enough to go looking for you." She sighed and dropped her forehead to her knees. "You win. I'm done playing."

He flinched as if she'd slapped him. "You're leaving." It wasn't a question.

"I don't know." She raised her head and met his gaze. He saw the pain in her beautiful eyes, the hurt and disillusionment he'd put there. "I want to believe it's going to be okay. I want to trust that I can win you over, but I don't know anymore." She shook her head. "I assumed loving you was enough, but it isn't, is it?"

"No," he said hoarsely.

"I thought as much. You have to love me back. You're not going to."

He didn't say anything. He couldn't. Love her back. Oh, God, and then what? Trust her? Trust that it was going to last? Trust that she could know the darkest, ugliest part of him and still be there every day? No, it wasn't possible.

He walked over to the window and stared out into the darkness.

"What do you see there?" she asked. "What do you stare at? The past? Do you relive those lonely times over and over again? Do you ever see me? Hear my voice? Do you ever allow yourself to believe?"

"I try," he whispered, fighting the emptiness clawing at him.

"But you don't yet."

"No."

He heard her sigh. The reflection from the lamp allowed him to watch her stand up and walk close to him. When she was directly behind him, he felt her hands on his back.

"I had this dream of a fairy-tale wedding," she said. "I

wanted to wear a beautiful white dress and be surrounded by all my friends and family. I wanted to be in a church filled with roses and sunlight, and ringing with the sounds of laughter and happiness. I wanted to marry my prince there, ride off on a white horse and live happily ever after.''

His chest tightened, making it hard to breathe. ''Then Wayne died and you lost your dream.''

''Wayne? No, Austin. You were the prince in that dream of mine.'' She leaned against his back and wrapped her arms around his waist. He stiffened at the contact, but she didn't pull away. ''It was always you. From the very beginning. Despite everything, I love you. I'll always love you. Even knowing the secret you try to hide.''

''No.'' He turned quickly and grabbed her wrists, setting her away from him. ''You don't know anything.'' Her gaze held his. Love and light radiated from her face, hurting his eyes, but he couldn't look away.

''You're wrong,'' she said. ''I figured it out. I thought it was about the way you watched me with the children. I thought you needed me to touch you and hold you, but that was only a symptom. The problem isn't that you're not worth the trouble. The problem is you believe you're not worth loving. But you are. You're kind and gentle. Generous. You treat me like I'm the most precious thing you've seen. You hold me in the darkness, you fight for me, you believe in me and what I want. The only part of me you won't accept is the part that loves you. Watch out, Austin. That's all of me. Every cell of my being is filled with love for you. You can't yell it out of me. You can't make me stop loving you.''

She pulled her wrists free of his grasp and touched his face. He jerked back as if burned. She smiled sadly. ''Be careful, though. You can't make me not love you, but you can drive me away.''

With that she turned and headed for the stairs. He watched her go, wanting to call her back, but unable to form the words. He felt as if his world had shifted on its axis. Nothing was as he'd thought it should be.

Rebecca knew. Somehow she'd figured out the truth. That

he wasn't worth loving. That he had a flaw so horrible even his own mother had recoiled from him. And yet Rebecca claimed to love him. It wasn't possible. He wouldn't let it be. He couldn't.

If he believed she loved him now, he would have to admit how much he needed that love. He would have to stare into the face of his empty life and know the suffering he'd endured. Better to turn his back on it all. Better to be alone than to risk it all.

He watched from the window, but she didn't appear. At least she hadn't gone for one of the cars. He closed his eyes and steadied his breathing. The silence surrounded him, pressing against his body. It deafened him.

There was a time when he'd enjoyed the silence. That was before his life had been filled with the sounds of Rebecca. Now the quiet tormented him. He would get used to it again, he told himself. He would have to if he was to survive without her.

Outside the circle. Alone. He'd been happy there. Outside the circle, where David now stood. But the boy wasn't happy. He hadn't learned how to pretend it didn't matter that he didn't fit in. How to pretend he wasn't in agony with every breath, knowing he would live out his days in mind-destroying silence.

"Rebecca," he whispered. Oh, God, what if it was too late?

He raced across the room and tore down the stairs. When he reached the foyer, he ripped open the door and stared out into the night, searching for her.

"Rebecca," he called.

"Austin? I'm right here." She sat on the steps, looking up at him. "What's wrong?"

"I thought you were gone." He was panting, barely able to get the words out.

"I was going to take a walk, but I'm too tired."

He leaned down and brought her to her feet. Tightly holding both of her hands, he said, "Don't leave me."

She sighed. "I was being melodramatic. I'm sorry. I won't leave you, despite your lack of belief in us. I love you, Austin. I'm going to keep saying it until you believe me."

He released her hands and cupped her face. He'd been given

another chance. A last chance. It wasn't too late. "You are so
beautiful," he whispered. "I love you, Rebecca Lucas. I love
you with my heart and soul, such as they are. Don't leave me.
Please. I would never survive the silence."

"Austin?"

He bent down and kissed her. Softly, tenderly, his lips pressing against hers. She trembled in his embrace.

"Austin, you're not kidding, are you?"

He smiled. "No. I've been frightened of caring, but I'm
more frightened of losing you forever. Of not seeing our child.
I don't know what kind of husband and father I'm going to be,
but I'll do my best."

"You're a damn fine husband," she said, holding him close.
"The best."

"Rebecca?"

"Hmm?"

He kissed the top of her head, then her nose. "You're far
too innocent to swear."

"I was trying to relate to you on your level." In the moonlight, he saw her smile.

"I love you," he said again.

Her smile broadened. "I'll never get tired of hearing those
words. The way you've fought me on this, you'd think I was
asking for blood. It's not so hard, is it?"

"No," he answered, lowering his mouth to hers. Now that
he believed, loving her, being loved by her, was going to be
the easiest thing he'd ever done.

Epilogue

The church was filled with white roses and sunlight. The sounds of laughter and happiness stretched up to the arched ceiling of the old building.

Rebecca stood at the altar, with her husband at her side. Her two sisters, her parents and Elizabeth stood on her left. Travis and his brothers stood on Austin's right. In front of them, the minister cradled their newborn son.

As the Reverend Johnson touched the holy water to the baby's forehead and proclaimed him to be christened Austin Jason Lucas—Austin after his father, Jason after his mother's father—Rebecca had to fight back her tears. She sniffed softly. Austin reached for her hand and squeezed it. She smiled at him and wondered what she'd done to deserve such happiness.

Everything was working out wonderfully, she thought as her eyes grew misty. The new home had been built for the children. She and Austin had remodeled his big house and were moving in this weekend. Their son had been born healthy and perfect, with his father's gray eyes and his mother's smile.

The reverend handed her back her son, then bowed his head for the final blessing.

The audience of well-wishers crowded around them. Austin accepted the attention easily. In the past few months he'd grown more comfortable with the people in town, more willing to be a part of the community.

"That was wonderful, dear," her mother said, giving Rebecca a hug. "Little Jason was perfect. Weren't you, sweetie?" She touched the baby's cheek.

Elizabeth congratulated her next. Julia observed the celebration solemnly from her mother's arms. "At least they're close enough in age to play together," Elizabeth said.

"Just eight months apart." Rebecca smiled. "Maybe they'll grow up and get married."

Travis came through the crowd to find his wife. "Matchmaking already? Don't you think they're a little young?"

"No," the two women said together, then laughed.

Rebecca looked around for Austin, but he was lost in the crowd. She raised herself on tiptoe trying to see him. Kyle came up to her.

"I just wanted to say congratulations," he said. "I can't come to the house for lunch."

"Why?" Rebecca asked, narrowing her gaze. Kyle had the oddest expression on his face.

"I have to help a friend move."

"*Friend?* Why do I know this friend is a female?"

Instead of teasing her about his prowess with women, Kyle simply looked uncomfortable. "It's not like that," he said. "Sandy is a friend of the family. All my brothers know her. I thought she'd left Glenwood for good, but she's moving back. I just want to help."

There was an earnestness about him she'd never seen before. "She sounds like a special lady."

Kyle bent down and kissed her cheek. "Yeah, she is. Or at least she used to be. I haven't seen her since I was sixteen. Take care of little Jason here and yourself. I'm glad you're happy."

She smiled at him. "You be happy, too."

"I am." But his dark eyes were tinged with sadness, the

way Travis's had been before he'd had the good sense to fall in love with Elizabeth. What was it about these Haynes men?

Rebecca watched Kyle leave, then turned to search for her husband again. She saw him on the outside of the crowd. He didn't notice her. He was looking around at all the people. She waited, knowing he wouldn't stay outside the circle. In the past few months, he'd allowed himself to love and be loved by her. He'd become the warm, tender man she'd always dreamed of. He'd changed.

Austin stared into the crowd, then ducked low. When he straightened, he had David in his arms. He stepped into the throng and began working his way toward her. She met his gaze and smiled, then focused on the eight-year-old boy who was talking animatedly. The adoption had been finalized earlier that week. She glanced at the baby in her arms and knew they really were a family.

Austin stepped around a young couple, then moved next to her. She held out her free arm and embraced him.

"I love you," he said quietly.

"For how long?" she teased, glancing up at him. His gray eyes held her own. "Just for today?"

"For always," he promised. "You and David and Jason. Forever."

He lowered his mouth to hers and kissed her. She clung to him, savoring the sweetness, trusting in the future. Austin had stepped inside the circle of their love to stay.

* * * * *

75¢ off

your next Silhouette series purchase.

If you enjoyed these two stories from Silhouette, visit your nearest retail outlet and take 75¢ off your next purchase!

75¢ OFF!

Your next Silhouette series purchase.

107716

5 65373 00075 5   (8100) 0 10771

Silhouette®
Where love comes alive™

75¢ off

your next Silhouette series purchase.

If you enjoyed these two stories from Silhouette, visit your nearest retail outlet and take 75¢ off your next purchase!

75¢ OFF!

Your next Silhouette series purchase.

RETAILER: Harlequin Enterprises Ltd. will pay the face value of this coupon plus 10.25¢ if submitted by customer for this product only. Any other use constitutes fraud. Coupon is nonassignable. Void if taxed, prohibited or restricted by law. Consumer must pay any government taxes. Nielson Clearing House customers submit coupons and proof of sales to: Harlequin Enterprises Ltd., 661 Millidge Avenue, P.O. Box 639, Saint John, N.B. E2L 4A5. Non NCH retailer—for reimbursement submit coupons and proof of sales directly to: Harlequin Enterprises Ltd., Retail Marketing Department, 225 Duncan Mill Rd., Don Mills, Ontario M3B 3K9, Canada.

**Coupon expires April 30, 2002.
Valid at retail outlets in Canada only.
Limit one coupon per purchase.**

52603541

Silhouette®
Where love comes alive™

FREE Refresher Kit!

With two proofs of purchase from any of our four Silhouette "Where Love Comes Alive" special collector's editions

Special Limited Time Offer

<u>IN U.S., mail to:</u>
Silhouette Quiet Moments
Refresher Kit Offer
3010 Walden Ave.
P.O. Box 9020
Buffalo, NY 14269-9020

<u>IN CANADA, mail to:</u>
Silhouette Quiet Moments
Refresher Kit Offer
P.O. Box 608
Fort Erie, Ontario
L2A 5X3

YES! Please send my FREE Introductory Refresher Kit so I can savor Quiet Moments without cost or obligation, except for shipping and handling. Enclosed are two proofs of purchase from specially marked Silhouette "Where Love Comes Alive" special collector's editions and $3.50 shipping and handling fee.

_____

Name (PLEASE PRINT)

_____

Address   Apt. #

_____

City   State/Prov.   Zip/Postal Code

FREE REFRESHER KIT OFFER TERMS

To receive your free Refresher Kit, complete the above order form. Mail it to us with two proofs of purchase, one of which can be found in the upper right-hand corner of this page. Requests must be received no later than March 30, 2002. Your Quiet Moments Refresher Kit costs you only $3.50 for shipping and handling. The free Refresher Kit has a retail value of $25.00 U.S. All orders subject to approval. Products in kit illustrated on the back cover of this book are for illustrative purposes only and items may vary (retail value of items always as previously indicated). Terms and prices subject to change without notice. Sales tax applicable in N.Y. **Please allow 6-8 weeks for receipt of order. Offer good in Canada and the U.S. only.**

Offer good while quantities last. Offer limited to one per household.

598KIY DAEY   © 2001 Harlequin Enterprises Limited
PSNCP-FORM